BUTTERSCOTCH BLUES

MARGARET JOHNSON-HODGE

St. Martin's Paperbacks

BUTTERSCOTCH BLUES

Copyright © 2000 by Margaret Johnson-Hodge.

All rights reserved. No part of this book may be used or reproduced in any manner whatsoever without written permission except in the case of brief quotations embodied in critical articles or reviews. For information address St. Martin's Press, 175 Fifth Avenue, New York, NY 10010.

Library of Congress Catalog Card Number: 00-024758

ISBN: 0-312-97630-5

Printed in the United States of America

St. Martin's Press hardcover edition / June 2000
St. Martin's Paperbacks edition / March 2001

St. Martin's Paperbacks are published by St. Martin's Press, 175 Fifth Avenue, New York, NY 10010.

10 9 8 7 6 5 4 3 2 1

I dedicate this book to my best friend,
George Walter Xaverian Bellinger, Jr.,
who diligently and faithfully works to
enlighten and inform people about the reality of AIDS,
and to our friends who fought the good fight, but lost. . . .

ONE

Sandy lay in bed, lights on, a rumble of snores beside her. *How did I get here?* all she wanted to know. She was trying to make peace, forgive herself for opening her door at five o'clock in the morning.

Sandy was trying to make concessions, her good sleep interrupted, Brian dozing the moment his head hit her pillow, lost to a slumber she could not find.

Life had dwindled down to fast moments, little leisure, and no real love. She never expected to be here. Never expected to find herself in a counterfeit relationship. *Never thought I'd fall in love with him.* But she had.

Brian didn't seem special enough, handsome enough, or classy enough to own her heart. But a heart doesn't think, just reacts, something Brian had known.

From the moment they met there had been little interest on Sandy's part. But Brian had ignored her initial dislike and poured on the charm. He bought her things, took her places, was there for her as if he knew what she had been missing.

Where's the harm, she'd asked herself so long ago when he asked her out on that first date. *He's nice,* she decided as the second date was ending and they were making plans for a third. *Treats me good,* she concluded when the third date turned into a fourth, and two months later Sandy was hooked, in love, and eager to take the sweet beginning as far as God and time would allow.

By month three the *good* bragging-on-the-phone-with-your-girlfriend moments began to fade. Two years later Brian was hit-and-miss, Sandy meeting up with him when she could, which these days wasn't often.

Now, as she recalled it all, she asked herself the question

of how: *How did you get me to love you so?* Because she wasn't supposed to. It wasn't in her nature to fall for a man like Brian. He wasn't even her type.

Sandy Hutchinson. There was nothing "sandy" about her. Her complexion was so deep-down chocolately brown, so flawless and satiny smooth her friends called her the Black Diva. As a counterbalance to her richly hued skin, her taste in men ran from butterscotch to café au lait.

Dark, short, and a bit on the rough side, Brian had been the exception. He had managed to change not only her mind, but the very operation of her heart. *Even after the good times disappeared I'm still here.*

She gazed upon his sleeping face, drew cool brown fingers along the slope of his chin and the fullness of his lips. It was her own brand of mojo, an etching of her desire, as questions she would never ask filled her.

Is this what you wanted? Me loving you and you not loving me at all? It isn't supposed to be this way. Not for me, not Sandy Hutchinson. She drew the covers over her shoulder, her face etched in pain. *Can you take us back to before, when times were good, when you seemed to love me?* The answer came before she could take the next breath.

No, Sandy, he can't.

Morning. When had the night disappeared?

Sandy squinted, saw Brian in her mirror, adjusting his shirt and fixing the waist of his pants. Sandy looked at the clock, then back to him. Still early.

"Where are you going?" her voice betraying disappointment. Nine in the morning was too soon to be *leaving my bed and getting ready to head out my front door.*

He turned away from the mirror. "Where you think?" appalled that she was even asking.

A battle moved through her, and her voice rose, meeting the challenge. "Why'd you even come?"

His eyes caught hers in the mirror. "You trippin'?"

"Am I?" she returned, defiance in every breath she took. She didn't know, only that she needed him to stay. But he had a different agenda, one that became apparent as he scooped up his keys, giving himself a last mirror check.

"Walk me to the door."

Moving past the hurt, her spine tingling with anger, Sandy got out of bed. Not bothering to put on a robe, she escorted him to the door. Easing past the rising grief, she pressed her body against his, one last effort to pull him back to her. But the moment their bodies touched, she knew.

He was not staying.

Life used to be so much better, Sandy thought, Monday coming as it always did. *I blink and it's here.*

There was nothing easy about a nine-to-five. It took real will, effort, and determination to go to a job five days a week when all you wanted to do was stay home.

Weekends had become a saving grace for her, a time to enjoy life, kick back. But the past few weekends had issued nothing but disappointment, Brian more out of her life than in.

His visits had become so incidental Sandy had stopped mentioning them to her best friend, Janice. In pursuit of a pipe dream with no chance of redemption, Sandy knew the hopelessness of the situation, and she was constantly on the lookout for someone new. But the search had not yielded any results, so for the moment she was stuck.

Outside of herself Sandy could see the wrongness, the inadequacies, the self-defeatedness of it all. Inside was a whole different arena, where she took the infidelities, the heartache, the overall lack of concern, convincing herself that one day he'd come around.

If nothing else, Brian was a name attached to a face, a voice at the other end of the phone line, and no matter how infrequently she saw him he was still in her life. It wasn't enough, she knew that, but until a real somebody came along, or at least the possibility of one, Sandy wasn't going to step up to the plate.

She had hope, the faith that one day life would turn around, and as she exited the train her eyes shot towards the ceiling.

Please, Lord, let me find somebody new.

So deep was her meditation she didn't see the column until she banged into it. Stunned and embarrassed, Sandy rubbed her shoulder and continued on her way, wondering if it was God's way of saying *Message received.*

Entering the world of Malgovy, Conner, and Dalton was like stepping inside a hyper cosmos of people in motion, ringing phones, and fast chatter. The casualness of the office attire belied the serious got-to-make-that-deadline frenzy, where keeping the wolves at bay was an everyday routine.

By the time Sandy had passed production and made her way down the corridors where the bathrooms and the water fountain were, the office grew less manic, a hint of civility in the air.

There had been a time in her life when she had longed for the mania she had just left behind. Had longed to be in the creative arena of advertising, where ideas were tossed around, revamped, revisited, and refined until they made their way to print ads and T.V.

She had had her eye on production manager like a hawk circling a chicken, but the dream had died quickly when she could not find anything beyond administrative work. A higher degree was needed to land such a job, and returning to school was not on her agenda.

She'd found contentment making appointments, answering phones, and handling correspondence. No, she never made vice president of marketing, but she had gone on to become secretary to one. It was not the glamorous in-the-trenches career she had dreamed about as an undergrad, but it kept her right on the fringes of that fast-paced world.

Sandy got the chance to experience the excitement without becoming victim to it, and that suited her just fine.

"Malgovy, Conner, and Dalton. Sandy Hutchinson speaking."

"Hey, girl, what's up?"

"Martha?"

"Yeah, it's me. Listen, plans have been changed for Saturday night."

Sandy looked at her desk clock, noted the hour, and knew Martha's workday was coming to an end. For an assistant district attorney for the County of Kings, four o'clock was the witching hour, and no doubt Martha was taking her first breath all day.

"We're not coming to your house?"

"No. We're going to hit the club instead."

"Who decided this?"

"Me. It's been a while since we went, and they're having seventies night. You know I can't miss that."

"Janice and Brit know?" The rest of their foursome. They had all been friends since their college days and in the years since had remained close.

"Yeah, they're good to go."

"How are we going to do this?"

"I've got the biggest car, so I'll pick everybody up. Hold on a minute . . ." The line went silent. Sandy wasn't sure how long Martha would have her on hold. She'd give her thirty seconds and if she didn't come back on, Sandy was hanging up.

Twenty seconds had passed when Martha clicked back. "Sorry about that. Real crazy around here today. Anyway, I'm picking up Janice first, Britney second, and you last. We should be there about eleven."

"That's fine."

"Gotta run. Catch you Saturday."

The phone went dead, her weekend half planned. Saturday night was taken care of, but that still left Friday and

Sunday wide open. She'd give Brian until Friday afternoon to call her. *And if he doesn't?* Sandy had no answer.

Tell me something good.

Chaka Khan was singing, but it was what Sandy was thinking as she stood in front of the bathroom mirror. Any second Martha, Janice, and Britney would be ringing her bell, and she was in need of some optimism about the evening ahead.

She was in deep thought, trying to predict the future, when the intercom rang. "On my way!" she yelled, grabbing her purse. *On my way to another Saturday night without Brian,* was all she could think as she left her apartment and made her way down the stairs.

"Ladies," she murmured, coming face-to-face with her girlfriends.

"My girl," Janice piped in.

"Looking good," Martha uttered.

"Let's do this," Britney declared as the four of them headed for Martha's car.

The beat of reggae music pulsed softly around the living room as Adrian held the phone to his ear with his shoulder and wedged his foot into a shoe. "Ya crayzee? Nuh, mon, me not coming all da way to Brooklyn, nuh? What far? Gotta nice little club 'ere in Queens, nuh? You go to dem shoot-tem-up, me make sure I speak well at your funeral."

He listened as his brother gave reasons why he should come out to Flatbush, chuckled, shook his head, and laughed some more. "No, me not go'wen." Adrian glanced at his watch, sucked his teeth. "Me got ta go . . . no . . . I telling ya no. Aw right, den. Peace."

The phone slipped back in its cradle, and Adrian headed towards the bathroom. He searched through colognes until he found the one he was looking for. Splashing his face, his eyes caught the mirror. "Ya look good," he told himself, feeling optimistic and joyful, things that had been gone from his life a very long time.

There were certain beliefs Adrian held dear: do unto others as you would have others do unto you, try to be the best human being you can be, and enjoy life to the fullest.

Once upon a time Adrian had been a testament to all of those beliefs, and his life had been fulfilling, with a few complaints. He had love, family, a good job, and the world was bright. Then two years ago everything he held dear was snatched from him, and it had been a slow steady road back to where he could even smile again.

Countless times he had found himself condemning God for the cruel hand that had been dealt him, and for months after he wallowed in self-pity, with no desire to see another day. But the saying of time healing all wounds began to manifest and slowly but surely Adrian found himself willing to step back into the land of the living.

He put himself back out there and managed a few relationships, but none of them could sustain themselves beyond a few months. In the aftermath Adrian realized he just wasn't ready, but even that was changing now.

He was in high spirits as he left his apartment. Found himself looking forward to a night of dancing. He felt optimistic about the evening before him. "Sumting good in de air," he murmured to himself. He couldn't wait to discover just what that something was.

Club Enchant was jamming.

Colored lights flashed, the mirrored ball spun, and the six-foot speakers vibrated with heady bottom riffs of the bass guitar. The crowd, three hundred strong, danced the Freak, the Funky Penguin, and the Latin Hustle. High-heeled women allowed themselves to be spun in dizzying circles, showing thigh beneath the twirl of full skirts, the fancy footwork quickening as their partners guided them like figure skaters across the floor.

The crowd had readily tossed off the reality of a mature

world for a trip back to the time of no mortgages, nine-to-fives, or real responsibility.

"Love Hangover," "Love Sensation," and "Love Train" played back-to-back, and James Brown's "Gonna Have a Funky Good Time" and Gloria Gaynor's "I Will Survive" got their due.

Sandy sat in her seat, head moving to the beat, eyes adrift about the room. She'd never thought she'd see the day she'd be swooning over records nearly two decades old. Never thought she'd find herself at a club, listening to *her* oldies and longing for the good old days. But here it was 1992, and she was watching couples hustle to "Doctor Love" like it was still 1978.

She finished her drink, contemplated another as she watched her friend move to the beat in her seat. *Britney . . . God bless her*. At 227 pounds and wearing that horrible floral print dress, Sandy understood why no one had asked Britney to dance. *Outfit makes her look forty years bold, and Lord, I wish she'd do something with that hair.* What Sandy couldn't figure out was why nobody had asked *her*. She was no beauty queen, but as a size nine and hair all her own, she got by.

Even Janice had lucked up tonight. She had been snatched up like the latest craze the moment they stepped into the club. Martha had been a close second. Both of them had been dancing most of the evening, leaving Sandy and Britney to table sit.

Britney seemed content, but Sandy was in need of diversion. She was scanning the crowd, wondering if her two friends were ever coming back, when she spotted Martha heading towards the table.

With small breasts and a tiny waist, Martha was all behind, just the way some men liked it. Whenever they went out she constantly got asked to the dance floor. Sandy was just glad to see her returning.

She slid in next to Sandy, leaned into her quick. "Brian's at the bar," she said, serious as anything.

"He see you?"

"No. Don't think so." Martha picked up her abandoned drink and sucked melted ice. "You're going to track him down or what?"

It wasn't a question. It was a call to action. If Sandy couldn't fight her love battles, Martha would gladly jump up and do it for her. But the last thing Sandy wanted was Martha in Brian's face. That was Sandy and Brian's business.

She had stopped telling Martha about the dramas long ago, when they became frequent and too much the norm. The telling of guess-what-he-did only made her more depressed and caused Martha to lip off, something Sandy was certain she wanted to do right now.

"Don't tell me you're just going to sit there?" Martha asked, irritated that Sandy was still in her seat.

She fixed Martha with a look that sizzled. "That's exactly what I'm gonna do." She was unprepared for this turn of events, and Martha antsy beside her wasn't helping one bit. "Things you don't understand," she warned, "and I'm in no mood to explain." Like if Brian hadn't invited her along, that meant he didn't want her up in his face tonight.

Another night, same club, Sandy had spotted the man that she loved on the dance floor. She hadn't even known Brian was coming, but the sight of him had infused her with the need to be by his side. Without thought Sandy had dashed over, wrangling herself between him and his dance partner. But her appearance had been met with cold eyes and hostile belligerency as he took her by the arm and dragged her off the dance floor.

"Whatchu doing?" he had asked, shoving her up against the six-foot speaker as if he was about to do a mugging. "If I want to hang with you, then I ask you along, you understand?"

Sandy did. Understood so deep and so well that it became a number-one rule. The rest of that night she had played hide and seek, trying to stay out of his line of vision.

It was two weeks before she saw him again.

She couldn't tell Martha that. Didn't want to tell Martha anything about Brian, good, bad, or indifferent. *It will just give her more reason to hate him.*

"I don't know why you're playing the fool." It wasn't the words so much that jabbed Sandy but the intensity with which Martha spoke them.

"My choice, now, isn't it?" But even as Sandy said that, she could not ignore the truth there. She *was* playing the fool. She took a deep breath, looking around for an out, *someplace to clear my head, get some breathing space,* when a man approached their table.

His age was indefinable, vague beneath the protruding belly, the jowly face. The pudgy hand he extended gave no indication either. "Wanna dance?" he asked Britney.

Sandy raised an eyebrow. *Well, I'll be damned. Britney getting a dance before me?*

It was obvious that Britney was, because she nodded and rose out of her seat. Depositing her purse onto Sandy's lap, she was off and gone, swallowed up in the crowd, leaving Sandy alone with the seething Martha.

"So? What are you going to do, Sandy?"

"I told you, not a damn thing," she answered, her voice cutting and defensive.

Martha pulled back. Turned away in time to see a man extend his hand her way. Martha's smile was automatic as she got up, the rhythm latching onto her swaying hips. She paused long enough to deliver her final words, "You are good, sister," and headed for the dance floor.

Sandy was at the bar. She had given up deciding what she was going to do if she saw Brian—*act like I don't*—concluding the evening was a washout. *Not even a single dance.*

She was sitting there with Britney and Britney's new friend Maurice. Not her speed, but he seemed to suit Britney just fine. He was buying, and the ladies were drinking as they sat listening to the buzz of other people's conversations.

Must be nice, Sandy mused, watching Maurice putting away the stack of twenties all crisp and flat as if they had just come from an ATM. *Must be real nice to have a wallet full of money that you can bring to the club and not worry about spending it all in one shot.*

The last time Sandy had had that much cash in hand, she was making a payment on her two-month-past-due cable bill. She made an adequate salary—twenty-eight thousand a year—had no children, and her car was paid for, but still Sandy had credit cards up the behind, and $550 a month went to the VISAs, Mastercards, and Discovery Cards of the world.

She had just gotten paid yesterday but still had to bum a twenty from Martha just so she could get in. It was the first of the month and her paycheck had places to go before she even saw it.

Rent took most of it, her one-bedroom garden apartment off the Laurelton Expressway, a hefty six hundred dollars a month. The utilities took another hundred. She had to buy groceries for two weeks and that had been another hundred, and that cute sexy velvet dress that she had put on layaway had to be paid for.

There was her six-week touch-up at LeAnn's House of Beauty, a payment on her student loan, and a ton of dry cleaning she had to get out of the cleaner's. Getting paid every two weeks was hard. Sandy's money disappeared quicker than she could think. "Late" was her middle name when it came to her credit card, phone, and student loan payments.

She was the middle-class working poor, two checks away from homelessness. She didn't look poor, didn't act poor, but she was. Her life was a system of robbing Peter to pay Paul, but nobody had to know that except her and Equifax.

Sandy yawned, the need for sleep catching up with her.

She picked up her glass and took a long sip, watching Britney and Maurice make a connection. Another yawn found her, and she blinked to wake herself, turning her head, in need of movement.

Fine. The only way Sandy could describe him.

Soft wavy brown hair, perfectly arched brows, and skin the color of butterscotch—he was a dream come true, and he was sitting at the end of the bar. *Stop staring.* But she couldn't, especially now, since he was staring back. He smiled; she smiled. Was still smiling when he got off his barstool and came over to her.

"Mind if I join you?"

"No . . ."

Thick tan fingers were extended her way. "I'm Adrian."

Sandy wanted to say that she knew that. Wanted to tell him that his name sounded like some kind of angel, and he certainly had the looks to go with it. But his close proximity had shorted out her circuits, and the most she could trust herself to say was her name.

"Sandy . . ." she murmured, her hand moving quickly around the small group. "This is Britney and Maurice." She made room for him, nervous, excited that he wanted to be close.

Their eyes met, each weighing the other's attraction. "Been here long?" he asked, a joyful smile on his face.

"Since midnight." She looked at her watch. It was quarter to three. "A while, I guess."

"Crowded tonight," Adrian offered, his eyes drifting from hers, came back. "Feel like dancing?"

Not anymore. Her great expectations about dancing the night away had died hours ago. She shook her head.

Adrian laughed. Put his glass down. Swiveled on the stool, his knee coming in contact with her thigh. "So, Sandy," he said, testing the sound of her name, "clubs your thing?"

Her answer came quickly, heart beat fast. "I like to dance, yeah."

His eyes twinkled. "I was a real disco hound in my youth."

"Youth? You can't be that old?"

Adrian looked into the drink. "Old enough."

"How old is old enough?"

"Let's just say I won't see thirty again," he said humorously.

"Me too."

"Back in the day I'd hit the clubs two, three times a week." Adrian paused, apparently awed by his own stamina. "Now I'm down to two times a month, maybe."

"I know what you mean."

Silence arrived, each settling back, sipping their drinks, aware of the delicate possibility between them. Something had drawn them to each other, but there was no exactness to what might happen next.

The sound of the Whispers' "If You Just Say Yes" filtered into the outer bar. His voice came to her, soft and hopeful. "You sure I can't convince you to go for one more spin? Nobody does it like the Whispers."

She looked up at him, at his sun-drenched eyes, the pearly white teeth. She glanced at his butterscotch skin and the naturally wavy hair and knew. She couldn't tell him no if she wanted to.

They stood on the sidewalk outside the club, the cold winter night nibbling at their ears, the skin about their necks. Britney had taken a ride with Maurice, Martha and Janice were waiting in Martha's idling Volvo, and Sandy and Adrian were feeding each other eye candy.

Few words spoken, hands jammed deep in their pockets, they stood there a long time, a thousand words they would never speak between them. "I better go," she said after a while.

Adrian looked up the block. "Yeah, it's late." Looked back at her. Reluctance as deep as the ocean gleamed in his eyes. "I'll call you," he said as he took her hand, gave it a squeeze, then turned and headed up the block.

Will you? all she could wonder as she watched him leave, then trotted off to the warmth of the idling Volvo.

Adrian maneuvered his car up the long slope of Parsons Boulevard, the engine of his 1991 Camry purring like a cat being rubbed, smooth. He was feeling mellow, easy. Light. Those many months of unhappiness and loneliness were falling away like autumn leaves knowing it was time to let go.

"Sandee . . ." He said her name as a whisper, a soft sigh that drifted up from his chest and eased from his lips. He could not believe his luck when he had spotted her unescorted at the bar. He had watched her, smitten with her rich beauty, wondering if she were alone.

There had been only one other woman he had been drawn to more, and the idea that life was giving him a second chance was that breath of fresh air he had longed for. Filling and complete, it infused him. The lost hope he thought he'd never recover, returning soft and delicate as a butterfly's wing.

Sumting good in de air. Adrian smiled to himself. *Yes, sur, sumting good.*

Nothing came without a price, Sandy realized as she lay in bed, dehydrated and fuzzy-headed. She had exceeded her three-drink limit last night and was feeling the effects of it this morning. It took ten minutes of just lying still before she was able to roll out of bed.

Into the bathroom she went, getting into the shower, letting the hot water work its magic. She brushed her teeth, slipped into sweatpants and a T-shirt, and went to put something in her churning belly. The crème de menthe had been fine going down, but eight hours later it was in serious revolt.

She ate one slice of buttered toast, drank half her coffee

and a full glass of orange juice. Started on the one thing she liked to do least—clean.

She didn't mind dusting, had no aversion to washing and scrubbing, but vacuuming always got on her last nerve. Quickly she did the carpet in her living room, the hall, and, just as quickly, her bedroom. With a sigh that came from the bottom of her soul, she shut the machine off, rolled it back to the closet, and hoisted it inside. *Kitchen*, she was thinking when her intercom buzzed. She wasn't expecting a soul, and company wasn't on her agenda.

Sometimes Sandy just wanted quiet.

Last night the fullness of her situation had been laid out on a platter, and there was no more denying the reality. What she had with Brian was so little that they had been in the same place and she couldn't even go say hello. *Which means we have nothing.*

At the other end of the spectrum she had met her dream come true, and she needed time to decipher what it meant.

She remembered her first impression of Adrian—*fine*— and was trying hard to hold back her hope. She didn't want to put all her eggs in one basket; meeting him could have been about nothing at all.

Adrian was not the first man to woo her. Others had taken on the role with just as much gusto. Buying her drinks, dancing slow, telling her bits and pieces of themselves until she felt she had known them all her life and wanted to be there for the rest of it.

Smiling at her, touching her, taking her number and promising to call, the majority never kept that promise. Sandy had no way of knowing if Adrian was in that group.

Then there was that other bothersome thought: could a man that fine ever be truly unattached? Could there not be some woman out there determined to have him or win him back? *Could he just find me and want me forever?*

Her intercom buzzed again.

Sandy studied the little eggshell-colored box with the red and black buttons. *Could be my knuckleheaded brother.*

And though he got on her nerves frequently, she hadn't seen him in a while. *Or maybe it's Janice.* Sandy found herself hoping it was. It would give her a chance to bounce around her Adrian theories.

She pushed the intercom button asked "Who?" with a smile.

"Me."

The joy left her, and it was a while before she buzzed him in.

This is how change happens, Sandy was thinking as she waited, front door open and one hand on her hip. *This is how it comes.*

There was nothing new to this situation as Brian closed the distance between them. It was old hat that he was showing up at her door after being out all night somewhere else. But it was one-thirty in the afternoon, and it was obvious from his clothes that he hadn't even been home to change his damn drawers.

"Wus doing?" he asked with a grin she could have slapped right off his face.

"Not you," she answered, eyes smoldering, feeling a rage towards him she had never allowed herself to feel.

His brow furrowed. "What's your problem?"

"My problem?" Her voice rose. "You, that's my problem."

"What you talking about, Sandy?"

"Talking about last night."

"What about it?"

"I know where you were."

"Wasn't nowhere."

She was glad to tell him differently. "Yes, you were. You were at the club and so was I. But you want to know the really sad part? We were in the same place and I couldn't even come over and say hello. You're supposed to be my man and I couldn't even come over and say hi. That's bullshit, and I've had enough. We're through."

Brian looked totally baffled. *Can't blame him, can I? Hadn't I loved him madly? Hadn't I taken his bullshit for nearly two years and sat around waiting for seconds?*

"Whatchu mean we through?"

"I'm not doing this anymore. I'm not sitting around waiting for you to spend some time with me. I'm not letting you into my apartment or my bed after you've been out Lord knows where. I've had enough of it and you."

Brian studied her, surprise dancing in his eyes. He went on another second fine-tuning his impressions before his face broke out into a bewildered smile. "You ain't meaning it."

"Oh yeah? You think I'm not? . . . you love me?" It was the one question she had always longed to know but was too afraid to ask. Some men ran from the L word, and Brian was one of them, but at this moment that's exactly what Sandy wanted. She wanted him gone.

"Do you?" she asked again, feeling him emotionally back away. "You don't," she decided for both of them. "If you did, you would have taken me with you last night, not come to my front door at one o'clock in the afternoon with leftovers."

He reached for her, but Sandy shrugged off his attempt. "A good thing," she admonished, her voice trembling with rage. "I was the best thing you ever had. You remember that, hear? You remember when you're out there all by yourself, how you blew this good thing."

"You mean this?"

She glared at him, allowing her eyes to answer.

"Don't do this," he pleaded, his voice a whisper. "You my heart."

She tried not to think about being his anchor, the one true thing he returned to again and again. But it was a truth they both knew and was hard to ignore.

"Please?"

Sandy saw herself letting Brian in and hours later his exit. He was needing her now, but how long would that

need last? *A day? A week? Then it'll be business as usual?*
This was the thought that found her, stayed, even as he
stood, heart on his sleeve.

She looked at him, sorrowed but more so determined.
"I'm sorry, but I can't, not anymore. It's over."

She did not say good-bye but simply stepped inside her
apartment. Gently she closed the door and locked it. She
leaned her whole body against the solid wood, the beat of
her heart easing over the sound of Brian's fading footsteps.

For two years Brian had been the half to her whole, no
matter how incidental, no matter how incomplete. He had
been the voice she had called after a hard day and the one
she sought during a lonely night, and now she had said
good-bye.

While some part of her rejoiced, it was too tiny to do
away with the sorrow that wedged itself inside. Regret, riv-
eting and overwhelming, covered her like rain.

Letting go . . . *Just let it go, let Brian go. Get beyond this.*
But Sandy couldn't do it alone. Needed help. She pulled
out her Phyllis Hyman CD, needing a voice, a reason,
something to pull her through the sorrow.

Her head wobbled, her eyes closed as she gave in to the
pain, the fire branding regret of it all. Because even in the
end, her love was no less potent, no less real.

That was the hard part. Beyond her pain, beyond her
sense of loss, Sandy had turned over her heart and had gone
on for two years hungry for more than he could give.

Now, in the aftermath, her yearning was no less tangible.
Deep inside her, the ache was the size of Vermont. *How
long? How long before the pain goes away?* she needed to
know as Phyllis Hyman's voice resonated around her. *How
long before the sadness is replaced with some joy?*

Ring.

The music was turned up so loud that Sandy nearly
didn't hear the phone the first time. *Ring.* Her head turned

in the direction of her side table, then back around as she reached for the volume control on her receiver.

Ring. She was slow getting to her feet, the pain, the music, and her forty-seven-minute powpow with herself making her bones stiff. Muscles protesting, spine slow to straighten, Sandy made her way, picked up, and swallowed, her voice choked with tears. "Hello?"

"Hi, can I speak to Sandy?"

She didn't recognize the voice. "This is her."

"Hi. This is Adrian."

Adrian. She swallowed again. "Hi."

"Busy?"

Sandy wiped her cheek. "No. Just listening to music."

"So, how are you doing?"

"Okay." But her voice was tight.

"You got a cold?"

"Cold? No."

"You sound nasal."

"I did some cleaning earlier . . . dust allergies."

"Oh. Well, listen, I was calling because I had a good time last night." He paused. "And figured I'd call to see if you had any plans for the day."

"No plans," she told him, her world shifting for a third time in less than twenty-four hours, the view brighter, clearer. She blinked away the last few tears, ran fingers over damp eyes. "Why?" she asked, eager to hear what he had in mind. Hoping it was something wonderful and good and fun. That he'd be special and kind and decent and loving. Sandy was hoping that this time around, her prayers would be answered.

"Well, I was thinking about taking you out to City Island. They've got the best seafood around."

"We talking shrimp and lobster seafood?" Her heart lightening, her taste buds coming to life.

Adrian chuckled. "Yeah, if that's what you want."

"I want," she said, holding back nothing. Wanting to be

there with him so fully that, in that moment, there was nothing she wanted more.

The car raced along the Throgs Neck Bridge. Tall steel girders and bridge cables loomed overhead. The lobster tail, baked potato, and salad were just a memory as Sandy looked towards her left, the distant shores of Manhattan twinkling in the night.

"Mind if I turn off the radio, play something else?"

"No, go ahead," she told him.

She hadn't thought it could be done. Didn't think that she'd meet someone who could take away her Brian Jones. Fifty-one minutes after she closed the door on Brian, Adrian had called. A sweet fate, a long-awaited destiny. Now, into the first few hours of her new life, Sandy couldn't believe how good she felt. She'd have to do double thanks to God tonight.

Adrian. Mr. Butterscotch.

Pisces by birth, he was single, with no children, the oldest of four. His father was from Trinidad. He fixed office equipment for a living and had a one-bedroom garden apartment in Flushing, Queens. Thought Sandy was beautiful.

"I wish I was a willow, and I could sway to the music in the wind."

"Who's that?" Sandy asked, pointing towards the car stereo.

"That?" His smile was easy. "That's my girl."

"Your girl?"

Adrian nodded. "Yeah, that's Phoebe Snow . . . 'Harpo's Blues.'"

Sandy listened, straining to hear the words. "What's she singing about?"

Adrian shrugged. "Kind of a lamenting song, y'know. Full of wishes and dreams never quite attained, that sort of thing."

Sandy sat back, the words filling her, tickling some lost

memory, imbuing her with longing. She listened, Phoebe Snow filling the air, and then the song was fading, coming to a soft end.

She wanted to hear it again. Felt she was on the edge of solving some great mystery within her. Felt the song could help her solve it if she heard it again.

"Can you play it again?"

Adrian smiled. "Sure." Reached over, hit the rewind button, his eyes never leaving the road.

In front of her apartment.

The engine idled, wisps of white exhaust drifting past the side passenger window. Phoebe Snow was on the car stereo, and Sandy was listening intently. She liked this Phoebe Snow. Was surprised she had never heard of her before, that the music was from an album released all the way back in 1974.

She black? Sandy had asked. *No, Jewish,* Adrian had told her. Sandy didn't want to leave the music. It was one of the reasons she was still sitting in Adrian's car ten minutes after he had pulled up to the curb. Adrian was the other.

Sandy didn't have any delusions about him and how she felt. Knew that if she invited him in now it'd be hard not to get in bed, and she didn't want to do that yet. Didn't want to risk a possible relationship for a one-night stand. He liked her and she wanted him to keep on liking her.

She hadn't kissed him. All Sandy had in that moment was his smile that was always there when he looked at her, the sparkle in his eyes. Sandy hadn't run her fingers through the soft, natural waves in his hair or even felt his fingers entwined with hers. Still, there was a potency between them that was tinder dry.

She unlocked her door. "Better go," eyes away from him.

The tips of his fingers found the space beneath her chin. "Not inviting me in?"

Sandy shook her head. "Can't do that yet."

He lifted her chin towards him. Sandy was surprised by the tenderness in his eyes. "I really like you, Sandy."

I know, her eyes answered back, as she leaned in and gave his lips a quick peck. "Good night," she said, getting out of the car.

He watched her go, taking a piece of his heart with her. Felt good things, sweet things between them. Looked forward to the next time.

life—being with a generous man—took some getting used to.

Now, as the end credits for *I'm Gonna Get You Sucka* began to roll, uncertainties still had her. Adrian had been kind and considerate, but just how far could they go?

For all her wants, for all her needs, her lifelong search to find someone just like him, she knew that, just as she had preferences—butterscotch to café au lait—the type of man she desired had preferences too, and often they wanted their woman just as light as they were, or lighter.

That Adrian seemed taken with her blackness, that he had a taste for the chocolate, was a kind of mystery to her. Sandy wasn't looking gift horses in the mouth, but she couldn't help but wonder if she was just the flavor of the month, a dance on the dark side to be wooed for a hot second and then dropped.

And what about the last woman that loved him? Whoever she was, how could she just go away and stay away forever? How could any woman ever walk away from a man like him? I would have never been able to let him go.

She knew this with every breath she took. Knew she would have gone through the fire and back just to keep him. It wasn't a pretty thought, but it was a real one.

Beyond his good looks, his intelligence, there was a wholesome tenderness to him, a gentlemanly quality that wafted through everything he did—opening doors, taking her hand, the easy way in which he spoke. Now that he was in her life, Sandy couldn't ever see him being anywhere else. Could not imagine him just walking away and never coming back.

She looked at the screen, then back at him. "Good, right?"

"Oh yeah . . . those platform shoes were too funny." A good choice, the day had turned into an easy afternoon. Adrian stood, slipped on his leather coat. "Ready?"

"Sure am."

They exited through the back door and stepped into the

TWO

The multiplex movie theater in Valley Stream was not one of Sandy's favorite theaters. While it boasted twelve theaters, surround sound, and free parking, there was always a long line, it was a magnet for rowdy teenage boys, and the seats weren't padded enough for her liking. The popcorn came prepopped, and the "butter" resembled motor oil. Still, this was where she and Adrian ended up for their second date.

It had been so long since Sandy had had this simple pleasure, out on a date in the daytime with a man, that it took a little while to adjust. It was strange watching Adrian pull out his wallet at the ticket booth, her hand on the gold fastener of her pocketook, ready to pay her own way.

It was strange standing at the concession stand, Adrian telling her to get whatever she wanted. There were so many choices, so much she wanted, but she didn't want to appear greedy or high-maintenance.

When she decided on a "small" buttered popcorn and a tiny cup of Sprite, Adrian urged her to at least get a box of Raisinets. "What fun is a movie without real junk?" he asked.

It was these little things, mere seconds in times that made Sandy realize just what she hadn't been getting during her time with Brian.

Who was that woman? Who was that person that inhabited my body and took so little for so long? Was that really me? Had I really gone on as long as I did like that?

When her popcorn was finished, he offered her some of his. He gave her a handful of his Gummi Bears and split his nachos with cheese. When he extended his large Coke her way, Sandy declined, thirsty as she was. This new parking lot, the chill and darkness taking them both by surprise. It had been sunny and the temperature in the forties when they arrived. Now the sky was midnight blue and the wind, brittle.

"I hate winter," she decided, the chilly air finding her easy.

"Cold?"

"A little."

"Come here."

She leaned into him, her head finding the space beneath his shoulder.

"Better?" he asked, holding her, his heart beating fast in his chest.

"Yeah," Sandy managed, a perfect fit.

Adrian took the curve around Kissena Boulevard a little too fast for Sandy's liking. His tires squealed in protest as she grabbed the ceiling strap. "Whoa," she uttered as the Village Mews Condos came up on her left and McDonald's on her right.

He looked over at her. "Didn't scare you, did I?"

"Yes," she answered quickly, her heart thrumming in her chest.

"Big Mac?" he asked as he pulled into the drive-through.

If she had been hesitant before, she wasn't now. The snacks at the movie theater had long ago faded and her stomach was singing its feed-me song. "*And* a large fry," she answered quickly. "Large Sprite would be good."

"No hot apple pie?" he asked.

"What you're trying to do, make me sleepy?"

Golden eyes sparkled her way. "It's a thought."

The speaker crackled. "Welcome to McDonald's. Can I take your order?"

"Yeah, let me have three Big Macs."

Sandy's brow raised. *Three*?

"Two large fries, a large Sprite, a large Coke." He

looked at her, then back at the speaker. "And two apple pies."

"Is that it?"

"Yep, that's it."

Adrian put the car into drive and eased around the corner, Sandy's head shaking, her voice sprinkled with delight. "You *are* trying to make me sleepy, aren't you?"

"Ain't nothing wrong with that."

Sandy looked away. *Nope, nothing at all.*

Sand-colored garden apartments took up the block on both sides. The pale bricks and black glossy trim gave the street a serene tempered feel.

Sandy squinted through the windshield, pointed up the block. "Queens College, right?"

"Yep. Parking's a real bitch sometimes." Adrian coasted, saw a car pulling out, and slid into the empty spot. "Welcome to my 'hood." But there wasn't anything "hoody" about it.

"You take the drinks. I got the rest." Sandy passed the bags over, got out of the car, and stood on the quiet street looking towards the dim lights of the Queens College campus.

Nice, she thought, letting Adrian lead the way.

Adrian flicked on the hall light, and the first thing Sandy saw was a huge sculpture of an African warrior. Made out of a dark wood, it gleamed softly under the ceiling light. The sharp chin, jutting cheekbones, and determined eyes held her attention. Adrian saw her staring and shared the history.

"Got that in Ghana."

"You went to Africa?"

"For my twenty-first birthday. A gift from my mother."

"Nice mom."

"Always on me to remember my blackness."

His living room held more sculptures, more pictures, Africa's influence everywhere. She recognized a Ghanaian stool made of a reddish hardwood, its seat looped with etchings on its base. Knew right away that the wooden doll with the elongated breast, round belly, and jutting penis was a fertility god.

"Don't tell me you brought all this back?" she asked, eyes drifting, taking in everything.

"Most of it. Some of it I got down on A-Hundred-and-Twenty-Fifth Street in Harlem."

"Back to his roots," Sandy said, a private thought that slipped through her lips.

"Most definitely," Adrian muttered, sizing her up.

The Hollywood kitchen offered no place to eat, so they took their meal in the living room, Sandy sitting on the edge of the sofa, Adrian preferring the floor.

With care Sandy bit into her Big Mac, determined to keep the sauce in her mouth and nowhere else. Adrian, at home now, dug right in. She watched for a moment as he took a huge bite, unaware of the sauce smearing the side of his face as he shoved a bunch of fries into his mouth. He went on that way for a while, a chunk of Big Mac, a wad of fries, before he realized Sandy was watching him.

"What?" he asked, oblivious.

"Nothing," she said, passing him a napkin. "Here, wipe your mouth."

Oh, she liked him. Sandy liked Adrian very much. She liked who he was, what he was about, and the way he looked. Now only one question remained for her—to sleep with him or not.

It was a question Sandy had been asking herself ever since he held her outside the movie theater. That perfect fit had her curious, and she wanted to know what it would feel like to lie naked against him.

She laughed at herself.

Adrian looked up at her from her lap. "What?"

Her smile was quick, her hands busy with the tips of his hair. No grease, no gel. Just soft, dry curls.

Sandy had wanted hair like that all her life. When the Jherri curl hit years back, she had been the first one in line, putting gels and sprays on her hair, wearing the plastic cap to bed like it was a newfound religion.

She had wanted Adrian's eyes. Had bought a pair of hazel contact lenses, too. Wore them twice before she got tired of folks staring at the dark brown sister with eyes of fire and ice.

Sandy wanted Adrian's butterscotch skin. Had always wanted to trade her dark berry complexion for Vanessa Williams's or Halle Berry's. She had grown up envying Lonette McKee, the pretty, white-looking black actress. Understood why Michael Jackson had undone what nature had dealt him.

Sandy looked down at the man who had everything she wanted. Wished she could do osmosis and vanish within him. Wear his skin for a day, just one day; then maybe the ghost of her past, of being the "dark one," of being called "Smoky" and "Midnight" would vanish.

"What are you thinking so hard on?"

"You," she answered, forcing a smile.

"Yeah, and?"

She shook her head, her voice feathery and in awe. "You're so fine."

He looked at her a long time before he spoke. "So are you."

Loving Adrian.

It wasn't hard, and it took so little effort as she lay beside him damp and spent. Loving a man who was beautiful and perfect and so together was easy for her. *'Cause I've been waiting for him all my life.*

His hand hit her bare hip gently. "So what you gonna do?" It was the sound of his voice in the darkness, the closeness of his warm bare skin, the I-need-you tone in his voice that made her shift, turn, roll towards him.

It was his eyes that were shimmering even in the darkened bedroom that made her caress his cheek, face stubble like soft sandpaper scratching her fingertips. It was the way his hand stayed on her hip as if it never wanted to disown it that made her smile, her teeth a flash of white in the dimness.

There was more intimacy between them in that moment than in all the time she had spent with Brian. She had been living in the land of the dead, and now she was back with the living.

"Don't know," she answered with joy. "What you want to do?"

He shrugged, eyes evasive. "Asking you."

"No," she insisted, "I'm asking *you*." *'Cause it feels so good and you got to tell me if there's gonna be more. You have to ask me to stay.*

"You staying?"

One eyebrow rose. "Am I?" Wanting to be sure, needing to know that the same need she was sensing from him now would still be there come morning.

"I want you to."

"Okay."

That simple word erased any doubt and took away any uncertainty of what morning would bring. That simple word, *okay,* a rainbow about them both.

The divvy, the dish, the dirt.

Martha, Britney, and Janice sat around Sandy's living room noshing on buffalo wings, smears of blue cheese dressing dotting the corners of their mouths.

It was Martha who asked what everyone else wanted to but wouldn't. "So was it good?"

"What good?" Sandy asked back, picking up her wine and drawing a long sip.

"You know what."

The question lingered in the air as Sandy reached for

another wing and dipped it into the creamy white dressing. She took a bite, rolled her eyes, moaning *umm*, refusing to answer. *Wasn't none of their business.* But the memory of it found her, and the smile she tried to hold on to escaped.

Martha didn't miss it. "Must've been. Look at her trying not to smile."

"Yeah, she smiling," Janice added, watching her friend. "He has any brothers?"

Britney laughed, chest heaving, hand fluffing the air. "Oh, you know it never works that way."

"Isn't that the truth," Martha said. "Remember Bill?" The others nodded. "You and his brother were just all into each other," she reminded Janice. "Then me and Bill hooked up. What happened?"

"We broke up, then you and Bill called it quits," Janice recalled.

"Right. See, that never works."

Britney took a long sip of her wine, her eyes dancing around the room. "Well, I don't know about the rest of you, but I'm very satisfied these days." Everyone looked at her as if she was drunk.

"No more wine for you," Martha said, moving the bottle out of her reach.

"I'm not drunk," Britney insisted, shifting half a pound of greasy hair off one shoulder. "Just happy."

Happy. When was the last time Britney had been? Ronald Reagan was doing his first term in the White House, and even then her relationship hadn't lasted six months.

Britney's eyes dusted the room. "I know when Maurice first walked up to our table, nobody was impressed . . . but I was. After not being noticed," her voice grew soft, "finally somebody was noticing me."

She was right, of course. Nobody had thought much of the heavyset man who had asked Britney to dance. But Britney had, and as a result, she was finding some joy.

Her eyes glistened. "And it's nice, real nice. Having

somebody caring about you, wanting you. Doing things with you."

Sandy nodded. "I know exactly how you mean."

"And I know he isn't the type of man you guys go for. He's not all lean and full of muscles, but he's treating me real good. Real good, and that's all I want."

"All anybody wants," Janice added, a tenderness filling the room.

Martha eased her arm around Britney's shoulder. "Well, you go on, then, go and be happy. You deserve it, Brit."

"We all do," Sandy added, her eyes fast on everyone.

THREE

The middle of March was living up to its reputation. A lion of a cold front was roaring down on Manhattan with a vengeance. Sandy strolled next to Adrian, head tucked and shoulders hunched. She and winter had never been on good terms, and today she was getting her behind whipped.

They moved down 125th Street, the most famous street in Harlem. Vendors from Ghana, Nigeria, and Senegal lined the sidewalk, selling everything from drinking gourds to handcrafted leather bags. Everywhere she looked, there was a face that matched her own dark hue, a shape of a head that had surely belonged to her grandfather Nelly, her great-uncle Alec.

Little Africa.

"Isn't this great?"

Great? I've been freezing my butt off since we got out the car. But Sandy wasn't about to tap-dance on his joy. If strolling down 125th Street at the end of winter with the temperature cold enough to keep ice solid was Adrian's quest of the moment, so be it.

"Yeah, great."

"Wait."

Sandy swallowed her sigh. They were nearly to the end of the block, the last vendor in her line of vision. She had hoped they would make it to the corner without another detour, but for the twelfth time since they'd started this trek, something was catching Adrian's eye.

Is this how it is for men when we women go shopping? Tagging along, hoping we will finish and not the least bit interested in what we're looking at? Because for all the afrocentricities lining the street, Sandy had no interest in any of it.

Adrian, on the other hand, couldn't get enough of it, something that was evident as he greeted the shiny-eyed vendor standing behind his table. Digging his hand into a rattan basket, Adrian gathered up a handful of cowrie beads and shook them.

Sandy had seen them stitched on leather bags, worn as necklaces, and dangling at the end of dreads, but Adrian didn't seem the pouch-carrying type, nor could she see him making a necklace. Couldn't be for his hair; he didn't have the type. *No, not my baby.*

Graduation had come quickly. Adrian had gone from some guy she'd met to *my baby* in less than three weeks. The gorgeous man beside her who loved her chocolate skin had done what no other had—made black beautiful again.

Adrian reached for his wallet.

"What are you going to do with those?" Sandy asked, cold, distracted, and in need of something hot.

"Not so much to do as to *have*."

The explanation went right over her head as Sandy spotted a misty-windowed diner. There on the breeze rode the smell of freshly perked coffee and meat being grilled. It called out to her most basic needs, and she knew as soon as Adrian was through, that's where they would be heading.

Belly full, boots off, and the car heater on high, Sandy leaned her head against the headrest, seconds from dozing.

He shook her gently. "Hey, no sleeping."

She waved him off, shifted her shoulders, and smacked her lips. Eyes closing, she drifted to the sound of the tires over the asphalt and the occasional jostle across potholed streets.

She must have slept because the next thing she knew, Adrian was cutting off the engine and asking her to grab the African mask out of the back. As with the cowrie beads, she was curious as to where he planned to put the three-foot carving.

"Right over my bed." He thumped his chest for empha-
sis. "I'm a warrior, don't you know?"

Lightest-looking warrior I ever seen. She tried not to
smirk. "What about the little beady things?"

"Cow-ree," he insisted.

"Yeah, those."

He held the foyer door open for her. "Put them on the
windowsill facing southeast."

"Why southeast?"

"Direction of the Motherland."

She saw so little "Motherland" in Adrian that she wondered if he was serious or joking. Not that it mattered.
Didn't matter one little bit.

Like a lid on a can slowly being opened, bit by bit Adrian
opened up Sandy's world. He had taken her to the Shom-
berg Museum in Harlem and crowded reggae clubs in
Queens Village. There had been the Latin clubs in the
Bronx where he taught her how to dance salsa and a Thai
restaurant on Main Street where she got her first taste of
Thailand cuisine. Their latest journey took them to Flatbush
near Nostrand Avenue in Brooklyn.

A half-dozen Caribbean dialects moved around her as
they moved through the congested streets bursting with Saturday shoppers. Two old West Indian women in knit caps,
brightly colored sweaters, long plaid skirts, and snow boots
stood on the sidewalk discussing news from home as they
sifted through sheets of stiff salted codfish and tested the
ripeness of plantain bananas.

Adrian and Sandy stopped at a shop that looked no bigger than her Hollywood kitchen. Leaning towards the
scarred, bulletproof Plexiglas window, Adrain ordered two
beef patties. Sandy took hers gratefully, the heat from it
warming her chilled fingers.

"Be careful, it's hot," Adrian warned, but Sandy ignored
him. Jamaican beef patties she knew. They were right up
there with pizza and Chinese takeout.

She took a big bite. Heat rushed her mouth and brown spicy meat landed on the side of her hand. She slurped it up with a fast tongue, nodding in agreement. "Hot but good."

"Bet you never got a patty like that from the corner store."

"You're absolutely right," she answered, going in for another bite.

Flatbush was as lively as a carnival. The entire spectrum of the Caribbean seemed to be represented as people from a dozen islands filled the streets. "This place is something. I never even knew it existed."

" 'Cause you a Yayn-kee, dat's why."

"Ain't nothing wrong with being American born."

"Never said it was . . . just that there's so much more to the world, things you never seen, heard, tasted." Popping the last of his snack into his mouth, Adrian stopped in front of a store. "Like goat-head soup."

"Goat what?"

"Head. Goat head." He reached for the door. "Come on."

The air was heavy with a slaughterhouse smell. The feel of sawdust wedging up under the soles of her sneakers, *to catch the blood*, caught her off guard.

A meat market? She couldn't remember the last time she'd been in one. *When I was a kid?* It took her back to bloodstained white aprons and the whisk of a knife being sharpened against a metal pole.

Sandy looked up and realized it had been a bad move. Hanging from a rack were a dozen animal heads, their done-away flesh revealing a textbook picture of skin, muscle, and tissue in pearly red, gray, and pale blue. Dead eyes fixed her with a stare, and her stomach churned. *Gonna be sick.* She looked away.

"You all right?"

She nodded towards Adrian, studied the wall, the shelves of spices. She studied bags of strange snacks stapled to cardboard, telling herself, insisting to herself, *I'm not going to throw up*.

"I," an older man said from behind the counter.

"I. Give me one of dem head, nuh? And make it fresh. Me want tit chopped. Making soop."

Sandy looked at Adrian, his perfect island lilt faded in the air. "What was that?" she wanted to know.

"What?" he answered, mischief dancing in his eyes.

"The accent thing."

He cuffed her lightly on the chin. " 'Oo I be, nuh? Trinnie to da 'eart." He drifted towards a cooler, came back twisting the top off a bottle, bringing the ginger beer to his lips.

Whack! The sound of the sharp blade cutting into the bone echoed around the store. *Whack!* Sandy jumped, the whole experience catching her off guard.

"What's he doing?" she asked, her voice a whisper, feeling foolish asking at all.

" 'E choppin' it up fine."

She hit his arm. "Stop that."

"Stop what?"

"Stop talking like that."

"Why?"

She didn't have an exact answer, only that he seemed to become a whole different person when he did. "Because."

"Scarin' ya?"

"No, not scaring me, just that it's weird hearing this whole other voice coming through you."

He slipped an arm around her. "It's a part of who I am, Sandy. Can't ask me not to be who I am."

"But you never done it before."

"When I'm down here, it's like coming home . . . accent just flows."

"Yeah, well, it's like you turn into somebody else, and I don't know you."

"Still the same." His eyes sparkled. "Wedder I tawk like dis or I talk like this. Same person."

"You were born there?"

"Trinidad?" He shook his head. "No, I was born right here at Kings County. But I spent my summers there, and my father is from there. My mom's poppa, too."

"You still have relatives in Trinidad?"

"Oh yeah."

"Anybody live on the beach?" Her curiosity up.

His eyes lost some of their glow. He shook his head, his voice less cheerful. "Nah, that's for rich folks and hotels. We're neither."

With the efficiency of a gourmet chef, Adrian moved around his kitchen, putting a big pot of water on to boil, chopping vegetables, and searching out spices in his cabinet. He seemed at home, at ease, as Sandy moved about, getting out of his way.

He had gone on about the soup he was going to prepare for her, a deep joy dancing in his eyes. She tried to change his mind, but he insisted that she would enjoy it.

"I'd rather have oxtail," she said as he tossed herbs into the pot, the plastic bag of goat head, eyeballs and teeth included, resting on the counter. "Can't you make oxtail? I love oxtail," she went on as Adrian dropped what looked like a tiny tree into the pot.

He squeezed her arm absently. "Ya gonna love it."

"Can't you leave the eyes and teeth out?"

One brow raised. "That's the best part."

"Teeth?" she asked. "How do you chew teeth?"

"You don't chew it, don't eat it, can't. But it's just a part of the soup. I'm telling you, Sandy, it's the bomb."

But she wasn't believing him. Couldn't. Her people didn't eat head, unless you counted head cheese, and Sandy knew for a fact there were no teeth in head cheese. Eyeballs she wasn't so sure, still.

"Look, why don't you go in the living room and relax.

I'll be finished here in a minute." But she wasn't ready to go. Wanted to see everything he did or didn't put into the big aluminum pot. Needed to know what she was about to eat.

She stood around until he took up the plastic bag of goat head. The sight of an eyeball falling in was all it took to get her feet moving.

With a pinched face and a firm touch, she placed her hand on Adrian's wrist. "No," she insisted, shaking the ladle free of meat pieces she could not identify.

He put her bowl down with a sigh and picked up his. Spooning out mounds of meat and vegetables, he didn't stop until broth lapped the edge of the bowl. He handed her the ladle. "Here, do your own." Picking up his soup, Adrian left the kitchen.

It did smell good. And maybe if Sandy hadn't seen the whole process she would have dug right in. But she had seen the skinned goat head being chopped into bits, and now, as she stared down into the soup, it was all she could remember.

May have been a dumb animal but it still lived, thought, and felt. Just don't seem right to be munching on its head like this. She stood there, deep in debate, trying to convince herself it would be okay. *Not like I haven't eaten "other" meat before. Chitlins, pigs' feet, and Lord knows what they put in that bologna I used to wolf down as a kid.*

She looked down into the soup and the soup looked back at her. *Eat me or stop staring*, it seemed to say. *This is too silly.* She stuck the ladle into the pot and began dipping out the soup. When her bowl was half full, she quit.

She went to the living room and made herself at home next to Adrian. Hesitantly she lifted the spoon to her mouth and sucked off broth. Hearty and rich. Her taste buds got a real treat. "This is good," she said quickly.

Adrian looked at her sideways, a smirk on his face. "See, girl, I told you."

Sandy nodded, got down to business.

* * *

"Goat what?"

She knew Janice would be surprised, was glad to share her day with Adrian and the delightful wonder of it all.

"Head," Sandy said again, going for the shock value. "Sounds real funky, but I'm telling you it was slamming."

"Sounds like it's going good." There was a slight hesitancy in Janice's reply, her words carefully spoken. Her sigh arrived, full of longing. "I remember those days."

In that moment Sandy knew her heart. Knew exactly where Janice was coming from. Had been there herself not so long ago. But she wasn't going to let her friend wallow. "They'll happen again . . . Gotta keep the faith," she insisted.

"Faith, smaith. Neither is keeping me or my bed warm at night . . . Been having those dreams again."

" 'Bout Brownie?"

Sandy's grandmother had a saying: *Nobody born with everything.* Janice was a perfect example. She was intelligent, pretty, and loving, but had gotten shortchanged when it came to affairs of the heart.

Most women had found and lost the loves of their life at some point in time and managed to get beyond it. Not Janice. She loved Brownie as if he had never been gone, carried his memory like a locket about her neck.

"Just because you're dreaming about him don't mean he's thinking about you." Anyone could see it was just wishful thinking, except Janice, of course.

"I know that, but I can't help but think that he is. Like something psychic is going on, like he wants to call but he's too afraid."

The whole time Janice was seeing Brownie, Sandy had bitten her tongue. Now it was time for the truth. "Let's say he is—thinking about you, I mean. Do you really want to go there? I mean, he put you through the wringer. You want that again? Him running through your life, just taking and taking and not really giving you anything? That's what you want?"

"Just want somebody, y'know?"

Sandy did.

"He don't have to be super fine, or rich, but I just want him mine. Don't want to have to share him. What happened to those days?"

"Still some good men out there," Sandy said softly.

"Yeah? Where? I walk around and see all these women with somebody and I say to myself, why not me?"

"The man of your dreams is right around the corner, isn't that what you were always saying?"

"Where he at? Haven't had a real relationship since Brownie."

"This isn't about Brownie, Janice."

"Oh yeah, then who's it about?"

Sandy sighed, her heart breaking. "You . . ." The truth hurt, but in reality half of Janice's man woes were her own fault. Still, Sandy apologized. "Didn't mean that."

"Yeah, you did," Janice answered, her voice choked with tears.

Silence came. Sandy just wanting to reach into the phone and draw her friend near. "You okay?"

"Yeah, I'm all right."

But Sandy knew her friend wasn't. Knew that she needed her. "I'm coming over," she decided, snatching up her keys.

Almond hands sliced through the air, shifting currents, disturbing the stillness. "What's wrong with me?" Janice wanted to know. In that moment Sandy felt a chasm as wide as the ocean, *because I have what she wants.*

She took in the soft, shiny black curls that encircled Janice's head, studied the full, wide brown eyes and the beauty mole over her lip. *What's wrong with you? Not a thing. I see you sitting there all torn up because no one wants to love you, and I don't know why either.*

Guilt found her, guilt about her life, what she had with Adrian. She swallowed it back, fixed Janice with a careful eye. "There's nothing about you a man wouldn't want," which was the real truth, as painful as it was.

"Then why am I by myself?"

Sandy had no answer.

Janice looked at Sandy with wide, wet eyes. "I'm so scared," she whispered. "I'm scared I'll never find nobody. Scared I'm gonna always be by myself."

"That's not true." But the reality of the situation, the absence of a real relationship since Brownie, took the validity right out of Sandy's words.

She got up and got Janice a tissue, her brain working overtime. *Think of something.* She couldn't bring a man to Janice, could not wave her hands and make one appear. *Must be something I can do.* She went on contemplating, face construed, brows furrowed, picking at the rafters of her mind for a solution. Suddenly one appeared. "Maybe you need a change of scenery."

Janice looked up, her face swollen with spent tears. "How do you mean?"

She wasn't sure, was winging it as she went along, but she could feel a shift in the room, a lightening of the despair. "Well, we always go to Club Enchant. Maybe we should check out someplace else."

Janice considered her. Her eyes were still wet but her cheeks were dry, and she was down to the sniffles. "Like where?"

Sandy shrugged. Felt an answer tooling around in her head. Just couldn't quite lay a hand on it. Something she'd heard—Mason's? Majesty? May something—on the radio.

She glanced away, trying to latch onto the loose thought. What was it again? It came to her, rushing out of her mouth like a new commandment. "Majett's!"

"Mah who?"

"Majett's. This new after-work club in the city. Heard it

on the radio. Y'know, ladies free before midnight, all that jazz."

Janice considered her. "The four of us?"

She hesitated, thought a moment. "Why not just us? Me and you?" She saw the doubt on Janice's face, read it. *Not how we roll.* But this was special, and it called for a different set of rules. "Been a long time since we went someplace."

"When?"

"Friday. We can meet in Manhattan after work."

"I don't know, Sandy."

"Why not? What's the worst that can happen? We go to Manhattan and get a dance or two. But on the other hand, what's the best?" She could see the wheels in Janice's head spinning, knew her words were taking hold.

Janice looked at her a long time before she answered. "Okay."

Sandy laughed, reached out, and touched Janice's shoulder. "We gonna be the flyest women in there."

Majett's was in full swing by the time they arrived. And while there were five women for every man, overall it was turning into a pretty good evening.

Sandy danced until her feet hurt, turning away drinks, phone numbers, and breathy alcohol promises. A month ago she had seemed incapable of buying a dance: now it was a whole different story. *Because of Adrian.* Nobody wanting you when you weren't wanted by somebody else.

She yawned, checked her watch, and watched Janice on the dance floor. *Looks like a love match,* she decided, picking up her drink and taking a lazy sip.

She yawned again, closed her eyes, thought about Adrian. *Didn't even blink an eye when I told him I was going out with Janice.* A test of a real man, as far as she was concerned.

She watched Janice head back towards the table, her dancing partner in tow.

"Sandy, this is Greg. Greg, Sandy."

She quickly sized him up. On the tall side, he was two notches below handsome. There was no ring mark on his left hand, and he had all his teeth. *Not bad, Janice,* she thought as he pulled out a chair for her friend, flagged the barmaid, and asked them both what were they having.

Stalls opened and closed behind them in a constant flux, strangers' eyes meeting theirs in the bathroom mirror. There was nothing private about the ladies' room, but outside of going into the street, there was no other place to have the heated conversation.

"You're not," Sandy insisted, one hand on her hip.

"Why not?" Janice tossed back, her voice scraping the ceiling like nails on a chalkboard.

"Because, number one, you don't know him from Adam. Number two, you don't know him from Adam, and number three, if you mean that much to him, he'll call."

"Just a ride home."

"With a stranger," she wanted confirming.

Janice's eyes danced from hers. "He's not a stranger."

"Oh, yeah? What's his last name? What's his favorite color? How many brothers and sisters he got? What's his momma's first name?" She exhaled, fire easing from her throat. She put both hands on Janice's shoulders, ignored stares from two women who entered the rest room.

"Look. I know you all excited and you just dancing with possibility. But he may not be what he seems. You get in the car, we may never see you again. Or he tries something, then dumps your ass in Jersey 'cause you wouldn't give him none."

"Britney did, and nobody said a thing."

Which was the absolute truth. When Britney announced she was taking a ride home with Maurice, no one batted an eye. *'Cause we were all just glad she met somebody, and if she wanted to go off and knock some boots, we were all with it.* But Sandy wasn't about to say that.

"Did you see Maurice? The man too big to be quick. Besides, you know despite her outward timidness, you back Brit into a corner and she's gonna come out swinging."

"Oh, I can't defend myself?"

"Not the point," Sandy insisted.

"But I like him." Yes, she did. It was all there in her eyes. Janice was half hooked for a man she had known less than two hours, half hooked and ready to go full speed ahead until she was fully fastened.

"I know you like him. And I'm sure he likes you too. But you can't take a ride with him. You exchange numbers and then you wait for him to call. If he's interested he'll be doing the calling. But don't take no ride from him, all right?"

Something in Janice's eyes faded, and something else moved into its place. Reason. Sandy silently thanked God. "Yeah, you right." She shook her head. "What is wrong with me?"

"Nothing, as long as I'm living and breathing. Gonna always have your back," Sandy insisted with a smile.

Out on the dance floor Greg had seemed a good antidote to her friend's blues. Sitting at the table with him had done nothing to eradicate that first impression. But the flash of disappointing anger in his eyes as Janice declined his offer was giving Sandy second thoughts, especially since he was looking back and forth between them as if both she and Janice had just tricked him out of something.

She considered him with cutting eyes. *No, you ain't taking her home.* He saw the look Sandy was giving, and his face shifted into an artificial smile. "The way it should be," he said after a while. "You came with your friend, then you should leave with her."

"I'm sorry," Janice said, touching his arm.

About what? You ain't got nothing to be sorry about. Janice's eyes were doing the "get lost" thing. Sandy started to protest, *ain't going nowhere,* but at the last minute she had a change of heart. If Janice was going home with her, the least she could do was give them some privacy.

She disappeared into the crowd. Seven minutes later Janice was joining her.

"Ready?" she asked, bubbly as a pot of perking coffee.

"Yeah." Sandy looked around. "Where is he?"

"He staying."

"Oh?"

Janice shushed her. "No oh. He gave me his home number and took mine. Said he would call." But something else had happened. Sandy could feel it.

"And?"

"No and."

Janice was definitely holding back. "What else, Janice?"

"Nothing."

"Janice."

"Sandy."

Sandy studied her. Lipstick a little smeared, a strange, buzzy kind of energy coming from her. She leaned into her, her voice a whisper above the din. "You gave him tongue?"

Janice smiled, but that was all.

"You did, didn't you? You gave him some tongue."

"Not tongue, you crude. We *kissed*."

"You tongued," Sandy insisted, laughing, ushering them both towards the front door, hoping it was the start of something good.

FOUR

Some things in life were certain: death, taxes, and Martha and Britney's reaction to Sandy and Janice's going out by themselves. Without the full story it would have seemed as if Sandy and Janice were trying to shut Britney and Martha out. But Sandy didn't want to tell them the real reason. Just couldn't see coming out and saying *Janice nearly lost it*.

It was a personal matter, something that had touched on their lives before Martha or Britney. Sandy and Janice had been best friends since ninth grade. There was a depth to their friendship that Martha and Britney just couldn't touch.

Add to that the fact that Martha and Janice had never been close but Britney and Martha were, and a meltdown was in the making.

No one would have been the wiser. They could have gotten away with it if Janice hadn't been so eager to offer up the details of how she had met Greg. Downright giddy with the telling, Janice missed all the signals that Sandy got. From the moment she said, "Me and Sandy went . . .", Martha had folded her arms and Britney got a peeved looked.

Oblivious to what was really happening, Janice went on with her little tale, either not paying attention or not caring about the hostile looks she was getting.

Sandy knew Martha was biting at the bit to cross-examine, but surprisingly Britney beat her to the punch. "You guys went out without us?"

Sandy didn't expect that. Didn't think Britney had the capacity to be faster than Martha when it came to words, but there Britney was, an indignant look on her face, waiting for an answer.

"Not a big deal," Sandy found herself saying, wishing Janice had kept her big mouth shut.

Martha entered the ring. "Since when?" The assumption, the one thing that had always been a bit of dirt under the rug—Sandy liked Janice best—was front and center, awaiting confirmation or denial.

Sandy didn't want to go there, didn't want to have go up against Martha and Britney, but she had no choice. *This is how wrong stuff gets started.* She looked around the room, catching the other women's eyes, determined to put it all to rest. "Look, she was going through a bad time and I just wanted to do something special for her."

"Without us?" Martha accused, in her best girl-you-done-really-crossed-the-line-this-time voice.

"Yeah," Britney added, which was so untypical of Britney. She never got into the little disagreements.

"It was a private thing," Sandy found herself saying, regretting the words the moment they left her mouth.

"Oh, I see," Martha answered, hurt and stunned in the same breath. "So me and Britney don't belong to that club, huh?"

"Oh, Martha," Janice piped in, coming to her own rescue. "It's not like that. Like Sandy said, I was going through a bad time and she decided she would treat me. It wasn't for spite or nothing."

"Then what was it for?"

"Yeah," Britney asked, shifting in her chair. Sandy wanted to reach out and smack both of them.

"Because," Janice said.

"Because. Yeah, okay. I'm getting you guys' drift. Are you getting it, Brit?" Martha asked.

"Sure am," Britney answered, animosity in her voice. "You guys have flipped the switch and left me and Martha to the sidelines."

Britney grandstanding? Sandy's eyes blazed. "What you say?"

"You heard her," Martha added in spirited backup. "You

two always rotated in your own little worlds. Me and Britney are just sideliners."

Sandy shook her head. "That ain't even true."

"Isn't it?" Martha wanted to know. Silence, a forbidden
truth coming into play.

Sandy forced the lie out of her mouth. "No, it ain't. And
if you don't know that by now, then maybe we should just
say our good-byes."

Martha's eyes widened. Sandy glared back. She was
holding on by a thread now, hoping Martha would not take
the threat to heart. Yes, she liked Janice best, but they were
still all her friends.

"Well, hell, maybe the fuck we should."

"Martha!" Janice barked.

"What? Tell me I'm wrong. Go ahead, Miss Janice, tell
me."

"You're wrong," Janice answered, but the conviction
was absent.

Britney stood, putting her plate down. "You know what,
I don't need this. I could be home with Maurice." There
was such a clarity, such absolute certainty in her voice that
it surprised everyone on two fronts: first, nobody could ever
recall hearing such force in Britney's voice, and second,
there was no doubt she meant every word.

But Sandy could not let Britney leave with the assumption undefended. She stood, arms spread out before her.
"Wait a minute now. Just hold up," she insisted. "You are
all my friends. Ain't nobody getting special treatment
here."

She took a breath. "Now, you know this is not how we
go. If I took Janice out without calling you guys, it must
have been for a damn good reason. This was not about
spite, not about leaving people out. It was about Janice. We
are supposed to be her friends, all right? I did what I
thought was necessary. You see how happy she was not
two minutes ago? Now you tell me what I did wasn't right."

The room grew silent. Britney stood, pocketbook hanging from her shoulder, breathing hard. Martha looked at Sandy, at Janice, and back at Sandy, deciding something. Janice sat, heartache on her face.

"I did what needed to be done," Sandy went on. "Now, if you two want to get on your high horses about it, then fine. But don't be insinuating something funky's going on, 'cause it's not. Like I said, Janice needed this and I gave it to her, and I will not apologize for it, not to anyone." She sat, leaving Britney standing.

Some of the steam seemed to have left Britney, her cheeks going rosy with embarrassment. Britney looked at Martha, but Martha was studying the wall. Slowly she slipped her pocketbook off her shoulder and sat back down.

"Well, I guess you did the right thing, but you could have least called us and told us you were going to do it. Didn't have to sneak," Martha decided. "Like you two are keeping secrets."

"Did hurt," Britney added, her voice less furious.

"But if I had done that, you two would have been hurt anyway, so what would be the point in that? Look, we've been friends forever, and every now and then somebody's toes are gonna get stepped on, but you know we always get past that. All y'all my girls, you know that. Nothing's going to change it. Am I right?"

Some of the air had left Sandy's balloon and her words drifted like smoke, too elusive to grasp. She looked around her, studied faces, chose the hard nut. "Martha?"

"What?"

"Am I right?"

Martha, face half moody, half smiling, rolled her eyes. "Yeah, I guess so."

"Britney!" Sandy called out. "I'm right, right?" She could feel herself changing the currents of the room, fixing things, healing the rift. Got charged. Britney wouldn't look at her. "Ask you a question, Miss Thing."

Which brought the smile to Britney's face. "Yeah, you right."

"Yo, Janice." To not include her would cause suspicion. "I'm right on it, ain't I?"

Janice smiled. "The white on the rice."

She clapped her hands. "All right, y'all, you know what this means." She opened her arms wide.

Martha gave her a leery look. "Group hug?" They hadn't done that since college.

"Yeah, group hug," Sandy insisted.

Martha was the first to yield. She stood, moved next to Sandy. Janice was third; Britney, last. Fitting arms over and under shoulders, the four of them hugged, laughed, and broke apart. Plates were dumped, more wine was poured, and they settled back in their seats.

"So what he look like," Martha asked after a while.

"Brownie," Janice said softly.

Sandy blinked surprise. Yes, that was exactly whom he looked like. She just hoped that wasn't who he was.

Janice happy. Janice in love.

Janice was calling Sandy on a near daily basis, giving her blow-by-blows of life with Greg. But beneath the joy was a whisper of desperation, and it made Sandy wonder just how good Greg really was.

She knew it didn't take a lot to get Janice started, to get her racing straight ahead into a future that might or might not hold possibility. Still, Sandy wished her well. Hoped that the relationship was really on the up and up. That Greg was truly all that.

Raising the roof, in high gear and determined to show the world, Janice suggested that they all get together and go to the Club Enchant. "Be me and Greg, you and Adrian, you and Maurice . . ." Her finger stopped in midair as she came to Martha. "I think it would be nice," she finished.

"You guys have fun," Martha said evenly.

"Aren't you coming?" Sandy wanted to know.

"Was I included?" Martha tossed back.

"Since when you need an invitation?" Sandy said, meaning it.

"I don't know. Ask Janice."

Janice's face blanched with guilt. "I didn't mean no harm. Besides, Sandy's right. You always getting dances. It's not like you won't have anyone to party with."

"But I won't have a man, now, will I?" Martha asked, unable to keep the bitterness at bay.

"Dancing's dancin'," Britney offered.

"Yeah, but at the end of the night, when you're heading home with Maurice, who do I get to go home with?"

Nobody had an answer, and there was no changing Martha's mind.

For the first time ever, Martha was not with her girls on a Saturday night. Her presence was missed as the six of them sat around the table, conversation stunted and the anticipated joy unrealized.

The women did manage conversation, but it always involved things the men weren't privy to. The men talked a little sports, but the women weren't that interested. By the time their drinks arrived, a pall had settled, interrupted only by the occasional trip to the dance floor or the rest room.

Sandy took advantage of the lull to watch Greg.

There was a secretiveness to him, hiding behind his gestures, the way he seemed to drift and then come back, *like he's constantly scheming*. She must have have been obvious in her observations, because Adrian leaned into her and asked if she was okay.

She turned, smiled. "Just thinking."

"Not supposed to be thinking, supposed to be having fun." There was irony in his voice, and Sandy knew she wasn't the only one not having a good time.

Greg whispered something into Janice's ear. A few seconds later he was rising from the table. "Just going to the bar," Janice explained, though nobody asked.

Janice followed Greg with her eyes as he made his way through the crowd. She picked up her drink, took a light sip, put it down. She twiddled her fingers, looked around, tapped her foot absently beneath the table. Looked at her watch, took another light sip of her drink, caught Sandy watching her, tried to smile. Couldn't.

Twenty minutes later, her searching making her weary, Greg returned, his hand empty of a drink. Janice gazed up at him in need of an explanation, but it was obvious he wasn't even considering one.

A woman drifted by the table, her wink at Greg unmistakable. His twenty-minute vanishing act lost all its mystery. Suddenly everyone sitting at the table knew.

"Who's that?" Janice asked, peeved.

Greg shrugged. "Hell if I know."

But they all knew he did.

It was the type of spring day the whole world waited for. The first real warm, sparkling, smelling of freshly turned earth and lots of sunshine riding the breeze day where people opened windows, breathed deeply, and marveled at the predecessor to summer.

It was lunchtime in lower Brooklyn, and floods of people emptied out of courtrooms, offices, and businesses in search of lunch.

Martha walked, Chinese food on the brain, accepting the feelings of inadequacy that plagued her. Her world was changing faster than she could think, quicker than she could blink. One minute her friends were right there for her; the next?

Her eyes grew hard, and she felt that ugly look settling on her face. *The Helen look,* she'd called it over the years. It was the expression Martha's mother had worn most of her life, and Martha had sworn she'd never get that way, would never let life overwhelm her to such a bitterness. But it had.

She was happy for Britney, Sandy, and Janice, happy they'd found someone to spend time with, but their good fortune had come at her expense. She had been the one sitting home alone Saturday night while the rest of them went out with dates.

She was the one who in the midnight hour was feeling so low she needed to talk but realized no one was home. Martha was the one who had sat by the phone all day Sunday morning waiting for one of them to call and give her a play-by-play of the evening without her, but nobody had.

Not Britney, not Janice. Not even Sandy.

That hurt, a lot.

But the feelings were as old as she was. *Should be used to it by now,* she reprimanded herself. But she wasn't. Never would be, and not by a long shot. *Just got to take it as it comes,* she decided, standing on the corner watching the sign blink *Don't walk.*

"Where are you going?" Janice was holding the sleeve of Greg's shirt tight in her hands, and while his frown was not the reaction she was looking for, she would not let up her grip.

It was late, but not that late, and she saw no reason for him to leave her now. That night at the club she had seen firsthand how quickly he got "distracted." *Sitting right by my side and he was looking at that woman like he wanted to gobble her whole.*

She knew then what she would have to do—keep him near and cut down on the opportunities for him to be "distracted" again.

Besides, she was still feeling the magic and she wanted Greg to reach back and feel it too, resurrect what he had shared with her not three minutes ago. But as Greg reached for his pants she knew he had other plans.

"Spend the night," she pleaded for the third time as he zipped up his slacks, worked the belt buckle closed, sat to put on his shoes.

"Can't. You know I got to get all the way to Jersey. Work tomorrow."

"You can leave from here."

"With no clean shirt?"

"I could wash it," she offered.

"You don't have a machine," he told her back.

"I've got two hands, some soap, and an iron."

Greg twisted, looked at her over his shoulder. Full perky breasts above the flat belly and dark down enticed him. He looked away, paused in his dressing. Wasn't how he wanted it go. Had no intention of staying the night, but damn, how could he resist her?

He sighed. She clambered across the bed, slipped her arms around his neck, and pressed against him. Even through his undershirt he could feel her full breasts, the hard poke of her nipples.

He sighed again, twisted his neck. Turned and studied her face so close to his. "What you doing to me, girl?" all he could ask as he kissed her slowly, uncertainty in his eyes.

"Just loving you," she offered softly, her face dusted with pain.

She slid around and stood in front of him. Linked her arms around his neck, his face moving into the soft place between her breasts. "All I want to do," she said, holding his head to her chest, caressing the top of his head, wanting to live in the moment forever.

Janice washed his shirt by hand, hung it in the bathroom to dry. Promised to press it in the morning. But when morning came, both the shirt and Greg were gone.

"Ring it again."

They stood in the lobby of the Manor Tower Apartments, laden with bags of food and drink. Sandy, in need of a rest room, was doing a little two-step, trying to convince her bladder that relief was coming soon.

"She's not answering?" Janice asked, the pan of lasagna heavy in her hands. She had made it for a special dinner for herself and Greg, but he had canceled at the last minute.

"No, she's not." Britney looked at her watch. "She should be home. It's five after seven."

"Maybe she's asleep?" Janice offered, the pan getting heavier by the minute, Sandy dancing beside her.

"Well, I wish the hell she'd wake up. 'Cause I got to go."

"Maybe we should go up," Britney suggested.

"How? We ain't got no key."

"We'll just wait until somebody comes through." But that was easier said than done. The first person coming out of the lobby refused to hold the door for them.

" 'Cause we're black," Sandy said under her breath. "I told Martha to live where some black folks live. If we were in the projects, we wouldn't have this problem."

The second person coming in eyed them with such disdain they knew better than to try to catch the door. Sandy crossed her legs and bent over. "Come on, y'all, we got to do something now. I can't hold this much longer."

The third person, a teenager with acne and bright orange hair, not only let them in but held the door for them. Their thanks were lost as they all ran for the elevator, relieved to see that it was waiting and empty. They hustled themselves inside.

Six floors, I can do this, Sandy told herself as her jig turned into stomps.

"Stop that. You making the whole car shake."

"Later for the car, I got to go!"

Out of the door they flew and hurried down the hall. They laid on the bell repeatedly until a grumpy, sloe-eyed—*drunk?*—Martha opened the door.

Sandy didn't say a word but pushed past her, racing down the long hall to the bathroom. A little later she came back, finding her three friends as she left them, Martha inside, Janice and Britney out in the hall.

"What's going on?" she asked, aware for the first time that there were no lights on in Martha's apartment and the smell of alcohol was strong.

"She says she's not having it," Janice said.

"What do you mean?"

Martha turned, her head scarf tilted on her head, her eyes watery, red. "Just like she said. I'm not hosting anything. So you all can just take your tired little asses home."

Sandy touched her arm. "Martha?"

But Martha shrugged away from her touch. "Martha what? Two fucks about me? Two fucks about you." She was weaving now, unsteady on her feet. Sandy nodded to Janice and took Martha by the arm. Martha gave no real resistance, allowing herself to be led to the couch.

Britney took her bags to the kitchen, Janice placed her lasagna on the counter, and Sandy turned on lights. They were going to be there a while.

They sat there, seeing Martha as they had never seen her before. They sat there, bits of guilt clinging in the corners of their eyes, around the pull of their mouths, as Martha talked about betrayal and abandonment.

"It's how I felt . . . nobody calling me, like I was nothing to anybody. You're supposed to be my friends, my *friends,* but everyone acted like I didn't matter."

They had gotten her to drink coffee, collecting the half-empty bottle of Chivas Regal off the counter. Britney had done a cabinet search, placing the Chablis, the Bacardi, and the uncracked bottle of scotch into a paper bag. Slipping it under their coats, Britney made sure the alcohol would leave when they did. If Martha wanted another drink, she'd have to go to the store and buy it.

Drinking wasn't a new thing to Martha. She had been known to get torn up from the floor up from time to time, but it had been a while since she had, and this latest incident took them all by surprise.

"The evening was a flop," Sandy reiterated for the fourth time, hoping Martha would hear her this time. "We didn't have any fun."

Martha stared at her, searching for the truth.

"It's true," Britney said. "Maurice said next time we plan an evening like that he's staying home."

Janice was silent.

"But somebody should have called me."

Sandy nodded, understood, "You right, and we're sorry." She looked around her. Decided things. "What do you say we all go out tonight?"

Hope and surprise glowed in Martha's eyes. "You mean it?"

"Yeah, why not? Middle of the month, I actually got some money."

"Maurice is expecting me home by eleven," Britney said firmly.

"And Greg is supposed to be coming over," Janice added.

Martha waved her hand, forced a smile. "It's all right. We'll just hang out here for a while."

Sandy maneuvered her car down Parsons Boulevard, Janice in the passenger seat. The tension in the car was tight, and not even the misty, warm spring night pouring into the open windows seemed to relieve it.

"Wasn't right," Sandy said after a while.

"What?"

"You, what you said."

"About what?"

" 'Greg supposed to be coming over.' Couldn't you see that Martha needed us more?"

"Martha is a grown woman. I can't be putting my life on hold for her."

"She'd do it for you. I did it for you."

"I didn't ask you to," Janice said defensively.

"Not supposed to ask. Friends are supposed to just do," she tossed back.

"She's just getting what she deserves for being such a bitch. Can't be hateful and not pay."

"Martha's not hateful."

"Not all the time, but enough to count. She's always trying to tell somebody what to do, how to do it. Her life is screwed? Well pooh-pooh on her. She's just getting what's due."

Sandy grew hot. "She's supposed to be our friend."

Janice shook her head, arms folded. "Yours maybe, but I never considered her a real friend."

"Well, she is. Nothing Martha wouldn't do for any of us."

"Her business."

As if she'd been slapped, Sandy's whole face stung from the impact of those words. *She didn't say that. I know she didn't say that, as much as we stood behind her and helped her through crap. I know Janice did not go there.*

She risked taking her eyes off the road, took a peek at Janice, wanting to make sure it was really her talking.

It was.

The question, weeks in the making, bubbled up off Sandy's tongue, quick and acrid, and nothing in her wanted to stop it from coming. "He worth it?"

"Worth what?"

"Choosing your friends over? I mean, is Greg really all that that you would choose him over us?"

"Not about Greg."

"The hell it isn't. All you had to do was pick up the damn phone and call him and say I'm going out with my friends, catch you later. That's all . . . but no, you wouldn't even do that."

"Britney didn't want to go either."

"Why should she? She's got the best man she ever had right at home. Maurice treating her royally. If she goes to the club, nobody is gonna ask her to the dance floor."

Silence came, the tension no less thick. Sandy turned onto Archer Avenue, stopped at the light.

"It's not like what you and Adrian have," Janice said after a while. "Not like I see him every day, so I have to take my opportunities as they come."

Sandy didn't respond.

"Everybody isn't you, you know what I'm saying. Everybody's not lucky like that."

"Don't get lucky by selling your own self short. You don't get lucky by letting some man walk all over you."

"No man is walking all over me," Janice said defensively.

Sandy let the comment slide.

FIVE

Oxtail.

Sandy could smell them, nearly taste them, as she stood outside of Adrian's door waiting for him to let her in. Peas and rice, a nice cucumber and tomato salad. She knew she was about to experience a little heaven. Couldn't help but smile.

But as the door swung open, her joy faded a bit as she took in the man before her. It wasn't Adrian, but he looked just like him.

He in turn appeared to be staring at her, just as curious, a mix of emotions going across his face. A second passed, another beginning when Adrian's face appeared over the impostor's shoulder.

He shoved his near-to-look-alike aside. "Man, move," he pulled her inside. "Sandy, this is my little brother Winston. Winston, Sandy." They shook hands.

Only Sandy offered a hello. Winston merely nodded. He turned towards Adrian, gave him a back-slapping hug. "You be good, man," then moved past her and out the door as if she were air.

"Don't pay him no mind. The boy got issues," Adrian said, closing the door behind them.

"Yeah? What kind?" all she wanted to know as she followed him into the living room.

"It's not important."

But it was to her. "Something wrong with me." Her first meeting with a member of Adrian's family had left a bitter taste in her mouth, and she needed to have things clarified.

"No, why?"

"Your brother. The way he acted."

"I told you, don't pay my knuckleheaded brother no mind."

"Which one is he?"

"Right after me. Got him beat by two years."

Sandy remembered there were three sons and one daughter in all. "All of you look that much alike?"

"Me and Wint do, more so than Junie and Rachel."

"Junie and Rachel?"

"Junie is the third son. Real name's Julius. And Rachel is my kid sister. She's the baby of the bunch."

"What about your folks?"

"They chilling in Brooklyn."

Brooklyn. They had gone there. Adrian had never mentioned it was where his parents lived.

"Down where we were?"

"What's with all the questions?"

"Just curious, that's all."

"My moms and pops live in East New York. We were in Flatbush."

"But Atlantic Avenue runs right by there, and we were definitely on Atlantic Avenue."

"Yes, it does." Peeved, annoyed. He was not going to tell.

Suddenly she didn't want him. Became certain it was something about her. Didn't want to think about what it could be.

"Hope you hungry," he said, heading towards the kitchen. "I put my foot in them oxtails." But as Sandy followed Adrian through the living room, all her anticipation of eating oxtail was gone.

She took off her jacket, laid down her purse. Rustled through Adrian's albums, found the one she wanted. Sandy lifted the dust cover off the turntable and slid on the cool vinyl. Carefully laying down the needle, she sat, closed her eyes as "Harpo's Blues" filled the air.

Lost in thought, she didn't hear Adrian return, a plate

of food in his hand. He tapped her leg with his knee. "Hey." Her eyes flew open.

Caught but curiously not embarrassed, she returned his greeting without much enthusiasm. Those feelings of lacking still with her.

"Plate's ready," he offered, a soft hurt in his eyes.

She sat up and took it, not the least bit hungry. Adrian left her, returning to the kitchen, Phoebe Snow's voice the only sound. Like summertime when the blue sky suddenly turned metallic, she could feel something bad brewing on the horizon.

The song finished, and Sandy felt its absence like a tender wound. She was about to go and play it again when Adrian returned and turned the stereo off.

"Enough of the sad music," he said, picking up the remote and clicking on the TV.

Since when? Phoebe Snow's supposed to be your girl. In that moment she knew: something was coming, and it would not be good.

The Poconos was a resort town that Britney had seen advertised on television, but she had never been there. She figured it was somewhere she'd never visit until Maurice told her he was taking her for the weekend.

Now, as she stood in the too brightly lit mirrored bathroom, she stared at her reflection. The black teddy, shiny and full of lace, didn't look as horrendous as she'd thought it would. Nothing she'd buy for herself, Maurice had gotten it for her.

She had been in the bathroom three minutes too long already, and she knew Maurice was on the other side of the door waiting for her. Waiting to see how his baby looked in sexy lingerie.

Eyes to the floor, she had put the garment on. With no cups, she was forced to hoist her breasts in, feeling like she was stuffing turkeys in the process.

She waited until she had fitted, shifted, and shaped herself into the teddy before she allowed her eyes to move towards the mirror. To her surprise the garment gave definition to her waist, and the spandex across the middle pushed her stomach in. Her breasts weren't sitting up high, but they weren't hanging as low as she expected either.

Britney turned sideways, peered over her shoulder, her wide behind and round hips flattered by the cut and fit. Not that bad, she was thinking just as Maurice rapped on the door.

"Just a minute," she called out, getting into the groove. She gathered up her heavily greased curls and pinned them on top of her head. One strand fell loose over an eye, and she looked so sexy she left it.

Seeing a Britney she had never seen before, she finished with lipstick and spritz of perfume. Laughing, she opened the door and stepped out, the look in Maurice's eyes telling her all she needed to know.

She took in the large belly stretching the material of his satin black boxers, the meaty thighs and bulbous arms. He had tiny breasts and as many rolls as she had, but that was all right. No, he'd never be an Adonis, but that was okay too because in the final analysis he was all hers.

Janice looked at the phone and let out a sigh. She really didn't have to check the time to know that it was a little after midnight.

She didn't ask herself where Greg was because she knew—*not with me*. He had canceled Friday night, had promised Saturday night was all hers, but Saturday night had come and gone eight minutes ago and he was still a no-show.

She went to her bedroom window, gazed down at the parking lot, saw a lot of parked cars, most indistinguishable from the rest. *Couldn't find his down there if I wanted to. And she wanted to.*

She needed to see him cut his engine and step from his car. Needed to witness him navigate traffic as he dashed across the wide expanse of Bedell Avenue. Nothing more she wanted than for him to head towards her apartment building and ring her intercom.

So much Janice needed. She couldn't remember not needing. Could not recall a single moment when she'd ever felt satisfied, complete.

Pressing her face to the cool glass, she closed her eyes and breathed mist against it. Pulling back, she drew a heart and placed two initials in the middle.

In her heart she knew he was not coming. *Did it again, didn't he?* But it took another minute before she could let go of the hope and abandon her window watch.

Martha sat in the dark, feet up, apartment silent, wondering if there was such a thing as having it all. Her professional life was stellar, but her personal one depended on the availability of friends. *Friends with lovers, friends with boyfriends, friends who have other places to be than with me.*

She had learned early in life that you couldn't go about life incidentally, that you needed a plan to succeed. And planned she had. Creating a narrow corridor, Martha had proceeded straight ahead with no detour. It had gotten her a good job, one that made even her mother proud, but there was so much more out there, and Martha wanted some.

She had never admitted her loneliness. Had kept her head, her chin forward. Masterful Martha, her coworkers called her. Don't let nothing stop her or get in her way. Yeah, right.

She snickered, and the sound ricocheted about the quiet apartment. *Is this why I work hard five days a week? To sit by myself all alone? Is this what I stayed focused all my life for—to attain nice things and not have a soul to share them with? Even my girls are out there having fun, Sandy with Adrian, Britney up in the Poconos with Maurice. Even foolish Janice has a little action going for her. What do I have?*

All her life Martha had planned, had known what she

had to do and done it. But she discovered that her life was just a glass halfway full, the tap suddenly gone dry.

Some anxieties never go away. Little demons, perceived flaws—they exist inside all of us.

Sandy was no exception.

While the gene pool had endowed both her mother and her brother with fair complexions and wavy brown hair, her own genetic makeup had taken the opposite route. As a result, her dark skin and short, thick mane became tokens of inadequacy, her own internal badge of shame.

When Adrian entered her life, he had changed all that. He deemed her a beauty to behold, a quintessential specimen of black womanhood. She had taken his opinion and run with it, erasing years of self-doubt.

But the slight from his brother and the antsy way he had reacted when she asked about his parents were suggesting something else. Hinted that she might have been good enough for Adrian, but not his family.

"You okay?"

She looked at the man who had everything she wanted— the butterscotch skin, the good hair. He had given her what she'd always longed for but, without even realizing it, had snatched it back.

She did not want to talk about it. Did not want to disclose the skeleton still hanging in her closet. She forced a smile, told a lie. "Just fine."

She watched him go into his nightstand, the condom package hitting the top with a thump. She understood its importance, knew its purpose, but tonight she wanted it gone.

It was just another thing separating them, another device keeping her world from his. A true barrier between her dark skin and his butterscotch one, its very presence made her angry.

But her anger was soon forgotten as Adrian reached for her and drew her near. Became a bad memory as he planted warm kisses and cool fingers upon her body, bringing forth a fire in her soul. His pulling away brought her back to reality, back to those feelings, the anger, as he opened the condom pack and slipped it on.

That she wanted it off did not surprise her. That she reached over and attempted to remove it made Adrian pull back as if burned.

"What are you doing?" he asked, eyes wide with fear.

"Do you have to?"

His voice was tense, strained. "The nineties, babe. I ain't dying over making love."

She knew he was right, but every fiber in her body wanted to have him inside her without it. She wanted his goldenness to enter her so that she would become golden too.

The moment sort of lost itself then, a halfhearted attempt at making love that was marked by her crazy notion. Afterwards, as they lay side by side, Sandy longed to speak what was in her heart. Longed to share her life of being too dark, of finding Adrian perfect and full of light. Of wanting some of his brightness to shine within her, if only for a few minutes.

His question came only seconds after they separated, but it seemed a lifetime before it arrived. "You been tested?"

She swallowed, surprised at the intensity with which he spoke and the question no one had ever asked her before. "For AIDS?"

Adrian heard the fear beneath her words but made himself go on. "Yeah." There was an urgency behind his voice. A deep-rooted need to know.

"No."

She felt the bed shift. Knew Adrian was turning on his side to face her. "And you were willing to take that risk?"

"I'm sorry." All she could say.

It was the first time he had felt anger at her, and it was showing in every breath he took. "Sorry, Sandy? Sorry? You want to go out that way? How could you choose a few minutes over the rest of your life?" *Because it happens in a heartbeat*—this much he was certain.

Sandy knew he was right, felt foolish and juvenile. Tears welled inside her eyes as his anger filled the bedroom.

"I go every six months like clockwork. And it's the hardest thing I have to do, but I do it, because I love life, you hearing me?" He had never expected this from her, and it took him for a loop. He never thought Sandy would be so careless, so unconcerned, would take that risk.

He fell back against the bed, raised an arm over his forehead. "You really shocked me tonight, Sandy. Damn, but you shocked me."

It took a while for her to think it through, Adrian's emotions churning, clanging against her own. *Most of the men I slept with never used them. Adrian uses them all the time . . .*

Ain't dying over making love.

It came together for her lightning quick, fast, furious, and without warning. The one conclusion she had never considered, did not want to consider, arrived, wedging itself squarely between them.

Sandy lay there, mute, thinking hard, afraid to open her mouth. She would have gone on lying there had Adrian not asked if she were ready to go. She nodded and got out of the bed, unable to ask the implied question, and Adrian, just as mute, seemed in no mood to supply an answer.

No words were spoken as they got dressed, nothing passing between them as he walked her to her car. He simply said good night and turned, not even waiting until she pulled from the curb as he hurried back to his apartment.

"Amen."

Her knees popped as she rose, twinged a little as she got into bed. For Sandy prayer was like breathing, automatic and without thought. Sometimes when things were really going rough, she would throw in a special request.

Tonight, she added a please-God: *Don't let Adrian have*

it. Not even in her head could she think the word. Tried to recall if Adrian himself had said it. Wasn't sure. The whole incident was muddled in dread, but without doubt it had been implied.

She was lying there wondering what tomorrow would bring when the phone rang. A little after eleven, it was too late for idle chatter. Whoever was calling had something important to say.

"Hello?"

"You know how much you scared me tonight?"

Adrian.

She swallowed. "I'm sorry." And she was, about everything.

His voice was nearly a whisper. "I got to tell you something."

Sandy could feel it coming, all of it—what she didn't want to know, what she could not ask, what she feared most. He was going to say it. *He's gonna open up his mouth and speak words and my life with him will be over.*

Her chest grew tight. "Go ahead." But she couldn't breathe.

"Grace of God is the only reason I'm still here."

"What do you mean?"

"An ex-girlfriend, Sandy. She's infected. We split up two years ago. Only protection we ever used was her diaphragm."

Her heart tom-tomed in her chest. "Are you—?"

"No." No hesitancy, no doubt, no pause. The truth. Sandy took a deep breath, then another, relieved.

"But this ex-girlfriend is," she needed confirming, shifting through the turmoil in her brain, trying to find a sanctuary, some steady ground to stand on, a place to decide what would be.

"Not full-blown or anything like that, but yeah, the virus is in her. Found out when she was trying to get life insurance. She had it. I didn't . . . grace of God."

"She all right?"

"She's fine. No problems. No complications."

"That's why you keep getting tested?"

"I don't have much of a choice. That's why I'm so careful, something you have to remember."

But Adrian could have kept his reminder. Because in that moment Sandy knew it was one thing she would never forget.

SIX

You got lucky. Isn't that what Janice told her?

Adrian, the wonder boy. Fine, sweet, and gorgeous. Had there been anybody else she'd wanted more?

Two days ago Sandy had operated in ignorant bliss, AIDS so far from her mind it was as if the word never existed. But the paradise had been taken from her, and in its place lived fear. No, Adrian didn't have it, *but his ex-girlfriend did.*

This was all she could consider as Adrian placed his lips to hers, her body tensing, lips gathering, retreating, closing off Adrian's tongue. Her whole being, her physical and emotional self, pulled away from him, taking her far away from his space.

He looked at her, sadness in every breath he took. "I've been testing negative for two years. No danger in kissing."

She looked away. Found herself wanting to be somewhere else, anyplace else but across from the man that not two days ago she had loved with all her heart.

That was the Sandy she wanted to be, the one without doubt, worries, or concerns. She didn't want to be the one who now played the game of "maybe he got it, maybe he don't."

"You afraid of me?"

Sandy willed her eyes to seek his. She didn't want to say it, didn't want to make it true, but there was no way she could keep it to herself. "Kinda hard now."

"If I hadn't told, you would have never known."

He was right, of course. If he hadn't told—and he very well could have kept the knowledge to himself—Sandy would be all *in his stuff.* But she knew now, and her words came fast and accusatory. "But you did tell me."

"Because I didn't want no secrets, and you needed to understand the risk."

She paused, her voice small. "And it makes me afraid."

Adrian stood, his hand sweeping the air. "There's brothers who haven't been tested and probably got it . . . other brothers who have it, know, and aren't telling. I came to you, telling you the truth, and now you're afraid. I should have known."

No, she wanted to say. *No, I'm not like that.* But there was a chill in her bones that numbed reason. "God knows I appreciate you telling me, Adrian. Appreciate you believing and adhering to safe sex, but it's hard for me. Hard not to be afraid. Like you said, I don't want to die over making love."

He studied her a long time. She saw his eyes slide into a soft and knowing sadness. "Can't make you unafraid of me, Sandy . . . just the way it goes. All I can say is, five months ago I got my test and it was negative. That I've had five in all, and no virus in my system was ever detected. Now, if that's not enough, then there's no reason for me to be here."

Yes or no, his eyes were asking. Make up your mind now, the golden irises demanded.

"I don't know, Adrian. Got to take some time and think." Which was the truth. She didn't want to see him leave her life, but she had to decide what kind of life it would be. *Platonic friends? Buddy pals? Take me out, drop me home? No kiss good-night, no skin to skin?* No, he didn't have AIDS, but he had been exposed to someone who did, and to her it was nearly the same thing.

"Need some time," she implored.

The hurt in his eyes was no surprise. "Thought you could handle the truth. Guess I was wrong. I'm outta here."

Sandy wanted him gone, so she didn't try to stop him.

Two things had brought her to this moment: Adrian and her own sexual history. Countless times had she indulged herself with Brian, who had been far from monogamous. During those moments she had relied on her diaphragm, when, in hindsight, a condom was needed. She never got pregnant, but she wasn't so sure about the other things. Then there was the fact that someone as loving and caring as Adrian had been exposed, which became the icing on the cake.

Sandy was stepping up to the plate, no matter how scared, and determining if she was okay. She'd searched for a discreet place to get tested and found a good clinic.

She had imagined a run-down facility with hard orange plastic chairs, scruffy and cracked linoleum floors, and municipal-green walls. She had imagined a room full of gay men, drug abusers, and hookers. She had expected an inhospitable receptionist who asked questions without looking at her and gave instructions like a drill sergeant.

Sandy was not prepared for the high-class feel of the medical office when she walked in. There was mauve carpeting, Levolor blinds discreetly half closed, and real plants in the corners.

She was pleased to see the office had an obstetrician, a podiatrist, an internist, an oncologist, and a general practitioner. *I could be here getting my corns checked, getting a Pap smear, having my blood pressure checked, anything. Nobody knows I'm here for an AIDS test, except me and the receptionist.* She wanted to laugh out loud with relief.

"Sandy?"

She looked up at the dark-haired white woman in the white doctor's coat. Nodded and stood.

The crook of her arm hurt as she made her way back to work. The bandage made the needle hole hot and itchy, and Sandy longed to scratch it but couldn't without taking off her trench.

Her mind was dazed. Her thoughts scattered and incoherent. Every now and then a *please, God* would filter through the madness. She had a war raging inside her head, one voice telling her she couldn't possibly be infected, the other telling her that was what everyone said.

One voice told her she could end up dying a slow, withering death and her parents would have to bury her; the other voice said there was a chance the spermicide she used with her diaphragm had killed the virus if she'd slept with someone who had it.

Sandy tried to feel the blood moving through her system. Tried to sense if the virus was inside of her, moving around, doing damage. She didn't know, was only certain of one thing: soon all doubt would be erased.

Tell no one.

That was her litany for the next couple of days. She had to keep it a secret, a big, hollowing-out-the-heart hush-hush that turned every nerve to glass by the time she went back for the results.

Moments came when she just knew she was dreaming the whole thing, that God would not be that cruel to her. Yet other moments arrived when she knew the real side of life that said nobody got guarantees and the best and worst of the lot were all up for grabs.

Worst of all was, had she not gone a little love-crazy and tried to take off the condom, she might never have found out about the ex-girlfriend who had tested positive. Adrian could have gone on with her forever, never telling, and she wouldn't have been the wiser.

It was this last scenario that she had longed for. Had her wishing Adrian had kept quiet. He used condoms, he got tested every six months—how much risk was that?

She opened the doctor's office door, heart beating fast, and walked across the soft mauve carpeting. Sandy gave the receptionist her name and took a seat when all she really wanted to do was run away. Act like none of it had ever happened. Pretend that the rainbow was still hers.

But it wasn't, not by a long shot, especially now as a young black man appeared at the door, calling her name with a smile that could have melted steel, and Sandy wasn't sure if it was good news or bad news he had for her.

She followed him through the door, down the hall, and took a seat in the chair. Tense, still, she breathed tightly, very much afraid.

"Hi, Sandy. I'm Joe. How are you doing today?" She blinked, her mouth stuck. Joe leaned over, patted her hand. Talked on. "I'm your health counselor, and as you know, you are here to get your results."

Tears came then, big fat warm salty ones, and Sandy could not even bring her hand up to wipe them. "Go ahead. It's okay," Joe told her, his eyes bright and soothing as he handed her a tissue. "Now, the first thing I want to say is, you've tested negative."

A sob escaped Sandy's lips. Relief so sweet and so swift moved through her. Joe plucked another Kleenex for her, and she took it gratefully. No, she didn't have it; no, she wasn't going to die young. Yes, she was okay.

It took a few more seconds to get her composure. To settle the gratefulness in her heart. Joe allowed her a moment. And when she was able to stop the tears, calm her trembling hands, her eyes darting towards heaven in gratitude, he spoke.

"Now, it's wonderful that you've tested negative, but judging from your reaction you've been involved in some risky behavior. Am I right?"

Sandy nodded, shamed.

"As a rule of thumb, we recommend testing every six months, because a negative test today doesn't always mean a negative test the next. Now I'm going to spend a few minutes with you going over information on all the diseases—chlamydia, syphilis, AIDS, gonorrhea, and all them other STDs that can really do a sister in, okay?"

Humor. Sandy appreciated that.

She left armed with pamphlets, condoms, and brochures. Enough reading materials to fill her pocketbook. Eyes still misty, she thanked God, her soul on fire. Grateful for a chance to live better and as long as she could.

Guilt, joy, relief, and sorrow were all mixing inside of her as she reached for the phone and dialed seven numbers. She was surprised she remembered them, surprised that her fingers moved with a fluidity, an unfaltering deftness her own heart seemed incapable of.

She listened to it ring, unsure of what she would say or how she would say it, knowing only that the only person she wanted to share her news with was him.

There had been moments when she decided to stay away, but just as many found her that said she couldn't. Scared as she was, she could not just say good-bye.

"Hello?"

"I went and got tested." She didn't say hello, didn't say *It's me.* Sandy spoke those words first, showing him off the bat just how deeply he affected her life.

"Sandy?"

"Yeah." She heard him sigh, and her own heart melted. "I'm sorry, Adrian, about everything, about the way I acted, all that stuff."

"People have the right to feel the way they feel." But his voice was tight.

"Should have handled it better. Didn't mean to hurt your feelings like that. Just scared, that's all."

"Not as scary as waiting for the results, I bet."

Sandy laughed, relieved. "Oh, God, Adrian, it was the worst three days of my life. Thought I was gonna lose my mind with all the crap running around in my brain."

"Tell me about it. Well, you sounding chipper, so I guess it was the big N."

"Negative, yeah. Got all these pamphlets, condoms, and a tentative appointment for six months from now. I found this great place near my job in lower Manhattan. Real classy, and the staff is wonderful."

"I use my family doctor."

"Oh."

"I went somewhere where nobody knew me that first time. But after the second, it wasn't such a big deal. After a while it's not so scary."

Her voice was tiny. "Still scared."

"Only natural."

"Don't want to be."

"Takes time, Sandy."

"Do want to see you," she admitted.

"Want to see you too."

"My place?" Sandy asked.

"Give me half an hour."

This is what it all boils down to. Me being here with him like this. She was trying to prove it didn't matter, trying to prove she wasn't afraid. Had purposely brought Adrian to her bedroom two minutes after he had stepped through her front door, probing the probability of their future.

He didn't ask why, but the question danced in his eyes as she lay on her bed and patted the empty space next to her. It was a stance, a stepping stone to get them back to where they had once been, but even as her laughter dusted the air and her fingers shifted various packets of condoms, he could sense her apprehension.

"Let's see," she said, a laundry list falling from her lips, "we got superthin, lubricated, French kiss, ridged, oooh bumpy, peppermint—not!—Mandingo, strawberry. Which one?"

Adrian reached over, willing to play sidekick in her masquerade, wanting to get over the hump as much as she did. "Mandingo." He held the condom up, wanting the bridge yet to be crossed behind them. "Let's see. Just how big does this thing stretch?"

"Oh, you're funny." Her laughter came, died quickly as she looked over at him, aware of his shirt, pants, and bare feet. "This is so damn romantic," the bitterness potent in her voice.

"Fun is what you make it," he answered, but it was starting to hurt now, things becoming less hopeful and more despairing with each passing minute.

Her hand hit the bed absently. "Nothing fun about lying in bed with clothes on."

He reached for her, hoping that his arms held enough magic to bring her back to him, that somehow touch would mend the rift.

She did not resist his embrace, sort of lost herself to it. Allowed him to hold her a long time, a fine heat coming where their bodies touched.

But it was not enough, and after a while she pulled away, sat up, feet on the floor, back to him. "I can't," she said, a real anguish in her voice.

"I know," Adrian answered, sorrowed to the bone.

The visit didn't go on much beyond that moment, Adrian putting his shoes back on, Sandy smoothing her wrinkled clothing. Then he was standing and asking her the one thing she always dreaded to hear. "Walk me to the door." There was something final in those words, something unfinished and incomplete, and if Sandy ever needed a wholeness, it was now.

She did not want to him to leave, wanted him to understand the new role she'd found herself in. *Have some patience with me,* she was thinking as they stood at her front door.

He didn't know what to say, wasn't sure what she wanted to hear, but as the moment went on too long, her standing there, holding on to him as if she never wanted to let go, he made a decision. "I gotta go, Sandy."

He was hurt again and Sandy didn't want to hurt him anymore. Didn't want him leaving angry at her. Didn't want him leaving. "Don't go, Adrian. Try to understand."

"I'm trying, but I just can't be here now. Maybe later, maybe . . . but right now . . ." His voice drifted, anguish settling behind it like dust.

"Just hard," she whispered, still in need of his understanding.

"I know . . ." Sighing, he moved from her embrace. "Look, take some time, think it out. When you're ready, give me a call."

She watched him go, her heart breaking, unable to shift the fear. She watched him until he disappeared around the stairwell, words, *don't go,* stuck in her throat.

Janice jumped up off the sofa, bopping her head and moving her arms to the music. "Now, that's the jam," she breathed as Tanya Gardner's "Heartbeat" came from the speakers.

Sandy didn't think it could be this way again. Was certain everyone was off into their own little lives. But the phone had rung and it was Janice calling to see what she was doing Saturday night.

Then Martha called, and when she found out Janice was headed Sandy's way, she said she'd be there too. Everyone assumed Britney was tied up with her love thing, but Sandy called her anyway. "Maurice's working overtime so I'll be over as soon I can grab a cab," Britney told her.

There had been a time when cab fare, like good shoes, had been out of her reach. But Maurice had come into Britney's life, heart and wallet open, freeing her up in many ways. Together they made a robust couple, but nobody could deny the love between them. Strong, solid, and good, there was no doubt they were in for the long haul.

The song faded, and Gloria Gaynor's voice filled the living room. "First I was afraid . . ." Sandy, Britney, Martha, and Janice jumped up, hitting stances, mouths open, singing loud and strong with Gloria Gaynor. "I Will Survive," their war song from the late seventies, racing off their lips.

They sang with gusto and strength, sang as if they had personally written the lyrics, all of them surviving a man who had left them, expected them to just lie down and die.

"Oooh, baby," Martha said, wiping her brow, finding a seat as the song finished. They fell back into their chairs, legs spread, catching their breath.

"Now that was the jam," Janice said, picking up her wine.

"Yes, it was," Sandy added. "Michael Richardson."

Martha nodded. "Leon Andrew Wilkins."

"Brownie," Janice barely whispered.

Martha saw Britney, silent, reflective. Left out. Pulled her into the fold. "Who was your love of loves, Brit?" There was genuine interest on Martha's face.

Britney shrugged, reluctant, self-conscious. "This boy from high school. Didn't even know I existed, but boy, did I love him."

"How's Maurice?"

"He's fine."

"You guys are going strong?" Martha went on.

"We're all right," Britney said softly.

"Have you met his mother yet?" was Janice's question, a joke that never hit its mark.

Britney's voice was uneasy. "Only known him a little while."

Janice fluffed her hand at her. "I'm just messing with you, Brit."

"Is he making you happy?" Martha asked.

Britney's smile came, filling her face. "Yeah."

Martha nodded, decided things for herself. "Well, that's all that matters."

Though the question—he treating you good?—was directed at Britney, Sandy couldn't help but consider an answer for herself.

Yes, she thought, *he did, didn't he? Adrian treated me better than I've been treated in a long time. Treated me the way I've always wanted to be treated. And I walked away from that.*

She looked around the room, longing to share. Sandy wanted to open her mouth, talk of her dilemma, seek advice. But it wasn't the type of thing you told. *Not even to my best friends.* So she remained quiet on the issue, smiled, tossed in a comment every now and then, and pretended that all was right with the world.

But it wasn't, not by a long shot. The man she had always wanted was away from her. And even though it had been her doing, she needed him to come back. Just couldn't find the courage to ask.

SEVEN

Grandma Tee lived in the Bronx. Grandma Tee had come north from South Carolina back in the 1930s, when jobs were plentiful and dreams still seemed within reach. She had settled in her two-story wood-frame house with the front porch and thick posts and, along with her husband, raised four children.

Even after her husband had passed away, after her last child had left, Grandma Tee stayed. It didn't matter that the three-bedroom house was empty of people and some days she drifted through like a ghost, that drug dealers disturbed her sleep with their late-night revelry of gunshots and boom boxes. It didn't matter that her mortgage had been paid off and she could get a fair sum for the property. That her middle son had asked her to come out to Queens, that her baby girl had tried to talk her into moving back south, or that her oldest son had found the perfect town house for her out in Patchogue, Long Island. No, Grandma Tee was determined to stay, and she'd tell you in a minute that the only way she planned to leave was in a box.

Grandma Tee was Sandy's paternal grandmother. It was Grandma Tee's smooth, dark brown skin, Asiatic eyes, and wide full lips that Sandy wore. It was Grandma Tee's slightly bowed legs and wide buttocks that Sandy walked with. Sandy was Grandma Tee all the way.

Grandma Tee was Gullah, and she had taught Sandy simple Gullah words and phrases. Sandy had gone to school, and for show and tell told how she was a descendent of real African people and how her roots went back to a fishing community off the coast of South Carolina called Daufuskie Island.

Back in 1967 Africa was Tarzan, Jane, and black bodies

in loincloths, with bulging eyes. It was a long way from James Brown's "Say It Loud, I'm Black and I'm Proud," and black people were still struggling with the idea that black was beautiful.

Sandy would never forget the snickers, would never forget the look on her classmates' faces as she spoke of her Africanism. Shock, then jeers.

Little Jimmy Patterson, who was the cutest boy and on whom Sandy had a mad crush, had done a Tarzan yell. Even Bonita Ellis, her best friend in the whole school, started laughing. It became too much for seven-year-old Sandy. All those words she had been ready to share jammed in her throat. Sandy started choking, hyperventilating, the class growing quiet as the unplanned second act began.

Sandy had clawed at her own throat, the hem of her red Scotch plaid jumper rising above her scabby knee. Mrs. Rainey had rushed to her, knowing enough to pull Sandy past the dusty green chalkboard, out of the classroom, and into the hushed hall. Mrs. Rainey had bent down, placing her hands on Sandy's shoulders.

"Breathe," she urged in a whisper. "Come on, Sandy, breathe. That's it . . . deep breaths." The words Sandy had been choking on faded. Her breath eased, her heart settled. Her wide dark eyes closed as Mrs. Rainey drew her in, the itchy material of the teacher's lambs-wool jacket scratching her face.

"Nothing to be ashamed of, Sandy," Mrs. Rainey had told her, the old southern dialect slipping through easily. "You be proud, hear? You be proud of who you are and where you came from," Mrs. Rainey had urged.

But it was too late. Her classmates had taken away her specialness, had made a mockery of her African roots.

Later Grandma Tee told her that her classmates were just ignorant little fools, that they didn't know better. But Grandma Tee didn't have to sit in school with them, didn't have to be the butt of jokes about Tarzan and feel the sting of hearing "boola-boola" every time she played at recess.

Grandma Tee was just an old darky who didn't know nothing, was how Sandy saw it. And for a long time Sandy resented her grandma for even filling her head with such tales. Her grandmother stopped talking to her about her Gullah roots.

Then Julie Dash made her movie about the women of Gullah, its truth and beauty transfixing. Sandy took her grandmother to see the film. It made Sandy ashamed of her years of denial and pulled her closer to her Grandma Tee. They both had tears in their eyes by the movie's end.

Her grandmother never discussed the movie for its accuracy. Didn't bad-mouth it for any improper depictions, either. The time of sharing Gullah was over, a bitter pill Sandy learned to swallow. Though Sandy longed to ask about this history she had grown up ashamed of, she knew her Grandma Tee would no longer tell.

Sandy exited off the Bruckner Expressway and made a right at the gas station. Up ahead the powder-blue porch fronting the old house stirred up memories so real Sandy could taste them.

How many hours had she spent playing with her Chatty Cathy and Raggedy Ann dolls, the covered porch shading her from the heat of summer, the pine floorboards etching lines along the back of her bare thighs?

The porch had been a haven from the traffic that raced up and down the street and the brutal July sun. Grandma Tee would come out with ice tea in metal tumblers that sweated tears against her palms, or icy cold milk and honey grahams, the squeaking of the screen door announcing the arrival of some treat just for her.

Now, as she made her way up the wooden steps, she saw the porch floor, worn of paint in spots and dirt in its crevices. *Everything changes,* Sandy found herself thinking.

There was a time when even on a cold day like today the porch would have been swept and scrubbed clean. It was her grandmother's pride and joy. "This is the first thing people see. Can't have a dirty porch speaking lies about me," she'd say. But Grandma Tee was old now. At seventy-two she didn't get around like she used to.

But Sandy knew before she even rang the bell that before the day was through, she'd brave the chilly day and get back to the porch with a broom and hot soapy water.

Some things were worth preserving.

Samuel Hutchinson was a medium height man with a sensible personality. Years of shaving had roughened his face, but the roughness was eased by his soft brown eyes. It was those eyes, his soft, dusky brown color, that had brought Sandy comfort growing up. Now, as he pushed back his plate and tossed his linen napkin to the side, Sandy eyed her father with reverence.

"Momma, you done outdid yourself again."

"You certainly did, Tee," Sandy's mother piped in, standing to clear the table.

"Ain't nothing but some chicken and rice and okra," Grandma Tee replied.

"Yeah, but it's the best food I've eaten in a long time, Gran," Sandy's brother Cliff declared, watching the huge dish of dessert headed towards the table.

Grandma Tee placed the pan down with care. Reached over for the serving knife. "Ain't nothing special," she said, taking a moment to look around the table. "Still, it is nice having y'all here."

"Gran, you know, hell or high water, we always come to dinner when you call. Wouldn't miss it for the world," Cliff said.

"Samuel?"

"Yeah, Momma."

"Been thinking."

" 'Bout what?" Sandy's father asked.

" 'Bout going back."

"South Carolina?" Sandy asked, surprised and heartbroken in the same breath.

"Y'all been after me for years to leave this place. Figured no time like now."

"Yeah, but . . ." Sandy managed, unable to stop a gathering of wetness in the corners of her eyes.

"Like I said, been thinking. Don't mean it's engraved in stone nowhere. But I tell you, this house too much for me now, and the winter don't do my hands no good. Thought I'd move in with Cleo and Sidney. You know they got plenty room and all." Grandma Tee's eyes drifted, found their own bit of light. "Be kinda nice to live my last days at home."

"Daufuskie Island, Gran?" Cliff asked, his voice full of concern.

"Ah, Cliff, you make it sound like Mars . . . Just down the way."

"Yeah, but I mean . . ." He couldn't finish. Silence filled the room as Sandy eyed her brother with contempt. He was what she considered a "progressive black," moving forward with no eye on where he had come from.

Grandma Tee sighed. "You always did think it was some scary place, filled with voodoo and ghosts. No matter how much I told you about Daufuskie, you always been fearful of the place. Ain't nothing to be afraid of."

Cliff looked down, embarrassed. Even at thirty-five, just the sound of it—*Daufuskie*—put a fear in him.

"Ain't your fault, Cliff. You was always a different child. You got that Cullim blood, and life done did you different."

Sandy had always thought half of Cliff's problems was the Cullim blood. Skin so faint you could see blue veins. Hair dusty brown. Not enough blackness to keep him real, was how she thought about it. Side by side she and her brother looked like strangers.

"Momma, don't start," Sandy's father pleaded.

"It's the truth. The bloods mixed, faded. Ain't nobody's fault, just the way it is. Jeanne's family did a whole lot of mixing, that's all. Don't love her any less for it."

Sandy's mother piled the last plate.

"Jeanne, you know I don't mean no harm. But you know what I'm saying is true. Cliff your child. Sandy's ours."

"If you say so, Tee," Sandy's mother said, resigned, as she balanced china and silverware.

"We're all family," Sandy added, seeing her mother's discomfort.

"Course we are. Never said we wasn't."

Sandy's father watched his wife carry the china to the kitchen. Studied his mother, no doubt checking for signs of senility. "So when you thinking about doing this, Momma?"

"Well, I figure by the summer. Contacted a real estate man, 'posed to be coming by next week."

"You know you don't sign nothing until I look it over."

"Course I know, Samuel."

"Well, okay . . . all right."

Grandma Tee stood, her hands resting on her wide hips, old age bowing her legs even more. "Now, everybody get rid of them glum faces. I said I was moving, not dying."

But to Sandy it was all the same thing.

Saturday night and Sandy was having her fifth dance on the dance floor. Her heart wasn't in it, and her partner, some man she had said yes to, wasn't helping. He danced all right, looked decent, but he was in her face like he was the best thing since white bread, and she wasn't pleased at all with his posturing. She didn't even wait until the song was over before she told him thanks and left him on the dance floor.

She made her way back to her table. Martha was looking around, bored. Sandy signaled the waitress. It was mid-month and she had a little money to burn. So she ordered a rum and coke, half listening to the lyrics, the thump of the bass, every now and then her eye catching the empty chairs. Britney was out with Maurice somewhere. Janice had never shown up. *Home on Greg watch, no doubt.*

Her world was changing.

Her eyes drifted, lost in thought. A roar went up on the dance floor. *They having big fun,* she thought as she watched the commotion, seeing a familiar figure partying down.

Adrian was on the dance floor.

Adrian was dancing with a Hootchie Momma. A spandex-encased, multicolored-weave-wearing, gold-dripping-from-her-ears Hootchie Momma. Sandy could not believe it was him leaning back and arching against the women's plump behind. That he was having a great time with someone else while she had been sad and in turmoil for two weeks.

The joy and rapture on his face tugged on her heart hard. Adrian, the man she had been lamenting over, whom she was afraid to call because she had no words within her to make it better, was having big fun with another woman.

Martha saw her staring, looked in the direction of her gaze. "That Adrian?" she asked.

Sandy picked up her drink. "Yep, sure is." She was ready, ready for whatever words Martha would throw her way. But surprisingly Martha was silent.

The song ended, and Sandy watched them walk off the dance floor. *Going off to fuck, no doubt,* came the thought, bitter and sour to the taste.

It was three o'clock in the morning and Sandy was ready to go. Martha, having no fun this night either, agreed. They got in line to get their coats, stifling yawns and shuffling their feet. One of the worst nights either of them had ever had.

"What a pissy poor night. Damn, but this night was jacked up."

"You right, Martha."

"We gonna stop for the breakfast thing or go straight home?"

"Tell you the truth, I'd rather go home. Besides, half the crew's gone, so what's the point?"

"I guess you're right."

They were three people away from the coat check room now. Sandy opened her bag to look for her ticket. Stifled another yawn as she found it.

Martha laughed at her. "You letting the flies in."

"I'm just beat."

"Sandy?"

She turned, looked up, and there he was.

"Adrian?" surprised and stunned that he was next to her.

"How long you been here?" he asked, his eyes moving all over her.

"All night." She was one person away from the coat room.

"Oh."

Her mind cleared. "Heading home." She turned. "Right, Martha?"

Martha smiled and nodded.

"You've been okay?"

The line moved, and she handed her stub to the cost check girl.

"Yeah, okay."

"Well, I better get back." But even as he spoke, he was hesitating, waiting for her to come up with reasons why he should stay. At the moment she didn't have any.

She took her coat and slipped it on. Waited for Martha to get hers. She dared a look his way and saw he was indeed looking back. Something went through her, drumming up her heart, filling her senses. Bittersweet and profound, it took a second to recognize what it was.

Love.

Pure, unadulterated, heart-stopping love, pouring into her like grain through a sieve. Sandy found herself lost inside the honey of Adrian's eyes, their pasts mixing, stirring, bringing on a need for more. *Say something*, she was silently imploring when Martha's voice cut through her emotional reverie.

"You ready?"

Her eyes dusted Adrian's once more, reluctant, yearning. "Good night," she managed, turning with Martha and heading out into the night.

Sandy shivered as she left Martha's car. Was still shivering as she got inside and undressed, cold. Lying in bed, chilled to the bone, she understood. She loved Adrian. Could not go another day without him.

She looked at the phone next to her bed—*call me*— stared in the dimness, invoking it to ring. *Call me, Adrian,* her mantra, the chain of thought that looped endlessly through her head. She needed it, needed him. Could not sleep. Could only think, want, and need as the sun made its ascent into the morning sky. Cold and forlorn, dawn caught her wide-eyed and aching.

She got up, decided on breakfast. Sat down to it but was unable to eat. Up again, fast and swift, she was into the shower and out in no time, dressing quickly in a sweater and jeans.

Then she was out the door and into her car, the world slipping by in sleepy wonder. On her way, quick with her approach, she knew now. God, how she knew.

Bzzzzzzz.

The buzzer rang loudly on the other side of the door. She knew Adrian was home because his car was parked outside. Her finger hit the opaque button, held it steady. She was determined to see his face.

"All right! Just a minute!" she heard him yell. The door opened and there he stood, looking annoyed and sleepy. Not even the sight of her moved his set expression.

Her reason for coming left her.

She stood uncertain, in limbo and in need. *Don't look at me like you're not happy to see me, like you've never known me or cared. Give me something, Adrian. Your voice, a smile, anything except the coldness dancing in your eyes.*

"Hey," she said softly, afraid.

Adrian rubbed his face, whisking away sleep. "Hey."

She peered past his shoulder. "Can I come in?"

"Got company," he said, dismayed.

"Company?" She nearly choked on the word.

Adrian looked perplexed. "What's this about, Sandy?"

He had extended her the offer, had told her to think about it and let him know when she was ready. But the fact her visit wasn't yielding anything more than surprise halted her voice.

She had been prepared to tell him, but now there seemed to be no point in admitting that she loved him so much her heart ached. That she had decided that she could sleep with him as long as they both kept on testing negative.

That they could possibly go on and live a long healthy life and never be HIV-positive and maybe get married and have cute cocoa-colored children that they would love with all their hearts.

She had been ready to confess that she had been so wrong about so much and didn't want to spend another second of her life away from him. That he mattered more to her than anything else in the whole world and she was certain they could do this.

But the look on his face, the woman in his bed, had changed the possibility of those words, and so she uttered what until thirty seconds ago had not been true.

"It's about nothing, Adrian. Nothing at all." With that she turned and walked away, anticipating but not getting the touch of his hand on her arm, that invitation back to his heart.

All Sandy's life she had had to struggle for what she wanted. Her place in her family, good grades in college, a decent job. Struggle wasn't new, but this business with Adrian was a different kind of tussle.

She left his apartment, her mind set, her soul determined to forget all about him. She burned rubber pulling out of the parking spot, nipping the back end of the Ford Escort she had squeezed behind.

It wasn't until Sandy found herself the target of oncoming cross traffic on the Grand Central Parkway overpass that she realized she needed to forget about forgetting Adrian for a while and concentrate on getting home safely. There was no sense in getting killed over some light-skinned man.

Butterscotch, came the thought, popping up from nowhere, but there had been nothing sweet about her experience twelve minutes ago. Adrian's eyes had told her everything she needed to know. No, he wasn't missing her. Yes, she could have saved herself the trip and stayed home.

Music was an old friend, and she reached out for it. Sandy fiddled with her radio, in need of something deep— Bobby Caldwell's "What I Do For Love" would have suited her fine. She turned the knob, and hip-hop boomed around her, all heavy quick beats and rapid-fire lyrics. She changed the station to WBLS and got commericals. WKRS, her third choice, was no better.

Her last option was the jazz station. She wasn't expecting much when a lone bass guitar filled the car and Phoebe Snow began to sing.

"I wish I was a willow, and I could sway to the music in the wind . . ." Sandy didn't know she was sitting out a green light until the man in the four-wheel-drive behind her blasted his horn. It was only when she checked the traffic light and saw blurry green did she realize her eyes were full of tears.

"So you giving me a number or what?"

She looked younger, maybe five years less than what she had told him—"twenty-five"—last night. Gone was the lipstick and the freshness. Left behind was a young thing in a tight dress, the large gold earrings and streaks of fake burgundy hair making her look as if she had gone into her mother's closet and decided to play dress-up.

Too young.

Adrian had known that. Had known last night that morning would come and find him just as he was now, standing at his door ready to dismiss the piece of ass he had clung to like Saran Wrap in the wee hours.

She was waiting, long dragon claws on the slim waist. No hips, but lots of booty, and that's what Adrian had wanted last night. A young thing with a big black ass that he could spank as he rode his demons into the sunrise.

What he didn't want was her asking for his number as if the few hours they had spent together on the dance floor and in his bed meant something. It didn't. She had to have known that.

Adrian looked into her dark brown eyes and saw that, yes, she knew she was going against the rules but he was someone that she could get with from time to time and she liked the idea of having his number in her digital diary in case she was bored or lonely or wanted to impress her friends.

She stood there, her lips dry and dusty, her tongue moving around her mouth as if she was trying to clean her teeth or was wishing for a stick of Juicy Fruit. She looked like the gum-popping type.

Her head did a circular motion, pointing to the four corners of the earth before it snapped back in place. And Adrian knew she was going to get black on his ass.

"Oh," her eyes growing wide as the lids stretched with disbelief, "I'm good enough to knock boots with, but I ain't good enough to get your number?"

Adrian didn't answer. He clicked the locks out of place and opened the door.

"You wasn't all that anyway."

But Adrian knew he was, at least to her. Knew that the

little girl had taken to him like white on rice. Knew that she had been impressed that he was light-skinned, had his own car, a nice place, and a job. That he didn't have kids and had liked her enough to invite her home. Adrian being fifteen years older was real icing on the cake; every little girl wanted a daddy.

There was no doubt she was impressed that he had gone to college, didn't talk like a gangster, didn't sell drugs, had some smarts and intelligence, and had actually gone to Africa. Adrian knew he was the type of man she would want when she really grew up.

"I took pity on your ass." Her words, as she knew it was time to go and that last night was as far as they would take it. He was about to close his front door when she stopped, turning on her clunky black platform shoes.

"What bus take me back to Jamaica?" she asked, serious as anything.

Knowing that her world didn't extend very far, Adrian pitied her.

Sandy was full of regret. She was so heavy with it that it took extra effort to climb the few steps to her apartment, to lift the key to the lock, step inside.

There was her coffee, now cold, with the swirly oily rainbow on top. The soft fried egg yolk had congealed on the white plate; the buttered toast had shriveled and turned up at the corners.

Her nightgown was still on the bedroom floor where she had dropped it, a dresser drawer half open, hanging on by a corner. The bathroom light was on, the toothpaste uncapped, her washcloth in the bottom of the tub.

Her need, her rush, her I-have-to-get-to-Adrian-right-away Jones had made her tear out of her apartment like a hurricane. And for what?

She shrugged her answer. She didn't know now, didn't have a clue. Didn't know what had happened that had forced her out into the streets so hastily, that had made her make the twenty-minute trip to Flushing to ring Adrian's door. *Always chasing after the promise of some man's affection.*

No, not just any man's . . . Adrian's, her heart whispered.

Powder blue.

The sky over the expressway was as clear and full and complete as new denim. Not a smudge, not a stain, not a puff of anything other than blue. The winter months of battleship-gray skies were gone now, and in the air hung the promise of spring.

Adrian sat in his car, engine off and deep in thought. He gazed out the window, studied the second-floor apartment, and looked away. He turned on the ignition, only to shut it off. Nothing in him wanted to do this, but he knew he had no choice.

The shame was still with him, the shame of his lust gone mad. No reason in the world for him to have done what he did, brought that little girl home. It was so unlike him, so totally out of character, and his pleasure had come with a hefty price. It had cost him Sandy. Had cost him the one thing that had been real to him in years.

There was no reason for her to see him, no reason for her to open her door and let him in. The damage had been done, and he was almost certain it was too late. But he couldn't walk away without knowing, could not skip out of her life forever without being privy to what had drawn her to his door after being gone all those weeks.

Maybe she'd tell him. Maybe she'd confess that she had been wrong and did want him, needed him. Loved him. And maybe, just maybe, things would all be all right again.

He had to at least try.

Sandy opened her door, expecting nothing, anticipating nothing, not knowing why Adrian had come, only that he had. She stood there, her eyes searching his face, trying to decipher the look she was seeing in his eyes, her heart thumping hard when the message was received.

This is the real thing.

"Can I come in?"

Sandy felt heavy, light. Trapped. Caught. A weird, strong powerful feeling had her, and there wasn't anything she could do about it. She was in love with him and could no longer hide from that truth.

She had never felt so potent, so full, so strongly connected to anyone, *not even Brian,* but she was and could not even consider holding those feelings at bay.

Her body was hot and cold, zipping, pinging and ponging, adrenaline zooming her into emotional warp drive. More than the air she was breathing, the face she was seeing, she was ready to take the moment as far as it could go.

But it couldn't be real, couldn't be right, and *what about the AIDS thing, don't you care about that anymore? Don't you care that this man may carry death deep inside of him?*

"Can I?" he asked again, and Sandy wanted to answer but her mouth would not work and all she could do was fall in his direction and be very glad that his arms were strong enough, big enough, and loving enough to hold her.

Sandy was no longer afraid.

EIGHT

"Didn't put no onions in there, did you, Sandy?" Mrs. Alston asked, blocking the door and lifting the foil off the large aluminum pan.

Sandy took a deep breath. "No, Miss Alston, no onions," which was a sin as far as Sandy was concerned. You couldn't make decent potato salad without chopped onion.

"Well, come on in. We only got an hour."

Sandy stepped up the back kitchen steps, Adrian behind her. She laid the pan on the countertop, reached for his hand.

"This is my friend Adrian."

Mrs. Alston stared at him, her expression focused and unforgiving. She went on to study him a little more, trying to find the personal flaws that seemingly only she was privy to. "Oh, so you Adrian? Yeah, Martha told me about you." She sounded as if he had been found guilty of something but extended her hand anyway. "I'm Helen, Helen Alston, Martha's momma."

The moment went on too long. Sandy gave Adrian a little push, enough to get his feet moving. Her hand, fixed in the curve of his back, forced him towards the basement stairs.

"Y'all got to hurry now," Mrs. Alston said. "She'll be here in an hour. And don't blow up all them balloons. Little Kenny got a party coming up next month and I want to save some for him."

Little Kenny. There wasn't anything little about him. Little Kenny was six feet tall, 187 pounds, and grown. Martha's oldest brother, next month he would turn thirty-six. Today Martha turned thirty-three. Not a difficult number like the all-encompassing fortieth year or that fiftieth when even the most successful, well-planned life still made you ask, is this all I will be?

Still, thirty-three implied some sort of mystical coming into oneself, but Martha didn't want to make a big deal out of the day. She wanted it to pass quietly and unassumingly. Didn't want a party, surprise or otherwise.

But Mrs. Alston had other plans. She had disregarded Sandy's suggestion that a surprise party wasn't a good idea, had insisted that Martha would get a kick out of it. She had asked all of them to help—Sandy, Janice, and Britney. Only Sandy had said yes.

Sandy flicked on the basement lights, wrinkling her nose against the faint moldy smell. The dark wood paneling must have shone in the fifties, but now it was dull and faded, swallowing the thin ceiling light, giving the basement a murky feel.

She had spent many college days down here with Martha, Britney, and Janice, windows open, incense burning, and music blasting, Mrs. Alston off to card games and church meetings. But now the rec room seemed small, confined, and abandoned.

"She for real or what?" all Adrian wanted to know.

"Miss Alston?" Sandy reached for the package of balloons. "You ain't seen nothing yet." She ripped it open, counted out half, and folded the bag up.

Sandy had no doubt Mrs. Alston would count how many were blown up and how many were left in the bag. Couldn't cheat little Kenny, now, could she?

There was nothing easy about being Helen Alston's only daughter. Just ask Martha. Growing up had been hard, painful. It wasn't that Martha's mother despised her; Helen Alston had treated her husband and her son the same way—with disdain.

Everybody was ignorant in her book. Nobody knew nothing as far as Helen Alston was concerned, "least of all you"—her favorite expression when addressing her husband and her kids. Martha had spent half her life trying to figure out why her mother was so bitter and the other half trying to forget the anguish it had caused.

Nobody was born mean, nobody was born miserable, but it was as if her mother had lived and breathed contempt from the moment she drew her first breath. She was the unhappiest person Martha had ever known, and only Helen Alston knew why.

Helen didn't talk about her life before marriage, what had or hadn't happened to her—good, bad, or indifferent. Both her parents had been long dead by the time Mr. Alston asked for her hand in marriage, and Helen's siblings didn't keep in touch.

Helen Alston operated in her own little orbit, and it had been nothing to suck her husband and children into its vortex of trepidation. It was no wonder everyone had planned their escape.

Martha's brother graduated from high school, went away to college, and worked three jobs so he'd never have to come back home. Martha's father waited until Martha entered twelfth grade before he left for work one day and never made it back for the evening supper.

Martha herself had planned early for her great escape. Had it figured out by sixth grade. She worked harder, faster, and better than anyone else in school so that she could get through high school and be out of her mother's house.

In many ways it had been Helen Alston who instilled the hard-work ethic Martha had come to live by. When she graduated from Cardoza High School with a 3.98 average, nearly every college on the eastern seaboard was interested in her, and Martha was ready to fly the coop. She didn't go as far away as she liked, but she was able to move out from under her mother's roof right before her freshman year at college began.

Working one full-time and two part-time jobs the summer before school started, Martha found a basement apartment and called it home. Some days she had no money for food or was too tired to eat, but she had freedom, and that was all that mattered.

In the years since, visits to her mother's home were reserved for holidays and birthdays. Martha had learned the ins and outs of her mother and tried to be a decent daughter, but when pushed to the wall she came back swinging.

Now, as she headed out for the "surprise" birthday party she didn't want, Martha had one thought: *I'm going, but damn if I'm going to be happy about it.* Because the evening ahead of her wasn't about the celebration of her thirty-third birthday at all. It was about Helen Alston. That much Martha knew.

Janice rapped on the back door, pulled it open, and stepped into the kitchen. "Hello, Mrs. Alston," she said carefully, Greg behind her.

"Couldn't get here no sooner?" Mrs. Alston asked, her face bitter, a drink in her hand. "Poor Sandy been running around here like a chicken with her head cut off getting things ready and here you come strolling in like Queen Elizabeth."

Janice's face flushed. "I told you before, Mrs. Alston, I wouldn't be here to help out."

"Yeah, but you got here time enough to eat up the food and drink up all the booze, right?"

It was old hat for Janice, but she could feel Greg confused and caught off guard. He did not know Mrs. Alston like Janice did. Had no idea that such words were commonplace. "It's not even like that," Janice answered back.

Helen Alston reared back, her eyes steely. "Ain't it? Always told Martha you wasn't no real friend."

Forget her. She's drunk. But there was a truth there that could not be ignored. For all her mean-spiritedness Mrs. Alston's perceptions could get downright uncanny.

"Come strutting in here like you give a damn about my daughter."

Janice was about to argue the point when there was a

rap on the screen door and it yawned open. "Hello?" Britney sung out as she came in, Maurice's hand tight in her own.

"Uh," Mrs. Alston said with disgust, taking in Britney, turning and walking out of the kitchen.

Britney looked confused, but Janice just shook her head. "Don't even ask." Together the four of them headed down to the basement.

Black, thick heeled shoes clunked down the basement steps. Everyone turned toward the sound as the polyester powder-blue dress came into view.

"She coming. Y'all get ready." Final instructions from Mrs. Alston. Twenty people clustered against the walls. Sandy took a sip of her Coke, wishing for something else in it.

"No drinking 'til she get here. Y'all have everything gone if I let you start with the alcohol now," Mrs. Alston had announced as she cracked the seal on the bottle of Gimlets, pouring herself a tall one. "I'm just gonna have a little taste, 'cause I'm about wore out readying this affair." Typical Helen Alston style. Sandy had been half tempted to open the Barcardi Dark out of spite.

She hadn't taken any mercy on Sandy's volunteering. "Too many balloons on that side. Spread them out . . . Why all these red ones? Get some other color on the walls . . . No, don't put out all the cups. Folks go through them like water," and had treated Adrian like an uninvited guest. "You here to hold up the wall, Adrian, or help out? I ain't seen you lift nothing but that cup of pop to your lips."

A frightened woman with a big bark, that was how Sandy came to see Martha's mother. Always afraid of getting cheated, shortchanged, left out. Always on the lookout for treachery, deceit, and wrongdoing.

Sandy wanted to tell her that Martha knew about the surprise. That Martha didn't want a party and had considered not showing up. But Sandy held her tongue. With her husband leaving her, her son hardly calling, and Martha keeping her distance, this was probably all the woman had to look forward to.

Mrs. Alston clunked back up the basement stairs. For a while there was no sound up or down. Then the back door opened and slammed shut. The sound of mumbled words tumbled down the stairs.

"Go on down there now," Mrs. Alston was heard saying.

The first surprise was how Martha was dressed: Timberland boots and faded blue jeans more suitable for a hike than a party. Martha hadn't even rolled her hair, leaving it flat against her head. Not a dot of makeup. There was nothing about Martha that said today was her birthday.

The second stunner was Martha's mood. Loathing was all over her face. Martha didn't even try to pretend she was happy or surprised as she ignored the two dozen guests who crowded around, wanting to touch and hug to show the gladness she was lacking.

Martha waved them off and away. Moved through the adoring crowd, feeling their expectations like a fever. She hadn't asked them to come, didn't want to be there herself. She owed them nothing.

Martha headed for the bar. Without fanfare she cracked open that bottle of Bacardi Dark Sandy had her eyes on and poured herself a drink. Downed it straight, no ice. That done, Martha put her bag down, looked over the food table, and picked up a plate.

It wasn't long before Mrs. Alston started in on her.

Should have brought my jacket, Sandy thought as she stood on the quiet street, rubbing her arms. There had been no time to get it. She had fast-tracked out the back door after Martha. That had been ten minutes ago.

Martha shook her head. "What a fucking joke . . . I swear this thing is so jacked up."

"What about all those people who came?"

"Fuck them. Fuck them, fuck my mother. Just fuck. A

damn surprise party? What's the surprise, huh? Then she's going to get on my case 'cause I wasn't falling out with appreciation? Just fuck her. I'm not staying."

"I know you mad, Martha, but she did it for you."

Martha looked at her, insulted. "Like hell she did. She did it for herself, that's who she did it for. Just an excuse to boss people around and get drunk." Martha's head shook. "I'm so fucking mad I could scream."

Sandy folded her arms. "Go ahead. It's your birthday."

An unwilling smile crept and faded about Martha's eyes. "Why does she always ruin shit for me? I planned to keep my black ass home, be by myself . . . I didn't want to do nothing." Tears made her dark eyes glisten.

"Don't cry."

"She makes me so goddamn angry."

"She's your mother."

"It still doesn't give her the right."

"Sandy!"

She looked up the block, saw Adrian waving at her.

"Yeah," she yelled back.

"Mrs. Alston said come back inside. She's going to cut the cake."

Sandy wouldn't look at Martha. "Tell her five minutes," she yelled back.

"She said she's going to—"

Sandy was really annoyed now. "Just do it, Adrian, okay?" She held up a hand. "Five minutes." Adrian vanished up the drive.

She couldn't fault her friend for wanting to leave. *If I had a mother like that, I'd want to leave too.* But Sandy knew those guests in the basement had come to celebrate Martha's milestone, and there was no way she could let her go.

"Please, Martha? Just come in, cut the cake, open your cards, and then we'll all go somewhere else."

Martha's eyes grew cold, calculating. The change swift

and complete. "You have your man with you, so where are you going?"

Sandy had expected this. Wondered when it would come. Wondered when the bitterness would be flipped in her direction. She stared at her hard. "Like I said, we'll do the cake thing and go somewhere, all right?"

Martha slid off the edge of her car. "I'm doing this for you, Sandy. Not Helen, you hear me?"

Sandy nodded, tugged at an arm. "I know, Martha, I know."

Mrs. Alston backed away from the table as Martha made her way down the basement stairs. Someone handed Sandy a match, and she lit the candles, all thirty-four. She raised her hand and began to sing, the crowd joining in.

Martha's eyes glistened.

Song over, Sandy handed Martha the knife and watched as she cut into one of the biggest, prettiest sheet cakes Sandy had ever seen.

After the first slice, Sandy directed Martha to the chair and pointed out her gifts. "Why don't you open them, and I'll serve the cake." Sandy made sure the first piece went to Martha and the second to Mrs. Alston, who stood by the stairs, drink in hand, her face hard and cold as stone.

Pathetic bitch, was all Sandy could think. *God, please forgive me,* a long time coming.

Martha was laughing by the time they left. Feeling better, she accepted hugs and kisses from her friends, her mind relieved, her soul a bit better. She had few words for her mother. "Thank you." was all she said as she headed out the door, arms loaded with gifts, her good friends trailing.

Adrian took her hand. "Nice to meet you, Mrs. Alston."

Sandy leaned over and gave her a kiss. "You take care, Mrs. Alston." Janice, Greg, Britney, and Maurice simply waved and moved out the door.

"Sandy?" It came out *Shanndee.*

She turned. "Yes, Mrs. Alston?" The wig was crooked, the eyes tinged red. The voice was brittle and slurry.

"I know what you thinking about this, but I was trying to give her something special."

"I know, Mrs. Alston."

Her head shook so hard Sandy was afraid she would lose her wig. "No, I mean it now. I was just trying to make it special for her. She all by herself, no man . . . I know what's that like, specially on your birthday, all alone, nobody to be with."

Sandy wanted to tell her that Martha wasn't alone, that Martha had friends who cared about her. But she merely nodded, letting the old woman have her way.

"You tell her I said so, okay? She listen to you. She likes you. You tell her, hear?"

"I sure will. Good night."

Martha leaned back against the sofa, a drink in her hand. They had come to Adrian's house to relax, listen to music, finish off the nearly failed evening.

Taking a long sip of her drink, Martha sighed, laughed, her finger pointing towards the small African statue in the corner. "Now, that's something I could use."

Adrian saw what she was pointing at. "A fertility god?"

"Hell no, just the dick part."

Britney blushed, Janice sucked her teeth. Maurice choked on his drink. Greg gave her a closer look.

"No lie, y'all, been a long time, and it's my birthday too . . . Hey, A., can I borrow that tonight? I swear I'll bring it back."

Greg turned towards Janice, his voice a half whisper. "She serious?"

Janice couldn't believe he was asking the question. Looked at him like he had lost his mind. Saw something in his eyes. Looked at Martha, looked back at him. Did not answer.

Greg smiled Martha's way. "Hey, if things that tough,

just let me know 'cause I know some brothers who definitely will be willing to hook a sister up."

Janice's cheeks reddened. Embarassed, she studied the floor. Even though the words were meant for Martha, they never hit their mark. Martha was lost in her own little haze.

"Seriously, A. I'd bring the shit back so clean and shiny you wouldn't even know I used it," which became the final straw for Sandy.

"No more for you, Martha," she said, reaching over and taking the drink out of her hand.

"No more what?" Martha slurred, eyes nearly closed, the alcohol sending her into a nod.

Sandy was tired and annoyed and didn't want to be here. Too wasted to drive herself, it had been Sandy who drove Martha home, Adrian had been none too pleased about it, and neither had Sandy.

The anger she felt last night was still with her this morning as Martha fussed around her kitchen, plugging in the Krups coffeemaker, arranging croissants on the baking tray. Sandy just wanted to be gone.

She had had enough of being Martha's "best friend," a title she didn't want and hadn't asked for. Didn't even know she was until last night when she undressed Martha and got her into the king-size bed. "You're my best friend, Sandy, outta all of dem, you my best . . ."

This litany had gone on until Martha had fallen off to sleep. This morning the assertion remained as Martha had dragged herself from her bed, struggled into her robe, and insisted on making them breakfast.

Best friend? Sandy liked Martha, admired her drive, and while her tongue did have the ability to cut, it also had the ability to tell things the way they were, which was needed from time to time. But that did not equal best friend, and Sandy felt uncomfortable with that title.

Sandy didn't want breakfast. She wanted to call a cab and go home, but Martha wouldn't hear of it. She had tried to escape last night after she'd gotten Martha into bed, but Martha had clung to her, begging her not to leave her. *"Don't want to be by myself, Sandy. Please stay."*

Now, as Martha placed the bone china cups and saucers on the bamboo place mats and laid the silverware on the linen napkins, it was obvious that this morning's meal wasn't meant to be a quick one.

"I could scramble up some eggs."

"No, Martha, coffee and the croissants are fine."

Like a worker bee Martha moved around her kitchen, her bare feet like whispers of silk on the shiny white floor. She was known for being a neat freak, and there wasn't a single smudge in the all-white kitchen.

All her carpets were lint free, and not even the light switches held fingerprints. Sandy didn't know where Martha found the time to keep her apartment so white-glove clean with all the hours she put in at the DA's office.

She earned enough to afford the Volvo, the nice apartment with the cute kitchen gadgets, and enough clothes to choke a horse. She was known for her no-nonsense approach to work and life, all of which hadn't made her happy.

This was what Sandy thought as she sat across from her, the coffee cooling and untouched, Martha staring off, wet silver tears falling from her face.

Sandy sat there, allowed Martha her sadness. Knew she needed to have it shared. Seconds went by, the sound of the grandfather clock ticking faintly from the living room surrounding them. It went well with the heavy, dark-stained furniture and the imported Persian rugs.

Sandy studied the design of the place mats. Not the flimsy get-wet-and-it's-all-over kind. No, these mats were made of thick shoots and were woven so tightly and intricately that their surface was smooth and without a ripple. Good things, fine things, they filled Martha's one-bedroom apartment like sequins, giving the simplest walls shine.

"Sandy?"

She looked up, the red eyes and sticky lashes no surprise. The smile that trembled like a pond ripple was.

"I can wrap it, the croissants, I mean. Wrap them and let you be on your way. Be ready in a minute."

Sandy sighed, caught and embarrassed, feeling a failure she never thought she could feel with Martha. She dared a look her way.

"I am tired, Martha, to tell you the truth. I don't sleep well in nobodies bed but my own."

Martha stood quick but not agitated. *Determined* was the word. With the grace of a gymnast, she reached up and opened the cabinet door over the stove, grabbed the foil, tore off a twelve-inch square.

Perfect.

Into the oven now, no gloves, no mitt, her fingers reaching for the hot little crusty bread that would be cold by the time Sandy got home.

"Use your phone?" Sandy asked, rising, wanting to get away from the kitchen, from the quick efficient Martha who was wrapping up the croissant Sandy had no appetite for.

"Sure. Living room."

The sound of foil being folded punctuated Sandy's eagerness as she moved out of the kitchen and towards the phone.

Home.

On the cab ride, Sandy had one thought—get in bed. But now that she was here, sleep was the last thing on her mind. She slipped off her coat, took off her shoes, padded stocking-footed to her bedroom.

She wanted to talk about anything and everything. Wanted the cloying, sticky remnants of the birthday fiasco to leave her. She wanted to pass the burden of Martha's sorrows on to somebody else, somebody who was willing to carry it.

But who else was there?

Not Britney, she wasn't strong enough. Certainly not Janice, or Martha's mother. *Just me.*

The thought depressed her.

She couldn't imagine what would happen the next time she ran into Martha, next time the phone rang and it was her. Sandy couldn't imagine what Martha would expect from her, now that she had been crowned best friend, because it wasn't mutual. It was lopsided and untrue. Sandy was Janice's best friend, not Martha's.

So where did that leave her? Where did that leave Martha? Sandy knew before the answer even found her.

Joined at the hip with no surgeon in sight.

NINE

"Busy?" It was the code word for "Are you alone?" There had been a time not too long ago when a conversation would have begun with "Hey, girl, what's up?" but the flurry of new relationships had put an end to such certitudes.

"No. Why, what's up?"

Janice paused, and Sandy knew it was something important, at least to Janice. "Greg . . . did you notice him checking out Martha the other night?"

Sandy thought about it, couldn't recall. "No, why?"

The phone shifted, Janice no doubt getting comfortable, ready to relieve a concern, Sandy receptive to hearing it. "When we were all at Adrian's, I just kept catching him looking at Martha hard."

"Hard how?"

"You know, *hard*."

"Like he wanted to get with her?"

"Yeah." There was a deep annoyance in Janice's voice, a declaration of whose side she would be taking—and it wouldn't be Martha's.

"I didn't notice, Janice . . . besides, you know Martha don't go like that."

"I know. Just that, well, I wanted to make sure."

"Sure what?"

"That, you know, him and Martha."

Sandy didn't mean to break out with a laugh, but it was too absurd for her not to. "Martha and *Greg?* You can't be serious. Number one, Martha won't do that, and number two, he doesn't have enough money or that Ph.D. after his name."

"I'm sure you're right," Janice said after a while. "Just

that on the way home he kept on talking about her."

"Well, she was the highlight of the evening, showing out like that."

"No, not like that."

Sandy was in no mood for twenty questions. "Like what, then?"

"Remember that thing Martha said about borrowing Adrian's statue?"

How could she forget? It was one of the most vulgar things that had ever come out of Martha's mouth. "Yeah."

"Greg talked about 'hooking a sister up.' Then on the way home he kept harping on it. Saying stuff like, 'Your girl a freak? She a freak, ain't she?' Like he really wanted to know, or find out."

"Like I said, you don't have to worry about Martha. But it sounds to me like you need to be worrying about Greg."

"I'm not worried about him."

"Yeah, you are. If you wasn't, we wouldn't even be having this conversation."

"I just want to know."

"And if he was, if him and Martha were knocking boots behind your back, would it make a damn bit of difference?"

"Of course it would."

"Yeah? How? Tell me how, Janice. What would you do? Curse his ass out, drop him like a bad habit, what?" The line was silent. "You want to play the fool? Then go ahead, that's your business. But don't be stirring up trouble where there is none. If Greg was staring at Martha a little too damn hard, that's on Greg, hear? Ain't got nothing to do with Martha, and don't you even think about asking her. Person you need to be asking is Greg."

"I did." That surpised Sandy. Janice had actually asked a man something?

"What he say?"

"Said no."

Did you really expect him to say yes? Sandy didn't have the strength to debate that issue. Tried to get the whole absurd matter dropped. "Then I guess you got your answer."

"You don't like him, do you?" There was a hissyness in Janice's voice.

"Haven't seen one reason why I should. Half in, half out of your life. Scoping out your friends and spending your cash. Beyond what I guess is a good lay, what is he doing for you, Janice? Tell me, please?"

"Everybody can't be like you, Sandy."

"Everybody's not supposed to be. But everybody deserves to be treated right."

"He treats me right." Back to square one. It was useless.

"You know what, Janice? For three years I sat back and listened to your Brownie sorrows, biting my tongue till it bled. I'm not going there with Greg. You want Greg the way you got him, fine. Just don't be calling up and telling me about the horrors. Keep the bad news to yourself."

"Fine, Sandy, I'll do that."

Just hang up the damn phone. But Sandy couldn't. This was not how best friends operated. Sandy sighed. "What are we doing?"

There was a tremble in Janice's voice. "Was just thinking the same thing."

"Since when we let some man come between us? We've never done that."

"I know."

"Janice, you know you my girl."

"You too, Sandy."

"Let's not do this anymore."

"Okay."

"We promise?"

"Yeah." But Janice sounded too weary to be sure.

"So we cool?"

"We're cool . . . I better go."

The phone clicked in Sandy's ear.

*   *   *

Guilt, a sourness between herself and Janice—Sandy wasn't sure why she dropped by Martha's house, only that she found herself ringing the doorbell unannounced. But Martha's response was receptive, and Sandy found herself glad she had.

"Just doing some homework," Martha told her, reading glasses perched on the end of her nose, thick manila folders scattered across her coffee table. She gathered them up quickly, efficiently, and slid them into her burgundy briefcase.

"I can go," Sandy offered.

"No, I need a break. Besides, the case is sort of open and shut."

"Guilty?"

"That's for the jury to decide. You want some cappuccino? I was just making myself some."

"That'll be good." Sandy followed her into the kitchen, the air filled with the smell of freshly brewed coffee from the intricately carved cappuccino machine. "Where did you get that?"

"They have these U.S. Customs sales down on the pier. I get some good buys there."

"Oh, yeah? Like what?"

Martha went to her cabinet and retrieved two demitasse cups. "A lot of things, like those Persian rugs I have in my living room, that grandfather clock. Most of it I got down there at the pier."

"Half the price?"

"Sometimes, but most of the time it's less than that."

"How come you never told us before?"

Martha shrugged. "I had a connection, this guy in customs. We're not on speaking terms anymore." Luther. Martha had broken her own rule, stepped out of her own boundaries on that one.

She had met him at a Christmas party, customs agents mingling with DEAs, ADAs, court officers, and the AFT; upholders of the law getting together, tossing back booze, dancing like fools and making connections if only for one night.

She had seen Luther watching her for a good hour before he approached her for a fast dance. The fast dance had turned into a couple of slow ones, and numbers were exchanged.

They went out on a few dates—movies, dinner, after-work discos, and the like. He told her about the customs auction and how he could let her know when the good stuff was going on sale. When the rugs came in, she was right there and made out like a bandit. Still Martha would not sleep with him. When the shipment of grandfather clocks came in, he called her and once again Martha got a good deal.

She liked Luther, could not deny the physical attraction between them, and decided she was ready to take things to the next step. So she went home with him, spent the night. Thought to herself, *Yes, I could get with this.*

It stopped mattering that he didn't have a doctorate, that he made twenty thousand dollars less than she did. It was the first time Martha had considered her standards a little too high for her own good, and she was ready to make that change.

But Luther had a different agenda.

Whatever need and passion had seen them through five weeks of platonic good times disappeared the morning after the slow drag across the sheets. Warm and funny Luther became cold, indifferent, and anxious for Martha to leave. Few words were spoken as she found her bra, her panties, her pantsuit, stuffing her panty hose into her purse, disillusioned and eager to get away.

She didn't call him and he didn't call her. It was her last attempt with working-class men.

Now, as the foamy hot milk bubbled down into the small cups of strong coffee, Martha shut down the memories the way she turned off the tap, with a push of her finger, asking Sandy how many sugar cubes she wanted.

"I guess three."

Martha gathered up three cubes with a spoon and carefully put them into the hot liquid. She handed the cup to Sandy, added sugar to her own, and then headed out of the kitchen.

Sandy considered her. "What you think of Greg?"

"He looks all right. Wasn't paying him much mind, though. Why?"

Should I or shouldn't I? "Just that Janice accused me of not liking him."

"Do you?"

"He's not treating her right, what's there to like?"

"Well, I guess you know more about him than I do. Janice doesn't tell me much."

"Believe me, it's nothing you want to hear," Sandy offered with a shake of her head.

"That's your girl, not mine."

"Sometimes I wonder."

"Oh, you know it's true. We all do. Janice is your ace coon boon. Me and Brit are just sideliners . . . but that's cool." Still, Martha's voice was a little too high to be believed.

"Me and Janice go back to high school. You and Brit came along later."

"You don't have to defend yourself to me, Sandy. Besides, you know by profession I know a lie when I see it." Martha laughed, shook her head. "You were standing up there grandstanding and talking about how we all your girls. I must admit it was one of the better performances I've seen."

"Just didn't want any stuff between us," Sandy said softly.

"Stuff between us anyway."

Sandy sighed. "Seem like every time I turn around, something out of sync."

"We all have our issues." Martha put down her cup. "But hell, life doesn't come with guarantees. Only thing we have

to do is keep on keeping on." She considered Sandy carefully. "I know you have my back, Sandy, more than anybody else, y'know. And there's nobody else I want to have
it more. I mean that."

Sandy looked away, embarrassed. "Oh, Martha."

"Nah, truth is truth. We may never be as tight as you
and Janice, but I know in a pinch you'll be there for me."

"That's what friends do."

"Real friends," Martha said emphatically.

Life had gotten scattered, but when the dust finally settled,
things fell back on track. Sandy found herself making calls
Thursday night, insisting to her friends that they all get
together Saturday night.

Martha was good to go, and Britney said she'd be there
too. Janice tried to wangle herself out of committing, but
Sandy insisted that she be there.

Martha was the first to arrive. "Bought us something
different this time," she said, handing Sandy a shrimp platter from Red Lobster.

"You hit Lotto or something?" Sandy asked with a
smile, glad for the variation.

"No, I didn't hit Lotto. I just figured I'd make it special."

Britney was the second one to arrive, Maurice coming
in to say hello.

The first thing Sandy and Martha noticed was Britney's
appearance. Her hair was permed, cut, and stylish. She
wore makeup that took ten years off her face. The standard
stretch pants were gone and replaced with jeans, leather
boots, and a sweater that was showing curves nobody ever
suspected she owned.

Maurice looked as if he had been working out, his pot-
belly a little less Santa Claus, a little more WWF wrestler,
retired a couple of months. He had gotten waves in his hair
and had grown a mustache, which gave him a sophistication
he didn't seem capable of those months ago when Sandy
had first met him.

"Looking good," Sandy told him as he gave a little wave to Britney and slipped out the door. "And you," she said, giving Britney the once-over, "girl, you looking like a million."

"That the same Maurice you met that night?" Martha asked, half in fun, half seriously.

"Yeah, that's him. Started going to the gym. The hair thing was my idea. That other style looked like he was wearing a black fuzzy helmet or something." Britney looked around. "Where's Janice?"

"Not here." The bitterness in Sandy's voice could not be missed.

A fifteen-minute grace period was all they gave before they cracked open the wine and dug into the shrimp. At quarter to eight, when Janice finally showed up, Sandy, Martha, and Britney were eating the chocolate silk pie Britney had bought.

Janice looked as if she had been crying.

"Hey," she said softly to her gathering of friends, laying her bag aside, eyes avoiding everyone.

"Are you okay?" Martha asked, rising.

"No."

Britney got up too. "What happened?"

Janice shrugged. "Greg."

"What about him?" Martha asked, looking Janice over for damage.

"Called things off." Like a deflated balloon, Janice crumbled into herself. Martha and Britney reached for her, but she shrugged them off, headed for a chair, and sat.

"You want something? Wine, soda?" Britney asked.

A tear rolled down Janice's cheek. "No, I'm okay."

Martha looked around for a napkin, saw none. "Sandy, go get her a tissue." Sandy got slowly to her feet. Went to the kitchen, came back, handed Janice a paper towel, their eyes meeting for the first time.

What she gets for being such a fool. Sandy could feel Janice's stare, could feel her thoughts. Sensed the I-need-you-Sandy emotions drifting her way. She sat, shifted in her chair, and tossed one leg over the other, offering her back.

"We have shrimp this time," Britney said, "and I bought a silky pie." Striking a pose, she added, "You haven't said anything about my new look."

Janice's eyes were slow to look up at Britney, her weak smile overwhelmed by sadness. "Yeah, you look good."

Martha crouched next to her. "Why do you want to give him the victory like that, huh? We know you're a good person, that you have enough love to fill the world, and if that knucklehead can't accept it, can't deal with it, is too scared or too stupid to love you, then that's his problem, not yours."

"You're right about that, Martha," Britney said softly.

"Now, you know when I was born the word *heartache* was branded on my forehead. You know what I went through, what happened to me, but I'm still here. If I could survive *that,* girl, you can get over some tired-ass Negro from Jersey. Am I right, Sandy?"

She heard her name, knew Martha was trying to force her into the mix, but pretended she didn't hear.

"I said am I right, Sandy?"

"Uh-hum." But there was no conviction in her voice.

Janice's voice rustled through the room, lost, bleak, and forlorn. "You were right, Sandy. You were so right."

Sadness. It rushed at Sandy like high tide. It was hard not to be moved, hard to remain neutral, hard not to care, offer words.

Sandy's eyebrows drew together as she turned and addressed her friend. "Why didn't you listen to me, Janice? Didn't I say you deserved someone better? The whole thing could have been avoided if you'd just listened to me."

"Now, hold up, Sandy," Martha interjected. "Let's be fair here. How long did you run after Brian? Yeah, Janice should have listened but she didn't. But you didn't either, so don't be trying to make it seem like she did something that none of us ever did."

"That's not the point, Martha."

"Yes, sista, it is the point. Now, we're supposed to have each other's back, and when times get hard we're supposed to support each other, not tear each other down. She's sitting over here hurting, and instead of trying to read her the riot act, you of all people should be trying to comfort her."

Martha the prosecutor sat down.

The room rushed into that off-kilter silence, the air thick with innuendo and judgment. Sandy found herself tired of it all, tired of the tit-for-tat that had become their way of life.

She considered withdrawing from all of them, the burdens of being together outweighing any good as far as she could see. *I don't need this shit,* she was thinking when Janice spoke directly into her heart.

"You said you'd always have my back, Sandy. What happened to that? I made a mistake. One stupid mistake. Can't you forgive me for that? As long as we've been friends, isn't that worth something? Thought I had something worth saving, and it turned out I didn't. You want me to say I'm sorry, then I'll say it. I'm sorry. But stop sitting over there like I don't matter to you."

The words were a knife plunged straight into Sandy's heart. She looked at her friend, saw the broken spirit, and didn't want to add any anguish. Knew in that moment she was the most important person in the world to her and accepted the responsibility.

"Apology accepted," she said after a while.

Britney leaned back, wiping imaginary sweat from her brow. "Whew. You guys had me worried there for a minute. I thought it was the end for sure."

Martha sucked her teeth. "There will never be an end to us. We will be friends forever."

But as Sandy stared deep into Janice's eyes and Janice returned the favor, things floated between them. Yes, they were friends again, but the foundation had suffered a severe blow.

TEN

Meeting Adrian's family.

It was an idea that had visited Sandy briefly and then vanished. Her encounter with his brother had left a bitter taste in her mouth, and she never even broached the subject with Adrian.

Their life together was going fine, and family introductions were not a necessity. But when Adrian announced he was taking her to his sister's party, the script got switched. Suddenly the idea held significance. If Adrian wanted to do this, then that meant he was in it for the long run.

Now, as he exited off the Belt Parkway, she glanced at the man beside her and sent up one of her silent prayers: *please let them like me.*

Adrian made a left on the overpass and made another quick left, entering a block Sandy never knew existed but had no doubt passed a dozen times. "The border," he explained as she took in the attached two-family houses with little half-circle balconies in front.

"Built in the seventies. More a Brooklyn/Queens mix than Brooklyn," he went on.

They coasted up the block in search of parking, cars filling both sides of the street. The next block over Adrian found a space, and together they walked, the spring night misty and warm about them.

"You sure this is Brooklyn?" Sandy wanted to know.

He laughed. "I'm sure." He looked at her with careful eyes. "You ready to meet my brood?"

"Your what?"

"Brood, brothers and sister. That's what I call them. When I was younger I had to look after them a lot, and I considered them my charges, y'know, brood?"

"Well, if they treated you like I treated my brother, they must've run your behind ragged."

"Tell me about it. I got more whippings because of them. My father didn't use his hands, didn't use a switch. Had this paddle from home, used to tear my behind up."

As a child Sandy could not recall getting beaten. *Slapped, yeah, sent to a corner, but beaten?* "Sounds like a sweet dad."

"Nah, he knew what he was doing. We grew up in a rough neighborhood, and he was determined to keep us on the right track."

"Did he?"

"Well, all of us have college degrees. Nobody ever went to jail or got hooked on drugs. I'd say he did just fine." Adrian opened the chain-link fence and headed up the wide brick steps. He rang the doorbell, and Sandy wondered who could hear it over the pulsating reggae music.

"Ready for some rubba-dub?" he asked with a smile.

"Yeah, I guess." But her eyes were fixed on the front door, anxiety with her.

A tall, light-skinned woman appeared. Broke out into a smile. With a scream of delight she pushed the storm door open and threw her arms around Adrian, hugging him tight, face filled with joy. "Paw Boy, ya made it, nuh?"

"Me here, right? Stop all dis fuss." But the gladness in his eyes could not be missed. He reached back and ushered Sandy forward. She stared into the honey eyes, the head of brown soft curls. Felt an envy in the presence of such beauty.

"I, dis me friend, Sandee. Sandee, dis me sister Ray-chill."

She tried not to react to the change in Adrian's diction, but every time he switched, it was like having a whole different person beside her. The smile on Rachel's face did not diminish an inch as their eyes met.

"Come in, come in," Rachel offered. "My home is your

home, so please, kick off ya shoes, eat, drink, have a good good time, eh?"

It was slow going through the thick crowd, the smell of curry heavy in the air, the bass guitar vibrating heavily through the carpeted floor.

"Where Wint and dem?" Adrian asked, following his sister.

"Dem downstairs, being deejays."

"I, mixing it up?"

"Dey tink so."

He squeezed Sandy's arm. "Be back." Headed down into the basement.

Rachel moved towards the kitchen. "You want something, Sandy? Rum? Beer? Stout?"

"I'll take some rum and OJ if you have it."

"Sure we do."

The older woman standing over the stove, stirring the pot, cast her eyes on Sandy briefly and looked away. Sandy felt it. Adrian's mother.

"Mommy, come now, meet Adrian's friend," Rachel cajoled. Mrs. Burton laid the spoon down, her face devoid of emotion. Her smile was the last thing to arrive. She extended her hand. "Hello."

"Hello, Mrs. Burton." Sandy took in the dark-skinned woman and felt things pass between them. *We kinda look alike,* she thought, Adrian's mother no doubt thinking the same thing.

"Was wondering when I would get the chance to meet you." But there was no real joy or anticipation in those words. "I know Adrian's been seeing you a while," she added, letting Sandy's hand go.

Rachel grabbed her mother by the shoulders, shook them. "Loosen up, Mommy. It's a party, not no funeral."

A small smile dusted Mrs. Burton's lips, faded as she went back to her pots. "Where's Adrian?" she asked no one in particular.

Rachel waved her hand. "Downstairs. No doubt showing

Wint and Junie how to mix records." She poured orange juice into a plastic cup. Called Sandy over. "I let people pour their own poison." She pointed to the Jamaica rum sitting on the counter.

Sandy didn't miss the American tone in Rachel's voice, knew it was her way of trying to make Sandy feel comfortable, but as she poured a digit of one hundred proof into her cup, she had already tallied the score. Two against, one for. She hoped Adrian's other brother would even the score.

If upstairs was crowded, then downstairs was violating fire codes. There was so little room, Sandy had to squeeze past people as she followed Rachel towards the bar. Seeing them before they saw her, she was startled by the similarities between the three brothers.

Rachel stopped at the bar. Considered her brothers with sassy eyes. "Enough of dat new stuff. Put on some Marley, slow tings down a bit."

Sandy caught Adrian's eye, and though he was smiling, little joy lay within it. She stood there, the bar filled with deejay equipment separating them, waiting to be introduced. It seemed forever before Adrian tapped one brother on the shoulder. "Eh, want you to meet Sandee." But Adrian said it as if it were a chore, and his brother's head bopped to the beat a few more times before he looked up, only to nod and look back down at the turntable.

"Junie," Adrian explained. He indicated the other brother. "You remember Wint." But if Junie was treating her like air, Wint was staring at her with such cold eyes they chilled her.

"I," Winston offered.

"Hello," Sandy offered back. She stood there, surrounded by dozens of people, feeling like the last person on earth. Even as Bob Marley's "No Woman No Cry" filled the air and Adrian came around the bar to take her hand and danced with her and she gave herself to him and the sensuous motion of his body, it was not enough.

Even as she closed her eyes, determined to lose herself, disappear into Adrian's embrace, make his brothers unimportant, forget the chilly response from his mother, it still hurt.

Sandy no longer had any doubt, knew it like she knew her first name. Something about her had offended them, and she had no idea what.

When Sandy was tired of dancing and not another drop did she want to drink, Rachel rescued her and took her for a house tour. She showed Sandy pictures of Adrian as a boy on trips to Trinidad, pointing out the stern-faced man who was their father.

"Him look tuff? Him is tuff," she said with a laugh. "But he my poppa, and me love em so." Rachel introduced her to the other guests as Adrian's lady, shared her recipe of oxtail. "Tuff ting, y'know. Got ta boil it and boil it and just when ya tink it ready, nuh, sar, it still tuff!" But of all the things Rachel shared, going out of her way to make her feel comfortable and at home, the one that meant the most was her advice.

"You can't pay my brudders mind . . . they tink dey know every ting and dowen't know nuttin'." When Sandy asked what exactly that meant, Rachel shrugged, smiled, and patted her hand. "Adrian is all ya need to be concerned wit, you 'earing me? You have made 'em 'appy like I haven't seen ina long time, and dat's all dat matters."

"Ray-chill."

They both looked up. There before them was the same brooding, icy-eyed man Sandy had seen in the photographs. Rachel jumped up, went over to the man who was without doubt Adrian's father.

"Poppa . . . ya made it."

She hugged him hard. Her whole body overflowing with joy. Gently he eased her away. "Ya mudder, where she?"

"Kitchen, where else?" Rachel took his hand. "Come, I w'an' ya ta meet Adrian's friend San-dee."

Sandy stood, forced a smile. Extended her hand, nervous and on edge. But her smile faded as Mr. Burton slipped his hands into his pockets, his eyes hard and unkind on her.

Rachel tapped his shoulder. "Poppa!" Tapped it again. "Poppa." But Mr. Burton ignored her and headed for the kitchen. Rachel looked at Sandy with sorrowed eyes. "He needs a little time, that's all."

For what, Sandy wanted to know as she stood there, stunned and hurting in the same breath.

"Wait here," Rachel told her, disappearing down the basement steps. Soon she was returning with Adrian in tow, his eyes saying he knew what had just happened.

He took her outside. They sat on the stoop. Still fresh and raw inside, Sandy could not speak about it, and, gratefully, Adrian didn't ask. He took her hand, looked deep into her eyes, saying without words what was important.

It gave her resolve, the guts to remain. She would not allow them to chase her away. She would stay at the party for as long as Adrian wanted to.

He stayed by her side most of the night, attentive, laughing, smiling. *Trying to make it better,* but too many times she saw his brothers whispering and looking her way, her very presence apparently insulting them.

It was nearly five in the morning when the last guest left. Adrian was downstairs with his brothers, breaking down equipment, and Sandy was upstairs with Rachel helping with the cleanup.

When they were finished, Rachel suggested Sandy go downstairs and get Adrian. "He'll be downstairs all night drinking stout wit my brudders if you dowen't."

But Sandy didn't want to go down there. If she never came face to face with Adrian's brothers again it would be too soon. "Could you go and get him for me?"

Rachel laughed. "Don't let my brudders or my farder scare you. D'are bark worse dan dare bite. No, you go down and get your man. You show 'em who's boss."

Sandy went, her shoes clattering on the hardwood steps. Her eyes danced around the room as she tried to spot Adrian but found Winston instead. She quickly looked away.

"Wondering if you were ready?" she said, Adrian sitting at the bar, a Guiness Stout in front of him. He extended his hand in a slow, weary fashion, and she wasn't sure if it was his heart or the alcohol that made him do so.

He nodded. "Come."

Two pairs of eyes followed her as she made her way, taking his hand, allowing herself to be pulled close. He kissed her lips, got up off the stool, and lifted her hand towards Junie. "Shake." Junie rolled his eyes. "Shake it nuh," Adrian insisted.

Sandy could not believe it when Junie took her hand. Was surprised at the gentle way he held it. She prepared herself for a jarring of her whole shoulder, but the shake was light, and too soon he was letting her hand go.

"Now you, Wint."

Wint sucked his teeth and said something Sandy could not understand. Adrian answered him back with fast, heavily accented words that also went right over Sandy's head. In the end, Adrian won. Winston shook her hand, but his grip was tighter and there was no gentleness in the motion.

Adrian smiled, nodded. "Good night, brudders." He urged Sandy up the steps. When they reached the top, he called out to his sister, telling her they were going. Rachel came from the kitchen, foil-wrapped plates in her hand. She held out the other arm to Sandy and gave her a parting hug.

"Don't be a stranger. Adrian, you bring her around as often as you like."

Adrian nodded, gratitude in his eyes. "Will do."

They were heading back towards the car when Sandy asked the one question she could not before. "How come they don't like me?"

"Who?"

"Winston, Junie, your mother." Her eyes grew damp, the memory fresh in her heart. "Your father wouldn't even shake my hand."

Adrian sighed. "Because they don't know you."

"Rachel didn't know me either, but she welcomed me right in."

"Sandy, my family's a funny bunch. And believe me, it has nothing to do with you."

"Then who?"

He turned his head, a melancholy look full on his face. "Me."

"What does that mean?"

"It means I like you and that's all that matters. It means Rachel likes you, and that means more to me than anybody else liking you. It means we are going to go on and live our lives and not worry about who doesn't like it, all right?"

Sandy swallowed, nodded, and conceded. But on the ride home the whole evening coated her like tar, hot, sticky, burning her to the bone.

It was the first time he had ever seen her cry.

Tears like spent jewels slipping down her face, eyelashes glittery beneath the bedroom lamp. So much pain there, so much anguish, it broke Adrian's heart.

"No, Sandy, don't cry," he whispered, kissing the damp cheeks gathering her in his arms.

But she could not stop her tears. "They made me feel like I was nothing." Her grief had caught her off guard, returning with fire.

She didn't want to have this conversation. Didn't want to be lying in her bed, Adrian beside her and in anguish. She had thought she had pushed it down and away from her, but the moment they had entered her bedroom and began undressing, it all came back. "Made me feel like a nobody," she added.

"They don't know you, that's all."

"What about Wint? I've met him twice."

Adrian wiped her tears. "It's not about you, Sandy. I told you that. It's about me."

"What about you?"

He looked into her eyes, his own filled with love and regret. "No matter what anyone else says, thinks, or does, I want you in my life. I'm in love like I never thought I would be again, and nobody's going to change that."

Her soul lifted, heavenbound. "Love you too," she managed as she drew his lips to hers and gave herself over to the love and the joy, bittersweet.

Janice held the steering wheel steady as she navigated her car over the George Washington Bridge. Beside her was a map, an address, and a scary kind of hope. She knew what she was doing was wrong, but in the moment it felt right. It didn't have to be this way, shouldn't be this way, but this was the way it was.

Those many weeks ago when she had done the unthinkable, when she had gone into Greg's wallet, found his driving license, and copied down his address while he was in the shower, Janice hadn't been sure what she was going to do with the information, only that the more he insisted she didn't need to know where he lived, the more she felt she did and took matters in her own hands.

She had looked at the paper often, trying to determine its worth, but when Greg said good-bye and kept to his word, a decision was made. Using the Cole's Directory, which listed every address in the country, Janice had found a business on the same street and gave them a call. When she asked the delicatessen situated in Teaneck, New Jersey, for directions coming from Queens, she had been met with suspicion, but a possible sale had erased any mistrust.

Now, as she headed towards the toll bridge, she scanned her paper again, verifying the exit that would take her where Greg would not. She had never been to this part of New Jersey, and there was a real possibility of her getting lost, but that was the least of her worries. *Just let me get*

there, she decided, stashing her token for the return trip
home.

There was something about apartment building hallways
that, no matter how clean they were kept, always smelled
of living: cooking smells, body smells, there was always
something in the air. As she made her way down the hall,
she became aware of old grease, floor wax, and incense.

12A, 12B. She passed a big black door and knew that
was the incinerator room, felt faint by the time she came
abreast of 12C. Straightening her clothes, smoothing down
her hair, she lifted her finger to ring the bell just as the
door swung open and a woman appeared.

Both of them jumped, both of them startled, two pairs
of eyes going from fear to amazement to certainty. They
took a second to decide things, took a bet, and each played
their hand.

"Can I help you?"

Janice looked at the woman, determining her worth, her
beauty, her relationship to Greg. Sister, cousin, friendly
neighbor all falling by the wayside as the woman's eyes
narrowed as she did her own sizing up.

"Is Greg here?" *There, I said it.* But there was a tremble
in Janice's voice that reached all the way down to her toes.
She had not betted on a woman being there. No scenario
for that in her plan of plans. She hadn't considered that
Greg had found someone else to take her place.

"And you are?"

"Janice." She couldn't say the rest because for the first
time she doubted who she was to Greg.

The woman turned and shouted "Greg!" over her shoulder as if she'd known him, owned him, forever.

She looked back at Janice, a pretty woman with few
flaws, making Janice feel small, incidental, and unimportant. There was a power to her; no doubt she handled a
wild oat like Greg with ease. The woman had her beat by
a mile.

No competition. But Janice could not turn away, could not retreat, especially since Greg was coming up behind the woman's shoulder.

"What the hell?" were his first words. "How'd you find me?" his second, which brought a smile to the woman's face. How much could Janice really have meant to him if she wasn't even supposed to know where he lived?

"What you doing here?" That hurt more than anything, because he should have known why she came.

"I came to see you because I still love you."

Her response was gasoline on a fire. Greg's voice sliced through her and echoed down the long empty hall. "You what? 'Cause you love me?"

He addressed the woman beside him. "You hear her? 'Cause she love me." There was an abhorrence in his voice, and for a second Janice doubted everything. *This can't be Greg.* But as his dark angry eyes came into focus, she knew. It was. "You crazy, you know that? Now get the hell away from my door before I call the cops."

But she wasn't crazy, she was in love. "I came all this way to see you," she insisted, trying to get him to understand.

Greg turned toward the woman. "Bring me the phone."

But Janice would not be moved. He would never call the police on her, they had shared a past, something had to have remained. She folded her arms, settling in, her stance—*ain't going nowhere*—full inside of her.

Then the phone was in Greg's hand. Determined, he tapped in three digits, looking past her head as he spoke. "Yes, there is a woman at my door and she will not go away. No . . . no . . . no. Ten-fifteen Moreland Avenue, apartment twelve-C. Yes, yes, that's right. Thank you."

He handed the phone back to the woman, glared at Janice. But she was determined to prove a point. *You still love me.*

"They coming," Greg warned.

"Let them come," Janice said back.

And true to his word, five minutes later two uniforms were coming out of the elevator.

Their sirens were silent, their lights still and unlit, but there was no denying the scene unfolding on the street in Teaneck. One police cruiser behind Janice's car, another in front.

I won't cry.

She held her head up, followed the brake lights of the police vehicle in front of her, trying not to tailgate, trying hard to swallow the pain.

At least he didn't press charges, the only thing she had to cling to now. Yes, Greg had summoned the cops, but he hadn't filed a complaint. *Has to still be feeling something for me.*

When the officers arrived, they had been ready to haul her off to jail. Seemed kind of disappointed that they couldn't. They had come, holsters unstrapped, hands on the smooth handles of their guns, ready to draw at a second's notice.

Had asked her, "Ma'am, please step away from the apartment door." Asked it twice before Janice realized they were talking to her. She took one step back, and they moved four steps forward. Then they were by her side, a hand on each arm, ready to wrestle her to the ground, slap on the handcuffs, and jostle her out of the building.

But a tiny bit of hope had come in that moment. Greg had flinched as they pulled Janice backwards. A millisecond, but Janice had seen it. A hot flash of concern coming into his face, the idea that he had gone too far, arriving.

His anger had all but dissipated by the time one officer took his notebook out, flipped to a clean summons, and asked Greg his name.

Greg had faltered, his eyes darting over Janice, who was pushed against the wall and held tight by the other officer. It seemed forever but was only a few seconds before Greg's words came. "Not pressing charges."

"If she's stalking you—" the officer began.

Greg cut him off. "She's not," his voice soft.

"But you said—"

"I know what I said, and I don't want to press charges. I just want her to leave."

"If you don't press charges, she can come back."

Greg had glanced at her again, a flash of pity in his eyes. Shook his head. "No, she won't be coming back."

Janice's arm was let go.

"Does she live around here?"

"No, Queens."

The officer tipped back his hat. "We'll make sure she gets over the bridge if you want."

Now, as her personal procession journeyed down the street, the girders of the bridge up ahead, the first tear fell, but she willed back the rest. *I won't let them see me cry,* she insisted just as the sirens came to life, red and blue lights swirling oily against the dark night.

It took a while to understand why. A while to realize they were clearing a toll lane just for her. They were making a path to get her on the bridge, wanting her gone from their town and their state. *Just like Greg.*

A white hand popped out of the police cruiser, directing her to an open token booth. Janice eased her car to the left, found her token, and handed it to the clerk. With caution she moved past the booth and towards the bridge, the police cruisers growing tiny in her rearview mirror.

Adrian seemed to be on a mission since his sister's party. He took Sandy out as often as money allowed. Every time she turned around he was calling her with plans to do something.

Tonight it was Latin night, and Sandy was all dressed up and ready to go. Her spiky high heels felt good on her feet, her short full skirt would allow it all to hang out on the dance floor, and her Carmen Miranda top made her feel as if she'd been born on the island of Puerto Rico.

She was a *mamacita*, and Adrian, Juan Carlos. They were going to the Bronx to dance Salsa till the sun came up.

"Ready?" Adrian asked as she clicked off the last light and reached for her pocketbook.

"Sure am," she answered, smiling brightly; feeling sexy and Latin and just *hot*.

"Let's go." Adrian opened the door, and Sandy stepped through just as her phone rang. She looked at Adrian. He nodded. Sandy went back inside and answered.

"Hello?"

"Sandy?"

Janice in tears. Janice in trouble. Janice's world coming to an end. *Don't have time for this nonsense.* "Was on my way out," Sandy said, none too kindly.

"Got a minute?"

She sighed. "Adrian's waiting." *Take the hint.* The line grew silent. Sandy took a breath. "Call you tomorrow, all right? We'll talk then. I got to go."

"Yeah, sure . . ."

Sandy hung up the phone.

"Who was it?" Adrian asked.

"Nobody," Sandy said quickly, stepping outside and locking her door.

Oh yes, she was a real *mamacita bonita* tonight. Everywhere she looked, honey-colored men of Latin persuasion were watching her maneuver on the dance floor. Air whisked through her legs; flashes of her black satin panties gave out fast cheap thrills. Sandy was on fire.

Drenched with sweat, fast on her high-heeled feet, Sandy was twirled and pushed and recovered at dizzying speeds, Adrian moving her about, a masterful salsa king.

The music never stopped, and neither did the two of them. They danced fast, slow, and well into the dawn. Later, on the trip home, Adrian drove to an abandoned pier, parked his car, and together they watched the sun rise.

*   *   *

They entered her apartment, giddy as children. Raced to her bedroom and fell upon her bed. "Can it always be like this?" She wanted to know as she reached for his hand and gave it a squeeze. "Promise me, promise me the fun times won't end," she asked, her eyes somber, needing.

He kissed the back of her hand, looked all the way into her soul. "I promise," he whispered.

In love, happy and at peace, neither of them suspected, had the slightest clue, that life was about to take a swift turn. That it would be weeks before they saw each other again.

Her feet hurt.

Even the sixty-dollar Reebok Walkers could not do away with the pain. *Too much being a mamacita.* Two days after her night out with Adrian, Sandy's feet were still in deep protest. Easing the sneakers off her feet, Sandy sighed, wiggled her toes, and was considering a foot soak when her phone rang.

"Hello?"

"Sandy?"

"Adrian?" But the voice sounded too desperate and scared to belong to him.

"Oh God, Sandy . . ." The rest was lost in one long moan.

"What is it?" she insisted.

"Oh God, Sandy." Yes, she got that part. Had gotten that part the moment she picked up the phone.

"What Adrian, what? What is it?" In the background she heard a flurry of voices and the jingle of chimes.

"Gen . . ." There was a long inhalation of air that sounded as if his throat was being sucked dry by a vacuum.

"Gin? Are you at a bar?"

"This can't be happening," Adrian moaned.

"What, Adrian, what?"

"Gen . . . she's dying, Sandy. She's dying."

Gin, not a drink; Adrian not in a bar. Those sounds in the background not patrons sitting around sipping Buds and vodkas. Gin was a person. Those sounds—a hospital.

"Gin?"

"Gennifer." His voice drifted off.

"Who's Gennifer?"

"My friend, the one with AIDS."

Sandy's heart skipped a beat. Her faced flushed hot with a rush of dread. *Dying?* Sandy swallowed as her legs gave away.

She slid to the kitchen floor, paralyzed with fear. Adrian had just said she was fine, no symptoms, no signs, no nothing. Sandy had taken that knowledge and used it as a yardstick against Adrian's own foreseeable wellness.

"How bad?" she asked, not wanting to know.

"Bad, bad."

"What hospital?"

"Booth."

"Memorial?"

"Yeah."

She knew where that was. "Where are you now?"

"On the ward."

"What floor?"

"What?"

"I said what floor?"

"They won't let you up."

"You got up."

". . . different."

"Why?" But even as Sandy waited for an answer, she half knew it. You had to be next of kin—a mother, father, sister, brother, or spouse.

She didn't speak, couldn't speak. Numb.

"I was going to tell you."

"Tell me what? Tell me when? That it wasn't some ex-girlfriend, but your fucking wife?"

She heard choking noises, the phone juggling. Sandy saw him standing there, phone clutched to his ear, shoulders shaking, tears squeezing out like rain. The need to curse him jumped her so badly her throat burned, but she took a moment to quiet her rage. Didn't want to add her ton of bricks to the weight she was certain he already carried. Found enough forgiveness to say, "Don't cry."

"This shit is so fucked up."

Sandy nodded. "I know . . . but right now you got Gennifer to worry about. Take care of what you got to take care of. Call me when you can."

The receiver slipped from her fingers. Sandy sat on the floor, feeling a locomotion of fear charging upward. She twisted from it, tried to clamp down her lips against it, but could not contain it.

Adrian has a wife and she's dying of AIDS.

The howl came out of her like a banshee.

If she had been invited, Sandy would not have known what to wear. If invited, she would not have known where to sit, how she would have been introduced. Wouldn't have known whether to bake a ham, send flowers, or hold Adrian's hand. But she hadn't been invited. All she had was the knowledge that the love of her life had a wife who had died of AIDS.

Gennifer died.

Gennifer Elaine Burton, wife of Adrian, had passed away. *No wonder they all hated me.* The puzzle that she had tucked away for a brighter day was coming together with Kodak-color clarity. Winston, Junie, Adrian's parents had all treated her with disdain, and now Sandy knew why. *Adrian was a married man, and I was sleeping with him.*

They had all disliked her, no doubt thinking bad things about her. All of them except Rachel, *because I made him happy.*

Sandy turned away from the thought. Pushed herself away as she had done for the last five days. Away from Adrian, away from fears, pain, agony, and distrust.

She had asked him *you want me there?*, ready to be by

his side, help him through. But his answer, *nah, that's okay*, had done away with the possible.

Alone he wanted to handle the wake, the service, and the burial. Alone he wanted to take the drive out to the cemetery and stand in the soft, warm April breeze, roses, carnations, and billowy chrysanthemums offering all the promises of spring.

Alone he wanted to pitch earth onto the lid of the coffin that held the woman he had asked to be his wife. A woman whose love wasn't strong enough to keep him when she tested positive.

Alone—to be physically, emotionally, and mentally separated from people and things. To lock yourself into a tiny box with no windows, no air, and no light for days. Sandy knew what it felt like.

I need some time, Sandy . . . things bouncing around in my head I gotta get straight. Sandy gave him what he wanted. Left him alone. But when the morning of the eighth day rolled around, services over, the body laid to rest, and no phone call arrived, Sandy was out of patience.

The lie, the big blow, had not been discussed or explained. It became just another thing she needed Adrian to do. Like call her and share his grief.

The lie, eight days old, took front stage that morning and was still with her in the afternoon. It ate at her, chunks of herself vanishing as she lay in bed, unable to do anything else.

Her intercom buzzed.

Sandy sat up, rubbed hands over her ashy face, aware of her appearance for the first time in days. She could not remember the last time she had showered, the last time she had done anything but roam around her apartment like a ghost.

For the last five days Sandy had been living like a hermit, calling in sick, refusing to step out her front door. The truth of Adrian's situation had devastated her to the core, but it didn't matter, not now with him finally coming, coming to explain, to hold her. Share.

She didn't bother to ask who, didn't bother with a robe, just waited, door open, eager for the sight of him. Her heart surged as she heard footsteps on the stairs, her whole body yearning in anticipation. And just as quickly the hope died as she saw who was heading her way.

"Here . . . take it."

But Sandy didn't want it. She pushed it away, spilling hot tea on both her and Martha's wrists.

"Girl, you scalded us both." Martha put the cup down. Stood over her, one impatient hand on her hip. "This isn't like you, Sandy." Martha considered her friend, who looked as if the world had come to an end. "You have to get out of this funk."

But Sandy had no intention of doing that. Her blues were a balm against all that had happened, smoothing out the rough edges, and she had no plans to let it go. "I don't have to do nothing."

"Yes, you do."

"No, I don't. Now will you just leave me the fuck alone."

"No, I'm not going to leave you the fuck alone," Martha said, taking a seat on the couch. "I'm going to sit myself right down here till you get over the fact that Adrian lied and his wife died."

Sandy blinked, surprised. So Janice had told.

She had been the only one Sandy called. And while she had not asked Janice to keep it a secret, she thought Janice would have at least honored her privacy.

But Martha knowing didn't change a thing. Sandy didn't want to be bothered; she wanted her gone. "I'm not up to your lectures today. Now will you just go?"

Martha shook her head no.

A pulse of anger moved through Sandy, her body becoming incensed to the core. She took in the woman who assumed too much, her words arriving bitter and sharp. "You think you know everything, don't you?"

Martha looked at her coolly, unfazed, determined. "I know sitting around moping isn't getting it. That it's not going to make anything better."

"You know?" Sandy laughed, a bitter rush of sharp edges. "What the fuck you know?" outraged by Martha's words. "Know how to get a man? Do you even know how to start?"

Martha's voice grew low, contained. "That's enough, Sandy."

But Sandy was too hot to cool down, too out there to reel herself in. "The hell it is. You come in here like you Big Momma or some shit trying to tell me what to do and you ain't had nobody since Leon? What the fuck you know?"

Martha's eyes were intense. Angry. "I know anger is making you nasty so I'm going to forgive you, that's what I know."

"Don't be forgiving nothing, hear? Just get the fuck out."

"I'm not leaving."

"Fine, sit there. I'm going back to bed."

Sandy took a step but Martha grabbed her arm, pulling her back. "You're not going nowhere."

Sandy pulled back, bringing Martha with her. They tumbled, fell, landed on the floor. Sandy scrambled to get to her feet but Martha was quick and grabbed her heel, sending Sandy crashing to the carpet.

"You fucking bitch!" Sandy yelled.

Martha's hand made impact with Sandy's face. It stunned them both, Sandy blinking, surprised and in pain, Martha breathing hard, hackles raised.

"That's right. I slapped you, calling me out my name like that. I don't give a fuck who died, you don't call me no name like that . . . Now, you want to throw the fuck down? Well, we can do it. Because I'm so ready to kick your ass I can taste it, you hearing me?"

Yes, Sandy was. Saw for herself the ferocity in Martha's eyes, and felt things draining away from her. Breathing hard, soft loose tears streaking her face, she laid her head down, the dusty carpeting tickling her nose. When she was able to sit up, Martha was holding out the tea.

"You gonna drink this now, or what?"

Sandy took the cup.

The stereo was turned down low. Wind instruments drifted around them on long, lazy, endless riffs. Martha had gone through Sandy's CD collection looking for mellow and unimposing. Kenny G. won.

Martha had forced Sandy to take a shower. Took the comb, brush, and hair grease when Sandy refused to do a thing to her wet, matted hair. Martha made her sit on the floor between her thighs as she worked healing into her scalp.

"Old trick, honey," Martha explained. "Believe it or not, Helen taught it to me. Sometimes I'd get so riled after she been on me I'd just be crazy. She'd send me in her room for the jar of Dixie Peach, that hard-ass boars'-hair brush, and put me between her thighs . . . worked magic on my head until all the anger was gone." Martha paused, looked down at her. "Feeling better?"

Sandy nodded. "Didn't mean those things, Martha."

"Yes, you did, but I forgive you. Know it was just your anger talking. But you did come within an inch of losing your life."

"So Janice told you." Sandy wanted confirmation, her head being pushed gently from side to side.

"Yeah."

"What she say?"

"Said turned out Adrian was still married and his wife died. Said you wasn't sounding all that hot . . . that you were depressed. So I asked her if she been to see you, and

she said you told her you didn't want company. That's
when I decided to make this trip, because I know how depression can do you."

"Janice say anything else?"

"Like?"

"Why she died?"

"Heart attack?"

Sandy nodded, relieved. "Yeah," her voice fading. At
least Janice didn't tell it all.

Martha shook her head. "Don't know why he lied, but
you can't be laying up over here letting his lie do you in.
That's on him, Sandy. Let him carry that load. You don't
have to take it on."

But it was too late. She'd done it without a thought. "He
hasn't called me."

"Man just lost a wife, he needs to deal with that."

"What about me?"

"What about you? You still living and breathing, aren't
you? He hasn't called it off, has he? So—what about you?"

Sandy sighed. Leaned her head back against Martha's
jeans, the black denim warm, carrying the faint smell of
body powder.

"Now, what you want me to do with this?" Martha
asked, grabbing up Sandy's hair in one fist.

"Can you do that French roll thing?"

"If you got bobby pins and some hair spray, I think I
can swing it."

"I got a bunch." Sandy turned around, looked up at Martha. Remembered how Martha's mother had reacted to
Adrian, as if she'd smelled something bad. "Your momma
ain't always wrong, Martha."

"I know. Now isn't that a scary thought?"

Patience was a virtue, but it was easier to spew such ideals
when you weren't the one waiting. Easy to say things like
if you love something, set it free . . . if it comes back, it
was meant to be. Easy to dole out timeworn slogans about

tolerance and destiny and fate. Easy. But Sandy was out of patience. She called Adrian, breaking her promise to let him be.

"I want to see you," Sandy said without so much as a hello. She was beyond formalities, all out of refinement and polite civilities.

"Not a good time, Sandy."

"You owe me answers," she said hotly into the phone receiver.

"Do I?" His voice was scary and far away.

"Yes, you do."

Silence came and went. "Sandy . . ."

"No, Adrian. Today."

"Look, I—"

"No excuses," she demanded. "Today."

"All right . . . give me a few."

She knew coming to see her was the last thing he wanted to do, *but it's not about what he wants anymore. It's about me this time.*

He needed a shave, his jeans looked slept in, and his shirt was rough dried. The tight jaw and red-rimmed eyes gave him a feral look. She couldn't believe it was Adrian at her door.

Sandy had anticipated so many other things at this moment, like the pressure of his hugging her so hard that her bones cracked, but the man before her was detached and haunted. He wouldn't even look at her, just gazed past her shoulder as if he was seeing something she could not.

For nine days Sandy had given Adrian his space. Favors were over. It was her time now. "I deserve answers. Let's go talk . . ." When he didn't make a move, Sandy forced herself to go on. "You coming in or not?"

He stepped inside and headed for her living room. Sandy closed the door and took a cleansing breath.

Beginning or our end? She wasn't taking bets.

ELEVEN

It wasn't how she wanted the conversation to go, but Adrian had started on the offensive, insisting that she hear the whole story before she passed judgment.

Hearing it, the tale of the wife who had come down with AIDS and the husband who had left her, Sandy had more questions than answers. Planted her feet first on the other side of the equation. "But why did you leave her?"

"It got hard on both of us, Sandy."

"Hard? How?"

"She having it, me not . . . I got scared and she knew how scared I was."

Sandy stared at him in disbelief. "So you left her?"

"She didn't want me to stay."

Sandy knew better. "She did."

"You weren't there, Sandy. Every time I was five minutes late she accused me of being with somebody else. She wouldn't let me hold her, touch her. She started sleeping on the couch."

Sandy's eyes grew wide. "But she *did*, Adrian. She wanted you to do all those things . . . she was just putting up a front. Didn't you know that?"

"I only knew what she told me."

"You should have listened with other things."

"Like what?" Adrian wanted to know.

"Like your heart." The room grew quiet. Sandy stared off, the moment hard. She could sense the cool rage inside of him now. Knew she had to defend herself.

"I didn't want to be a part of this, Adrian. You made me a part of this by not telling the truth. You didn't have to lie, didn't have to tell me it was some ex-girlfriend. We didn't have to end up here."

He shifted, resentment surging through him. "Wanna know why I lied? You want to know? 'Cause I knew you'd blame me. That no matter what I said, you'd blame me."

Her eyes grew moist, Adrian's words stinging. "Did you think I was that shallow? That I wouldn't at least try to understand?"

Adrian moved his hands over his face. "Don't know what I thought, Sandy. All I knew was that everyone else blamed me, accused me of abandoning Gen. After a while I felt like I had."

"And now?"

He looked miserable and lost. His gold eyes were haunted.

"I needed her forgiveness, Sandy. I needed her to tell me that she forgave me, but she couldn't talk, couldn't even open her eyes . . . A squeeze was all she could do. One squeeze of my hand, all she left me. Then she died, and I didn't know what to do. About you, me, her. Nothing. I felt like I didn't deserve anything . . . least of all you."

Sandy swallowed, sensing the answer to the question she had been holding on to for over a week. "What about now?"

His eyes gave it all way. There was no now.

Exile.

Adrian wouldn't let her make him dinner, wouldn't take a cup of coffee. Wouldn't watch a movie with her. Wouldn't stay.

"But what are you going to do at home? Nothing to do there."

"I'll be all right."

He touched her face, that place beneath her chin. Her tears gathered, pooled, fell over his wrist like rain.

"Don't," Adrian asked for both of them.

"I need to know."

"I don't know, Sandy."

"You *have* to know."

"I need more time."

Her voice steamrolled out of her. "No! No more time. You tell me now." She was trembling, shaking, and out of control. But the truth found her in her moment of madness. After days of waiting, he had nothing for her. Not a wish, not a desire, not even the promise.

"Everything's changed, Sandy. You get on with your life, okay?" The knob turned, the door opened, and Adrian walked out.

She slammed the door shut, turned, looking for things to tear, things to throw. She spun herself in a circle, seeking out something to smash, to destroy, her soul on fire.

The phone rang. She turned towards the sound. It rang again. She stared at it, livid and enraged. It rang again. "Shut up!" she yelled, moving towards it, determined to rip it off her kitchen wall.

Her hands grabbed the base, fingers clinging to its smooth, shiny sides. It rang again and she pulled hard. The phone came away and crashed to the floor. Two puncture wounds decorated the wall. Two holes with dusty sheetrock crevices, all she got for her efforts.

Not enough.

She kicked the phone clear out of her kitchen. It slid into the dining room and banged against the wall. The base on one side, the receiver on the other.

Better, she thought, as she turned and headed towards her bedroom.

Her eyes opened, adjusted to the darkness. Sandy's mouth was dry, her back and chest damp. She felt hot, threw back the covers. Lay there waiting for a cool breeze to find her. She turned her head. 2:48 A.M.

She sat up, her head spinning from the effort. What day was it? She couldn't remember. She lay back down, closed her eyes to stop the spinning, opened them to the darkness.

The image of her broken phone on her dining room floor

found her. She picked up the receiver next to her bed. It was dead.

Tears gathered, rolled down her cheeks in huge drops. Her legs itched. She touched her stomach, found her T-shirt. Inched down further, found sweatpants. She was fully dressed and in bed.

Sandy sat up, looked at the clock again—2:49 A.M. What day was it? Sunday? Saturday? Wednesday? Her mind flipped back to the last thing she remembered—the dead, broken phone. Skipped back some more—her apartment door slamming. Back some more—*I don't know, Sandy . . . stop.*

She had come in from work, straightened her apartment. Ate a bologna and cheese sandwich, waited for Adrian. All day at work she had been anxious and struggled to keep her mind on the bimonthly report that was due in two days, on Thursday. Two days before Thursday was Tuesday.

It was now Wednesday. It was after two o'clock in the morning. Her phone was dead. Adrian said he didn't know . . . no, that's not what he said. Go back.

Get on with your life.

How?

She saw the repairman looking at her. Knew what he was thinking. *None of your business,* she thought, cutting her eyes and walking out of the kitchen. She'd seen his eyebrow raise the moment he saw her kitchen wall with the gaping wound and the brightly colored, tattered wires. Was certain he knew exactly what had happened to the phone.

She let him to do his job. A few minutes later he was peeking into the living room. "Need some new wire. NY-NEX's gonna bill you for it."

"How much?"

"Well, the service call is seventy-five. Wiring is another eighty."

Quick math filtered through Sandy's head. "One hundred and fifty-five dollars?"

"Can I make a suggestion?" He had to be one of those technicians—young, cute, and black. "I can change the outlet to a jack plug. If it happens again, all you have to pay for is a new phone. Wiring would be okay."

"Just do what we already agreed to," her eyes steely as she turned and walked down the hall.

A long breath surged through her, reviving her as the end of her story arrived. She waited for Martha to say something, but the silence told her that even Martha was at a loss for words.

"Damn."

Sandy nodded, reaffirming her feelings.

"No wonder you were so messed up . . . You told anybody else?"

"Just you and Janice."

"Figured you told her . . . I liked him, thought he was cool."

"But he *was*, Martha."

"No, he wasn't. He was just like all those other fools out there, putting on the good face. Nobody is without secrets. No one's closet is clean . . ." Her voice drifted. "So you okay?"

"Well, I broke my damn phone and have to pay a hundred fifty bucks, but outside that, I'm here."

"All you can be, considering. You eat dinner yet?"

"Hadn't thought much about food. Why?"

"I feel like some down-home cookin' and don't really want to eat alone."

"Momma's Place?" Sandy asked, suddenly excited.

"Where else can you get cooking like you wished your momma made?"

"You treatin'?"

"Do you ever have money?" Martha said, laughter rich in her voice.

*   *   *

Momma's Place didn't look like much from the outside. A storefront with big glass windows, spider plants, and country kitchen curtains, it was easy to miss driving down Merrick Boulevard.

Inside, the cement walls were painted a cool beige, the floor, hardwood, the lighting was soft, and the tables were round and sat four easily. Baskets of corn bread were complimentary, as was the lemonade. Weekends you couldn't get a table, but it was Thursday, so Sandy and Martha were in luck.

The glossy menu felt cool beneath Sandy's fingers. She studied the offerings, mouth watering. "What you getting?"

Martha's eyes moved over the menu. "I feel like some smothered pork chops and collard greens. Candied yams on the side. How about you?"

"I was thinking about some white limas with ham hock and corn bread, but now that I'm here, them baby back ribs got my nose."

"Their ribs are good, but you can get ribs anywhere." Martha gave her a conspiratorial smile, and Sandy knew that she was about to have her mind changed.

"Think roots. Think way back. Think way back to them summers down south where Antie May Jean spent all day slaving over that cast-iron stove, and how the whole house filled up with the smell of simmering collards and chopped barbecue, or chitlins and corn bread."

Sandy jumped in. "Or a country ham and potato salad . . . that pound cake she whipped up from scratch."

Martha took over. "No, wait . . . that lemon coconut cake she spent all morning grating fresh coconuts for."

Sandy licked her lips. "Sweet potato pie."

Martha shook her head, closed her eyes. "A Seven-Up cake."

"Ladies?" The waitress hovered over them, pen and pad ready. Neither Martha nor Sandy knew how long she had been standing there, but her expression told them she had heard half their dream journey.

Martha went first. "I'll have pigs' feet, collard greens, potato salad, and a lot of hot sauce."

Sandy put down her menu. "I'll have the same." She looked up at Martha. "And who in the hell is Antie Mae Jean?"

Martha shrugged, her laughter large and infectious. "Hell if I know."

They slapped palms over the candle.

Martha put the good-feeling, boxy, luxurious Volvo in park. A year old, the interior still looked and smelled showroom new. The leather upholstery was warm and rich, *just like Adrian's jacket the first time he held me*. Sandy turned away from the thought.

Martha looked at her, her eyes knowing all of it. "Adrian?"

Sandy looked away guiltily.

"Takes time."

"Yeah, I know."

"He's going to be a hard one to get over."

"I know."

Martha changed directions, lightening the mood. "We need to hang out more often, you know that?"

She smiled. "It was kinda fun."

Martha reached into her large leather bag, searched around in the dark recesses and pulled out an invitation to a club. "There's this guy on my job, told me about this club . . . admits two before midnight and it's free."

"Me and you?" Sandy asked, unsure.

"Only two . . ."

She pictured herself and Martha at a dance club in Manhattan. It had been a long time since she had ventured out of Queens to party. The change could do her good.

"What you wearing?" Sandy asked, her mind dancing with the possibilities.

*   *   *

The whole world was there—that was the only way Sandy could describe the massive crowd that jammed into the warehouse-turned-dance-club. The push-pull journey of trying to find a table, a place to rest her feet, sip a drink—*chill*—took away Sandy's excitement and any real hopes of having a good time. People occupied every nook and cranny, holding up walls, drinks, each other. Black and brown faces were everywhere.

Sandy and Martha plodded on, clothes getting crushed, hair getting mushed, belly-rubbing with strangers. It was Martha who spotted the red neon sign that said REST ROOMS and headed towards it. Sandy, a few bodies behind, followed. The deafening music vanished as the bathroom door swung closed behind them.

"Whoooo!" Martha said, heading towards the mirror to check her hair.

"Damn, it's like a zoo out there, Martha."

"You telling me. What did they do, send free invites to the whole isle of Manhattan?" Martha turned sideways, her eyes busy on the left side of her face. "Too damn crowded in here. We have to go somewhere else."

"Where?"

"Bentley's?"

Sandy shook her head hard. "Hell no. Bentley's is just as crowded and is full of snobs."

"Place round the corner has a nice crowd."

They both looked up and over at the six-foot-two glamour girl in the mirror applying fresh lipstick.

"Where around the corner?" Martha asked.

"There's an OTB right around from here. They having a thing tonight and it's only six bucks."

Sandy was confused. "The offtrack betting place?"

"Yeah."

"They having a party?"

"The betting windows are locked down, but yeah, there's a party going on."

"Music?" Martha wanted to verify.

"Jammin'. I just left there to check this place out. I'm going back. You can follow me if you want." The woman paused, her false eyelashes fluttered together. One long hand with manicured nails so slender and red they had to be fake came their way. "I'm April."

It took a while for Martha to reach out and take the hand, her eyes probing the heavily made-up face, the massive hair, and that knob in the middle of the throat. There was something wrong with the picture. The longer Martha stared, the stronger the feeling got.

One hard long look later it came to Martha like a jolt of electricity. She smiled, tickled, surprised. Her eyes widened, giving away her discovery. Her hand rose to meet April's, the grip light and soft.

"I'm Martha. This is Sandy."

"Nice to meet you," April told them, her Adam's apple bobbing twice.

Tall.

Martha didn't really get a sense of how tall April was until they stood outside the Broadway Diner in lower Manhattan, a hint of dawn in the Manhattan sky.

It was hard remembering that April was a man. Hard to keep in mind that beneath the short tight dress lay something Martha never owned but had longed for many times in her life.

Girly-girl, but in true diva style, April held Martha in a perfumed, padded embrace. "Girlfriend, I had a ball," April said, pulling back and giving an air kiss. Her eyes dusted Sandy's. "Well, come on, Miss Thing, Momma ain't got all night. Come on over here and show me love."

There was no way Sandy couldn't. April was so alive, so smart, so witty, so joyful. Being in her company had been the best medicine. For a few hours Sandy had forgotten her woes, and in that moment she was truly feeling all that April had given her this night.

She moved in close, wrapped her arms around the tiny

waist, hugged April long and hard, appreciative of the person beneath the drag. She pulled away, reluctant, heart open. Looked up at April with grateful eyes.

"Well, ain't you cute," April said, moving a long red nail gently across Sandy's face. "You too, Miss Maw-tha. I think I'm gonna have to just crown you both Miss April's girls." She raised her hand. "Poof, poof. So this means you two got to keep in touch with Mother"—she placed her hand at her heart—" 'cause once Mother claims you"—a smile blossomed on her face—"Mother will never let you go. Now," she said, fluttering her long dragon nails, "you two get home safe, okay? And don't forget, Mother will be waiting for your call." With that April turned and began strutting down the street, her high heels clicking to an uncertain rhythm.

"She's wonderful," Sandy found herself saying.

"More woman than any woman I ever met," Martha added, just as awed. A faint smudge of pale pink morning was lingering on the horizon. "I ain't been out this long since I don't know when. Listen . . . the birds are tweeting."

Sandy took her by the arm, feeling a closeness she'd never anticipated. "Come on, girlfriend, let's take our behinds home."

Sandy dropped a chicken leg onto her plate, scooped up some potato salad, and grabbed a chunk of corn bread.

"Give me one," Martha ordered, her plate extended. Sandy dropped a golden square on the paper dish and reached past Janice to get a cup. "Martha, hand me the Sprite."

"Diet or regular?"

"You know I ain't down with no diet."

The table was laden with fried chicken, macaroni and potato salad, and butter-topped corn bread. There was chocolate cake, kiwi, strawberries, and Reddi Wip. The soiree was back in swing.

"Coming through," Britney called, her hands full of nap-

kins and forks. Janice stepped out of her path. It seemed
as if she had been waiting at the edge of the table forever,
biding her time as Martha and Sandy piled their plates as
if it were the last supper.

"All right, Ms. Thang," Martha said, studying the new
and improved Britney.

Even her apartment had gotten a makeover. Gone was
the lumpy orange plaid couch and the lopsided wall unit.
The heavy, full-length sateen drapes had been replaced with
soft gray miniblinds that brought a richness to the shiny
new black sofa and the large obsidian entertainment unit.

Maurice had come into her life fully, changing Britney's
whole world, from how she dressed to how she lived. Nobody said it, but everybody knew: Britney had hit the jack-
pot.

"You should have met Maurice years ago," Martha said.

"Oh, Martha, stop it." But it was easy to see Britney was
pleased, that her life had taken a good turn and she was
coming into her own.

"Stop what? You looking good, sister."

"Yeah, she does," Janice added, but her opinion was cut
off as Martha reached past her to get a fork, diminishing
Janice to the bone.

"Did he show you?" Britney asked, getting comfortable on
the floor.

"His stuff? No, Brit, course not. But I *was* sort of curious."

"A drag queen?" Britney shook her head. "And all those
men trying to hit on her."

"Child, you should have seen them."

Britney poured more wine. Took a sip. "And he slow-
dragged?"

Sandy jumped in, eager to share. "Slow-dragged this
man down, all the way to the ground. Me and Martha was
hysterical."

Martha put down her wineglass and picked up the story.

"After we left the dance, she took us down to the Village to this all-night diner for breakfast. She talked about everybody who walked in—and I mean everybody. Talking loud and not caring who heard. I tell you, we had a ball."

Britney raised an eyebrow. "You gonna see her again?"

"We exchanged numbers."

Britney set her plate aside and got up from the floor. "Time for music." She gathered up a handful of CDs. Martha looked on in amazement. "You have a CD player too?"

Britney slipped "Shai" from its box, her smile quick. "Dinette set coming next week."

Martha shook her head. Sandy smiled. Janice picked up her wine and took a long sip.

The brake lights of the car in front of her glowed feral in the darkness. Sandy tightened her hands on the steering wheel, waiting for the light to change to green.

She had not expected Janice to ask for a ride home. She knew her car was in the shop and had taken a cab to Britney's but was certain she would take a cab back. Sandy had figured her deliberate cold shoulder would discourage Janice. A month ago asking would not have been an issue. She would have said "You ready?" and Janice would have nodded, following out behind her.

Tonight she had been almost out the door when Janice hurried to her, eyes wide, apprehensive. "Giving me a lift?" Sandy didn't have the heart to tell her no.

They had been silent for most of the ride, which seemed to suit them both. Sandy thought she'd get Janice home without words, without confrontation, without disturbing the hurt and pain that lay buried beneath every breath they took. But five blocks from Janice's apartment Janice spoke and the gates were thrown wide open.

"Are you going tell me what I did?"

"Nothing, that's the problem."

"What are you talking about?"

"When I was going through that thing with Adrian, where were you?"

"I offered to come over and you told me no."

She risked her eyes off the road. "So you just left it at that?"

"You told me you didn't want company."

"Yeah, so you just said oh well, right?" Sandy was getting hot. She'd known this was coming, but still the anger moving through her took her by surprise.

"Well, if you wanted me to come, then why didn't you say so?"

"Because I didn't know myself," Sandy admitted, feeling feeble just saying it. "Didn't know I needed somebody until somebody got there . . . Martha knew, why didn't you?" Which was the part that hurt.

"Because I had my own stuff to contend with," Janice said softly, turning her head for the first time to really look at Sandy. "You don't know what I had just gone through. I put myself through some ridiculous mess, Sandy, crazy-out-of-my-mind mess, and when you called about Adrian and his wife, my heart was too broken up to even think about somebody else."

The word *excuse* filtered into Sandy's brain. Her thought must have reached her face, because Janice went on the defensive.

"You don't believe me? You think I'm lying? I drove all the way to damn Jersey for some man to call my ass crazy because I loved him. I went all the way to Jersey for Greg to call the cops on me and have a damn police escort me to the bridge."

Janice shook her head. "Don't know how I made it home . . . I called you but you were on your way out. Next thing I know you calling me all sad and tore up but I was so depressed about Greg I couldn't even think about helping somebody. And I know that was wrong, and I'm sorry. But there was nothing else I could do."

Sandy blinked, her eyes dampening. "But you called

Martha, right? You sorry? Well, Janice, I'm sorry too. I'm sorry every damn time I need you, you off chasing some man. I'm sorry that you couldn't put your tired little woes aside and come because I needed someone and you supposed to be my best friend."

"You and Martha, is that it now?"

The question was not expected, but Sandy had her answer ready. "Martha was there for me. Where the hell were you?"

She slowed her car in front of Janice's building. *How long have we been staring this day in the face, trying to stave it off, fix things?*

Janice fiddled with the lock, swung the door open. She stepped out of the car and bent her head so that she and Sandy were eye to eye. "You know what, I thought we were better than this . . . Guess not." She closed the car door and Sandy pulled away from the curb, refusing to look back.

TWELVE

Sunday morning came too soon.

One minute Sandy was closing her eyes, falling into a fitful sleep, and the next the sun was coming up through her bedroom window, presenting the first day of her life without Janice. Even as she lay there trying to determine how the pieces fitted together, a cornucopia of what had been filled her heart.

There before her were the endless trips to Jamaica Avenue she and Janice had taken as teenagers, hunting out the best bargains for silver bangles and trying on the funkiest pairs of Faded Glory jeans they could find.

There had been that chilly September morning in 1979 when they stood cold, hungry, and sleepy at the ticket window of Madison Square Garden, determined to get front row center seats for the Earth Wind and Fire concert. A month later they lost their minds when Philip Bailey fixed his eye on them and belted out "Reasons."

At fifteen, when Sandy had gotten her first boyfriend, Janice had been the first person she called. Three years later, when he called it quits, Janice helped to put her world back together.

That's when she was a real friend. Because no matter how Sandy tried to twist it or turn it, it always backed up to the same fact—*she wasn't there when I really needed her*—so Sandy had let her go.

The other part of her troubles wasn't so simple.

Adrian. Not a day went by that she didn't think about him. Not a day passed when she was not aching. Sandy wasn't going to get desperate about it, but her heart was still very tender.

Get on with my life. That's what he told me. And I won't

trespass where I'm not wanted. Still, what he had advised was a hard thing to do, and moments came when she didn't think she could handle it, when she didn't want to handle it. Moments came when she wanted to pick up the phone and call him just to hear his voice, ring his doorbell just to see his face.

Check on him, make sure he was okay, confirm that he could live without her, that she had stopped mattering to him at all. Moments coming where she thought about Janice and her man dramas and, despite it all, understood.

The truth will set you free.

Adrian had held on to it for years, had hoarded it like a deep dark secret, but now as he sat before his sister he unburdened himself, glad to relieve at least part of the load from his shoulders.

"You got to tell dem, Adrian. You got to tell Mommy and Pop da trut."

"What, nuh? What you wa'n' me to tell dem? Gen was de one 'oo 'ad de affair, she da one dat bring dis ting on her so? You wa'n me to say dat?" He leaned back against the kitchen chair, shook his head. "Me not gonna do dat. Why should me, eh? I'm dare son, no?" He thumped his chest hard. "Me dey suppose to love, nuh? Me dey suppose to believe. An' in if I say da marriage was ova, dey suppose to accept dat, dey suppose to trus' me."

The day Gennifer Ellis had become Mrs. Adrian Burton, there was no doubt in Adrian's mind it would be forever. But their marriage did not turn out to be the heaven they sought. There had been troubles early on, and what had started out as two hearts beating as one soon became two individuals unable to really connect.

Still, her confession two years into their marriage had taken him for a loop. They had problems, yes, but he never thought Gennifer would step out of their marriage into the arms of another man.

It had been a wake-up call for both of them. Had made

them do what they had both resisted during the first year of their marriage—take a long hard look at who they had become to each other and who they wanted to be. Within the soul-searching they realized that they did in fact love each other and decided to start anew.

They drew closer, made plans, talked about starting a family, buying a real home. They met with a financial planner to help carve out a secure future. Decided to get additional life insurance to help support their retirement. There had been no fear, no reservations on the day the insurance rep came and drew blood.

Standard practice in the industry, Adrian and Gennifer were both certain that they would get clean bills of health. But when Gennifer's test came back with traces of the HIV virus, suddenly what Adrian thought was forgivable wasn't.

Anger turned to sorrow, and sorrow turned to fear. When Gennifer began pushing him away, it wasn't hard to resist. Trepidation had him, and it was easier to run away than deal with the reality that his wife had cheated and gotten a death sentence as a result. Adrian left.

Months passed, and he learned to think and act like a single man again. By the time he met Sandy, it was who he was. He did not consider himself married, did not consider that somewhere out there he had a wife. The marriage was committed to paper only, and whatever hopes and dreams he and Gen had shared no longer existed. But Adrian's family didn't know this, only that he had left his wife and had declared the marriage over.

Those many years back he had vowed to tell no one about Gennifer's disease. He felt it was a private matter. But with Gennifer's passing, the burden had become too hard to bear. So he told Rachel, the only family member he felt close enough to share it with.

Rachel reached out and touched her brother's face, her eyes soft with compassion. "Dey do luv you, dey do trus' you, but dem don't know, see? All dem know you left Gen and she die. Dey don't really know 'ow she die, only dat she did. In dare eyes you da bad one, and it not so."

Adrian picked up his fork, brought his plate towards him. Pushed around peas and rice.

"What about Sandee? You cawl her yet?"

He lifted food to his mouth. Rachel sucked her teeth. "Lawd, boy! You want to go on dis unhappy, nuh? You wanin' to live your life dis misrable? Why you not call her?"

Adrian looked up from his plate. His sister stared back. They went on staring until he blinked and looked away. He pushed back his chair and stood, anger making his whole body pulse. "Everybody tink dey know what's best for me. Everybody tink dey know what I'm feelin', how I should be acting. Nobody ask me, nobody say Adrian, how you feeling. How you being. What you wa'n ta do."

Rachel looked up at her brother. " 'Cause what you tink ya should do, you too scared to do it. What cha need to do, you too frighten to do it. All I see ya doing is hidin' from da world. Well, ya know what? It ain't gowen no-where. Gonna be right dere before ya every time ya look."

She sighed. Stood, took him by the shoulders. "I love you, Adrian. Wouldn't tell ya wrong. Sandee? She love you too. She made you real happy, seen it wit me own eyes. All I'm saying is, why you wa'n to keep dat happiness away?" Slowly she pulled him near, holding him in a warm embrace. Adrian found himself hugging her back.

It was the first time he allowed himself to feel since Gennifer died. It was the first time he released the hold on his sorrow and let it flow. It was the first embrace he'd opened his soul up to, setting the pain free, restraint falling away like a long sigh to his feet.

Rachel held her brother, urged him on. "Yeah, you go'n and cry. You let it out. Go'n be all right, see? Go'n be all right."

A good release, a deep release, when there were no more tears, when the pain had been wrung from him, Adrian released her, unburdened for the first time in weeks.

"Now," Rachel said, "ya gonna sit right down here and eat dis food I made for ya and den ya gonna call Sandee. Den we gonna leave here and march home and ya gonna sit down and tell Mommy and Pop da truth."

He shook his head. "I can't."

Golden eyes blazed at him. "Yeah, you can."

"Sandy?"

She did not expect his call, but she had needed it, and now that it came, sweet relief filled her. She swallowed. "Hey."

"I never wanted to hurt you, never my intention. Just that . . . I didn't handle it very well, and I'm sorry."

The first tear spilled from her eye, her emotions rolling. "It was bad enough when you called me from the hospital talking about your wife was dying. Then you pushed me away. Without asking me how I felt or anything, you just pushed me to the curb."

"Just rough for me."

"Rough for you? Imagine how I felt. Imagine what I went through. I waiting around for you to come and explain it, for you to come and apologize, and when you do finally show up you tell me to forget about you and just go on with my life?"

"Because I thought it was best."

"Best how?"

"I was wrong, feeling guilty. Felt like I was responsible."

"For?"

"For everything. And I just couldn't deal with any of it. You, Gen, my family, nothing. I was wrong, can see that now, and I just want to apologize for it." Rachel made hand signals at him. He shrugged. She mouthed words his way. Adrian understood, swallowed. "Can I see you?"

It took a while for her to answer. She could not stand another slow entry/fast exit; knew her heart would not be able to take another changing of his mind. "Are you really ready to do that?"

"Be with you, you mean?"

"Yes."

"I'm ready, Sandy, if you are."

Am I ready? She remembered the first good time they had had together, the last good time, and all the times in between. She remembered how he made her feel, her world spinning more perfectly. Could not deny herself another chance. Another chance to get it right, get it strong, get the love flowing again.

"You there?"

She had never been gone, *not even when I left you, you left me. I was always here waiting.* "Yeah. I'm still here."

"Do you?"

Yes, she did.

It could be so much better now, the secrets out in the open, no more puzzles to figure out. They were free from this point on, and Sandy wanted all that that freedom held. "Yes, Adrian, I ready."

His relieved laughter filled her ear. He paused, no doubt collecting his thoughts, optimism and hope in his voice. "I got to make a stop. Don't know how long I'm gonna be, but I'll call when I'm on my way. Is that all right?"

"That's fine."

"Sandy?"

"Yeah?"

"I do love you."

"I love you too."

They stood in her open doorway, on the threshold to something more. They stood there holding onto one another as the past few weeks faded like a bad dream.

They held each other for dear life, held each other in need of all they had ever given and received. Here was the love they had sought, temporarily lost, but so gratefully had found again.

"I missed you," Adrian murmured. "God but I missed you."

"Missed you too."

"I'm so sorry about everything."

She nodded. "I know."

He pulled back, looked at her a long time. "You understand now, don't you?"

"Your family, you mean?"

"Yeah."

"Saw me as a home wrecker." She moved past it. "Behind us now."

He released her, a plastic bag in his hand. "Rachel sent you something."

"I like her."

"She likes you too." They headed for the kitchen.

She took the bag. "What she make?"

"Some peas and rice, plantain, jerked chicken." He stood there watching her inspect his sister's cooking, aware of what had not been discussed. "Tomorrow," he said softly.

Sandy was confused. "Tomorrow what?"

"Go for my test."

"You are gonna be fine."

"How can you be sure?"

She looked at him deeply. "Because I love you too much for you not to be."

Words he had never spoken out loud found him. "I'm scared, Sandy."

She nodded. "I know you are, and so am I, but it's okay." She swallowed, pressed on. "Because I know God would not do this to us."

He wanted to believe her, needed to believe her, but the prospect was too real, too in his face. "Don't have your faith."

"You're okay. I know you are."

"But suppose I'm not," he insisted, needing her to consider the what-if, needing her to go into it with her eyes wide open. "As much as I want you in my life, I couldn't hold you to that."

"I love you and I'm not going anywhere. Period. The end."

"You love me that much?"

"Yes, Adrian, I really do," her voice betraying her own amazement.

Sandy helped herself to a second glass of wine, paced her living room floor. She rubbed her arms even though the apartment was warm, eyed the clock, and stared at the phone. Her stomach was in knots, and not even wine could undo the tangle. It had been a long three days.

She fell to her knees, wine spilling from the glass. She scuttled over to the edge of the sofa and clasped her hands together. Closing her eyes, bending her head, she prayed. "Dear Lord"—her chest heaved with unspent tears—"I know it's not up to me, it's not up to Adrian, but I'm asking you—" The phone shrilled. She lunged for it. Her heart was thumping so loud she was sure the caller heard it.

"Hello?"

"Doctor just called."

Sandy inhaled sharply, her heart thundering like a tom-tom.

"Negative."

She screamed, dropped the phone. Jumped up and down, her eyes raised to heaven. Whispered *Thank you,* whooped, danced, heard Adrian's voice far away, and raced to the phone.

"Oh, thank God, Adrian, thank God."

"Oh, yeah." He laughed and it was good to hear his joy. "We got to celebrate. You dressed?"

"Not *dressed* dressed."

"Well, put on your finest clothes. We're going to dinner, and then we're going dancing all night till our feet ache, and then we're going to go park somewhere and watch the sun rise. I'm not wasting another day. You hear me? Not another day am I going to waste."

"How was everything, sir?" the maître d' asked.

Adrian nodded. "Everything was perfect, thank you." He looked at Sandy, the black velvet dress and faux pearls giving her a rich look. "You want anything else?"

She shook her head.

"I'll have the check now," Adrian told the maître d'.

She wiped her mouth with the napkin, took another sip of her champagne. *Pinch me,* she thought, her eyes steady on the gorgeous room.

The Rainbow Room on top of Rockefeller Center was as elegant as you could get in Manhattan. She couldn't believe it when Adrian told her that's where they were headed.

"Going to the ladies' room." The bottom of her short dress popped to life as she stood; crinoline and satin whispered against each other as she made her way across the floor. *French maid effect*, the saleswoman at Saks had told her. Sheer black stockings and spiky heels completed the effect.

The outfit had cost her a fortune, and it had hung in her closet so long she was tempted to take it back and pay a bill. Tonight she was glad she hadn't.

She tipped the bathroom attendant five dollars because she felt anything less would be insulting. She found her perfume—*Red*—on the complimentary tray and gave herself a quick squirt.

She checked her hair and reapplied her lipstick and then made her way back to the table. Didn't notice the small gray jewelry box until she had taken her seat.

"Go ahead, open it," Adrian said.

She pulled back the spring lid. The diamond catching the candlelight, taking her breath.

"Will you marry me?"

It was a good thing she hadn't put on mascara.

THIRTEEN

The heavy oak door shuddered open, and her mother's face appeared like a full moon in the night sky. The smell of cinnamon and baked apples drifted past her, and Sandy knew her mother had made her famous apple pie.

She had purposely kept her family in the dark about Adrian, didn't really know how they would react. Bringing Brian home to dinner had left a bad taste in her mouth, and she didn't want her parents having another crack at someone she liked and they didn't. But with Adrian asking for her hand in marriage, it was time to face the music.

Now as she ushered Adrian up the stairs, she was amused to see the look on both her mother's and Adrian's faces. She hadn't warned Adrian, hadn't told him about her mother made of light and air.

You made of the earth and the sun, Grandma Tee had told her. *Your momma, well, she's light and air.* Jeanne Hutchinson was so light-skinned, so ivory, it was hard to see any brown in her color at all.

"Nice to meet you, Adrian," Mrs. Hutchinson said.

"Nice to meet you, Mrs. Hutchinson," Adrian replied.

Sandy watched her mother's face, knew her thoughts, the tiny joys she was feeling. *Yes, Mommy, he's caramel, got those honey eyes, the good stuff like you.*

Sandy looked beyond her mother, searching out her father. She saw him standing in the foyer and made her way. There was the face she had looked to a thousand times. There was the understanding and the knowing. Sandy nearly ran to him, her arms outstretched, eager for his embrace.

"Hi, Daddy," she murmured, feeling a sweet surrender in the arms of the first man she had ever really loved.

He pulled back from her, his arm going easily around her waist. "I assume this is Adrian?" he asked, trying hard to hold back his smile. But her father had never looked at any boy or man she had brought home so. And suddenly things clicked into place.

From a young age Sandy could remember her father being indifferent to any brown-skinned boy she dared to bring home and falling all over himself for the damn near white ones. After a while, it was all she came to want for herself.

But what does that say about you, Daddy? she found herself wondering as she motioned for Adrian to come over. *What does it say that the very person you are is the very type of man you never wanted for me?*

It was a question Sandy knew she'd never ask as her father took Adrian's hand and shook it wholeheartedly. "So very good to meet you, son."

"Good to meet you too, sir," Adrian said.

"Cliff just called. He's running late, but he's on his way," Sandy's mother told them, her delight still evident. "Well, if you will excuse me, I'm going to check on dinner. Please, make yourself at home."

Adrian started for the sofa but stopped by the wall of pictures. There before him was a time capsule of the school days of both Sandy and her brother.

"This you?" he asked, taking in one of her earliest school photos.

"Yeah."

It was her least favorite, the one where she looked mad at the world. Not many school memories stayed with her, but that particular day, forever mounted behind glass, was one she'd never forget.

She had been eight.

That morning so many years ago Sandy had been excited and delighted, eager for the moment her mother would put the hot comb to her head for the first time ever. That morning, one she had waited for forever, Jeanne Hutchinson would give Sandy her first hot press ever, making her cute, adorable. Special.

Sandy had sat through the hair washing and scalp greasing the night before. She had sat quiet, obedient, barely flinching as her mother combed the tight coils from her wet hair and box-braided three-inch plaits for the morning milestone.

With breathy anticipation Sandy had watched the gas flame wrap itself around the metal-tooth hot comb. Had flinched a bit as her mother tested its hotness with a damp finger that made the comb sizzle briefly.

She had witnessed the miracle on her mother's hair. Had watched with amazement as Jeanne Hutchinson pulled the hot metal through her own coily crown, leaving the hair long, smooth, and luxurious. Sandy had no doubt the same would be true for her, and after years of anticipation, her hair would hang past her shoulders too.

She would arrive at school, Shirley Temple ringlets about her head, long and shiny as jumbo black licorice. She would fling her hair and make the curls shiver. She would hit Bradley Mormon's hand with bull's-eye accuracy when he attempted to pull one and bask in the adoration of her classmates.

But the reality hadn't even come close.

The heat of the curling iron made her jumpy, and in the process both her ears and her neck got burned. The length, the fullness, the volume Sandy's eight-year-old mind had anticipated never materialized. Yes, her hair was straight, it was shiny, but it wasn't much longer than it had been the day before.

The Shirley Temple curls turned out to be a pitiful imitation that clung to her head and refused to budge an inch past her ears.

These were the memories that were stirred up as Adrian studied the picture. "Bad day?" he quipped.

She looked at his wavy hair, unable to ward off old truths that still maimed. "Cut it, all right?"

"You two are fussing already?" her father teased, a joviality in his voice Sandy could not taste. She stared at him a long time, wondering if he had a clue about the life she'd lived, born to a mother of light and air to whom she could claim no resemblance.

Sandy loaded the last dish into the dishwasher and closed the door. Her brother Cliff leaned against the counter, picking crust from the edge of the last slice of apple pie.

"Must say, sister, you did good. Just knew he was gonna be some stone-cold homeboy from around the way, with a beeper hanging off his ass and a scarf 'round his nappy head."

She laughed, picked up the dish towel, and threw it at him, eyeing him with contempt. "Why his hair gotta be nappy? You're such an asshole," she said, cutting her eyes.

"Ah, you know I'm just playing with you . . . I like him."

"Didn't think I needed your opinion or your permission."

"Hey, you my baby sister, my only sister. I get props."

"Save the street slang for your Hunnies, okay, homie?" she answered, turning the dishwasher to wash.

The pie was too good, and Cliff picked up a fork. Tossing a chunk into his mouth, he eyed his sister with casual interest. "Well, Mom and Dad are relieved . . . They thought you and Martha had something going on."

A twilight moment, her mouth fell open. "What?"

His brow raised. "Seriously. They told me they hoped you wasn't going 'the wrong way,' quote unquote."

Her hand moved to her hip. "Me and Martha? Why would they think that?"

"Well 'cause y'all been real tight lately. You ain't brought nobody around in a long time, and Martha ain't never had no man, far's I remember."

Her blood boiled. "That ain't true. That ain't even true. She was engaged."

Cliff waggled his fork at her. "Yeah, what, seven years ago?"

"Oh, come on, Cliff, you know me better than that."

He nodded. "Yeah, but Mom and Dad don't. Well, they can stop worrying now." He tossed the fork into the sparkling clean sink Sandy had just wiped dry and squeezed her shoulder. "You marrying old Redbone in there and y'all gonna give them a whole bunch of yellow babies."

"Not funny, Cliff," she said, staring him down and hating him. "That's not funny at all."

"Yeah right, it's not funny 'cause you know it's true. What did Daddy use to say? Don't be bringing no black-ass pickaninnies in here?"

Sandy walked out of the room.

Black-ass pickaninnies . . . then what was I, Dad? What was I if I wasn't that? Was I special 'cause I was your daughter?

"Hey, you all right?" Adrian asked, taking his eyes off the road for a second.

She wiped her cheek. "Yeah, I'm all right."

"What are you crying about, then?"

"Not crying." But even as she said that, fresh tears fell.

"Want me to pull over?" he asked.

"No. I want you to keep on driving."

"Where we going, your place, or mine?"

She shook her head. "Don't matter."

Adrian didn't press her about her tears, and she was grateful. How could she even begin to explain what it felt like, being a little black girl born to a mother of light and air?

Martha, Britney, and Sandy had come together to celebrate Sandy's engagement, Janice nowhere in sight. Sandy had prepared herself for this first encounter, had been mentally hyped, ready for the full dismissal of her ex-best friend, but when she arrived and saw Janice was a no-show, she was surprised to discover it hurt a little.

Britney reached under her side table and withdrew a small gift-wrapped box. "This is just a little sumpin' sumpin' we got for you."

"What is it?" Sandy asked, shaking the box.

"Open it," Britney insisted, her smile wide.

Sandy looked at Martha but Martha discounted herself. "Don't ask me. Britney bought it."

She tore into the wrapping and lifted the lid off the box. Inside was a pair of handcuffs, complete with duplicate keys. Her jaws opened, her eyes fixing Britney with surprise. "What kind of freaky thing is this, Britney?"

"Don't knock them till you try them. Besides, you know how some men like to stray once you say 'I do.' These here are in case you need to keep his behind in your bed, not somebody else's."

"I wasn't in on that, Sandy. Brit came up with this gift all by herself," Martha said, lifting the cuffs out the box. She slipped one on her wrist and clicked it in place. "This here is some real freaky shit, Brit." She wriggled her wrist. "But I like it."

Sandy handed Martha the key, no less astonished. "Take that off." Martha gave them back. Sandy considered them one hot minute—*no way*—and put them back in the box.

With everyone staring, Britney had to defend her choice. "Figure I'd give you something to keep things hot," her smile full of secrets.

"We're definitely into hot, but handcuffs? You got the wrong sister."

"Ain't nothing wrong with a little freaky deaky every now and then," Martha insisted.

Sandy laughed, Britney joined in, the sound of hearty cheer filling the room. But as the moment faded, things less joyous filled her mind.

How am I going to say this? She knew she was going to tell it, relay what her brother had revealed in her mother's kitchen, but the implications were none too kind, *even if they ain't so*, and she wasn't sure how Martha would take it.

Just tell it. "Y'all ain't gonna believe this," she began, her eyes avoiding Martha.

"What?" Britney asked.

"Y'all really ain't gonna believe this," she said again, giving herself some breathing room.

"What, Sandy?" Martha asked quickly.

"My parents . . . thought . . . me"—she pointed to herself—"and you"—she pointed to Martha—"had a thing going on."

Britney choked. Martha's face grew dark. "Say what?" she said.

"You heard me. Told stupid ass Cliff that they were worried I was going in the 'wrong direction.' "

"No lie, Sandy?" Britney asked.

"No lie, Brit."

"Why would they think something like that?" Britney wanted to know, her eyes searching Martha's face.

"Some nonsense about how I hadn't brought a man around lately and how Martha, well, you know, ain't really had a steady in a while."

Martha sat up. "Excuse me? What the fuck is that supposed to mean? What the fuck do they know about who I'm with?" Her face was full of disgust and grief. Hurting. "I can't believe they'd think that about me."

Sandy was quick to respond. "Me too." But she could feel things shifting in the room. It was true that Martha hadn't had a steady, not since her fiancé had dumped her. And she and Martha *had* become tight lately.

Martha's eyes were glassy. "That really hurts."

"I know, Martha, but we know it ain't true."

"But they thought that? I can't believe they thought that."

Britney waved her hand. "Well, don't matter now. Sandy's getting married and that's the end of that."

"What's that supposed to mean?" Martha asked quickly.

Britney looked perplexed. "Nothing. What you think I'm trying to say . . ." She trailed off. "Come on, Martha, you know me better."

"Yeah, well."

Sandy interjected, "Look, I'm not paying it no mind, so don't none of y'all pay it any either. Just a bunch of nonsense. Besides, we got to start planning this wedding." She smiled, shifting the focus to something better. "I set the date."

"You have?" Britney said, delighted.

Sandy nodded. "September twenty-one, first day of fall."

"This year?"

"No, next. Gives us a whole year to plan."

"Why wait so long? You know people change their minds," Martha told her.

"If a man can't wait a year to marry me, then I don't need to be married."

"You decide who's going to be the maid of honor?" Britney asked.

"Yeah." She took a deep breath, her eyes lingering on Martha's. "I've decided it's gonna be Martha."

Martha's eyes fluttered in surprise, her hand landing on her heart, her mouth hanging open. "Me?" she said, surprised.

"How could it be anybody else but you? How could it be?" Sandy asked her softly.

"I thought—"

"What, Janice?" She fluffed off the suggestion, but her throat grew tight. "Is she even here? Not like she didn't know. You did call her, didn't you?" Martha nodded. "I don't have time for nonsense, not now, not when the most important day of my life is coming up. No, girl, you the one."

She was waiting for Martha to say something, but Martha seemed to be paralyzed. She took her hesitancy as reluctance. "You don't have to be, if you don't want, Martha."

Martha looked up at her, grateful. "Ain't nothing I would want more in the world."

"Am I in it?" Britney wanted to know.

"Of course you are. How could I possibly get married without my girls right there by my side?"

A second chance, an opportunity to make things right again, make things work—that's what it was supposed to have been about. And though Greg's kiss had faded from her lips minutes ago and he was in the process of leaving, Janice was still optimistic. Still hopeful.

She had been all ready to go to Britney's. She had thought long and hard after Martha called her about Sandy's engagement and the get-together they were planning, and even though she didn't say it, Janice was ready to make amends. She had even bought a gift. But Greg had called just as she was heading out the door.

"Can I come by?"

If he hadn't asked as if he had never called the cops on her, as if there wasn't some other woman in his life, maybe Janice would have told him no. But he hadn't. *He asked like he had to see me, like I was something good.*

She had hopes and dreams that Greg would one day realize what she had always known—that he loved her, cared about her. *That final scene at his door told me so. If he didn't care, he would have had me arrested.*

Love could hurt, and Greg had hurt her badly. But love could also heal, and she wanted that healing. Wanted to do away with the nightmare, have them truly come together, be as one.

So she did the unthinkable. She canceled her plans to surprise and make up with her best friend in favor of a visit from Greg. She put on the nightgown Greg liked and waited for him to show up. Surprisingly he arrived, as promised, at nine-thirty.

He didn't talk about the unkind things he'd said, the cops he had summoned, just sort of snapped her up and took her to her bed.

Now, the twenty-minute go-round fading fast, she watched him get dressed, waiting for him to speak the magic words that would set their life back in motion.

He caught her staring, her expression open and honest. "Just wondering," she managed, caught up.

"Wondering what?"

"When we're gonna hook up again?"

"Hook up?" He seemed genuinely surprised.

"Yeah."

He shook his head. "Nah, it ain't like that."

Janice stumbled. "But I thought—"

"Them days are over." He went back to his dressing. Slipped on one shoe, then the other. Stood, took her in. Something in him changed, transformed; a different Greg but one she'd seen before. A cruelty was coming into him and it would come her way, crushing, devastating. "Ain't learned nothing, have you?"

"Learned how?"

He shook his head again, a private thought moving through him. "Despite all that drama, your ass almost getting arrested, you still don't get it." He slipped his wallet into his back pocket. "Any other woman would have cursed me out for even thinking about trying to get back into their bed." He chuckled, and it was a demeaning sound. "But not you."

Janice swallowed, her throat gone dry. "Because I thought you wanted me."

"Yeah, I wanted you. And I got you, don't I? Tell you to jump and I bet you'll ask me how high." He looked at her, as if for the first time. "Don't you know a man has only one use for a woman like you?"

She wanted to answer, wanted to defend herself, but her mouth would not work. Her mind was too busy sorting out other things—how he was acting, the words he was speaking, all of it being stuffed into a bottom line.

"Know what we call women like you?"

She wasn't certain but had some idea. "Not who I am," she defended.

"Oh, you not? Could have fooled me. One thing I don't have time for is a stupid bitch. And damn, baby, you as stupid as they come."

His words landed with a mighty blow, knocking so much out of her. It was like a fist to her face, the impact taking her off her feet. Janice sat there, breathing hard, struggling to recover as Greg delivered his final words.

"Well, it's been real." And with that he walked out of her bedroom and out her front door.

Long after he had left, long after the silence had encompassed her, Janice felt as if she were in some twilight zone, everything surreal and overwhelming.

An easy lay, that was what she had become. Nothing more, nothing less. Her hopes, her dreams, the very notion of who she was fitting into three appalling words.

Janice sat there, Greg's words and the cruelty with which they had been spoken hanging in the air like muslin, tough and resilient. He had stripped her to the core—*Know what we call a woman like you?*—she a willing participant, and now she wasn't sure how to reclaim herself.

She began to tremble, realized she was naked. Grabbed her comforter, pulled it around her tight. But she could not find the warmth, could not find the shelter, a means to get past the moment.

He never loved me—the truth coming, sticking to her like burrs. She had pursued Greg, turning her life upside down for the sake of him, and had lost herself in the process.

All she wanted was to be loved. *Will anybody ever love me?* She looked at the clock. A little before ten. A slice of hope wiggled inside of her, moved towards the surface.

Maybe they were still there. Maybe they were waiting

for her. If she hurried she might be able to be with them, her friends, the ones who really loved her.

Britney answered the door, pajamas on and a scarf around her head. "Janice?"

Janice eyed the dark, quiet apartment, and her heart sank. "They're gone?"

Britney frowned, puzzled. "Yeah, a good forty-five minutes ago. Where were you?"

Sometimes reality becomes so pressing, the truth so evident, you cannot keep it to yourself. Janice gazed into Britney's eyes, feeling the weight of the world on her shoulders, and spoke what was in her heart. "Where was I? Getting nothing and giving away a whole lot of something."

Britney chuckled, took her by the arm. "Come on in, girlfriend. Sound like you need to talk."

Janice hesitated, then entered. "I was coming tonight, earlier I mean. Martha called me about Sandy getting married and how you guys were getting together tonight. After I got off the phone I found myself just sitting there in my apartment all by my lonesome, missing Sandy. Missing all of y'all. I mean I haven't seen any of you guys in weeks."

"Your choice, Janice."

Janice could not disagree. "Yeah, I know . . . but I was so looking forward to tonight. I was going to apologize my ass off, you hear me? I was going to say sorry to everyone for every wrong thing I ever done." Janice went into her bag. "Even bought Sandy a gift. I was nearly out the door and what happens?"

"Some man calls?"

"Yeah, exactly. Stupid ass Greg." Janice shook her head. "I should have known what it was about. Should have known it wasn't about me, or who I am, or anything. But I'm thinking yeah, he still loves me, wants me . . . trying to prove something that just wasn't so. Put on the sexy nightgown and everything. Twenty-three minutes he is in and out my front door, calling me the B word." Anger coursed through her, but her eyes were dry. "That Negro was between my thighs for fifteen minutes just taking his and he calls me a stupid bitch?"

Britney shook her head. "He was talking about himself. You shouldn't pay that any mind."

"But that's the thing. He *was* talking about me. I'm sitting there, butt naked, unable to defend myself. Couldn't call him a liar or nothing because it was true."

Britney looked at her, said nothing. Allowed her to talk. "I'm getting real tired of it, y'know? Tired of how I'm living. Tired of falling for bad men. Just tired."

"Least you know that. There are a lot of women out there who don't have a clue, and couldn't buy one if you gave them a dollar."

Janice laughed. "Girl, you are too funny."

Britney smiled smugly. "Yeah, when I want to be." She looked around her. "Being with Maurice has changed a lot of things for me, how I see myself, other people. Never thought I was smart, never thought I was sexy." She looked off, lost in it all. "I never thought nobody would ever want me, but he did. Like he gave me back a piece of myself. I stopped worrying about how big I was, stopped worrying if other people liked me or not. Just became free."

Janice was right there with her. "I've been noticing . . . like that time me and Sandy went out and you jump up grandstanding. You never acted like that. I was like, damn, where that come from? You cut your hair, got a perm. You're looking real good these days. Yeah, I'd say he freed you up."

"Wouldn't trade him for the world."

Janice's tone was careful. "Did anybody mention me tonight?"

"Well, yeah. Sandy asked Martha to be her maid of honor and Martha was surprised because she figured it would be you, and Sandy was like, 'Is she even here?' " Britney looked at her carefully. "People have to take responsibility for their own troubles."

"I guess I really blew it this time."

"Maid of honor, oh, yeah . . . Friend? Now that something maybe you can fix."

"How?"

"You've got that gift there. Why not take it on over to her house? Maybe she'll let you in, maybe she won't. But you've got to try. She's getting married next year, and she said specifically, and I quote, 'How could I possibly get married without my girls right by my side?' End quote."

Janice's eyes grew bright. "She said that?"

"Sure did."

She put the gift back into her bag. Stood. "Think she home now?"

"Said she was going to Adrian's."

"His wife died of AIDS, y'know," Janice said, contempt in her voice.

Britney nodded. "Yeah, Martha told me."

"And you cool with that?"

"That's Sandy's choice. If she's cool, I'm cool." Britney looked at Janice carefully. "And if you planning on getting back on her good side, you better be cool too."

FOURTEEN

Swlap . . . swlap. The sound of laminated cardboard pages hitting each other was the only sound inside the apartment. Martha sat flipping through the photo album, the yellowed strips of sticky glue telling its age.

Images of her younger self, short Afro hair, large gold hoop earrings, something between a smile and a dare, *my focused expression,* looked back at her, possessing a wisdom so long gone Martha had forgotten she even owned it.

Yeah, you was gonna save the world, she thought with a despondent smile. *You'd never have taken a job in the district attorney's office. No, you'd be operating out of a dinky, dilapidated storefront, living and breathing pro bono to an obsession. You were going to flip the United States judicial system on its behind, weren't you? Go boldly where no other twenty-something black female attorney had ever gone before.*

What happened to you?

The photo album, worn and forgotten, tucked away and out of sight for so long, gave up the answer. When Leon left, everything got changed.

Marry me, Martha. She heard the words, took in Leon's bearded face, and remembered. *Grew that beard to save money on razors.* Financially strapped but emotionally rich, Martha and Leon had been students in law school at the time.

The picture, taken outside the civil court on Chambers Street, had caught them taking a break from the mandatory courtroom observations. A stranger had snapped the picture with the pocket Instamatic Martha used to always carry. *Never left home without it, did I? Like I needed proof of who I was.*

They had known each other for four years by then. One year as undergrads and three years being side by side, in the trenches, indifferent professors and endless hours in the law library, until their eyes burned, their brains simmered, and their minds grew numb with names, dates, and decisions.

They were going to be attorneys, and their eyes had been on the future. Maybe that was why Leon asked her that last year of school. Maybe he figured two legal eagles were better than one.

They had talked about their foreseen greatness, had had midnight discussions about setting up a firm and what type of law they would practice. "Defend the undefendable" had been their motto. Together they were going to take on the world.

Martha had loved Leon for his passion and his determination. She had loved him for his intelligence, his savvy, the way he could turn a phrase and make it sing. She had loved him because he knew how to tame her, knew how to bring a calmness to her fierceness, a tenderness to her determination. And when moments came that she doubted her own abilities, Leon had been there telling her she could do whatever needed to be done, that he had faith in her.

Despite their closeness, the solidity of their relationship, his proposal had taken her by surprise. Martha didn't think he wanted to settle down yet. Had figured graduating and passing the bar had been his main concern. That everything else would come after.

But he asked me, didn't he?

The years had robbed Martha of so many things, like exactness and joy. She could no longer pinpoint what she did when Leon told her he had changed his mind, only the consequence of his decision. Six thousand two hundred and seventy-nine dollars, that was how much it cost Martha not be married. Limousine companies and catering halls didn't care that Martha hadn't made it to the altar. Payment due was payment due.

A lot of things happened on the day Leon said he didn't have enough love for her. Martha lost her fiancé, her future husband, a new last name. Martha lost her Rock of Gibraltar, the only one who had truly loved her, and the brightness of the world.

For years Martha had toted it around, forcing it deep inside. For years the old photo album had rested on the top shelf of her closet. *Couldn't even bring myself to look at it.*

Now as she came upon the final page, the shot of them taken their last Christmas together. *God, I was happy then,* Martha closed the book and moved towards the hall. She opened the closet and put the photo book back on the shelf. Closing the door with a finality that resounded through her heart, she knew the time had come. Embrace the loss, then let it go.

Jules was the brother from another planet. He was smart, dread-headed, and for the past three years hard at work trying to bring a sense of civility to the criminal court system in the County of Kings, State of New York.

Jules and Martha had known each other for all the years Jules had been an ADA, and Martha often told him he was working on the wrong side of the fence.

"Your heart's not in prosecution, Jules. You need to go on over to Federal Defenders and help the poor and downtrodden," she'd tell him, to which Jules would give that smile, shake his head, and study the woman who seemed to know him all too well.

There had been innuendos, fast brisk tangos, Martha and Jules sidestepping and gliding around each other. Neither of them seemed willing to take their office association a step further.

Jules was the laid-back, jazz-listening, black-studies-reading, yoga-practicing, meditating black man whose lifestyle seemed the exact opposite of Martha's. He didn't do clubs, didn't drink alcohol, and dug experimental theater.

He liked Farrakhan, Ellis, and Miles. Martha was more in tune with Jesse, Terry, and Janet—Jackson, McMillan, and Jackson, respectively.

Martha's last "friend," if two weeks counted at all, had been a fast-talking liability lawyer named Henry. The romance lasted all of one date, three trips to his day bed, and a real nasty phone call that ended with Martha calling him names that you couldn't say on TV.

That affair had been so brief that it came and went without Martha mentioning a thing to her friends. She knew she had been running scared since Leon dumped her. Knew that the few entanglements she had had in the last seven years were wrong from the start; the men she dated had nothing more on their agenda than bedding the fierce, dominating Martha. A notch on their belt, regret and shame on hers.

Sex was supposed to be the passion that sustained itself into the next hour, the next minute, the seconds after separation. Like fertilizer it was supposed to help the love grow. Yet too many times she found herself, the last passionate kiss fading and no hint of it remaining as she said good-bye, closing an apartment door behind her.

Men were from Mars, she knew that. She also knew that at thirty-three she wasn't getting any younger, and she didn't want to end up one of those career women who at forty looked around and convinced themselves it was okay not to be married, okay not to have children, that they could go on and have their career and not much else and be happy.

It was for that reason that Martha came to work with Jules on her mind. *Got to start somewhere,* she figured as she rapped on his office door, waiting for him to ask her in.

Youngsters whirled around the cul-de-sac, the metal of their rollerskates and the wood of their hockey sticks scraping the pavement like a dull axe. A couple hugged at the railing as they took in the skyscrapers of Manhattan across the water. Brooklyn Heights, sandwiched between the edge of Brooklyn and the isle of Manhattan, offered its own bit of suburban life.

Hugging the shores of the East River and facing a majestic slice of Manhattan skyline, the Brooklyn street was as familiar as Martha's childhood backyard. She had seen it a dozen times in dozens of movies. Could not believe this was where Jules lived.

As Martha followed Jules up the brownstone steps, the bag of Nature's Own fruit drinks clinked gently. She paused, looking around her, knowing she'd never see this block the same way again.

Sex was going to change things.

Martha knew that and was willing to take the chance. Changes had come already, with Martha coming to Jules's place instead of him coming to hers as she had suggested. That nice meal she thought they could have was no longer possible because Jules was watching his protein intake and couldn't eat meat but knew a great vegetarian restaurant that she would love just as much.

This evening Martha was going to have her first brown rice with vegetables. She couldn't begin to imagine what it would taste like, her mouth still longing for barbecued ribs, fried rice, and egg roll from the Chinese restaurant on Montague Street.

Jules's second-floor apartment was a dim, claustrophobic affair with dying cactus cluttering the windowsill, bare wood floors in need of cleaning, and dust bunnies taking refuge in the corner. The pull-out couch was still open, showing off dingy twisted sheets and pillowcases that were greasy in the middle.

Jules must have burned incense all the time, because the air was heavy with it. The whole apartment smelled as if a fresh breeze hadn't entered it in a long time. It was so tiny Martha felt she could spit from one end to the other without effort. The nicest thing in the whole place was the bay window, even if its beauty was hidden beneath a layer of dirt.

Martha looked at the dingy sheets, the beat-up dirty pillowcases, and thought about eating something called brown rice with vegetables.

"Be up in a minute," Jules called from somewhere in the back.

Martha got all sorts of feelings then. Her mind became a computer as a hundred bits of information began to flow. In the three years she had known Jules she had never taken the idea of being with him beyond the thought process. *Because we are different,* came the thought. *And just because I've been accused of being a lesbian and I haven't been in a real relationship in seven years is no reason to forfeit what I am about, what I want, or what I deserve to get . . . I deserve at least clean sheets and food I want to eat.*

Martha turned and walked down the short hall, finding the kitchen. Jules stood dishing out the vegetables and rice into matching bowls. His dreads, black licorice hiding half his face.

She studied him for a moment before she spoke. "Jules, thanks, but no thanks."

As he looked at her in utter surprise, Martha knew this wasn't about her. It was about getting some.

My bag, she thought, remembering how she had come on to him like a cat in heat because at the time that was how she'd felt. Martha had been *down* with getting down with Jules. Ready to take the workplace into the bedroom. But her mind was clear now, and no way would she go through with it.

Surprise still had him. "You're leaving?"

Martha nodded, tight-lipped. "Yeah, going to take myself home."

"What about the food?" he asked, the thick veins in his wrist and forearms whispering her promise.

"Sorry, but vegetarian stuff ain't me. Being here like this

isn't me either. So I better be going before I get involved in something that I'll regret."

"I could run out and get Chinese," he offered.

Yeah, and I bet you'd sell your momma to get your nut too, came the thought. *Wouldja dance butt naked down Broadway? Sing me a rap song? Recite Terry McMillan? Would you change yourself over into something I need and stay changed? Would you love me and respect me ten seconds after you came?* Martha shook her head. "No, you go ahead and dig in. I'll catch you tomorrow."

With that Martha headed for the front door, anticipating the sound of it closing swiftly behind her and the sweet cool breeze that would herald her getaway.

"Mo?"

Maurice looked up from his copy of *Sports Illustrated.* "Yeah, baby?"

Britney paused, uncertain if she really wanted to go there, then decided to give it a go. "You know your friend Calvin?"

He casted her with suspicious eyes. "Yeah, he my boy. What about him?"

Britney paused again, feeling as if she was messing in somebody else's business. "I was just wondering."

"Wondering what?"

She smiled, took a deep breath, looked away. Let the words flow. "If he was seeing anybody." She looked back at Maurice and blinked.

"Why?" But his question had a little less suspicion than anticipation. *A good sign.*

"Well, because, you know, Martha. She hasn't had anybody in a while, and I know how it can do you."

Maurice smiled, put the magazine aside. "You talking about hooking them up or something?"

"Or something." She was careful with her words, couldn't appear too vested. Maurice hadn't said no, but he hadn't said yes yet. He loved her, but he could get real stubborn if something went against his grain.

She had met Calvin, thought he was a real fine cutie. Had the kind of temperament that Martha liked, smart and compassionate. Only problem was he hauled garbage.

Still, it had been an idea dancing in Britney's head for a while, mostly every time she looked at Maurice. She didn't know how she had lived all those years alone, with no one to love her, but now that she was with a good somebody, it was all she wanted for Martha. And out of all Maurice's friends, Calvin seemed the best candidate.

"Be seeing him tomorrow. Want me to ask him?"

Britney shook her head. "No, not yet. I have to clear it with Martha. She has this thing about dating only professional men. No offense, honey, but hauling garbage isn't one."

Maurice laughed, smitten with her honesty. "Yeah, but some of us make as much money." Which was the absolute truth. Maurice had been picking up the toss-offs of the people of the city of New York for fifteen years. He was five years from retirement, and the raises had been steady. In a few years he'd be able to sit back and not lift another finger if he had no desire to. Garbage collecting was not a pretty job, nor was it easy, but in the final analysis it made the bank account sing.

He rubbed the back of his neck. "Calvin's been hauling longer than I have, and you know how much money I make." That Britney did. The first time she saw his pay stub she couldn't believe it. Being single with no children was eating into his take-home, but that gross column had looked real sweet.

Maurice had been hinting with more frequency that he was ready to change his status. " 'Bout time I settled down,' " he'd confessed. A good man and three years older than Britney, Maurice was fun, he was pleasant, and she loved him. She knew the question wouldn't even get halfway out of his mouth before she'd say "I will."

"Check with Martha and let me know," Maurice said,

picking up his magazine. Britney picked up her book, but
her eyes fell on Maurice. *This is what love really is, isn't
it? Just sharing space and feeling the joy.* She sighed,
found her place on the page. When the time was right she'd
ask Martha if she was interested.

FIFTEEN

Marrying Adrian.

It changed the parameters of her life and brought back old adversaries. Sandy had gone to Adrian's parents' house soon after Adrian had asked for her hand in marriage. Despite knowing the full story of what had happened between Adrian and Gennifer, certain members of his family still held a grudge.

Winston managed to say hello, but Junie said nothing at all, something between hostility and awe dancing in his eyes. Mrs. Burton wore a Madonna smile the whole time as if she knew some great secret, and Mr. Burton downright scared her.

"So, ya tink ya go'wen marry an lib a 'appy 'appy life?" he'd asked, cornering her in the kitchen. He had been so close she could smell the bay rum on his neck. "Well, ya do'went know nutten' ya 'earing me? *Nutten'*," he had said vengefully.

Sandy had reeled back from the intensity of his words and hurried to the living room where Adrian was. She mouthed a few words in his ear, they left soon after, and the visit to the East New York street became a bitter memory.

It had taken time to shuck off her concerns, her worries, convince herself *no monkey is gonna stop this show*. It had taken conviction, deep faith, the utmost belief that her wedding could come off without a hitch, with or without Adrian's family.

They could talk about her, despise her, be rude all they wanted, but there was no way she was going to let them take away what she'd wanted all her life—marrying the man of her dreams.

She had faced greater challenges, suffered other indignities, *gone through that fire, I can handle this*. But as she sat looking up at Adrian and Adrian stared down at her, suddenly she wasn't so sure.

"Is this you or your parents?"

"Don't even go there, Sandy."

Sandy closed the brochure for the Astorian Manor and got up from her dinette table. A year and a half to their wedding and already they were arguing over money.

Sandy never remembered him having such a tight fist. Hadn't he taken her for real seafood and not that Red Lobster mess for their first date? And what about the dinner at the Rainbow Room, not to mention the nice-size stone she was sporting these days?

She didn't understand his reluctance. Their wedding day was the most important statement they would ever make. "All we need is another four thousand dollars. We got sixteen months to come up with the money. That's what?" She reached for her legal pad, ran her fingers down the page of numbers. "Two fifty a month, one twenty-five from each of us."

"We don't need a big wedding, Sandy," Adrian admonished her for the third time that evening, wishing she'd see his point, or at least trust him enough to even consider it. "Look, it's about me and you and making a commitment, that's all. The rest is secondary."

"Easy for you to say, Adrian, you've been married before. You had your big day, but I haven't. It's important to me." Her own words tripped her. *Why am I even saying this out loud? He should know.*

"Nine thousand dollars, Sandy? Do you know what we can do with nine thousand dollars?"

The indignation she had been trying to hold back arrived. "I already cut the guest list from two twenty-five to one fifty. My folks are giving us five thousand dollars. The least we can do is come up with the other four." She took a breath. "A lousy one hundred and twenty-five dollars a month from both of us. That's like thirty-two dollars a week, not a lot of money, Adrian."

Adrian sighed. "You just don't get it, do you?" The look on her face told him that she didn't and had no intention of doing so.

"It's not about money, Sandy."

"It must be."

"I have money." He looked away from her. "Look. When I asked you to marry me, it was with the idea we'd have a simple little ceremony somewhere and a small reception. All this talk about stretch limos and steak and lobster at the Astorian Manor and a honeymoon in Aruba, that's not what I had in mind."

But that's exactly what I did. That fire was dancing along her spine again. It burnt, but it also revitalized, filling her with might. "Oh, so it doesn't matter what I want."

"Not what I'm saying. I've already gone the route you want to take, and I'm telling you, Sandy, you end up regretting all that money you spent. Nine thousand dollars could be a down payment on a house, a new car for you. Why blow it on a day that lasts all of six hours, and after it's all over all you got is some pictures and a video?

"You talking about this big-ass wedding. My father already told me he's not coming, which means some other relatives aren't either. We don't need to make it a big affair." Adrian's voice grew soft, pained. "A small thing . . . something small and simple, and then we can just get on with our lives."

"Your folks don't want to be there, so be it, Adrian. This is about me and you, not *them.* You don't want to give a dime towards this, then fine. I will get a second job at fucking McDonald's if I have to."

Her tears came. She knew they would and let them fall as her fingers jabbed her own chest as she left her chair. "*My* day, Adrian. Not your momma's or your daddy's, but *mine*. Now, if you don't want to do this, just say so."

Sandy stood there waiting, arms folded, tears running,

waiting for him to understand, give in. She refused to take another step, utter a single word until he did.

Adrian stared at her teary face, his heart breaking, *what am I doing?* Sighed. He moved towards her. Eased his arms around her tight. "You right, Sandy. I have no right to deny you, parents or no parents . . . Don't worry about the money. I'll get a check to you soon as I can."

"The whole thing?"

"Four thousand dollars, right?"

Sandy swallowed. "Yeah."

"Okay, it's done." He released her and took a seat. Patted the chair next to him. "Come."

There it was, the man she loved, the man who was kind, gentle, flipping that Caribbean accent her way at just the right moments, like now, his face dusted with a sleepy smile as if the last three minutes had never happened. As if she were the maker of all his joy. Before her was the Adrian she loved with all her heart, making her world golden again.

"I was thinking," she said, taking the seat, "about fall colors—y'know, rust, sienna, and maybe a soft yellow."

"Sounds good."

Her eyes sought his approval. "And maybe Kente cloth for the guys and Kente cloth ribbons for the bouquets?"

Adrian nodded. "I like that."

"I got these from the bridal store," Sandy said, pushing the brochures out of the way, digging under papers to find the color swatches, slips of silky material lying across her palm, soft and gentle as a promise.

The phone call Sandy never wanted arrived on a Sunday afternoon.

"Baby?"

"Grandma Tee?"

"How you doing, sugah?"

"Been just fine."

"Well, good. Already called your daddy and your uncle

Zeke. They said they'd come and help next Saturday."

"Come?"

"Here, to my house. Didn't want to mention it till I signed the papers, but your grandma done sold her house. I'm leaving by the beginning of next week."

Sandy's heart dropped. "So soon?"

Her grandmother laughed. "Been here on this same street for over forty years. Don't call that soon."

"I know, but—"

Her grandmother hushed her. "No but. Like I said, I'm going back home. It's a done deal. Ain't gonna be nowhere but down the road. Come visit anytime you like."

"South Carolina ain't down the road, Grandma Tee."

"Nowadays it is . . . Now, everybody done met your fiancé but me. Figured if you bring him along next Saturday your grandma Tee get the chance to meet him too."

"Adrian."

Her grandma chuckled again. "That's his name, right?"

Sandy smiled. "Yeah, that's his name."

"Well, then, good. Want to get an early start. Got lots of stuff I got to pack up, give away. Your momma and daddy said they'd get here about nine if I make breakfast. That sound good?"

Sandy swallowed back tears. "Yeah, Grandma, that's fine."

There was a joyful noise up in the old wooden house on Croes Place in the Bronx. Shouts, curses, memories, and laughter drifted about as furniture was hauled, cartons were lifted, and windows were stripped of their modesty.

"Momma Tee?" Aunt Edna called, her brown fingers warming the sides of the bone-china server.

"Yes, Edna."

"Momma Tee, I was just wondering . . ." Edna paused, her wet black Jherri curl accenting the moles that dotted her cheek like peppercorns. "This old server, you taking it with you?"

Grandma Tee chuckled, a sound she had been making most of the day as her sons' wives vied for things Tee "maybe" didn't want.

"Lawd, Edna, you better put my server in this here wrap and make sure it gets on that truck."

"Well, now, Tee," Edna began, "you got two others, figured with you moving in with Cleo, what you need with three? 'Cause you know Cleo like to entertain and she must have three down there already."

Grandma Tee grabbed her porcelain dish. "It's mine, Edna, and it's going." She pointed towards the coffee table. "Sandy, hand me some of that wrap." Sandy cut off a large square, placed it carefully around the server as her grandmother held it steady in her hands. "You'd think I was laying up here dead and buried the way these women clucking after my stuff." She handed the wrapped platter to Sandy. "Make sure that get in the box marked 'fragile.' Your grandma Tee gonna go upstairs and start on her bedroom."

Edna watched her mother-in-law make her way up the long stairs until she was gone from view. "She don't need three servers. What a woman need with three servers?" she wanted to know, picking up her glass and settling back on the sofa, her spot from the moment she'd arrived.

Despite the early season, May still flexing its wings, the day was hot and moist with a slurry breeze. Outside it was about eighty; inside, despite open windows and four air-circulating fans, the temperature was closer to eighty-five.

Grandma Tee was famous for a lot of treats, but her homemade boiled lemonade was everyone's favorite, and on a day like today, it was just what the doctor ordered.

Sandy spied it in front of her aunt Edna, who was known for her love of simple pleasures—a nice hat for church, a good movie, tasty foods. You could always judge how good or how bad a meal was by how Sandy's aunt piled her plate.

There were few things Grandma Tee made that Edna didn't devour, her lemonade one of them. It should have been for the hard laborers, the ones packing and hauling and working up a sweat. But Edna had barely lifted a finger this day and had drunk nearly half. Sandy took up the pitcher, *no more for you,* and headed towards the kitchen.

"That's all the lemonade left?" her father asked as she set it on the counter. The other men, her uncle Zeke, her brother Cliff, Adrian, all wiped their brow, disappointment on their faces as well.

"Aunt Edna," Sandy said matter-of-factly.

Her father headed for the freezer before he realized it had been cleaned out and disconnected. "Damn . . ." He looked around the kitchen full of boxes, cupboards open and stripped bare. "We need something to drink." Considered his future son-in-law. "Adrian, why don't you and Sandy run to the store." He dug in his back pocket, pulled out a misshapen leather wallet. Pulled out a twenty. "Get two bags of ice and something cool to drink."

But Adrian waved off the money. "It's all right, Mr. Hutchinson. I got it." Lifting the edge of his undershirt to wipe his sweaty face, he looked over at Sandy. "You ready?"

Sandy nodded, and together they left.

There was more to this day than helping Grandma Tee move. Sandy had been waiting to be summoned upstairs, help pack up things, and get some of her grandmother's personal effects. But her gran was a mountain; there was no moving her until she was ready to be moved.

Out of all Grandma Tee's grandchildren, Sandy was her favorite, the one closest to her. There was no doubt in Sandy's mind that her grandmother was going to give her some family heirloom.

There was that extraordinary white embroidered tablecloth that had been in the family since the turn of the century. There was the old photograph of her grandparents, faces so stern and set they looked as if they'd been made from mahogany. There was that quilt twice as old as Sandy, and a couple of gold bangles her gran owned but no longer wore.

Sandy had been waiting for her grandmother to holler down the stairs for her so they could hole up in the privacy of her bedroom and talk. They'd dig up old memories—mud pies and sweaty cups of ice-cold milk—and future memories—how great her wedding was going to be and how Adrian was the perfect choice. Her grandmother would praise her for coming up good and strong, hug her for her accomplishments, and share the love that had been forever.

This was what Sandy anticipated, looked forward to when her grandmother finally called for her. But it wasn't anywhere close to what she received.

Grandma Tee sat surrounded by piles and piles of starched white bedsheets that had sat folded and unused for so long their edges had turned ecru. She seemed a bit bewildered at the quantity as she glanced around her bed. "Lawd, when did I ever get all these sheets?"

"I'll take some home," Sandy offered, even though she didn't have much use for them.

"You can ask your aunt and your momma if they want some," Grandma Tee decided, easing up slowly off the high bed, her hands going on her hips as a little moan escaped her. She took her time righting her spine, looked around the room as if deciding what she'd do next. Then she seemed to abandon the idea, her eyes fixing on her granddaughter.

"What you know about him, Sandy?"

The abruptness caught Sandy off guard. *She talking about Adrian?* She struggled for an adequate response, came up with the best she could find. "I know I love him, that he loves me."

"What else?"

What do you mean what else? Her grandmother was scaring her. "I don't understand what you mean, Grandma." And she didn't, not at all.

"He come to you with a lot pain, didn't he? And you think you can heal him."

How did she know that? But the answer came to her quickly. *Like she's always known things . . . that time I took one peppermint out of the candy dish without asking and she had been upstairs sleep but knew I took it. When Cousin Grace died, she knew before the phone rang. When Mommy lost her ring, Grandma Tee told her to look in the can of flour.* There was no point in trying to lie. "His ex-wife died."

Nobody in her family knew that. Now her grandmother did. Sandy was wondering if the knowledge would leave the room when her grandmother spoke.

"And he's afraid," Grandma Tee said matter-of-factly.

Sandy's voice got testy. "Not afraid. He *was* upset."

Her grandmother pulled back, taking some of her anger with her. A soft weariness that had seemed impossible just seconds before lined her face. "I know you see a million dreams every time Adrian looks at you. But out of that million, how many gonna come true?"

"Grandma Tee, you're not making sense."

"Making all the sense in the world, Sandy. You know I am . . . You about to commit to something that bigger than both you and him and you won't win."

Win? Win what? "Just what are you trying to say?"

"Already said it. Ain't repeating myself."

Her grandmother shifted, her whole being leaving behind her warning, confusion and doubt fixed squarely in Sandy's mind.

Grandma Tee went to the antique highboy, took down a mother-of-pearl jewelry box, reached inside, and withdrew three gold bangles. "Know you've had your eye on these a long time. Was my intention of passing them on to you long time ago." She considered her granddaughter, something other than joy dancing in her eyes. "I guess now is as good a time as any."

But Sandy no longer wanted them, no longer wanted

anything but for her grandmother to take her words back. She looked at the bracelets, looked at her grandmother, knowing she would not take the gift. Her refusal would be a first between them.

She steeled herself for the tongue-lashing, for the bitter words she was certain would come her way as she said, "No, thank you."

But her grandmother seemed neither shocked nor surprised by it and simply turned and put the bracelets back in the case. Spoke. "Ain't much to this room. I can manage it ma'self . . . You can go on downstairs."

But Sandy couldn't move. It shouldn't be like this, not between them. This was supposed to be their special time, filled with love, joy, not animosity.

"We done here," her grandmother insisted.

Sandy's eyes glistened. *We can't leave it like this. You going away, don't know when I'll see you again. We can't part this way.*

"Grandma," Sandy implored, her heart breaking.

But her grandmother stopped her. "It's done. Your mind is made up, good or bad . . . we got nothing else to discuss." She turned. Opened a bureau drawer. Started humming something upbeat, spiritual. Sandy could not catch the melody, though she knew it.

She watched her grandmother go on for a few seconds, humming, taking things out of drawers, finding space inside boxes, the edge of her bed. Her grandmother moving around her, about her, as if she didn't exist.

Sandy left the room.

Down the stairs she went, a hurricane in the making. Through the parlor she journeyed, not stopping until she was out the front door. She came to rest against the porch rail, leaned against a pole for support.

She stood there hurting in the worst way, tears streaming down her cheeks. Sandy was still standing there when she heard the screen door yawn open.

"You're out here," she heard Adrian say. "Was wondering where you went off to."

"Just taking a moment to myself."

"So what you thinking on so hard?"

She couldn't look at him. "Nothing. Just this place . . ."

"You gonna miss her."

No, Sandy thought. *I'm not.* Because her grandmother was a witch woman. Her grandmother *knew. Knew things I've never uttered to nobody but my friends. Knew the whole of Adrian's story without me whispering a word.*

Ten years. That's how long the virus could hide and wait before showing up on an AIDS test. Just because Adrian was testing negative today didn't mean he would tomorrow.

Seven and a half years ahead of them, seven and a half years of not having children, not really getting skin to skin. Could she do that? Could she wait until she was past forty to give birth to her first child?

You won't win . . . Sandy hugged herself, wanting it all to go away.

"You all right?" Adrian asked.

"No, I'm not all right." Sandy turned and faced the man she was engaged to marry. "I'm scared."

She felt the bed shift, knew that Adrian was turning towards her, towards her body gone cold, dry, and burdened with dread. There was no desire, no need, no wanting of the man beside her. She lay there still and barely breathing.

Adrian's head dipped under the covers. He licked her flesh, made a snail's trail between her breasts. He kissed her navel, and Sandy's breath caught, held as his tongue snaked lower, the hairs of her pubis bristling against the wet invasion.

Sandy could not believe Adrian wanted to do this. Could not believe he wanted to put his mouth where his penis could not enter unsheathed. She rolled away.

"I wasn't going to do that, Sandy," he said breathlessly, surprised at her withdrawal. "You know I'd never do that," he insisted, reaching for her. But again Sandy pulled away, and he knew the reluctance, was familiar with the disdain. Adrian had been there and done that, but its return took him by surprise.

She was afraid again, and there wasn't much Adrian could do. He could not crawl into her head and rearrange her thoughts, could not wave his hand and make the fear go. Could only step up to the plate and face it. Offer up that option she had once upon a time refused to even consider.

"You want to call this whole thing off? 'Cause I can't do this, Sandy. I can't be having you afraid of me. This is no way to begin *jack*, especially a marriage. So you tell me, right now, right here. What you wanna do. And don't tell me you don't fucking know, either, 'cause that's not good enough, not now. Not anymore."

Her mouth opened, her lips moved. It was her words, "I can't marry you," but not her heart that spoke them. She had no doubt. She still loved him.

Adrian blinked, blinked again, stunned. He had offered the option but hadn't expected her to reach out and grab it. Had not expected her to turn her back on their dream. "What's going on, Sandy?" He had never felt so confused. "Can you please tell me what's going on?"

"I can't marry you."

"Why?"

"Just can't, all right?"

She was expecting him to just nod and go on with his life without any explanation. But he could not do that. Could not leave without knowing why.

He reached for her, determined to see her face, look into her eyes, because eyes didn't lie. And there, like always, deep in the depths was her love for him. "You telling me you can't but I'm looking right at you . . . you still love me."

She turned away, tears running down her cheeks. "Just go, okay? Just go." Her plea, so painful, so stripped of hope, dissolved all of Adrian's convictions. He released her, got out of bed, stood, the moment surreal but sharply focused.

He became aware of the carpet under his feet, every coil pressing against his bare soles. The bedroom lamp glowed morning-sun bright. The air, dangerously thin. "You told me you loved me, no matter what happened or didn't. That's what you said."

It was true, but now she was an Indian giver, taking it all back.

"You don't want to marry me, Sandy, fine. Sure can't make you, but I love you with all my heart. And if you can walk away from me, if you really mean this, then I'm gone. But you tell me, you tell me you don't want to marry me."

Her eyes found his. "I don't want to marry you."

It took a moment for Adrian to comprehend it, to understand she was sticking by her decision. It took a moment to concede, accept the fact that all the mountains and mole-hills they had overcome together, in the end, added up to nothing.

It took a few seconds to understand that despite the love he was still sensing from her she was not going to marry him. Only then could he get dressed and leave out her front door, the absence of her saying even good-bye haunting him like a kiss that has faded, too elusive to reclaim, too heartfelt to forget.

It had been the hope that sustained, the belief, the utter faith that had allowed her to forge ahead with her plans to marry Adrian. It had been Sandy's optimism that they would go on and live that happy-ever-after life that had kept the dream going.

Sandy had backup, reasoning, probability—two years, six tests, all negative—supporting her, doing away with doubt, the worry. That fear.

But in a heartbeat her grandmother had stolen it all

away, had pulled the faith-filled rug right from under her feet.

This was the whole of it, the summation of why she called off her wedding to the man she loved. But only her friends knew of Adrian's past, so the real cause of her action could not be shared with everyone. Her mother was one of those whom Sandy couldn't tell the why to.

"I called off the wedding."

"You did what?" her mother screamed over the phone.

"Called off the wedding."

"Sandy, are you crazy? You pick up that phone right now and you call Adrian and tell him you wasn't thinking clearly, that you do want to marry him."

"No, Mom, I'm not. We're not getting married."

"But why, Sandy?" There were tears in her mother's voice. "Can you tell me why?"

"Just aren't, okay?"

"Oh, baby, you sure about this?"

"I'm sure . . . I've got to call my friends, all right? Talk with you later." Sandy hung up the phone and decided she'd tell one friend. Let the news flow from there. She called Martha.

"Guess what?" she began, with a gaiety so false it made her throat ache.

"Sandy?"

"Yeah . . . guess what?"

"What?"

The giddiness was bordering on hysteria. "The wedding's off."

Martha's scream beat her mother's by an octave. "What?"

"You heard me, wedding's off!" The teetering-on-the-edge mania was still with her.

Martha cleaved it in half. "You're not happy. Stop trying to pretend you are."

Sandy blinked, coming into herself, coming fully back

into the here and now after traversing a twilight zone from the moment Adrian had left.

Like an avalanche the reality began raining down on her head, hard and without mercy. Tears came, fast hot drops. She wiped them, swallowed and swallowed again, her voice raw. "You are so right, Martha, you are so right."

"What happened?"

Sandy would never tell how it had really gone down. She would never speak the scene between her and her grandmother, say out loud what her Grandma Tee *stole away all my hope* had done. Instead Sandy shared the bottom line. "I got scared."

She was grateful that Martha didn't ask of what. Grateful that Martha was wise enough to put two and two together, offering her gentle advice. "You got a right to be scared, Sandy. AIDS ain't no joke."

"Thank you," Sandy said softly.

"Ah, girl, you more than welcome. It's a hard place you're at now. I know because I was sort of there myself. But don't let your sorrow mess you all the way up. If you paid people, you better call them and cancel. You know not getting married can cost as much as getting married."

Martha had never been so right.

The little white card arrived in a little white envelope. No return address; the envelope had been hand-penned.

On the little white card that arrived in the little white envelope were three initials, *L. F. C.*, and four words: "Time for your checkup."

Where had six months gone?

SIXTEEN

Sandy didn't want to pick up the phone and dial the number she had scribbled in the back of her address book. She didn't want to be put on hold as the receptionist found a date and time that was suitable for her.

Sandy didn't want to return to the lush office with the comfy chairs, dim lighting, and enough magazines to fill a library. Didn't want her blood drawn, the bandage that made the wound itch, and the seventy-two-hour wait to find out if she could possibly see old age.

Sandy wanted to forget that segment of her life—*it's over, right?*—and move on to her *before*, when AIDS hadn't known her up close and personal.

She wanted to forget about the man the color of butterscotch. Forget about grief and pain and death and killing fields. Sandy didn't need any more reminders of how close her dream had come before it was taken away. Didn't have room inside her heart for the sorrow.

Don't want to do this, Sandy thought as she made the appointment. Didn't, but she did.

Adrian had been right; it did get easier after the first time. Sandy was sure her results would be the same as before. Worry only found her when a counselor she didn't recognize called her name.

Her eyes revealed her concern as she sat in a different office, in a different chair, and studied the different face.

"Joe's out for a while," the young white woman told her.

Sandy didn't know why that worried her, only that it did. She liked Joe. Liked his wit, his humor, and his familiar brown skin.

"He's okay?"

The woman smiled, nodded, and opened her file.

"You're negative."

There was no drama like the last time, no tears, no eyes raised heavenward, thanking God with all her heart. There was no joy that lifted as she left, no pep in her step, no pledging to live life better. But mostly, no phone call to Adrian to tell him the news.

Nobody should have to do this.

Sandy hung up the phone, placed a check mark next to "Astorian Manor," took a deep breath, and picked it up again. She knew she wasn't only person in the whole wide world who had to make these calls, but at the moment she felt like it.

After dialing the seven numbers, she waited for someone to pick up. Cleared her throat when they did. "Uh, yes, my name is Sandy Hutchinson and I had a reservation for three stretch"—*beautiful, long, luminous gray;* she swallowed, pressed on—"limos for September twenty-first of next year?" This was the hard part, the part that stuck in her craw. "I want to cancel that reservation . . . Yes, I'll hold."

Except for five hundred dollars, the Astorian Manor was refunding all their deposit. Sandy wondered if Larry's Limousine Service would be willing to do the same. "Yes, that's right. Yes. One hundred dollars? Okay, yes, that's fine. Thank you."

She hung up, another check mark. More breaths of air. She was about to pick up the phone to call the photographer when her intercom rang.

Crazy hope, that's what she'd called it these last few days every time someone rang her bell. *Just crazy hope it's Adrian,* she thought to herself as she went to answer, her heart thundering in her chest.

It's not Adrian, her litany as she pressed the button and asked who. "It's me, Janice. Can I come up?" No, it wasn't Adrian, but in that moment it was almost as good.

Her smile trembled through her tears, matching the wetness streaming down Janice's face. She ran to her friend, embraced her hard, feeling like she could never let go.

"Oh, girl," all Sandy could say, "Oh, girl, you just don't know," she moaned. "Oh, Janice," the joy falling away to reveal a broken heart.

"It's okay, Sandy, it's okay."

Sandy pulled back, wanting to make sure it was real. Wanting to make sure it wasn't a mirage, a trick of her imagination, that Janice was standing there, right in front of her, *here for me when I really need her.*

She stomped her feet, head shaking, her voice going high. "I'm so happy to see you. So happy." She clung to her old best friend, the one who knew her most.

"I'm sorry I've been gone so long, Sandy. Sorry I was ever away from you," Janice returned in the same singsong way. "Never leaving you again, you hear me? Never."

They stood in the hallway, crying, hugging, making sweet promises, afraid to ever let go. The two old friends reaching back to who they had been before, their hearts seeking old comfort and the sweet promise of new joy.

Sandy didn't think the sadness could go any deeper. Thought she'd hit rock bottom with it all, but sitting across from Janice she was feeling pain in places she'd never thought possible. Like a toothache, the sorrow pulsed with every beat of her heart.

"Know what it's like, Sandy. You know I know."

She nodded.

"And I know it hurts, real deep inside, and I know there isn't much I can do besides sit here with you, but I'll stay as long as you need me to, if you want."

Sandy shook her head, wiped her wet cheek. "Felt wrong but so right, y'know? Like there was nothing else I was supposed to have done . . . but now I wake up every morning wondering if it was the right thing, wanting to take it back."

That seemed to surprise Janice. "You mean take him back?"

"Yeah."

"Aren't you scared?"

"I was, still am. Maybe I've always been." She shook her head. "I don't know. But now, sitting up here, everything changed, my life just diced up, I'm not sure."

"We were scared for you," Janice confessed, seeing the surprised expression on Sandy's face. "The AIDS thing. Didn't want anything to happen to you, not like that." She grew silent, looked away, guilty of so much but needing to share it all. "I was kind of glad you changed your mind, even if we weren't talking. 'Cause I never stopped thinking about you, wondering about you, worrying. Even though we were apart I didn't want anything bad for you."

Sandy blew her nose, sniffled. Sat in deep silence, her eyes very far away.

"You still love him?" Janice asked after a while.

Sandy lowered her head, lifted it back up. "As much as ever."

"Have you called him?"

She shook her head. "Can't bring myself to."

"Why?"

Sandy looked up, her eyes wide, wet, and afraid. "Because I'm still scared."

Life tipping the scales.

While Sandy's world was on a downswing, Britney's was heavenbound. "He did it," she began, a flurry of joy rushing her words.

"Did what?" Sandy asked, easing her ear from the phone. Britney was close to screaming.

"Asked me, Maurice asked me!"

"To marry you?"

"Yeah!"

"Oh," was all Sandy could manage.

A pause. "You doing okay these days, Sandy?"

These days. These days had stretched into these weeks. Soon it would become these months, *my whole lifetime.* Was she okay? It was hard to say. Her daily life had changed a bit, but she was still living, breathing, being, and sometimes moments arrived when she forgot she had broken off her engagement, had been in love with a butterscotch man. But those moments were rare, too uncommon to matter and too infrequent to make a real impact.

Janice was taking up a lot of slack. She had practically moved in. At least three times a week she was doing something with Sandy, window-shopping at the mall, taking in a movie. Life wasn't as sweet as it had been, but it was no longer as bitter either.

"I'm doing fine, Brit, and hey, congratulations, girl," Sandy answered, meaning it.

"Thanks, Sandy. Means a lot coming from you."

"What's the date?" Sandy asked, taking Britney's joy and pushing it to the limit, her own personal litmus test of how well or badly she could function in the face of lost dreams.

"April. April twenty-eighth."

"Spring wedding?" Her throat grew tight.

"Yeah. I already called Martha and Janice. Martha's gonna be my maid of honor."

Sandy blinked back tears. Made herself speak. "Two for two." She forced a laugh.

"Don't want you to be torn up about this, Sandy. If you want me to shut up, I will."

"No, Brit, I'm all right. World can't stop spinning just because I'm not getting married."

"You sure?"

"Sure as sure can be. We've got to get together, the four of us."

"Well, actually, that was the other reason I was calling. We're planning to go to Club Enchant this weekend. Maurice and his friend Calvin's coming."

"Calvin?" Sandy wasn't ready to meet anybody new. "Not sure if I'm ready for that."

"No, not for you."

"Then who?"

Britney paused. "Martha."

Martha? Sandy felt a moment of envy. *Why not me?* It took a second to see the absurdity of her feelings, some soul searching to let the jealousy go. *About time Martha met somebody.* "You gonna hook her up?"

"Yeah."

"Well, that will be a good thing," she answered, swallowing back much.

He better have it going on, Martha thought as she stood in her mirror, applying the hot curling iron to her hair. *Don't know how I let Britney talk me into this,* she concluded, clicking and twirling the wand like castanets.

This is crazy, she thought for a minute as she left hair curled-up hair and began applying foundation to her face. *Probably the craziest shit I ever done . . .*

A damn garbage man.

Slop hauler, pooper scooper, waste gatherer—Martha had a slew of nicknames for the man she had yet to meet. *Britney says he's fine and smart, has a paycheck as big as mine, but hell, how does she know what he earns? Has she seen his stub?*

Martha smoothed the foundation with a damp sponge. *If he's a creep, I'm leaving.* She finished her face, styled her hair, and settled on the black dress.

Martha got into her Volvo, turned on the engine, and pumped up the stereo. She was picking up Sandy first and Janice second. *They better have cab fare,* her final thought as she pulled away from the curb, because if Calvin wasn't all that, Martha would definitely be calling it an early night.

Trading barbs about what Calvin would look like as they sat at the table, drinks by their sides, waiting for Britney,

Maurice, and Calvin, everyone gave their two cents.

"Black pants, black shirt, and maroon tie," Martha said.

"Black pants, black shirt, and white tie," Janice tossed in, happy to be back amongst her friends.

"No, y'all got it all wrong. It's gonna be some black pants so worn out they shine, a dusty black shirt, and a bright red tie," Sandy decided, eager to see the man who would be Martha's blind date.

She felt a genuine happiness about it, glad that her envy had dissipated into a general pleasantness. Sandy found herself happy to be out and about again.

Martha was the first to spot Britney, looking unbelievably sexy in a low-cut, tight-fitting jacket and loose silky pants. Maurice was the second stunner, because for the first time that any of them could remember, he had on a suit, charcoal gray and tailored.

But Maurice's friend was most surprising of all. A nice height, the short-sleeved, collarless cream shirt and tobacco slacks showing his goods. Even from across the room Martha could see how well put together he was. *His momma and daddy did just fine.*

Britney, leading the way, glided up to the table. A new role, she was wearing the shoes of Queen Bee very well. "Hi, hi," she said quickly, all smiles. She pulled Calvin forward. "This is Calvin. Calvin, this is Janice, Sandy, and *Martha.*"

Martha extended her hand. Calvin took it and kissed the back, something about him familiar but Martha uncertain what. She had seen him somewhere but couldn't finger where. *I know that face,* she decided as he slid into the seat next to her.

Law school? Some store? Martha's brain was working overtime when a name clicked into her head. *Joe Morton.* An actor with as much talent as Denzel Washington, Joe Morton was one of Hollywood's greatest secrets.

Calvin had the same soft droopy eyes, the prominent nose, the pull of the lips, and the color of skin. Only thing

that was missing was the face mole. Martha could not keep
quiet about her discovery. "You look just like that actor,"

He nodded, slightly embarrassed. "Yeah, I know, Joe
Morton." He laughed. "Wish I had his money."

Martha took the moment to fine-tune her impressions.
He wasn't ugly, had a good command of standard English,
and knew how to shop for clothes. *He's passed my first
test.* But now it was time for her second one to begin. She
fanned her face. "Hot in here. I sure could use a drink."

The words were hardly out of her mouth before he was
flagging the barmaid and telling Martha to order whatever
she liked. She didn't know if he was making a show of his
wallet, which was full of money, or if she had just been
looking too hard, but as he pulled a twenty out, Martha
gave him another A.

Relaxing for the first time all evening, she asked the
barmaid to bring her a seven and seven on the rocks, not
stirred, Calvin's gaze like cool fingers on her profile.

Everybody off and gone to the dance floor and Sandy feeling in no mood to join them, she sat at the table by herself,
nursing her drink. She had turned down four offers for
dances, suddenly feeling so out of the mix it was as if she'd
never belonged.

Feeling far removed and away from everything, the sensation had snuck on her without warning. One minute she
was sitting bopping her head to the beat, the next a funk
had descended and she found herself wanting nothing more
than to go home.

Sandy was trying to find a source, a reason, for her
change of mood when her eyes moved towards the dance
floor. And there below her was her answer.

Adrian.

He was on the dance floor moving to the beat with a
woman who was light-years from being a hootchie. He was
not supposed to be down there having fun. Not supposed
to be down there laughing, smiling, grooving like every-

thing was okeydokey with his world. *He suppose to be hurting and in pain like I am.*

A month after she'd broken off their engagement, he was out there looking happy for all the world to see and had found a nice normal woman to party with. Somebody his age, someone on his level. *Someone like me.*

Sandy took a long sip of her drink. Didn't see Janice return, only felt her nudge her shoulder. "See 'em?" Janice whispered.

"Yeah, I see him."

"You gonna go say hi?" Sandy shook her head. "Girl, I was out there dancing with some fool and I saw Adrian and had to cut the dance short."

"Did he see you?"

"No, don't think so."

Sandy realized what she was doing—*playing I Spy again,* except she was the one hiding this time. She shifted in her seat, giving her back to the dance floor, encouraged Janice to do the same.

"Can't hide from him forever, Sandy," Janice said, scooting her chair around.

"Just not up to seeing him now."

Sensing Sandy wanted the matter dropped, Janice changed the subject. "Martha lucked up tonight, huh?"

"Yeah, looks like she did."

"He's a cutie."

"Yeah, he is . . ." Sandy replied, feeling Adrian behind her like a fire.

"I like him," Martha was saying on the phone the next day.

"He definitely got the goods," Sandy told her.

"I mean the brother is fine, he's smart, he works. Single, no kids. Has a place. And a car."

"And a San man."

Martha paused. "Yeah, right. Isn't that a kick in the head."

"Never thought I'd see the day. Ms. Assistant District

Attorney admitting she can get with a garbage man."

"Yeah . . . did you see Adrian?"

"On the dance floor."

"He didn't come by the table?"

"No."

"That surprising. He said he was."

Sandy swallowed. "You talked to him?"

"Yeah. A good minute. He asked all about you, and I told him where you were sitting. He still loves you, Sandy."

"Don't make me feel any worse than I do, okay?"

"Not trying to get on you, make you sad or anything, but love doesn't come every day. I know you got your reasons, just that, well, it's so much better when there's a *him* in your life."

Sandy had no comeback for that.

The park was crowded, the sun was high, and a warm breeze rustled the leaves of the maple and oak trees like silk. WBLS-FM had set up its remote near the bathrooms, and music was blasting loud enough to be heard a quarter of a mile away.

The normally empty park was now crammed with people. Folding chairs lined the perimeter of the basketball court like ringside seats. Babies in strollers dozed in the sun, toddlers dashed through the thick crowd, wanna-be ballplayers coached from the sidelines, and the smell of reefer filled the air.

Sandy adjusted her straw hat, fixed her sunglasses, and shouted to her brother as he ran down court, the ball in his nimble fingers. "Your left, Cliff, watch him." The ball was raked from her brother's hand, leaving Cliff dazed for a second. Then he shifted, his sneakers skidding on the cement as he turned, heading the other way.

"Damn," Janice muttered beside Sandy.

"It all right, it all right. Down by two, a minute left, it all right."

If Sandy's brother had forsaken his black roots, basketball still had him. Cliff loved basketball with a passion. Every chance he got, he played and played hard. Was known for his skill around the courts in Hollis, Queens. Every year for the last eight, Cliff had participated in the summer tournaments. Today was no different.

He had brought his high school to the championships two years in a row during his high school days. Had been seriously scouted by St. John's and Michigan State. But Cliff had dreams beyond basketball and chose Morehouse instead.

Then Morehouse became a dream deferred when a knee injury interrupted his playing in his sophomore year. Returning to New York to finish his studies, he enrolled at Stony Brook, where he played ball, but no longer as a major player. With a degree in computer science, Cliff secured a well-paying job and played basketball during his off time.

The ref blew his whistle, and the players broke up and moved off the court. Sandy watched as her brother took the bottle and squirted his head, water like diamond dust glittering in his sandy brown hair. Summer hadn't been around three weeks and already her brother was getting toasty; pale brown skin seeking out its African roots.

Cliff shook his left leg, rubbed the knee beneath the brace. When he shook it again, Sandy knew he was in pain.

"He's all right?" Janice asked.

"His leg probably acting up."

It had been a last-minute thing, Sandy and Janice coming out to see Cliff play. Neither of them had anything else to do on this gorgeous Saturday afternoon, and with folding chairs and a minicooler they had headed out to the park.

Cliff seemed glad they came.

The whistle blew again, and the players ran back to the court. Sandy checked faces and saw her brother was out. Found him sitting on the bench, undoing the brace. She caught his eye and mouthed "You all right?" Her brother shook his head.

"Let me take him some juice," Janice said, reaching into

the cooler, finding a Mystic Strawberry. Adjusting her sun-glasses, Janice moved down the sideline and headed Cliff's way.

Sandy watched her friend. Wondered when Janice was ever going to give up the dream. Janice had had a crush on Cliff since she was fourteen, and nearly twenty years later it was still evident as Janice smiled pretty teeth his way.

She wasn't the first friend to drool over him and probably wouldn't be the last, but she was only one who appeared to be still caught up in it.

It had been annoying the way her girlfriends fawned over Cliff. He treating them as they were, little girls a millions years away from the orbit in which he rotated. *Give it up, girl,* Sandy was thinking as she watched her friend try to engage Cliff in conversation. His eyes, his mind, his soul were still with the game, and eventually Janice gave up.

"His knee is hurting him bad," she said, taking her seat next to Sandy. But Sandy knew Cliff's knee was the last thing on Janice's mind.

Permanently benched, Cliff sat out the rest of the game. By the time they headed home, his knee had cramped up so badly he needed both Sandy and Janice just to make it to the car.

He didn't get the MVP, but his team won the title. Still, the trophy, over three feet tall and weighing a good twenty pounds, didn't seem to lighten his mood. Cliff held it shot-gun between his thighs on the ride back to Sandy's parents' house.

Janice leaned towards the front seat, slipping her head between Sandy and Cliff. "Good game," she piped, her eyes bright.

But Cliff merely grunted and looked out the window.

It wasn't the curl of smoke rising from the back of the house that gave it away, but the undeniable smell of grilling meat that told them Sandy's father was barbecuing.

At the ready, Sandy and Janice both went to help Cliff out of the car, but he pushed them away. "I'm all right," he insisted, the pain in his knee making him grimace.

Sandy's mother stood at the front door, her face furrowed with worry. "What happened?" she asked, taking in her limping son, his stern expression.

"Knee gave out," Cliff said as he hopped on one leg up the stairs.

"Daddy grilling?" Sandy asked as she moved past her mother.

"Yeah, figured you guys want something to eat."

"Smells good," Janice said, coming behind her.

"Got burgers, ribs, and some chicken. I was just making some potato salad. Be ready in a minute."

"Anything I can help with, Ms. Hutchinson?" Janice asked eagerly.

"Well, I hate doing onions."

"I don't mind," Janice said, going off to wash her hands.

They sat around, full and content in the backyard that was an oasis of shimmering leaves, warm breezes, and sunlight dappling through the trees. From far away the sound of children playing filtered through the air like childhood revisited, the quiet tree-lined street their unbordered playground.

"Samuel, better check that grill. Foil's smoking," Mrs. Hutchinson warned.

Sandy's father rose, putting his beer aside. Taking up the cooking fork, he folded the edges of the burnt aluminum and pitched it in the garbage. Looked at his watch. "Mets are on," he said, excusing himself as he went into the house.

"Can't miss my Mets," Jeanne Hutchinson decided, putting the last piece of melon in her mouth and rising too.

Sandy got up and began gathering used plates, napkins,

and cups. Janice went to join her, but she shooed Janice away. "I got it."

As Sandy took the ketchup and mustard from the table, there was no missing the look in Janice's eyes as she gazed at Cliff. But the real surprise was how her brother was returning the look.

Somebody could have knocked Sandy over with a feather.

Missing Adrian.

It had been faint at first, *better this way,* but as the warm season moved into the hot season and she began seeing couples everywhere, her longing was taking on a new fever.

Sandy had grown optimistic. Knew Adrian would call her soon after that night at the club. Martha had said he asked about her. Martha had said he was going to come over and say hello, and when he hadn't she found reasons and excuses why.

He didn't want to do it with Janice there. He was waiting for me to be alone. He was scared of a face-to-face and will call me. But that had been two weeks ago.

Now Sandy was experiencing a new emotion, and its name was doubt. *I did what I did because I'd convinced myself it would be better. But here in the aftermath, who has it been better for?* She didn't know, only that she had taken her grandma Tee's warning and run with it.

But had it really been a warning, or had Sandy simply read too much into it? Had Grandma Tee really been suggesting that Adrian was going to get real sick and die a slow death? That he would infect Sandy and Sandy would die too? Had Grandma Tee suggested that, or known that?

Or was Grandma Tee simply putting her own feelings about dark-skinned black people marrying light-skinned ones on Sandy's shoulders, trying to do away with a tradition her daddy had started?

Everybody had their own agenda. Even sweet dear old

Grandma Tee. Just because Sandy had latched her own fears onto her grandmother's omen didn't mean it was true. Didn't mean it wasn't.

In hindsight Sandy realized she should at least have found the courage to ask her grandmother why.

SEVENTEEN

The pen clattered against the tabletop. The check, freshly inked, read: *"Payable to Adrian C. Burton, Three thousand one hundred dollars and 00/100 cents."* Sandy got her pad, scribbled a quick note—*"refunds from the caterer, limousine service, and photographer, less nonrefundable deposits of $900"*—her strokes barely legible, haste making her writing slipshod.

She put her pen down, took a deep breath. Found it wasn't enough air and took another. It was the only tangible between them now, the envelope, her note, the check. It was the only bridge they both would cross, she retreating by the time he took the first step.

She would never address another envelope to him, never jot another note. Sandy realized she would never pick up the phone and dial his number or answer hers and find him on the other end. This was their last and final connection.

She slipped the papers into the envelope. Licked the flap and pressed it closed. Her hand shook as she wrote his name, *Adrian,* paused at *Burton,* the name she had forfeited.

She scribbled the address and headed out the door. The post office was closed, but they had a mail slot and she needed to have the envelope gone from her before she tore it open, wrote another note, adding those words she longed to say.

It had been planned days in advance, Sandy and Janice doing the mall, but when she called to confirm, Janice didn't seem to know what Sandy was talking about. Recovering quickly, apologizing profusely, Janice asked for half an hour with the promise of being ready. Something was going on, but Sandy didn't know what until she arrived at Janice's front door.

Close your mouth.

But she couldn't, especially now as her brother come out of Janice's kitchen, a glass of juice in his hand. "What's up, Smoky?"

"Cliff?" All she could say, the sight of her brother making himself at home in her friend's apartment downright bizarre.

Janice got her pocketbook. "We'll talk on the way. Be back later!" she yelled, moving herself and Sandy out the door. "Now, don't go acting all surprised like you didn't know."

"I knew, I mean, after the barbecue, but I didn't *know* know."

"I'm taking it easy, Sandy. No head first about this at all."

"How do you mean?" The elevator arrived, and they got in. Both of them reached for the lobby button but Sandy made contact first.

"What I mean is, it's no secret I've had a crush on Cliff since forever. Now, I'm not pressing no issue here. I don't call him, he calls me. I don't go and see him, he comes to see me. We've gone out twice and I haven't spent a dime."

Sandy couldn't believe Janice was talking about her brother. She had to be lying. "We talking about the same knuckleheaded fool?"

"Yeah, I'm talking about Cliff."

"You telling me that my brother is treating a woman with real decency?"

"That's what I'm saying." The elevator door opened, and they stepped out into the hall. A quick left and they began their journey down the long, snaky corridor.

"Oh, he tried it. That night he dropped me home, he asked if he could come in and I said yeah, sure. Wasn't in my apartment ten seconds before he's all over me. And I told him that's not how I go anymore."

She shook her head. "So much crap, been through so much nonsense. Never dawned on me to tell somebody what I wanted instead of waiting for them to tell me. But I know it now, and it's the way I'm going from this point on." There was no denying Janice had not only decided it, she was living and breathing it.

"And my brother accepted that?"

"At first he was kind of mad, talking all the bru-ha-ha about leading him on and he's too old to be playing games. We ended up talking. Did what I never done. I broke it down to him, told how I wanted things to go, and I mean we just *talked* till like four o'clock in the morning . . . Your brother's got a lot of issues."

"Yeah, he's an arrogant high-yellow creton."

"That's part of it . . . but there's other things going on with him."

"Like?" Because as far as Sandy knew, Cliff's world rotated on a perfect axis.

"Promised I wouldn't tell."

"Not even me?"

"Especially you. I will say that he loves you and is very glad you're his sister."

Sandy shook her head. "Janice, you blowing my mind over here. I can't believe we talking about my brother."

"You know, just because a person come off one way doesn't mean they that way at all. Cliff hides a lot of stuff. Some of the stuff he's concerned about is like ridiculous."

"And I guess you can't tell me what."

Janice looked at her. "No, 'cause I promised."

They got into Sandy's car. "So it's a love match now, is that it?"

Janice laughed. Shook her head. "Believe it or not, no. Since ninth grade I had this thing for him." Her eyes searched the horizon. "And it's like now, after all this time, I'm getting to see the man behind the mask, and he's nothing like I thought."

"So it isn't a love match." Sandy needed confirming, still tossed up by it all.

"We're just friends. Like I said, he's the one doing all the calling, all the visiting. And if I want to see him, I do; if I don't, I don't." Which was the real joy. The day had finally come when Janice could allow herself the choice.

"What about him? How does he feel?"

"Know what he told me?"

Finally something. "No, what?"

"Said I'm the first woman he ever met who had a real sense of herself."

The doubt was full in Sandy's voice. "And you believe him?"

"Well, it's been three weeks and he's still here, still calling, still coming to see me. What you think?"

Sandy shook her head. "Don't know what to think." It was too surreal, out there somewhere. Truth or pipe dream, she wasn't sure, but she offered her friend some advice. "Just be careful, all right?" Sandy started her car, pulled out of the space, and when they got back hours later, Cliff was right there waiting.

Calvin took their cups and headed towards the kitchen. "Justice is supposed to be blind," he reminded her as he poured cappuccino in both.

"Yeah, and I'm the president of the United States," Martha tossed back, removing her glasses and rubbing the sides of her nose. Her eyes were aching a little, but her very soul was on fire. She was energized by the brisk, lively debate she and Calvin had just embarked on.

Martha had no intention of talking about the *State of New York v. Ernest Weaver*. Had no intention of going into any details about the man who had shot an intruder with an illegal handgun. But Calvin had been watching TV and she had decided to get back to her work when he strolled over, casually took up the file, and, before she could protest, started asking her questions.

She had attempted to snatch the folder back, but the questions he raised were ones she had never considered, things too important for her not to examine. Before she knew it, the cappuccino machine was going and they were sitting at her dining room table playing defense attorney and prosecutor.

His knowledge of the law stunned her. Martha found herself asking how he knew what he knew. "At one time I was in the police academy. Took my law courses at John Jay seriously. Found I liked the law, and even after I took the job with Sanitation, I read up on as much as I could." He had laughed. "Nowadays a brother can't know too much about the criminal justice system. Got to know your rights out there or the police will stomp all over them."

Which surprised and delighted her to no end. Calvin knew her world, had a real passion about it.

"Here you go," he said, placing the demitasse cup before her and taking a seat.

He knew things. Not just everyday things but names of people who had taken on the law and won rights not just for themselves but for everyone. It had started out as a game, Martha wanting to test Calvin's knowledge of her professional creed and Calvin up to the challenge.

"Who argued and won *Brown versus the Board of Education*?" she'd asked, starting off easy.

Without blinking, pausing, or even taking a breath, Calvin had answered, "Thurgood Marshall, who later went on to sit on the Supreme Court." Then he totally flipped the switch and asked her, "Who was Norma McCorvey?"

She smiled. "I know, do you?"

"Course I know."

"Say it."

"No. I asked, you say it."

"She was the plaintiff in—"

Calvin cut her off. "*Roe versus Wade*."

"Which was?"

"One of the most groundbreaking historical court decisions since Emancipation, legalizing abortion in all fifty states in one single sweep."

Impress me and there was no doubt she was. Intelligence and knowledge had always been a major turn-on for her, *reason why I loved Leon so much.*

Now, as she scrutinized Calvin, she wondered if she was being given a second chance for that greatest love. "Ever think about going back to school?"

He smiled into his cup. "I got four more years with the city, then I'm looking at retirement. School?" He shook his head. "Nah."

"But you should," Martha found herself saying. "You're smart, know enough about the law already. You'd be done in no time."

He considered her, his words carefully spoken. "Just 'cause I like law, know a little sumpin' sumpin' about it, don't mean I want to be a lawyer."

Point well taken. Martha sat back in her chair. Sighed and picked up her strong coffee. *Nobody's perfect,* she thought, *but damn if he doesn't have the potential to come real close.*

EIGHTEEN

She'd felt his eyes, that heat that said she had sparked an interest. Sandy wasn't out to be noticed; she was just trying to get home.

He had come up behind her, tacking himself to the long line of people waiting for the bus. She sensed he was going to say something to her. Hoped he took rejection well.

She gazed up the street for the sight of the blue and white bus, her eyes skittering across the man's profile as she did. In an instant she had a sense of him, a feel for him, had determined his attractiveness, the gentle soul that rested inside.

In another lifetime she might have smiled his way, opening herself up to the fuzzy possibility that was nudging against her. But her heart was locked and the key thrown away.

If leaving Adrian was supposed to have brought her comfort, the only thing it had brought was a new longing. Where she had once anticipated peace, she now found nothing but turmoil.

She had hoped calling off the wedding would allow life to start anew. But all it had done was proved there was no getting over true love, and there was no doubt their love had been true.

"Don't tell me you're taken."

For a moment she'd forgotten about the handsome stranger beside her, her own little world encompassing all her thoughts. But he was right there, taking in the circle of precious metal and stone, a wondrous expression in his eye.

Sandy covered the ring with her hand.

"No sense in hiding it now. I've seen it."

She chuckled, not with joy but bitter irony. "Don't mean

much," she found herself saying. "This ring is just a ring," she concluded, turning away, showing her lack of interest.

But despite her turned back, the stiff shoulder, he was not deterred. There was a sadness to her that made her wholesome, attractive even, and he wasn't willing to let her slide by so easily.

"If the ring means nothing, why are you still wearing it?" There was such a gentle knowingness in his voice it touched her. For a second she felt the need to turn towards him, open her mouth and utter what she now knew—*I've been such a fool*. But the moment passed as the bus arrived and she prepared to board.

She found herself wondering about Adrian. Wondering where he was and what he was doing. She wondered if his heart was still aching or if he had managed to heal the wound.

Sandy juxtaposed him in all sorts of scenarios until she ran out of settings and a simple truth filled her. *It doesn't matter where he's at or what he's doing, because the reality is I love him still.*

Even in the most vigilant households parents grew tired, loosened their hold, relaxed the reins with which they once ruled their children's lives. Adrian's parents were no different, and as the years passed Rachel began taking up the slack.

Passing the twenty-one-year mark years ago, Rachel began stepping out of the shoes of baby sister into the shoes of knowledgeable womanhood.

With keen eyes and a sharp mouth Rachel began instructing her older brothers in the fine art of humanity, everything from how often they were to call their parents to what not to expect on a first date. They had balked at first at their baby sister trying to run their lives and rule their worlds, but as time passed and her words always managed to land on the right side of wrong, they began to heed her advice.

"The General," her brothers called her. When they stumbled, dragged, got caught up, she was right there, laughing, chiding, demanding them back on the straight and narrow.

Like Adrian.

She knew he would hole up somewhere and lick his wounds after Sandy called off the wedding. Knew that, left to his own devices, if he never saw the sun shine again it would be too soon.

He's grown, her brothers said, relieved that he wasn't going to marry after all. *San-dee made de right choice,* her father insisted. *Must have had her reasons,* her mother surmised.

Everyone accepted the breakup, but no one lifted a hand to help him along. That was when Rachel swung into action. She began calling him almost daily. "Ya need to come and see ya sista, nuh? We sit and chat. Whatcha say?" But time and time again Adrian refused. No dummy, he knew what Rachel was really up to, and it took time before he was willing to allow her to do it.

Now, as he laid down his fork, he leaned back and considered her, belly full, gratitude in his eyes. "Yah chasing your mudder's skirt tail, ya know dat, dontcha?"

A smile blossomed on her face. "Ya tryin' to chummy up the cook?"

"Just offering my appreciation."

"So when ya go'wen ta?" Rachel asked.

"Go'wenta what?"

"No twenty questions, nuh? Ya know what me tawkin' about."

He smiled, reached out, and cuffed her chin. "Such a cuttin' tongue ya got for such a fine fine laydee."

She flicked his hand away. "My tongue speak da trut, cuttin' or udderwise." Her flash of anger faded, shifted into something else. "Poppa tinks ya sick."

"I'm fine, Ray-chell. Jus fine."

"But Poppa don't tink so, and him got Mommy and da rest of dem justa trudging in his shoes."

"Everywan but you."

" 'Cause I know ya fine . . . nuttin' bad gonna happen."

But it was more question than statement. Adrian tried to allay her fears. "No, Rachel, nuttin' bad."

She stood, took up his plate. "I dreamed her, dreamed San-dee," she said, scraping bits of meat and rice into the garbage pail. "I dream her just lawst and cawlin' cawlin' cawlin' ya name." Adrian lowered his head. "I felt her love, Adrian . . .'ere in me heart."

"She do'n w'an ta marry me."

"But she still love you."

"A dream tell ya all dat?" he chided.

"No, she tell me."

"Oh, she cawl you on the telephone?"

Rachel sucked her teeth. "No, she not pick up da phone and ring it. But I know. I know she out dere, lost and looking for ya. Dat she be wan'tin ya . . . just cairn't find her way."

Adrian shook his head, pushing away the words that were too close to his heart. "She know where I live. She know my numba. She ain't cawl, she ain't come."

"But she still loves ya, and dat wort more dan any udder ting."

"You say," he accused.

"Nah, she say. Even when she broke up wit cha, she say she don't luv ya? Nah, I know she didn't. Cause she do . . . ain't gonna force ya to no phone. Ain't gonna scream or shout or nuttin'. Not ta nudder word I'm speaking but dis. But don't keep holding on to da lies tinkin it da best way, 'cause it's not, not at t'all." With that Rachel began the dishes.

My wedding folder.

Standard legal, the folder was crammed with contracts, pictures of wedding dresses, shimmery gossamer strips, hand-scribbled notes, and wedding invitation samples. Just holding it in her hands felt strange. *Does paper hold magic?*

It had drifted around Sandy's apartment like a finicky breeze, going from her dinette table to her entertainment unit, traversing on to her nightstand and finally under her VCR cart.

She had no real memory of moving it, didn't even realize she still had it until she was cleaning up, throwing out old bills and television guides, and it appeared.

She didn't open it. Didn't flip through it, just headed for the garbage can ready to toss it in. But once she got there, she could not let it go. *Just a stupid folder,* but in her hands it felt like so much more.

She looked at the worn, bent edges, the ink stains. Took a deep breath, *don't need it anymore*, ready to release it when the phone rang.

"Hello?"

"Sandy?"

Her breath caught.

"Sandy, you there? It's me, Adrian."

"Adrian?"

"Yeah. Look . . . this is awkward as hell . . . I just need to know."

"Know what?"

"Do you still love me?"

That he was asking at all surprised her. She had always loved him. "Always . . . even when I said good-bye."

"But you walked away from me."

"Because I was scared."

"Are you still? Scared, I mean?"

"Yes . . . I am."

"I see."

Her voice came, a rush of desperate need. "Hear me out, please."

"Okay."

"These past few months have been the hardest thing I've ever lived through. Not a day, a moment, a second goes by when I don't think about you, sorry about the choice I made. I wear the ring and tell myself it means nothing. I go around and pretend I'm just fine, but I'm not fine. I miss you, Adrian. Miss you so much I don't think my heart will ever stop missing you. Am I scared? Yes, but I'd rather be scared with you than not scared and without you."

A final chance, they were both thinking. A final chance to make it right.

He swallowed. "You still want me?"

"Only if you still want me."

She trembled beneath his fingers, a hunger deep and raw racing through her like a live wire. She was wet and open, filled with passion and need.

Adrian pulled away.

Sandy waited.

Concentrating on other things, on the anticipated pleasure, the moment they would become one. She sought out images of blue skies, better days, a new future. Sandy filled her mind with rainbows and star-filled skies, banishing the fear and welcoming the love as he entered her, a slow motion that made her spine arch, her thighs quiver.

He lay there a while, holding his weight, searching her eyes, needing to know her thoughts in this moment. Adrian needed to be sure she was not turning away, running scared. Afraid.

"Hey," he said softly.

"Hey back," she answered, just as hushed.

"You love me?" A secret he needed divulging.

"Always," she whispered, drawing his lips to her parted mouth, their tongues intertwining and complete.

Martha and Britney arrived at the same time Janice did, the three friends gathering in the apartment foyer, curiosity and concern lining their faces.

"What she tell you?" Janice asked.

"Just that she wanted me to come over."

Britney nodded. "Told me the same thing."

They headed up the short flight of stairs. "Wonder what it's about?"

"I don't know, but I hope it's good news," Martha decided as they rounded the bend, the sight of Sandy standing in her doorway, her smile unmistakable, erasing some but not all the concerns that found their hearts.

"You sure?"

"Absolutely, Janice."

"No more changing your mind?"

"Nobody I want to be with more."

"But what about the other thing?" Britney's question.

"He's still testing negative, and we're very cautious." But the look on her friends' faces said their fears were still with them. "Am I supposed to just tuck away the most important thing in my life on a maybe? Is that what I'm supposed to do, just say oh well, he could have AIDS and he could die, so I'm not going to take a chance, just go on without the love of my life? Go on being miserable, unhappy, and alone? Is that what y'all want me to do?"

No one would answer.

"Well, you know what? I tried it that way. Broke my own heart in the process . . . I love him and he loves me just as much, can you understand that? L-O-V-E, love. Not like, not maybe, not one-sided, but a complete three-sixty." She took a breath, imploring her friends to understand. "I've tried to walk away from it, but I can't. I'm not gonna try anymore, either."

She looked at Martha. "Didn't you tell me that life was so much better with a him in it?"

"Yeah, I did."

She looked at Britney. "Can you imagine yourself just walking away from Maurice? Can you?" The look on Britney's face said she couldn't.

"And you, Janice. Suppose Cliff was in Adrian's shoes— would you just say no?"

"Not the same thing," Janice insisted.

"Like hell it isn't."

Wide eyes danced her way. "We just don't want to see anything happen to you, Sandy. Can you understand that?"

Sandy blinked back tears but remained firm. "I appreciate that, love you for it even, but this is what I'm going to do. Now you can be with me on this or not at all."

The room grew quiet, each pulling away, cocooning themselves in their own personal thoughts. It was Britney who broke the silence. "I understand just how you feel, Sandy. No way I could just walk away from Maurice, no matter what happened. You want to do this, you got my blessing."

"Thank you, Brit," Sandy said softly.

Martha sighed. "You haven't pitched the question to me, but I asked myself the same thing. If Calvin were Adrian, I know I couldn't just walk away either. So I'm with you."

Sandy wiped away a tear.

"You my heart," Janice said, her voice choked. "I just don't want nothing to happen to you. Promise me you'll be safe."

"I promise. I'm not planning on going nowhere anytime soon."

"Same date?" was Martha's question.

Sandy nodded.

Martha swallowed on the next question. "Same maid of honor?"

Sandy held her eyes steady. "Yep. Just like it was before."

Martha had doubts. "You can change it if you want, Sandy."

"No, I asked you and that's that. Stuck by me like white on rice. No way you can't be."

Weariness found her. Sandy never thought she would have to defend her choice, and in the aftermath she was tired, wanting the matter finished. She shifted the focus. Offered a diversion. "I was going to order pizza."

"Pizza? This ain't no pizza moment," Martha said, offended. "We need real food. Momma's Place, not pizza."

Janice perked up. "Momma's Place sounds good."

"Sounds good to me too," Britney added.

"Fine. Momma's Place it is."

Dream maker.

Sandy didn't realize she was until she arrived early one Saturday morning to help her mother "get the house ready."

As old as time and as steadfast as tradition, this day the Hutchinson household would see no corner unscrubbed, no table unpolished. It was spring cleaning in the middle of October as Mrs. Hutchinson readied her home to be presented to her daughter's future in-laws.

There was an energizing anxiety to her mother's narrow face, a certain unassuredness as she rubbed the dining room table, determined to see a clear reflection in its surface. Sandy stood there watching her, a bucket, sponge, and Pine-Sol in hand.

"Especially around the base, and the bottom. Don't want nobody thinking I keep a nasty house," her mother instructed as she applied a second coat of Pledge to the sofa table.

Any more and she'll have them thinking we grow lemons. The air was absolutely infused with the scent of them. Leaving her, Sandy went through the kitchen, stepping to the bathroom off the back. She chuckled to herself as she got down on all fours, half amused but mostly understanding her mother's mania.

"Trinidad?" Her mother had balked as Sandy tried to relay as much of Adrian's family history as common courtesy allowed. "You never told me his family was from Trinidad." Till then Sandy had seen no reason to. But with the peppery, disagreeable Mr. Burton coming to visit, she was trying to warn them of what they could possibly expect.

"Well, just his father. Adrian, his brothers and sister, and his mother are all American born."

"So Adrian not an alien or anything?" her father had asked suspiciously.

"No, Dad, he didn't come sneaking into America on a banana boat. He was born right there at Kings County in Brooklyn." Sandy had paused then, unsure of how to proceed. She hadn't wanted to leave her parents vulnerable to whatever mood Adrian's father would bring, but there was no way she wanted to tell it all either. "Don't think his father cares for me much."

Her parents had looked at her in horror. "What do you mean? How could he not?" her mother asked, indignant that anyone would be offended by her only daughter.

"I don't know why, and I really don't care . . . just that I wanted you to know. In case he says something."

"Like what?" The blood vessels had began to pulse in her father's head by then.

"Dad, who knows? And who really cares? Adrian loves me and I love him, that's all that matters. But I just wanted you to know, that's all." Which was far from the truth.

"Tidy Bowl's beneath the kitchen sink," she heard her mother shout. Sandy grunted an answer, squeezed between the vanity and the toilet to reach the space behind it.

A tight fit, but she managed to attack whatever dirt had accumulated there, *and it must be invisible, 'cause nothing's coming off on this sponge.* It would be just their luck that Mrs. Burton would come in later, wedge herself down as Sandy was doing now, and do a white-glove test.

With gusto Sandy wiped, dipped, rinsed, and wiped some more. *Last thing I need is her thinking my mother keeps a dirty house.*

"My hair all right?"

Sandy looked at the woman whose beauty she had always envied and could not help but smile. "Yes, Mother, you look perfect."

In that moment Jeanne Hutchinson *was* perfection in her daughter's eyes. In that moment Sandy could see and feel all the love her mother had ever had for her. She had found the special someone to live her life with, all any mother wanted.

Jeanne Hutchinson reached out, adjusted the lay of pearls across her daughter's dress. "You look so beautiful," she murmured. "You are going to make a gorgeous bride." She hugged her. "So happy for you."

"Don't cry. You'll ruin your makeup."

The doorbell rang.

They both turned and stared towards the doorway, then at each other. It was too early for guests, the appointed time another twenty-five minutes away. The doorbell rang a second time as they debated what to do.

"Oh, Lord, is that them already? They're too early. Why are they showing up early? Haven't even finished getting ready."

"Go ahead," Sandy decided. "I'll go down and answer."

Down the stairs she went, a delicious current finding her. She felt light, delicate, *because it's my day*, and, good, bad, or indifferent, she was determined to shine.

She was on her own stomping ground, would allow no one to take anything from her. Not her importance, her beauty, her future role as Mrs. Adrian Burton.

Not even the *tuff* gruff Mr. Burton would do her in this day.

Sandy swung the door open, her face fixed with a smile. But it was not the grumpy-faced Mr. Burton she saw, not even the leery Junie. It was Winston, alone and ahead of schedule. "Can I come in?"

"You're early," was all she could say.

"Hope you don't mind." Through the door he came, looking around, taking in the home she had grown up in.

"My parents are still getting dressed."

"Actually I came early to talk to you."

She wasn't certain what he was going to say but knew that it would require privacy. She moved him towards the kitchen and offered him a seat.

"I love my brother, Sandy. No man I love more, not even my father." That surprised her. She thought undying love for the father was a requirement for being a Burton child. "And when Adrian first talked about you, I disliked you off the bat, Gen being alive and all."

Sandy looked around, got a funny look. Winston caught her drift, nodded, went on. "I didn't know you, not really, but Adrian was talking about you like you were the best thing, better than . . . well, y'know. Gen? We loved her. Wasn't just a sister-in-law, she was like a sister. Her family, my family, close tight . . . she wunna us, Trinidadian, y'know?"

"And I'm not," Sandy interjected.

Winston looked at her. "No, you're not."

"But neither is your mother."

"Her father is." He considered her. "More than Adrian and Gen, it's about island roots, the traditions. Old ties."

Sandy looked around her. It was the second time he had mentioned Adrian and Gen in the same breath. She stood. "Let's go downstairs." Made her way, distrustful of what else Winston would say. *This man hated me,* all she could consider as they settled in the basement, Winston taking a barstool, Sandy standing, not wanting to wrinkle her dress.

Winston went on. "Adrian and Gen? They were perfect in our eyes, destined from childhood to be together. Next thing I know Adrian's talking about they're apart. Wouldn't say what, why, how come, or nothing. So I go to Gen and I ask her why?" His lips pulled down the same way Adrian's did from time to time. "Wouldn't tell me. Just said it was how it had to be and it wasn't Adrian's fault."

Sandy spoke. "It wasn't."

"Yeah, yeah, I know that now, but I didn't then. So time goes by and my brother's back to hanging out. Wasn't meeting anybody serious and we all praying he and Gen would get back together. Next thing I know he's all excited and happy about some woman he met."

Sandy interjected. "Me."

Winston looked at her with accusing eyes. "Yeah. And I could tell he was really digging you, I mean really digging you. But all I could think was 'What about Gen? What about his wife?' " His eyes lit into her. "My father went absolutely nuts."

Sandy threw up her hands. "I don't want to hear any more. I want you to shut up and get the hell out of my parents' house. How dare you come and tell me this! How dare you!"

He shook his head slowly, grabbed her wrist. "No, Sandy. Please . . . just hear me out."

She wrenched her wrist free. Had one thought. *Just walk away. You don't have to stand here and listen to this bullshit. Just turn and go upstairs.* But she couldn't. Winston was right, she did want to know.

She swallowed, her eyes hot, wet. Angry. "Go ahead."

"All right. All of us were stewing, hating you like we haven't hated anybody in a long time. Then my brother brings *you* to Rachel's party. It was like a slap in our faces." Winston sighed. "Next thing we're getting a call—Gen's dead. Gone. Poof! Like that. And suddenly it comes to me that no, Adrian and Gen won't be getting back together . . .'cause she dead. And even when we found out why, it was hard to swallow. We kept saying no, Gen wouldn't do that . . . just knew Adrian had made the whole thing up."

"But you realized it was the truth."

"Yeah. Well, *we* did . . ." Winston looked away. "My father's still spinning his wheels about you. Says you're an 'outsider' trying to shove your way in. Everyone else has sort of come around."

Winston took a deep breath, sighed. Considered her with regretful eyes. "So I came here today, Sandy, to apologize. I will never treat you that way again. I've seen Adrian with you, and I seen him without you. And if there's one thing I now know, you make him very happy." Winston's eyes glistened, his words grew choppy. "My brother's been through enough." He swallowed down the lump in his throat. "Don't want him to suffer through nothing any-more."

She was moved in a way she never thought possible and didn't know what to say. She was feeling Winston's pain, more so than her own. *I won't cry*. But even that thought could not stop the tears that seeped.

"No, no," Winston uttered softly and tenderly. "No, don't do that," he insisted, gently wiped the side of her eyes. "Adrian gonna be here in a minute. You don't want him to know I had you in tears now, do you?" He lifted her chin, those eyes, *Adrian eyes*, looking back at her. "Him find out I don made ja weep, him kick my arse from 'ere all da way to Brooklyn."

Sandy couldn't help it, couldn't hold it back. The smile she felt from the bottom of her feet to the hairs on her head tingled through her. Grateful, overcome with relief. "Thank you, Winston," all she could say.

"Nuh, sir, ya gonna be family soon. Got to cawl me Wint."

"Thank you, Wint."

He extended his arms. "Now, come. Give your brudder-in-law a beeg hug." His arms found her, a slow draw into his embrace. Familiar in a way she never thought possible, it was a very long time before either of them let go.

Her mother was holding her hand for dear life. Her father seemed to turn into stone as Mr. and Mrs. Burton came through the door.

Sandy moved forward, minding all her manners, her p's and q's. "Hello, Mr. and Mrs. Burton. I would like to in-troduce you to my parents, Samuel and Jeanne Hutchin-son."

Sandy's mother stepped forward and extended her hand to Mrs. Burton. But Mrs. Burton opened her arms and gave her a hug. "So very nice to meet you. Jeanne, was it?"

Sandy's mother nodded, smiled, mildly surprised. If Mr.

Burton didn't like Sandy, then as his wife Mrs. Burton probably didn't like her either. "Why, yes. And your name is—?"

"Alice."

Mrs. Hutchinson pulled back, studied the woman with careful eyes. "Nice to meet you, Alice."

Samuel Hutchinson considered the man who had found fault with his daughter. Mr. Burton seemed to be looking back just as intently, but he stepped forward and extended his hand. Sandy's father took it. "I, I'm Aldridge, Aldridge Burton."

"Samuel."

They shook, dropped hands.

"You have a lovely home, Mrs. Hutchinson," Adrian's mother was saying as she took in the picture-filled walls, the leather modules, things made of glass and brass.

"Why, thank you, Mrs. Burton, and please, call me Jeanne."

"Can I get you something to drink, Aldridge?" Sandy's father offered, taking in the proud yellow man before him.

"Got stout?" he asked.

"In fact we do, in the kitchen. I'll show you the way." Like foot soldiers the two men moved, spines straight and arms barely shifting, towards the kitchen.

There was a tap on the screen door. Sandy turned and saw Adrian, loaded down with a cake box. "Black cake," Mrs. Burton explained. "No celebration is complete without it," she added as Sandy went and let Adrian in.

"Hey," she said with a smile.

"Hey back," he answered, finding her lips.

"You got that?" she asked, reaching for the large white box.

"Yeah. Just point me towards the kitchen."

But she never got the chance. The doorbell rang again. "I'll get it!" Sandy yelled, the afternoon moving into high gear as her cousin Della arrived, eyes about her, quick, darting.

"Where is he? Where is this fine man my cuz about to hunker down with?"

"Della, stop it. He's right over there."

Della's mouth dropped open, closed. Opened again. "Girrrl," all Della could say as she took in the man Sandy had snared.

"I know, right." Sandy turned to greet her uncle Zeke, her aunt Edna, her cousin Jasper, and his wife Bernadette. Like a train passing through a station, people flowed in one behind the other until the house was filled with faces.

Aunts, uncles, and cousins arriving, offering words like "He's so fine," "Girl, where you met him?", "His brother married?", "A fine couple you two gonna make."

Everyone there, happy, glad. Everyone except Grandma Tee. Sandy hadn't called her, but her mother had and was told, "The ride down justa bout killed me, Jeanne. Don't see how I could try and take one back."

Sandy knew why even if her mother didn't. *I'm marrying him despite her.* But she feigned ignorance when her mother asked.

Jeanne Hutchinson had known Tee a long time, knew about her funny ways, her backward thinking. Could have been anything and nothing that turned Tee away, and she wasn't going to worry about it too much. Her daughter was marrying Adrian, and that was all that mattered.

"Lawd, gal, tawt I never see dis here day."

Sandy turned, saw Rachel standing there. Hugged her hard.

"Don' you ever let my brudder outa ya sight again, ya 'earing me?"

Sandy laughed. "This time around, I'm sticking like glue."

The late afternoon turned into a mild evening, so pleasant they took chairs and went outdoors, enjoying the last of the Indian summer.

Sandy ate the last bit of her black cake, watching Adrian

converse with Winston and Junie. Her mother and Adrian's mother were getting along well, and even Mr. Burton was decent. He hadn't done much beyond nurse his stout and nod at the introductions, but that was good enough for Sandy.

Rachel nudged her. "Now ya got tree men loving ya," she said, taking in her brothers. Her eyes turned towards Cliff, who stood across the yard. "And dat brudder of yours, tell him if he wa'n ta talk to me, just come up and talk. I don't go for all dis incognito nawnsense."

So it wasn't just me. Sandy had seen the look in Cliff's eyes when she introduced him to Rachel, but she had convinced herself it was just because of Rachel's looks. Now she knew different.

"My 'brudder,' as you call him, is currently involved, and he needs to stop scoping you out."

Rachel smiled. "Well, den, in dat case, don't tell him I said a ting." She scooted forward in her chair. "Gonna go get some punch. Be back."

Feeling her absence, Sandy looked around for a connection. Found one. She leaned forward and called out to the Burton brothers, "Hey, what you guys talking about over there?" When three guilty smiles came her way, she knew. *They're talking about me.*

One minute the house was full of noise, and the next there was hardly any sound at all. Company gone, Sandy found herself cleaning up, her brother staying to help.

They had gathered up the empty cans and bottles, trashed the paper cups. Together they wiped counters and were tying up the garbage when Cliff made the ultimate confession. "All right, I'm busted."

Sandy pleaded ignorance. "Busted about what?"

"Looking, a little too hard."

"At?"

"Rachel. I know what you thinking, and I'm asking that you don't."

"Oh yeah, Cliff? What am I thinking and what is it you're asking me not to do?"

"You thinking that I'm back to my old ways, and first chance you get you gonna tell Janice all about it."

Sandy addressed the trees. "The man's a psychic."

"I'm serious, Sandy. Not like that for me anymore."

"You sure was looking ready to turn back the clock."

"All I did was introduce myself. I didn't try to rap to her, didn't try to get her number, none of that."

"So you say."

"It's the truth."

"Yeah, uh-huh."

"Was I checking her out? Yes. But when a woman's that fine, it's kind of hard not to notice."

"Well, at least you admit that much."

"Me and Janice is going along good, okay? So don't be talking up stuff that ain't happened, all right? You want to call her and tell her how I stared at Rachel, then do that, Sandy. But make sure you tell her that's all I did."

Sandy fixed him with a dare. "No, Cliff, why don't you? Show me how much of a real man you are and tell her yourself."

NINETEEN

With no hello, no "it's me," no formalities or even a slow ease, Janice came right out and asked, "Adrian's sister, Rachel . . . she seeing anybody?"

Well, I'll be, he did it. Cliff actually told. There was no doubt it had been discussed, argued, yelled about, even cursed over. No doubt Janice had wrung herself dry over it, this phone call, her question, not the easiest thing for her to do. So Sandy was careful. Played ignorant, offering and asking nothing. She'd let Janice tell it if she wanted to. "I don't really know."

There was a revving in her voice, each word sharp and cutting, dicing and slicing through the phone wire like a Ginsu. "Cliff told me he was staring at her, and I just wanted to know."

"All he did, Janice."

"Yeah, that's what he said."

"And you got to give him credit for telling you." *The little cretin, taking up my dare and coming out smelling like a rose. Even got me coming to his defense.*

"I was surprised . . . must admit, it pissed me off and I had a few choice words for him. Seeing as she's gonna be your sister-in-law, just wanted to know."

"Well, like I said, I've never seen her with nobody, but that don't mean there ain't a nobody."

"She really that fine?"

There was no sense lying; Janice would see her for herself soon enough. "Think island beauty and then some."

"Sounds gorgeous."

"She is. But she's also upfront, straightforward, and she knows Cliff's involved, so I don't think you have to worry."

"Don't want to, y'know."

"You're human. Adrian came home talking about some other woman he was staring at all night, I'd be pissed too."

"I guess you right . . . So it went well?"

"Better than I expected. You really should have come."

"Suppose to have been family, Sandy."

"Since when you stopped?"

"Oh, I'd say a couple of months ago when we weren't speaking."

It was an old painful bridge, and Sandy had no intention of treading back across it. "That don't mean nothing . . . you always gonna be my sister."

"But not your maid of honor, right?"

Sandy laughed, relieved. "Well, thank God. You had me worried."

" 'Bout what?"

"How well you took the news that I didn't change my mind. I was like, well, damn, she ain't even batting an eye. Thought maybe you didn't care about me as much as you said you did."

"You know you my heart, but it was *my* fault . . . Anyway, I couldn't do that to Martha."

"Yeah, me either. She was there for me." There was an excitement in her voice that could not be missed. "Guess what?"

"What?"

"It finally happened."

"What finally happened?"

"All of us, all four of us. We finally got a somebody in our lives."

"Me and Cliff are just friends, Sandy."

"No, you and Cliff *were* just friends. The parameters changed on that a while ago."

"Really, we're just friends."

"My brother was making eyes at another woman and he actually came back and told the woman he was with? He ain't never done no mess like that, Janice."

"We never talk about it," Janice confessed.

"What? The L word?"

"Yeah."

"But you feel it, right?"

Silence. Sandy knew her friend was thinking, debating, shoring up enough hope to say it out loud. Sandy was right there with her, mentally, *just say it,* urging her along, but then Janice bailed out. "We're just friends."

"And I'm Whitney Houston. Don't be afraid . . . what you wanted for a long time. Janice, my brother is in love and it's with you."

"I thought—" Janice hesitated. "Didn't want to rush things, make the same mistakes."

"And you're not. 'Cause if you were, Cliff would have hit and run by now. But he hasn't. It's love, Janice, and it's yours."

"You think?"

"I know. There's a whole bunch of women who want what you got, but you want to know the really sweet thing?"

"What?"

Sandy's voice was soft, poignant. "Only person Cliff wants is you."

The house on 132nd Avenue boomed with the sound of music, laughter, voices, and dancing feet. The Christmas lights twinkled to the beat, and happy sweaty faces filled the living room.

A week after Thanksgiving Britney had had no idea where Maurice was taking her, only that they were "going for a ride." They had gotten in his car and driven through the streets of Jamaica, New York, until he pulled in front of a Cape Cod home.

He had cut the motor, reached into his dash, and extracted a set of keys. "Merry Christmas, baby," he said, depositing them into her hands.

When Britney finally made the connection between the

drive, the keys, and the house, she had let out a howl, thrown open the door of Maurice's town car, and raced up the drive to the front door.

Looking around, taking in the block with the brown lawns, the empty boughs of the trees, she knew come spring it would be an oasis of green. Nervously she had inserted the key into the front door and pushed it open. Stood taking in the dining area, the sitting room, the living room, and the stairs. In ectasy she had peeked in the kitchen, the bath, and the two bedrooms on the first floor.

Ran up the staircase and discovered two more bedrooms with a bathroom between. Down into the basement she had ventured, Maurice catching up as she made her descent. The finished basement with blond wood paneling and carpeted floors made her weep.

It was not a new house but it was *her* house, and after weeks of painters, wall paperers, and moving men, the house was officially opened, and her closest friends and the men who loved them had all come to celebrate.

Maurice stood in the middle of his living room, a beer in one hand and Britney caught up in the other. " 'Cause I love her," he repeated for the third time that evening. "I got her this house because I love her, I adore her, and she deserves the best."

Her friends were as stunned as Britney had been. Men bought you jewelry, gave you flowers, took you on trips. But Maurice had surpassed all that and bought his future wife a home. It was like pulling down the moon, incomprehensible, but Maurice had done it with no regrets.

"Hey, Mo!" Martha called, her derriere perched on Calvin's lap. "You got four bedrooms—does that mean four kids or what?"

"Hell no. We talking tribe, woman. Dozens of little Maurices and Britneys just a-running around the place." He indicated Britney. "In fact, might be a bun a-cookin' in there as we speak."

Britney blushed, looked away. Maurice was breaking his

promise to keep it secret until she knew for sure. Just three days late, all they had was the hope. She'd planned to take a test in two weeks, then tell, but Maurice's personal joy had changed that plan.

If she was, she was. Only problem she foresaw was that her wedding was still four months away and her belly would be full and round by the time she walked down the aisle.

Martha left the confines of Calvin's thighs and planted herself firmly in front of Britney. "You didn't tell me. You never even mentioned you were planning one."

"Yeah," Sandy added, feeling the mixed emotions of sadness and joy. She and Adrian were years aways from such a moment.

"So what's the deal, Miss Thing," Janice said with a smile. "How far along are you?"

Britney raised her eyebrows. She hesitated. Knew that three days late didn't even qualify, but told the truth anyway. "I'm just three days late, that's all."

Martha screwed her face up. "Three days? Oh hell, girl, that could be anything from stress to the waning of the moon."

"I know that, Martha. That's why I didn't call you."

"My bag," Martha said, stepping back like tacks were in her shoes.

"Well, I'm just going make it so," Janice decided, waving her hands over Britney's stomach. "Poof! You are pregnant." Bringing laughter. " 'Cause nobody's getting any younger, and shucks, we need some babies up in here," she said with real attitude. "I'm ready to be an auntie."

"How 'bout a mother?"

Seven heads turned towards the sofa, towards the cool and collected Clifford Hutchinson. Three sets of eyes blinked. Two mouths fell open.

Sandy pivoted on her heel, looked at Janice hard. "What he say?"

"I know he didn't say that," Martha suggested, unsure herself.

Janice heard Cliff speak it but couldn't believe it. "Did you say something about being a mother?" She wanted to make sure she wasn't hearing things. Because if that was what he'd said, and she was 99 percent sure he had, everything was about to change forever.

Everything. What she thought—*he doesn't really love me.* How she felt—*we're just friends.* Everything. No more lying, no more denying, it was going to be out there for all the world to see. And even though it was scaring her—*he can't be serious*—more so it was infusing her with love, hope, and the possibility of a real ever-after.

"Yeah, I said it. Now are you going to answer my question?"

The whole room grew silent. Adrian, at the turntable, lowered the music. It was one of those moments when sparks could fly or something deep gets explored. He knew enough to keep any distraction to a minimum.

"No, you answer mine first."

"Ah, sukie, sukie," Martha murmured, barely breathing, waiting for the conclusion of this unplanned confrontation.

"What's your question?" Cliff asked.

Her first response—*don't even ask it, not here, in front of everybody, because he could be joking, then you're going to look like a real fool*—was abandoned as she felt something stirring, mixing up between them.

"Well, Mr. Hutchinson," Janice began, "in order for me to answer that question I would first have to know your intentions in both the making and raising of a child."

Sandy laughed. Martha grinned. Britney silently applauded Janice's stance.

Cliff rose from the sofa. "In order to fully disclose my plan of having said child, I would have to determine your availability to be both a mother and a lover."

Janice's head cranked back. Her finger waggled. "Oh no, no, no, Mr. Hutchinson. See, I cannot be a mother unless

I am a spouse." He started to say something, but Janice cut him off. "And I will not consign myself to being just any kind of spouse. I demand that any husband with whom I engage with for the rest of my life commit to loving me, honoring me, protecting me, worshiping me—"

"You tell him, sister, drop that science on the brother," Calvin tossed out.

"Be faithful to me *and* only me until death, his or mine, do us part. If said husband cannot, has any doubt, any objections, any reflections, any dejections, corrections, selections, or other digressions, then I, Miss Janice, will have to say no, I am not ready to be a mother."

Sandy and Martha slapped five. Britney grinned. Maurice whistled.

It was all over his face: Janice had Cliff cornered. He rubbed his chin, as if deep in thought. Glanced about the room, aware of the silence. Took a deep breath. Probably the deepest breath of his life, Janice thought. "Then I, Clifford Samuel Hutchinson, will have to say to that, Mizz Janice, point well taken. And I will futher consider this matter and let you know my final decision."

A chorus of seven voices shouted, "When?"

Cliff jumped back, startled. "Damn." Recovered. "December thirty-first, thirty seconds from midnight, when else?" He clapped his hands together. Looked at Adrian. "Yo, A., where the music, man? Put on something slow for me." He extended his arms towards Janice. "And my lady."

"Something, huh?" Sandy was saying as Adrian took Rockaway Boulevard fifteen miles faster than the speed limit.

"Oh, yeah." He took his eyes off the road. "You okay?"

The lie came easily. "I'm okay."

"I'm sorry, Sandy."

" 'Bout what?"

"Having kids."

She swallowed, looked out the window. She had done her best to mask her disappointment, but she must not have succeeded. If Adrian had picked up on it, no doubt everyone else had.

She wanted to say "It's all right," but feeling Maurice's joy, Janice's anticipation, the whole excitement that had raced around the room, made her needy for such a moment.

"Children aren't everything," Sandy found herself saying. "And seven years is not a lifetime," she decided, turning towards him for the first time. Her voice grew cocky. "Besides, while Britney's changing diapers and Maurice is getting up for three o'clock feedings, it'll just be me and you . . . our time for ourselves."

But that was not compensation enough. Adrian would go a thousand sleepless nights for the gift of just one baby. *For one sweet, good-smelling bundle of joy.* Knew Sandy would too. But she was reaching out for a silver lining, and he would not hinder her efforts.

"You're right," he declared, taking her hand and kissing it. "Our time . . . just me and you."

The Christmas holiday arrived as it always did—blink and before you knew it, it was New Year's Eve. For a whole week Janice's friends had been burning up the wires about the arrival of this day. Now that it was here, the anticipation had turned into something else.

Worry.

Loving, confident, assuring, Cliff had left Britney and Maurice's house on a high, happy note. Burning to ask in the privacy of his car, wanting nothing more than to grill him about the unbelievable conversation they had had in front of everybody, Janice made herself be quiet.

"Not far," Cliff had told her as he stopped at a red light.

"What's not far?"

"December thirty-first, thirty seconds to midnight."

She had gazed into his eyes, trying to ferret out the truth. Had been surprised—*he's serious*—by what lay within. She had felt all sorts of things in that moment—relief, confusion, fear—but she wangled herself out of the bad and hesitantly stepped into the good.

Christmas Day had been as good as it got, and while there had been no ring under the tree for her, there had been everything she'd asked for on her Christmas list, down to the book light that allowed her to read while he slept.

A week later, when the thirty-first arrived, Janice hadn't thought much when Cliff said he was dropping by his parents' house for a few hours. "It is the last day of the year, just want to see my folks." He had promised he'd be back to her place no later than eight. "Not leaving till eleven. Gives me plenty of time to get dressed."

She had believed him, had spent the week and a half since Britney's party looking for that change of heart, the slightest reservation, but he had been the same wonderful Cliff he'd always been. Everything had gone on fine, until now, as the clock flipped to 8:37 P.M.

Going more on gut instinct than fact, Janice went to the phone and called Cliff's parents' house. Yes, he had been there, but he had left two hours ago. No, hadn't said where he was headed.

A dozen explanations danced through Janice's head. *Off to pick up my ring, getting me something special,* but none of them stuck to her like the one thing she didn't want to consider.

He's changed his mind.

She had worked on this scenario a thousand times. Had decided that she would allow him that and not hold it against him. Janice had decided if he wanted to take back the grand display he had provided at Britney's house, it was his right to do so. That she would not cling to someone who did not want her—*not anymore; those days are over.*

Janice had convinced herself that she would allow Cliff out of her life the same way she had let him in—with finesse. It would hurt, sure, but she had survived worse, and she wouldn't make a fool of herself over him.

These were the solutions she had decided on, the

backup, the get-through-this, if the worst of her fears were realized. But now, as the clock clicked to 8:39, her gut was full of acid and her head was in turmoil.

He's not coming.

She swallowed this bit of news and didn't hold back her tears. A real loss, she allowed herself to mourn its passage. She picked up the phone but just as quickly put it down. Would not call on the support of her friends. *This one I have to do alone.*

To say that she loved Cliff was an understatement. In these last few weeks she had come to adore him. After so many years of bad relationships, he had shown her how wonderful it could get.

He was funny, smart, fine, sexy, kind, and understood her. He was honest, told her things he had never shared with anyone. They had something special—*rare,* isn't that what Sandy called it? And if that magic no longer existed for him, Janice knew she did not have the power to bring it back.

He had come into her life and shown her her worth. Had done what no man had ever done before. The idea that it would all go away was a knife in her heart, but Janice was determined to adjust to the pain. She had come a long way, and the struggle had been too hard to turn back now.

More than New Year's Eve at Le Club, more than four friends coming together to celebrate the end of one year and all the hopes and promises of the next, more than champagne and wall-to-wall people, and a deejay who was mixing music like it was all he knew, tonight was about Cliff giving Janice a final answer.

It had been hard to put on her dress, fix her hair, apply makeup, and put on perfume. Harder still to slip on her coat, get her keys, get into her car, and drive the four miles to Merrick Boulevard. But in that moment it was more important to be there and face the crisis head on. Not hide at home hoping it would all go away.

"Smile, please," Adrian instructed, leaning his head towards hers, catching her eye. Her feet were moving, her arms were waving, and the music was pumping, but there was little enthusiasm.

"Not the end of the world," Adrian said, stopping his dancing and taking her hand. "Come on, looks like you need a drink."

There were no seats at the outer bar, but a café table became available. Adrian pulled out a chair for Janice, asked what she wanted, and returned three minutes later with their drinks.

He sat across from her, feeling much like the older brother he had been all his life. It could have been Rachel sitting before him, eyes dour, heartbroken, as he took up her hands.

"Hey," he said softly, "him not being here could be a whole lot of something or a whole lot of nothing, you understanding me?"

Janice shook her head. She didn't understand. Needed to but didn't know how.

"Look, I haven't known Cliff long." At the sound of his name she drew her eyebrows together. "But even Sandy's told me what you have done for him. Wherever he's at, whatever else the hell he's doing right now in this moment, he has only one thought and it's you."

Janice looked up, surprised, felt the truth in Adrian's revelation. Knew he was absolutely right. As she sat there sad and brokenhearted, wherever Cliff was, he was thinking of her and the promise he had broken.

"My guess is he got scared."

"Scared?" It was the first word Janice had managed.

"Yeah, scared. Y'know, sometimes the very thing you need is the very thing you'll run from. Women have the capacity to dish out love like breathing. Makes some men frightened, starts them doubting, do dumb stuff like not showing up tonight."

"But why? Why would he be scared? Of me?"

Adrian sighed, collected his thoughts. "A woman, if she feels like crying, well, she's gonna throw back her head, open her mouth, and just sob. She feels like laughing, she gonna laugh. Men?" Adrian shook his head. "Men weigh all the angles, think of all the consequences before they even fart."

"But you're not like that."

Adrian smiled. "Not like that now, but I was. Just holding back, holding tight, scared to open up . . . my heart, my emotions, everything. Then I met Sandy." His eyes drifted. "And for the first time in a long time I allowed myself to feel. The rest is history."

He watched her, waiting to see if any of his words were sinking in. He could see her thinking, sensed the little wheels in her head churning, went on. "So all I'm saying, Janice, is there's a good chance Cliff hasn't changed his mind, just got scared. The fact that he approached the subject of marriage at all in front of all of us says a whole lot. Not many men would . . . hell, I know I wouldn't."

"So when does he stop being scared?" Janice needed to know.

Those golden eyes looked deep inside her. "When he realizes that his world is a sweeter place with you in it."

She was supposed to go, but no one could make her. Not even Sandy. A day ago it would have been unheard of, turning down a New Year's Day dinner at Cliff's parents' house. But the whole world had changed overnight, and Janice could not see herself being there.

"For what? What's the point?" she asked Sandy over the phone. "Not like I'm gonna be their daughter-in-law."

Sandy understood her point, but felt there was a bigger point to prove. It was important for Janice to show Cliff that her life had not stopped because of his no-show. He was expected at her parents' for the New Year's Eve feast, and Sandy was hungry for a showdown.

He had stood up her best friend and there was no excusing that. None. If he hadn't been serious about marriage, he should have just kept his mouth shut. Pissed, Sandy wanted revenge.

"But he'll be there."

"Who?" Janice asked.

"Cliff. It's your chance to curse him out, tell him off."

Janice sighed, wearied by the whole thing. "As much as I want to do just that, I'm not, Sandy. Because the simple truth is he does not want to marry me. If he did, he would have showed."

It was the first time Sandy longed for the old Janice.

"So how you doing?" was Martha's question, the four of them holed up in Janice's apartment, sitting shiva for the recent arrival of bad news.

Janice smiled. "Better than I thought."

"You sure? I mean, you loved Cliff like forever."

"No, Martha, I *longed* for Cliff like forever. Didn't really know him, love him, till recently."

Britney considered her with proud eyes. "You're handling it well. Because I think I would have tracked him down, cut his tires or something." Gave in to the looks of disbelief. "Okay, maybe not cut his tires, but at least try to see him face to face."

"Which definitely shows how much you've grown," Martha added.

The phone rang. All eyes turned toward the sound. Janice got up, went to answer. She was gone a long time.

TWENTY

Adrian said Cliff had gotten scared. Janice decided he didn't want to marry her. No matter how she sliced it, it still came up bitter pie.

When she had first agreed to see him, talk things out, Janice had been optimistic that Cliff would provide her with something she could grasp, keep, hold on to long after she told him good-bye. Thought maybe hearing it from his mouth would soothe the wounds, heal the hurt, allow her no regrets. But twenty minutes after his arrival he still hadn't given her anything she could use, just his plea that he did want to marry her.

"But you didn't show, which means you didn't," she insisted a final time.

She looked away from him, gathering bits of her back from him, readying herself for departure, the quiet leaving from his soul. There were some things she did not know, but a few that she did like. She could not stay with him if she wanted to, and a part of her wanted just that.

Just close my eyes, forgive him. Close my eyes and open my heart back up. Tell him it's okay, I understand. We can still be. But that was the old Janice trying to emerge, not the one who knew better.

She laughed, a tiny thing that escaped her lips, faded from the room. "You know I'm going to say something that you probably won't understand and I know I'll regret. But after I say it, just take me in the back and shoot me to put me out of my misery. We need to call it a day."

"Just like that?" Cliff wanted to know.

"Yeah, Cliff, just like that. We had something special but you've taken that specialness away. Now we got nothing. And I'm not settling for nothing."

"I asked you to marry me."

"You most certainly did. But if you really wanted to, you would have shown up like you promised."

A weighty silence filled the room. Truth was truth, and there was no hiding from it. He looked up at her. "So we're done?"

Her heart broke a little. Her words, wrinkled and rough-dried, arrived. "Yeah, we are."

Britney's wedding was pushed up.

"Can't wait till April," she explained. "I'm only a month and I already gained five pounds. I wait any longer, my dress won't fit."

On February second, Britney and Maurice said "I do."

Sandy was the next bride up.

August 12 dawned bright and sunny. Birds sang in the early morning breeze, sunlight dappled through the trees, people packed cars and lunches and headed for the beaches of Long Island Sound. In Flushing, Sandy lay listening to the world outside, studying the smudge on Adrian's neck.

The smudge had had her attention for over a week now. She thought it had been a hickey given in the heat of their passion, but the discoloration had not faded. If anything it had grown in its darkness, marring the otherwise butter-scotch skin.

Adrian had a doctor's appointment on Tuesday, the mark causing concern, cutting into the six months between checkups. Could be nothing, could be something. The only thing they knew for certain was that their wedding was six weeks away.

The days dragged their feet, and by Wednesday evening Sandy was anxious and disagreeable. She and Adrian began fighting over things that had never mattered before. A sock on the floor, a glass in the sink. Where to eat, what to eat. When to eat.

By Thursday morning, their fear rode their faces like

masks of clay, the joy lost, the love hard-pressed to be found. They had not talked about "what if," but it rode every word they spoke, every motion their bodies made.

On Friday Adrian's doctor called. He wanted Adrian to take another test. Just to be sure. But Sandy and Adrian both knew that the results would be no different.

Adrian was HIV-positive.

I wish I was a willow . . . Me too, Sandy thought, as Phoebe Snow filled the air, jettisoned her back to her and Adrian's beginning. Sandy understood now so perfectly, it was as if she had written "Harpo's Blues" herself.

A hundred wishes. *How many could come true?*

Tears streamed down her face, sprinkling Adrian's cheek, the tip of his nose. Adrian looked up from her lap. "It's okay Sandy."

But God, it wasn't. It was so not okay that Sandy wanted to scream, throw things. Wanted to curse God and Gennifer and everything in between. Her hands rushed to her face, catching tears, her moans, the pain that etched itself down her spine.

"Don't, baby, don't."

How could he ask her not to? How could he be so calm and so certain that in the end everything would be fine, when it wouldn't be? No babies, no skin to skin. Illness, death, and Adrian *poof*, gone.

Sandy looked down at the man who had everything she wanted. The person who had brought her so much joy. She took in the butterscotch face, the eyes of melting gold. How could God be so unfair?

"You're so fine," Adrian muttered, his fingers against her skin, tears on her ebony face like drops of silver.

"So are you," Sandy whispered, her heart breaking. "So are you."

It was hard facing the new reality. Hard to swallow, digest, and adjust to what life had become. Where once serenity reigned now laid confusion and chaos, full of dire questions for which there were no real answers.

Whom do we tell? Do we tell? Do we still do this? How long will you live? What is safe, what is not? Can our skin touch at all? Can we drink from the same glass? Do we kiss dry-mouth?

Her life became full of morbid thoughts: Where do I bury him? Next to Gennifer? How will I live when he's gone? Will he linger or go quickly? Do we have six months or ten years? Will a cure be found in time? How much at risk am I? Will I die too? How can I live without him? How can I live with him?

In those first twenty-four hours after the call from the doctor, Sandy found herself slipping into bouts of denial. *It can't be. It just can't be.* Moments coming where she implored God to give her a miracle. *Please, God, don't make it real.*

But when Adrian came home from the doctor, vials of medicine clattering in the white pharmacy bag; when he lined up the three bottles in his medicine cabinet and slammed the door hard; when Sandy went in after him to read the labels and saw the initials *AZT,* she knew.

It was as real as it got.

Sandy walked.

She wasn't sure how far she'd go, where she was headed or anything. All she knew was when she left work the last thing she wanted was to board a crowded subway. Realized that she needed air, light, and space, a place to put her burden, if only for a little while.

She was dancing in a twilight zone where nothing was the same, familiar, or absolute. She felt as if the last few months of her life had been a beautiful dream and she had just awakened to a terrifying reality.

She longed for the ignorance of those days, the sublime indifference and unconcern she had dwelled in. She wanted to channel away her fears, do away with her distress. *I want God to take it back.*

Her feet took her, her destination not exact. She found herself slipping down to the riverbank under the Brooklyn Bridge, drawn to the rough, choppy waters of the East River.

She leaned against the rail, stared across the swells, Brooklyn smokestacks and warehouses filling her vision. She wasn't certain when the first tear came. Didn't even realize she was crying until a homeless man, old enough to be her grandfather, stopped and cautiously asked if she was all right.

Sandy blinked, surprised by the stranger and the extent of his concern. *He doesn't know me,* aware only then of the wetness on her cheek. She shook her head, looked away.

There was only one thing she wanted, just one thing she needed: for Adrian to be all right. *All I want, God,* her eyes pleaded to the open sky, *all I need. I need you to fix it, make it better. I need you to make a cure, heal my Adrian, give me that life I've always wanted. Can you do that for me?*

A seagull flew into her line of vision, its gray and white wings painting the sky. It released one long, mournful cry. Death, she was certain, her heart beating fast.

But You have the power, You can perform the miracle. You can make Adrian well again, keep him here with me. All my life, I've waited all my life for him. Please don't take him away from me. Please don't take him away.

She stood there, tears streaming down her face, begging a God she had never seen but had believed in all her life. It seemed forever before she got a response, an answer to her plea. *He's already taken,* echoing deep down in her soul.

"You okay?"

It was the second time Janice had asked her since they

had begun their outing. Sandy wished she would stop. "I told you, I'm fine." But she wasn't. Didn't want to be on Jamaica Avenue, fighting Saturday shoppers in search of that bargain.

Sandy did not want to go into Gi-Gi's and find cutesy baby things for Britney's baby shower. She wanted to go home and get into bed and never come out, but there was a front she had to keep up, no matter how difficult or how demanding. Had to pretend all was right with the world.

"What do you think?" Janice asked, holding up a tiny sailor suit, complete with a matching white hat.

"Cute if you know it's definitely going to be a boy." Sandy's voice was edgy. "But we don't know that, do we?"

"Well, damn, Sandy."

Sandy's eyes rolled. Too agitated to apologize, she simply walked away. Being in the baby department was chafing her to the bone. She looked around in disgust, her eyes cutting and full of loathing. *Baby stuff. I'm never gonna need this crap. Not a stroller, a car seat, sleepers. Not any of it.*

There was no more hope on her horizon, no more brass rings to reach for. Yes, she and Adrian were going to walk down that aisle, but that would be as far as their dream would go.

Even if he lives long enough, I can't have his baby. Can't do what fat, simpleminded Britney's doing.

Sandy did not try to ease the jealousy she was feeling. Instead she opened herself up to it. She was angry, felt cheated, had been denied. Bitter with a capital *B*. She didn't want to be bothered, didn't want to buy baby gifts, go to a stupid baby shower, nothing.

She wanted to scream.

Wanted to stand there in the baby department of Gi-Gi's on Jamaica Avenue on a Saturday afternoon and open her mouth and howl. But she caught Janice watching her, concern and worry deep on her face. Pulled back from the edge.

Sandy blinked. Blinked again. Got herself grounded, shifted the pain. She swallowed back the bitterness, forced the envy out of her heart. Looked up at Janice, apology on her face.

The need to tell it right there, to fall to the smooth, polished tile floor and spill her guts was inside every breath she took. But telling would not change anything, would just make it worse, so Sandy kept it to herself.

Big.

Britney was all belly and a good helping of nose, one seemingly trying to outdo the other.

The sight of her, a beached whale in white linen, was such a surprise that Sandy's mouth fell open.

"Close your mouth, girl," Britney demanded, bringing Sandy into an embrace, the massive belly getting in the way. She pulled back. Sandy took in her face, the nose that seemed to be trying to reach Britney's ears on both sides. "Yeah, I know. You should see my belly. It turned three shades darker."

"Sorry I'm late," Sandy offered a feeble excuse even to her own ears. She had no reason for not arriving on time. *Just couldn't get myself out the door.*

It was hard to be happy, hard to feel any joy. Sandy's world was tied up in a million knots. Felt it would take a lifetime to undo them. A prisoner of her mind, a prisoner of her heart, she was drowning in a whirlwind of helplessness, and no one could help.

Britney considered her wisely. "Don't matter that you're late, only that you're here."

Britney's mother came up to her, a straight pin in one hand, a boutonniere made up of tiny pink and blue watering cans in the other. "Thought you weren't going to make it," Mrs. Weller said.

Sandy took in Britney's mother and thought what she always thought. *Mrs. Weller just spit Britney out.* They were the same right down to the heavy eyebrows and the

round, high haunches. No hint of her father anywhere. Britney was every bit her mother's child. "Well, go on in.
Everybody's there."

The living room was full of crepe paper, hanging paper
storks, and pink and blue balloons. A high-back white
wicker chair was adorned along the edges with silk flowers.
A banner nearly fifteen feet long was strung across the ceiling, the words BRITNEY'S BABY SHOWER running end to
end in big, glowing silver letters.

There were the faces she knew—Martha, Janice, a
cousin—but just as many faces she didn't know, white
ones, beige ones, a woman of Asian extraction. Coworkers,
Sandy realized, adding her gift to the pile, wedging herself
on the floor between Martha and Janice.

Martha leaned in to her. "Girl, I thought you was gonna
miss Mr. Lickety Split," a stripper well known in the bor-
ough.

Sandy looked surprised. "That's who her mother got?"

"Yeah, honey," Martha whispered. "I called her to give
her some suggestions, and she told me she already had one
picked. Always knew Brit's mom was a freak," she said
with a sly grin, which brought the first real smile Sandy
had felt in a while.

"You missed the introduction game, the name game, and
some other game we had to play. We were just getting
ourselves settled for the real action," Martha went on, as
Britney came back into the living room and eased herself
into the chair. "Hope she don't go into labor before he starts
'cause I swear she looks 'bout ready to deliver."

Adrian looked at the clock. It was after ten. It was late,
later than the time Sandy said she'd be home. An hour and
twenty minutes later, to be exact.

He lay in the bed, aching, nauseous, and stared at the
ceiling. The drugs had debilitated him, bed his refuge these
last few days.

He was dying. No longer had any doubt. It might not

be tomorrow, or even next week, but that future he and Sandy had struggled for no longer existed.

His throat was raw from vomiting. Every muscle, every bone he owned ached. Eating was nearly nonexistent. Going to the bathroom alone, a difficult feat.

It was hard to believe he was only thirty-seven years old. Hard to believe that a month ago he could jog seven miles, cook, go to work, drive a car. *Bathe my damn self.*

But that life, hanging like a picture on the wall, was just a memory. He could see it but he could never live it again. Moments came when he wànted to give up, but Adrian struggled against it.

He did not want to die.

Didn't want to be bedridden, didn't want to be sick. Didn't want to leave Sandy, didn't want Sandy to leave him. But as he waited for her return, he couldn't help but wonder how much longer she could go on like this. Tending to him. Helping him to the bathroom and cleaning him up when he didn't quite reach it. How much longer could she go on being nursemaid to an invalid, brave-faced and determinedly so?

This was not the life he wanted, was not a future he ever foresaw. Even after Gen had tested positive, he never thought he would become incapacitated, but here he lay, not quite forty, with death dancing in the wings.

Adrian wondered what death would feel like, if Gen would meet him on the other side. Would she say sorry? Would his heart in the hereafter be able to forgive what she had done to him? Because he hated her every time he was too weak to eat, too weak to make it to the bathroom. Hated her every time he looked in his bathroom mirror and saw his gaunt face looking back at him.

Was the dick worth this? he wanted to scream at her. *Was it the best damn fucking fuck of your life? Do you see me now, what you've done to me, to Sandy? Has God forgiven you? Because I don't think I can.*

Such moments would leave him weak, physically and

mentally. Adrian tried not to succumb to them, but being bedridden and immobile gave him nothing but thinking time. Some days he thought so much he thought his brain was going to explode, fear and loathing just running rampant through him.

He looked at the clock. 10:29.

Sandy told him she'd be home by nine, but it was less than one minute till 10:30. His heart ached anew. *Come on, Sandy. Come on.*

The clock slipped to 10:30. The sound of keys in the door echoed from up the hall. Relief washed over him, his heart hammering in his chest. Adrian attempted to sit up, couldn't.

"Sandy?" he called out, desperation raw in his voice. It hurt to speak, hurt to swallow, but he called out again. "Sandy?" needing to hear her reply.

"Yeah."

He waited for her to close the door and lock it. Waited for her footfalls coming down the hall. His whole world stopped as he waited, and then suddenly she was standing there before him.

Her eyes danced across his, taking in the room that had become his home for the last week. Adrian was aware of his state, the sweat dappling his forehead, the day-old beard. He was aware of the smell in the room, the bucket of vomit beside him, the pajamas he had soiled.

He swallowed, the motion making him wince. Weak, tired, scared, he sought her eyes, needing so much and not feeling worthy of any of it.

He saw her as she saw him, knew it was a lot to stomach. In that moment he wasn't certain if she could go ahead with the wedding, and the need to know grew strong. "You still want to marry me?"

She could see the tears in his eyes. He looked pale and old and very tired. It was not the Adrian she had fallen for, but he was still the man she loved.

"Of course I do," she managed, making herself look at him.

"Are you sure?" his question twisted her gut. She did not want to answer now, Adrian so sickly and gray. *Ask me when you're feeling better, when death isn't everywhere I look.*

Her voice was tight but she answered, "I'm sure," knowing the reason for his dismay.

She had taken the long way home. Leaving Britney's baby shower, Sandy had started off for Adrian's apartment as promised, but when she came to Kissena Boulevard, she just kept going. Driving deep into Flushing until she found herself at Flushing Bay, she sat there, head in her hands, sobbing for a very long time.

It was never about choice, never about not marrying him. It was about shifting aside the gloomy present to allow herself to go on another day.

It was about the hopes and dreams they had nurtured together and holding on to them tightly even as they slipped from their fingers. It was moving beyond the here and now and being strong against tomorrow. Was about a lot of things, but not once had it been about leaving.

"I don't have the right to hold you to this. You can change your mind," he said softly.

She longed to touch him, hold him, but his skin was sweaty. Fevers had started coming on him like hot rain. Side effect, the doctor told her.

She forced a smile. "Don't you know I've been waiting"—her voice broke—"all my life for you? No way am I going to let you go."

Adrian turned, suddenly heaving, missing the towel by his head. She could smell feces and knew the sheets had to be changed again, knew that she would have to wear gloves and put the linens into a plastic bag and take them to the laundry, using hot water and a lot of bleach.

Her heart pumped tears as the reality of the situation

found her. Three weeks ago Adrian was fine and fit and well. How would it be a year from now?

"Want some water?" Sandy asked, glancing at the bucket of vomit on the floor by the bed.

"No, don't think I can keep it down . . . damn AZT."

The side effects had started slowly, Adrian feeling a little dizzy and not very hungry. By the end of the first week, he was down to Nutriment and baby juice. He had dropped five pounds without trying. Work was off, but Adrian had a lot of sick time for the moment. It had only been three weeks since the diagnosis, but their wedding was three weeks away.

Sandy didn't see how he'd make it.

She'd moved in to look after him, sleeping on the couch, ears perked for his calling her. They had taken more tests and discovered that Adrian had a strain of HIV that went undetected in normal analysis. He had no idea how long he'd been positive. Neither did Sandy.

The thought scared her, everything scared her. When he kissed her neck, it scared her. When he coughed, it scared her. When he put his used dishes in the sink, it scared her. When he lay covered in sweat, it scared her.

When he talked of dying, the dreams he'd been having about Gennifer, how bad he felt, how much he loved her, her whole world just grew scary.

These days Sandy was absolutely petrified, but nobody knew it but her.

"Girl, where you been?"

Sandy clutched the receiver tightly to her ear. "Adrian's."

"Been trying to reach you for two days."

"Yeah, you know."

"Everything okay, Sandy?"

"Everything fine, Martha."

"Well, you wasn't looking too fine the last time I saw you."

Sandy forced a chuckle, but tears found her. "Just tired, running around for this wedding."

"Sandy, are you crying?"

"No, I ain't crying."

"So how come I hear tears in your voice?"

"I told you, Martha, I'm not crying."

"What is it, Sandy?"

They had agreed to keep it to themselves, but she knew it was just a matter of time before she broke that promise.

"Adrian's sick."

They met at the Forest Hills Diner, Sandy picking over a salad, Martha digging into her medium-rare burger.

"You think it's the medicine, or just . . . you know?"

"I'm hoping it's just the combination of drugs working in him. I swear, Martha, I don't know what to do."

"You love him, I know that, Sandy. But have you thought about the future?"

Sandy's eyes were steely. "Every fucking day of my life."

"What about the other part?"

"What other part?"

"You know, body fluids and stuff."

"You talking sex, Martha?" Sandy said indignantly.

"Yeah, I'm talking sex and kissing and everything in between. No sense in both of you dying."

Sandy wanted to smack her. She didn't realize it until she felt her nails digging into the palm of her hand. Her voice lunged at Martha like a steamroller. "Nobody's dying, all right, Martha! No fucking body!"

Sandy sat back, spent and trembling, ignoring heads turned her away, the tears that rushed down her face, and mostly the tears that glistened back from Martha's own.

The television was on, but every single light was out. Adrian sat on the couch, an empty teacup on the coffee table. His head was back, sounds coming out of his mouth.

Laughter.

Sandy stood, confused and not knowing why. Watched his head again and heard the sound: laughing. Adrian sitting up, drinking tea, watching TV, laughing.

Sandy rushed to him, her eyes a searchlight hunting out beads of sweat on his forehead and in his scalp. But his skin looked smooth and dry. She reached out, touched it, found it cool to the touch.

"Hey," he said, reaching up and touching her arm. "Wondering when you was coming back. I'm so hungry I could eat two horses." His face was sort of gaunt, but Sandy could see life pulsing beneath the skin, in the sparkle of his eyes.

"You feeling better?" she asked.

"Yeah. Woke up, felt thirsty, and smelled real bad. Got up, took a shower, made some tea. Turned on the TV. Now I'm hungry," he said with a smile.

"You want something? Just tell me what you want," Sandy said, dropping her bag on the sofa.

"I'll start with some soup, then maybe have some of that meat loaf and macaroni and cheese from the other night. And if I have room, I'd love some Rocky Road ice cream." Sandy couldn't get to the kitchen fast enough.

But hopes sometimes die quickly.

Adrian was on the second spoonful of soup when he raced to the bathroom and slammed the door. His retching tore her heart like a knife.

He didn't want to go back to the doctor. A part of Sandy knew why. Just giving up, just giving in seemed the easiest solution. But Sandy was not giving him that option, and they went together.

Dr. Mathias was an internist, and the intricacies of AIDS were not his specialty. He recommended a specialist, and they drove out to Massapequa to see her. She did a complete exam and changed his prescription.

"Sometimes the doses are too high," Dr. Rowen explained to them both. And then she asked Adrian to wait outside. "Just want to have a few words with your fiancée."

Adrian nodded and left the room.

"Must be hard," Dr. Rowen began.

"It is."

"I understand that you're negative."

Sandy nodded.

"When was the last time you were tested?"

Sandy watched the raised eyebrow carefully. "A month ago."

"Did they do specific testing?"

"I don't understand your question."

"Like for Adrian. Did they test you for specific strains?"

Her vision dimmed. She faltered, her mouth moving, but no sounds came out.

"Then they probably didn't. It's not uncommon. I could do it here, now, if you like. Have the results back in three days."

Sandy shook her head. "No, I'm fine."

The hand on her wrist was firm. "We're all fine until we test positive."

Sandy pulled her hand away. "I'm fine. We use condoms, never had unprotected sex, not into anything kinky. Don't do drugs, don't sleep around. I'm not the one with lesions on me. I don't have fevers and chills and can't eat." Sandy was so close to hysterics spots appeared before her eyes.

"You love him?" Dr. Rowen asked.

What the fuck you think? "Of course I do."

"Then do it for him. If you can't do it for yourself, do it for him."

It took a while for the anger to leave her, a while to accept the validity of that suggestion. Defensiveness left in one long sigh. Then Sandy nodded, and Dr. Rowen prepared the vials.

She watched the test tubes of blood leave the office, wondered what answers, what secrets hid within. "Here are some support groups in your area," Dr. Rowen said, handing Sandy the brochures. "I'm not suggesting that you need it, but in case it ever gets too hard or you're feeling overwhelmed, well, you'll know."

But Sandy didn't want them. She stood and walked out of the doctor's office. Could not look at Adrian, could not even risk a glance his way, because in that second, she absolutely hated him, deeply and without compromise.

Her test came back negative, and the new prescriptions landed Adrian back on his feet. One week before the wedding he had gained his weight back, was eating like his old self, and was back to work.

"Then the organist will start the wedding march," Georgette, her wedding coordinator, was saying, "and Sandy, you'll come down the aisle . . ." Sandy went to step, but Georgette's arms fluttered about her. "No, no, you can't walk down the aisle now. It's bad luck."

Sandy started laughing. Hysterical wild laughter that shook her shoulders and juggled her breasts. They all turned and stared at her—her parents, Janice and Martha, Adrian, his mother and father, Cliff, Junie, Winston. All eyes were on her as the laughter turned to anguish, as moans replaced the joy, as Sandy fell to her knees and whimpered, the eight-foot stained-glass Black Jesus looking down at her with lifeless eyes.

The women rushed to her, took her outside of the sanctuary, leaving the men, nervous and confused, to tend to themselves.

"Nerves," Adrian said apologetically. His eyes locked with his father's, gold circles of fire and ice that seared Adrian's soul.

September 21 arrived chilly and gray, rain falling somberly. An omen, Sandy was certain as she rolled out of her old bed and planted her feet on the chilly floor. She glanced at the clock—not quite seven—and knew she could not go back to sleep.

Putting on her robe, her wedding gown hanging on the door like a headless white ghost, she went out into the hall and towards the bathroom.

She heard her father snore.

She paused outside her parents' bedroom, envying them the full life they had led. She recalled talk of children she and Adrian had had. How they would give each one a trip to Africa. Not happening, she thought, eyes spent of tears. Not a single drop was left in her. Sandy was all cried out.

"Oh," all Adrian could say, the sight of Sandy standing at the end of the aisle stealing his heart for a second time. "She's beautiful," he uttered, awed by the beauty she possessed even from twelve yards away.

"Yes, she is," Winston added. "Yes, she is."

And then she was at the altar. Through the fire they had gone, through the depths of a private hell and back, but now they were going to be together for as long as life allowed.

This is all that matters, Adrian thought as Sandy's father gave her away and she moved in close to him, the beating of her heart matching his own as the minister began.

The rain forced the outside pictures at the Botanical Gardens indoors. Janice stood next to Martha as she watched the photographer shift Sandy's family in various positions.

Despite herself Janice's eyes fell on Cliff. Thought what she had thought from the moment they had lined up in the church vestibule: *he looks real good in a tuxedo.*

She knew old dreams would find her this day, and though there had been no surprise when they did, it still shook her a bit. *Could have been me,* she thought as she took in Sandy, a vision in white. *Could have been my day,* she had felt to the bottom of her soul as the wedding march began. *Us,* she had thought when the minister introduced the new Mr. and Mrs. Adrian Burton to the congregation.

But it wasn't—*with good reason,* she tried to remind herself. More reason finding her as Cliff did not so much as say hello to her. *He's not reliable, remember? He didn't show up to give you the most important answer of your life. You should be glad you didn't marry him, glad you told him no. What kind of life would you have?*

"Wonder how Britney's doing," Martha said.

Janice blinked, coming back into herself. "I was going to call Maurice after we got through with the pictures. Shame she's not here."

Martha laughed. "But isn't it just like her? Go into labor the night before the wedding?"

"Can I have the groom's family?" The Hutchinsons changed places with the Burtons, Rachel and Cliff moving past each other, something intense sweeping their eyes.

Martha squeezed Janice's hand. "You doing just fine, girl . . . doing just fine."

But Janice knew so much better.

". . . introducing bridesmaid Rachel Burton and her groomsmen, Julius Burton."

Janice studied the back of Rachel's upswept hair, the curves of her tight satin dress. If she had any doubt, she had none now. Cliff and Rachel had a thing going on.

It was in the way they talked, laughed, touched. Could be heard in Cliff's voice, Rachel's rich Caribbean laughter; an intimate mixing of the two, a personal realm in which only they moved.

The applause died down. It was their turn.

She turned her head and glanced at Sandy, who mouthed "You're doing fine," but Janice was feeling anything but, as Cliff moved in close and took her arm, not a hint of kindness in the motion.

He hadn't uttered a single word to her all day. Janice could not recall his eyes meeting hers once. It was as if she didn't exist, as if she were simply air.

". . . bridesmaid Janice Duprey and groomsmen Clifford Hutchinson."

They walked into the reception hall to pleasant applause. They plastered smiles on their faces as the photographer snapped their picture.

Cliff held her arm until she arrived at the dais, pulled her chair out for her to sit. She knew later he would hold her as they danced to the wedding song, fake a smile at the photographer's request. But that would be all Cliff would do with her, no more, no less. And when the party really got started, she knew to whose arms Cliff would go.

He did not disappoint.

TWENTY-ONE

The sunny Dutch island of Aruba became a paradise realized the moment Sandy's and Adrian's feet hit the tarmac
at Reina Beatrix Airport. The sun was out, the trade winds
constant, and palm and divi-divi trees rustled in the breeze.

For the next five days they would play tourist, lie out in
the sun, and take in the sights, New York and the world
far away. It was a much-needed respite from battles fought
and won, a shoring up for the struggles still ahead.

Adrian had gone into his bathroom and Sandy into hers.
Finishing before him, Sandy sat on the king-size bed awaiting his return.

She felt uncomfortable in the tiny satin panties, the
matching bra, and the short, sheer white jacket. Seven
weeks since they had made love, the positive test had put
an end to any more attempts. But they were on their honeymoon in Aruba, and it was time for the bout of celibacy
to end.

How do I do this?

It was one thing to confess love, feel love, but it was a
whole different arena turning that love into physical action.
Sandy's heart was the same, but her mind was playing its
deadly game of *don't*. The risk was too great. Adrian would
understand. A slipup could mean the end of her.

These were the things she was considering when the
bathroom door opened and Adrian appeared, towel around
his waist and nothing else. The splotch on his neck was the
size of a quarter. The swelling beneath his towel telling her
much.

She could not hold back her fears, and they shone in her
eyes like dull diamonds.

"We don't have to, Sandy."

But she knew there was nothing he wanted more. He had not reached for her in nearly two months, but moments had come when his need had been a fire beside her.

Too late now, because the moment found everything else a go—the two condoms on the nightstand and the female version she wore. *Got to at least try.*

Carefully she stood, the white mules with the ostrich-feather tips making her feel whorish, cheap. Sandy made her arms lift, forced them open. She pushed a smile on her face and said, "It's okay."

He came to her tentatively, giving her the chance to change her mind. But Sandy needed to do this, needed to cross the divide.

His hands touched her back. She jumped at the contact, heart pounding in her chest. His lips moved towards her ear, the lesion on his neck away from her. "I love you so much," he whispered, his warm breath making her shiver.

He laid his head on her shoulder, her arms laced around his back. They stood there, still, breathing and feeling, this simple pleasure missing for so long.

Sandy pulled out of his arms, lay on the bed. Adrian moved next to her. She stared deep into his soul. *Help me,* her eyes were saying. *Help me want you.*

He sat her up, eased the jacket off her back. Undid the front hook of her lacy bra. Warm fingers across her cool skin, she reacted to the touch, parts of her pulsing, swelling, growing damp.

She forced herself to go deep inside to uncover her bottom line. *I love him, will always love him, no matter what.* Standing on that unshakable ground, she reached for the towel—"It's okay"—and pulled it from his waist.

She waited while he put on one condom and then the other, drew him close, his skin pressed against hers. Yes, Adrian was HIV-positive and moments like this could kill, but there was a soothing to the warmth of his body, one she had missed all too long.

She burrowed her nose into his chest, drawing in the sweetness of his cologne. Her tongue, on automatic, eased past her lips, wanting to taste his butterscotch skin.

She was halfway there, her mind *warm, soft, salty,* anticipating the moment, when she suddenly remembered, closed her mouth, pulled away. Turned her head. Cried a little, in mourning for things gone by.

Adrian moved off her, gathered her into his arms. Comforting her the best he could, her tears wetting his arm. He held her till her tears finally stopped, was still holding her when her gentle snoring filled the room.

Only then did he get up and go to the bathroom, the two unused condoms coming off with ease. Wrapping them in toilet paper and then in a plastic bag, he tossed it into the garbage and went to put on his pajamas.

Quietly he got back into the bed, lying awake a long time, wondering about their life ahead. *For better or for worse*, they had promised, but in that moment, a better could not be found.

It was hard picturing Adrian ill as he lay on the white beach chair, a drink in his hand, his baggy bathing trunks revealing a perfect belly button. It was hard to imagine the buttery copper skin turning dark, moldy, and wasted as she watched him drink the virgin rum punch.

He didn't realize Sandy was staring until he felt her smile. Turned his head a degree, the hot Aruba sun making the sand whiter, the ocean water crystal blue, and Sandy so mahogany she glowed. His words left him in awe. "You look so good."

She blushed, growing warm and moist and open beneath the Aruban sky. The ocean was at her feet, the white sand beneath her chair, alcohol flowed in her system, and her husband was beside her.

Suddenly she wanted him in a way she hadn't in a long time. Her need making her nipples hard, her skin flushed.

"Let's go take a nap," she said, carefully getting up off the lounge chair.

Together they rode the elevator, one-skinned, eager to do what had not been possible in weeks—reconnect in a real way, experience that loving touch.

God's gift, that's how Sandy came to think of their honeymoon in Aruba. God, the knower of all things, knew exactly what was up the road for Sandy and Adrian and had made their honeymoon a wonderful thing.

Adrian got sick when they returned home. A simple little parasite that lived in shellfish and that most people could ingest without so much as a stomach cramp had attacked Adrian's system.

It was the first time he was hospitalized.

Sandy told her family and friends that he had contracted a bug down in Aruba. "Bad seafood" was the explanation she dispensed like medicine to those who called or dropped by.

But who knew and who didn't no longer bothered her. All she cared about was that Adrian had survived.

It took ten days for Adrian to get better. On the eleventh day he was discharged from the hospital. Still, the lapse had weakened him terribly, and most of the time he could do nothing more than lie in bed.

They had the conversation Sandy never wanted. Where the important papers were, where he wanted to be buried—"with Gen, because after I'm gone I don't want you to stop living. Still young, Sandy . . . got that whole life ahead of you."

She got up and left the room, unable to comprehend Adrian gone, his final resting place with his first wife. It took a few minutes to come back, finish the talk she had never wanted to have.

Adrian went on, a knowing look on his face. "It's hard. Anybody knows how hard it is, it's me. But one day I'm not going to be here, and I don't want you sitting around like I'm coming back."

Her brows drew, wetness glistened in the corners of her eyes. "How can I? How can I go on without you?"

He smiled feebly. "Because you have to. Can't spend the rest of your life clinging to what we had."

"Have," she insisted. Tears ran down her face. "How can you lay there and talk about me living without you?"

"Because it's the way it's going to be. Can't change none of it."

But the notion was ridiculous. She wouldn't even consider it. Hadn't she been through enough? She didn't want to consider a future without him now. Just wanted to have him there with her. "I don't want to talk about it," she said stubbornly.

"But we got to. We have to get things in order." He was talking about preparing for death—his and the life they longed for and would never receive. "We have to, Sandy," Adrian implored, facing head on what she could not. "Okay?"

It seemed a lifetime before she gave an answer. Seconds passing, different emotions coursing through her. She did not want to concede, did not want to cross the final threshold, but knew she had no choice now.

She nodded somberly, slowly. "Okay."

Papers were drawn up, documents signed. Everything he owned becoming hers. *Everything but the one true thing—a long life with the man I wanted forever.* No piece of paper could give her that.

Jeanne Hutchinson looked past Sandy's shoulder. "Where's Adrian?"

"Not coming."

"He's still sick?"

Sandy searched her mother's face, could not stop the tears that spilled from her eyes. "Yes, Mom. He still sick. And more than likely he's going to die."

Her mother extended one hand behind her, her face paler than Sandy ever remembered seeing. "Samuel, get down here. Get down here now."

Her father came running down the stairs, fastening his pants, his face bewildered. He looked at his daughter, saw his wife. "What's wrong?"

"It's Adrian. Sandy says he's dying?" But it was still more question than reality, the whole of it not sitting anywhere with Sandy's mother.

Her father looked just as stunned. *Must be some mistake,* his eyes were saying. He shook his head. "No, that can't be right." He fixed his eyes on Sandy. "What is your mother talking about?"

Sandy swallowed, the weight of it all heavy on her shoulders. *How do I tell them? How do I open up my mouth and let go the secret I've been hoarding, wishing away for so long?*

She looked at her father, at her mother, and knew that more than her dreams were about to be done away with. "Adrian has AIDS." She blinked. "And he's dying."

Silence. Mouths hanging open, strange things dancing in their eyes. Automatically her parents drifted towards the living room, plunked down on the sofa, the news breath-stealing.

"How?" It took effort for her mother to utter that word, her eyes searching Sandy's face, looking for signs of disease, illness. Transgressions.

Sandy did not want to tell the story. Did not want to reveal the hidden truth. Did not want to go into Adrian's being married before and how his wife had had an affair and died.

Suddenly, sitting there in her parents' living room, the whole story seemed absurd. She had married a man who had been exposed to AIDS; what else did she think would happen?

"His ex-wife."

Her father was the first to react to that bit of news.

"What?" he shouted, looking at his daughter with hot angry eyes.

"Ex-wife?" Her mother was shouting too. "Ex-wife? He was married before?"

"Yes, he was. They had been separated for two years when we met. Adrian tested negative until recently. We thought we were safe, but we were wrong."

Sandy had told the truth. It was their turn to speak.

Her mother's mouth trembled, a tear like a spent diamond glistened on her cheek. She glanced at her daughter, looked away.

Her father leaned forward, elbows to his bony knees. "I raised you better," he said, his voice tight, accusatory. "I raised you so much better," he uttered again, as if Sandy had committed some horrible, unforgivable sin.

But it wasn't what she needed. She didn't need condemnation. She needed their love, their understanding, shoulders to lean on. His response drew her fire.

"Better? Better than what? Better than who? I love Adrian. He loves me despite what happened, what didn't." She shook her head furiously. "Ain't no 'better' there, Daddy. If there is, then please show me where, how."

Samuel Hutchinson considered his daughter, trying to determine other secrets, other things he did not know. "What about you?"

There was no compassion in his eyes, just bitterness. Sandy resisted the urge to tell him none of his damn business. "I've been tested and I am fine."

Her mother shuddered. "I hope you're still not sleeping together. A simple scratch—"

She cut her mother off. "Yes, I know, but like I said, we were always careful, and I have my own bed." But these matters were trivial to her, had nothing to do with the real issue.

"I loved him, can you understand that? Against all odds I was willing to go. And I did, and I won't regret it. Hate me, call me names, curse me, but whatever you're thinking, whatever you're feeling, all your worries, your concerns, your *fears* cannot, will not, change it."

Her father raised his hands. "Now, Sandy."

"Now Sandy what? What?" Her eyes blazed at him. "All my life the only boys you liked were the light-skinned ones. Right or wrong I spent most of my life looking for one—someone I could bring home with my head held high. Someone you would approve of, not turn away from. And I did." Her eyes bored into her father's. "Poor little tar baby me."

Her parents looked as if they had been slapped hard.

"And you both adored him. Well, he's not so pretty now. And there's sores on him. He's skinny, frail, weak, but he's still the same man I fell in love with and you fell for. AIDS hasn't changed that, won't change that, and if you two are going to be so damn shallow as to hold it against either me or him—if the idea of your daughter married to a man who is going to die soon is too scary for you—then just stay away and leave us alone. 'Cause we don't need your pity or your fears. We need your support." She paused, breathing hard. "Your love."

Her mother looked sorrowfully at her. "We're scared for you, baby, can you understand that?"

No, not anymore. "Scared ain't gonna help me. Scared ain't gonna heal Adrian. We don't have the time for scared. My husband is dying, can you understand that? Dying."

Her father stood slowly as if his bones ached. He did not look at her but somewhere past her head. He extended his arms wide, said, "Come here," and waited for her. But Sandy wasn't going to concede until she was certain they understood it all, every miserable hopeless bit.

"Come on now," he said with a flick of his wrist.

"Can't you even look at me, Daddy?"

He did, glanced away, and finally looked squarely into her eyes. Gave a sad chuckle. " 'Course I can. You my baby girl and I love you, Sandy." There were tears in his eyes, in his voice. "Be there for you, I swear I will."

It was what she needed to hear.

She moved into the expanse of her father's embrace.
Wallowed there for a long time. When Adrian was finally
gone, these would be the arms she would need to hold her,
soothe her, help her through. Her father's arms, that first
place she'd experienced that wondrous thing called love.

She let herself in, the apartment dark and gloomy, quiet
and still except for the spill of light from the bedroom doorway. She put down her bag, went to the bathroom, and got
the rubber gloves.

She moved down the hall, coming face to face with
Adrian, checking him visually for signs of distress. The
days of searching for signs of improvement were over.

"You all right?" she asked, donning the bright yellow
rubber gloves and reaching for the edge of the bedsheet.

"Am now," Adrian answered, getting off the bed and
into the chair slowly. He ached most of the time, his body
abandoning him bit by bit. Some days were okay, some
days were worse, but there hadn't been any real good days
in a while.

Sandy tugged at the end of the sheet. It resisted her for
a second but eventually sprang free. Taking care of Adrian
wasn't easy, but she did it because there was no way she
could not. Both of them were on leave from work; only
Sandy had plans of returning.

Adrian had learned ways to pass the time in his debili-
tating condition. Took up reading and watching as many
videos as he could. When he was up to it, Sandy took him
on long car drives, but those times were all too rare.

Four months after testing positive, his body now had a
slew of quarter-sized markings that lived across his back
and down his legs. He had lost forty pounds, and his face
had taken on a hollowed look most of the time.

The disease was moving fast.

But there were still moments when he would look at
Sandy and his eyes would sparkle and dance. She would

stand there looking at him looking at her and remember how life used to be.

She stripped the bed, carefully rolling up the corners, and put the sheet into a plastic bag. She had bought a washer and dryer out of necessity, and there were days when both of them ran all the time.

Her life had become a constant struggle of staying ahead of the germs, of the virus that killed. It was a losing battle in Adrian's case, this much she knew, but Sandy attacked with all her might.

They had not made love since their honeymoon, and in the months since, Sandy found herself filled with dreams of just that, waking as she came, Adrian's rattling breathing across the room.

Her husband was dying.

The secret was no longer a secret. Now that she'd told her parents, everybody knew. Martha came and watched over Adrian when Sandy needed a break. She'd sit in the chair across from him, trading jokes and making him laugh.

Sandy would go out, wander the malls, see couples and babies and think about the cheatings of death. She wanted a baby, wanted a husband to grow old with. But Adrian was dying.

He had bought a fifty-thousand-dollar insurance policy on Gennifer right before they got married, and there was still thirty thousand dollars left, which Sandy would get.

Adrian himself had a $130,000 policy that would be Sandy's too. The bitter irony did not escape her. Sandy, who never had enough money, who had played the rob-Paul-to-pay-Peter game, would suddenly have more than enough. But she'd give it all away if it meant Adrian could live and be well.

Britney came and visited a few times; Janice could only manage one. *Too much for me to bear, Sandy. I love you both and it breaks my heart*. Sandy allowed her that.

Rachel came by sometimes with Winston and Junie and sometimes by herself. She sat and shared long-ago stories with her brother, heated conversation flying through the room. And though Adrian would engage with gusto, often he would be exhausted by the visits end.

Adrian's parents came twice a week, his mother holding his hand, his father sitting strong-shouldered in the chair.

Some people lived a long time with HIV. Some people were asymptomatic and fine. But Adrian wasn't some people.

It was a blur.

Sandy was awakened by Adrian's rattling breathing, the room warm with the smell of heat and feces. Hearing Adrian gasping, she sat up and turned on the light. Across the room her husband lay clutching his chest, the pajama top too big, open, revealing the ugly blotches.

"Oh, God!" She jumped up, dialed 911. She took Adrian into her arms, pressing him against her. Sandy kissed his face like she hadn't done in a long time. *The last time?*

Holding him, rocking him, wanting him to find the breath he was struggling for, wanting him to find the hope and the strength to make it, she whispered, "Don't die, Adrian, please don't die" over and over again because she was not ready. Not ready for his leaving, not ready to say good-bye. *I need you.* "Please God, don't take him away." Time lost all meaning, Adrian nearly lifeless as she cradled him in her arms.

Suddenly there were quick raps on the front door. *Help.* But she didn't want to let him go. Didn't want to leave him for one second. Needed to keep him close, keep him here, *right here with me.*

The knocks grew frantic, the shouts of EMS personnel filtering down the hall. She released him, laying him as carefully as she could down on the bed, raced to the front door, wanting the medics to come and save her husband, his life in their hands.

She opened the door quickly, pointed down the hall. Her

words came fast as she told what she knew and gathered his medication for their inspection.

The stretcher was opened up. Her husband's too-big pajamas fell loose from his tiny waist, his narrow, hollowed chest. Sandy reached in and tried to fix his clothes, give him some decency, but she was forced away.

An IV was started, needles filled, and a defibrillator plugged in. The words "We're losing him!" found her over the din of the madness going on in the room.

"Clear!" Something like the sound of a bug being zapped filled the room. Sandy saw Adrian's whole body leave the stretcher and slam back down. "Again! Clear!" Another zap, the impact forcing his eyes open, glazed golden irises finding her across the room.

And then everything changed.

Grew picture still. Like a three-dimensional snapshot, everybody, everything stopped. Sandy looked about her, saw the paramedics' mouths frozen with silenced shouts, their bodies in weird in-between poses.

Nothing's moving except me, she realized, looking down at her hands, moving them through the immobile space. The sound of the pad creaking caught her attention, and suddenly Adrian was getting up off the stretcher.

With ease he drifted through the paramedic holding the defibrillator and came to stand five feet away. He looked more beautiful than she could ever recall. Perfect, healthy, and fit.

He smiled, his words arriving on a soft warm breeze, infused with all the love they had ever shared. "I got ta go now, ya know dat. Ya keep dat head up, nuh? Ya stay strong for me, ya 'ear? 'Cause I'll be a-watchin' ya and a-watchin' ya and luvin' ya until de end da time."

Another zap of power crackled in the room, and suddenly Adrian wasn't before her but was back on the stretcher, sickly and comatose. The whole room was bursting with motion as the defibrillator was put down, the ends of the stretcher were grabbed, and in the blink of an eye he was wheeled past her and out of the room.

Sandy turned, stumbling. She jumped into her sweats, threw a T-shirt over her head, and grabbed her coat. Snatching up her shoes, she dashed out of the apartment.

Ran like a demon was after her down the short flight of stairs. Burst through the door and saw the swirling, flashing lights. She hurried to the ambulance and banged on the door. But it pulled away from the curb without her.

She stood there on the suddenly eerie quiet, street, ears buzzing, heart pumping, and screamed, "Adrian!" until she could scream no more.

The overworked, weary, bleary-eyed intern named Joshua Akumbe did not have to waste his time to come and find her in the emergency room. He did not have to speak words he didn't feel—"I'm sorry, Mrs. Burton"—didn't have to tell her things she already knew—"He went into cardiac arrest and was DOA by the time he arrived."

She knew Adrian was dead. Knew when he died. *Because he came and told me so*, she wanted to say, but didn't. *He loved me that much. Loved me so much he stopped time, giving me those few precious seconds to say good-bye, so there, Mr. Tired African Wanna-Be Doctor, so there.*

She swallowed, her mind fuzzy as cotton. "Can I see him?"

Intern Akumbe looked away. "Considering what he died of, we had no choice but to send him down to the morgue right away."

She glared at him. *No, you are not scaring me. No, I will not go away. And yes, I will see my husband even if he died of the bubonic plague.* "Can I see him?"

"You will have to go to the morgue."

"So?"

"Wait here. I will get you an escort."

But Sandy wasn't waiting another second. She wanted to hold Adrian's hand while it was still warm, while the last little bit of heat remained in his body. She wanted to see him for herself, by herself, one last time.

She took the elevator to the basement, found herself in a place with two walls and a locked door. Riding back up to the front desk, she asked where the morgue was. Following the directions as best she could, she finally found the morgue and was surprised to see it was not as dark, dingy, or smelly as she'd assumed.

Less than half an hour into her new role—widow—Sandy was feeling very much like her old self as she walked the long, brightly lit corridors, following the arrows suspended from the ceiling. She still felt married, still felt in love, even felt a weird kind of peace. It was shock, but Sandy didn't know that. All she knew was she was feeling fine.

For a moment she forgot where she was going and why. The only thing with her was the sense that she'd left home without a bra and her hair had not been combed, but that was incidental as she made a left, the soles of her sneakers squeaking against the shiny tiled floor.

Nope, don't matter, 'cause I'm going to see Adrian, and he loves me no matter what I look like. She would tell him about her mishap in finding him. *I just, liked, hopped the first elevator I saw, went to the basement, but it was like this dead end.* She would laugh at her own stupidity. *So I finally had to go up to the lobby and ask them where you was at. Took me a while, but here I am.*

And Adrian would laugh with her and be glad that she came. Feeling super good now, Sandy found herself humming.

"Can I help you?"

Suddenly the corridor didn't look so bright, the floors not as clean, and the walls not the pretty peach she thought they were. Suddenly the anticipation of this moment, the high she'd ridden on the way, left her as she stared into the bifocals of the hospital worker whose name tag she could not read.

Her eyes were full of tears.

"Are you lost?" Mr. Blurry Name Tag asked.

"My husband . . . I've come to see him," she managed, feeling a sudden chill permeating the walls.

"Name?"

"Sandy Burton."

"Wait here."

He left her outside a door marked PERSONNEL ONLY. Came back two minutes later, a dire look on his face. "I have a Burton, but it's not Sandy. It's Adrian."

She nodded furiously, eager to go through the special door. Eager to go to the room made of steel and cold. Eager to lay her hand upon her husband's warm flesh. *And I better do it soon 'cause it's cold in here, and pretty soon Adrian's going to be cold too.*

"Yes, that's him." Her eyes feverishly scanned the closed PERSONNEL ONLY door.

"Come with me." But he did not lead her through the special door, instead took her down the hall to a small room with a few seats, a box of tissue, and a television hooked into the ceiling. A white dusty curtain hung over it. *Been up there a long time,* she surmised.

"Wait here."

Mr. Fuzzy Name Tag left, closing the door behind him. Sandy looked around the tiny room, wondering how the big metal gurney she'd seen on TV would fit inside.

She was still wondering when the lights dimmed a little, the little dusty curtain slid back from the television, and her husband's face, eyes closed and death-kissed, filled the screen in grainy, live video color.

It was in that moment that the whole of it found Sandy, when the realization of what would not be fixed its claws into her heart and would not let her go.

She was still screaming when Mr. Fuzzy Name Tag returned. So far gone Sandy didn't even realize he was not alone.

TWENTY-TWO

"Feeling better?"

It was Dr. Name Tag, except now she could see the blue chunky letters stuck to the shiny pastic tag. Could read the name N. NILSIN as clear as anything.

She felt the starched crisp sheet beneath her, became aware of the heavy cotton blanket on top. Realized she was in a hospital room. Licked her lips, thirsty beyond belief. Dr. Nilsin took a cup of crushed ice and offered it to her. Sandy shook her head. "Water, I want water."

"Not a good idea. We had to sedate you, Mrs. Burton. And unless you want to be throwing up, it's best you stick with ice."

Sandy conceded, tossed the frozen chips into her mouth. Sucked, chewed, sucked, chewed, more thirsty than she'd ever recalled being.

Seeing some of the color returning to her face, Dr. Nilsin parked himself on the stool on wheels and rolled close to the bed.

"You've had a bad shock. Is there someone we can call?"

Her eyes closed, a tear tickling down the side of her face.

"Someone, Mrs. Burton . . . your parents, a friend?"

Sandy wiped her face, tried to figure who should be there. Adrian's parents. They had to be notified. "His father, Mr. Burton. He lives in Brooklyn," she softly added.

"Nobody closer?"

"My parents, I guess." But she felt no desire to see them now. "My friends . . . Janice Duprey, Martha Alston." She reached for the clipboard, but he seemed hesitant to hand it over. "Their phone numbers, I was going to write them down for you."

He extracted a tiny pad from his jacket pocket, a flat-tipped pencil. Sandy took it and jotted down the numbers, aware of his steady gaze.

Not crazy, you asshole. My husband's dead.

The misery was back on her, and it was all she could do to finish writing, tears dropping onto the paper like rain, making the smooth surface pucker.

He took back the pad and the pencil. Suggested she lie back down and get some more rest. "I'll be back in a few," he promised, leaving and closing the door, a lock clicking in place echoing behind him.

She heard Martha and Janice before she saw them, their voices loud, screechy, moving down the corridor in angry bursts. ". . . I don't give a fuck what you think. Just tell us where she is."

Sandy got up, found her feet bare. Looked around for her shoes, but they were nowhere in the room. She went to the door and tried to open it, but it was locked from the outside.

Without thought she began pounding on the hard wood surface, calling out for her friends. "In here, I'm in here!"

Two faces appeared at the glass panel in the door, each determined for the sight of her. Her friends were at the door, ready, able, and willing to take her away, and in that moment it was all she wanted.

"Open this door, and now," she heard Martha insisting. "We're taking her home."

The lock was turned, and Martha and Janice were through it in no time. They hugged hard, the three of them, whimpering and moaning, caught in the reality of it all.

"Hey," Janice said, smoothing Sandy's wild hair, caressing the slope of her shoulder.

Martha took in her bare feet. "Where are your shoes?"

"I don't know. I woke up and they were gone . . . They sedated me."

"For her own good, Ms. Alston, I can assure you," Doctor Nilsin stated.

"Look, I don't give a fuck why you took them. All I want is for you to bring them back, and now." She whipped out her badge, something Sandy and Janice could never recall her doing. "I am an ADA for the County of Kings, and I swear to you I will have a full investigation as to why you not only allowed her to view her deceased husband by herself, you went on and sedated her without her permission. Am I making myself clear?"

All too clear. Not only did Dr. Nilsin bring back Sandy's shoes, he actually got down on his hands and knees to put them on her feet.

They pulled up to the quiet street, and Janice and Martha helped Sandy out of the car. When they got to the apartment, the front door was wide open, the lights burning. *Must have left in a hurry*, Martha surmised, taking in the scene.

Sandy faltered.

"Come on, Sandy," Janice urged softly. But Sandy seemed rooted.

"I know this is the last thing you want to do," Martha said, "but you got to do it. You got to do this. There's nothing to be afraid of." Martha placed her hand firmly on Sandy's back. "Come on, now."

Three hesitant steps and Sandy was through the door. She began to tremble. Janice came up behind her. "I'm going to run you a hot bath, okay?"

But Sandy shook her head, eyes wide, body spasming, Adrian's death still fresh inside her.

"I know you don't want one," Martha said gently, "but you're going to need one. We're going to be making some phone calls, and in a little while a lot of people are going to be crowded up in here. I know you just want to crawl

into a hole and never come out, but people are going to
need you to help them through."

Martha pulled her ear away from the bathroom door, satisfied that Sandy would be okay for a while. She went to
the kitchen, looked at Janice's backside humped up in the
air as she searched the space beneath the sink.

"You found another pair?"

Janice rose, two sets of rubber gloves in her hand.
"Whole bunch. Guess she had to keep them handy." Her
eyes met Martha's. "You know I'm scared shitless."

Martha nodded. "So am I, but we have to do it or it
won't get done. His people are going to be here soon, and
though they may want to see where he died, I'm certain
they don't want to see all the drama."

They slipped on the gloves. Each took a plastic garbage
bag. Together they walked down the hall and eased open
the door, the smell of death sickly sweet in the air.

Martha wrinkled her nose. "Damn . . ."

Janice took in the soiled bed, the discarded latex gloves.
Three hypodermic needles littered the floor, as did wrap-
pings from medical equipment. "Looks like a M.A.S.H.
ward."

"Let's get this sheet first," Martha said, her stomach
churning.

"No, let's open a window," Janice decided, wanting
some fresh air.

The room looked more like a hospital ward than a bedroom. There were adult diapers stacked in one corner, big
squares of leak pads piled in a chair. Bottles of alcohol, a
tube of bacitracin, box of rubber gloves, gauze pads. Two
beds.

How did Sandy do it? they were both thinking as they
got down to business.

Not what she needs, Martha was thinking as the Burton
clan arrived, extending their misery Sandy's way. *She needs*

them to be strong, Martha decided, a bit annoyed as the drama unfolded anew.

"He's gone, Sandy, oh Jesus, he's gone," Mrs. Burton moaned, holding Sandy tightly.

Rachel was next, and Janice turned her eyes away, feeling things that had no place in the moment. She crushed down the anger and bitterness. *Because it ain't about me right now, it's about Sandy.*

Junie could not speak at all, Sandy holding him more than he was holding her. Only Winston seemed capable in the moment, strong-willed, eyes damp but cheeks dry.

"You okay?"

Standing there, looking into the eyes that were Adrian's, the turn of the mouth that was Adrian's too, a brief peace filled Sandy. It did not last long, but it was the first glimpse she had that maybe she'd be all right.

Gathering up her will, Sandy turned towards the last visitor. The golden eyes were shimmery with tears. "I tank ya," he said, wringing callused hands. "I tank ya for lubbing me Adrian so. Ya gave 'em so mowch joy, so mowch." He tapped his heart. "An' I just wan'n tank ya."

In that moment their bitter past stopped mattering. In that moment Sandy's heart reached out to embrace the man who had given her so much grief.

She corralled him inside her arms, the father of the man she loved. Together they held on, a healing, long overdue, arriving, filling them both.

Too much hoopla.

Too much planning, too much energy, too much everything. Sandy wanted it just to end. *Death shouldn't be so complicated.* The passing of a loved one was drama enough.

Sandy didn't want to sit in the funeral director's office and select things, from what the casket would be lined with to how the obituary should look.

She just wanted to lay her husband to rest and try to

make it another day. But there were papers to process, things to decide, clothes to pick out, services to be attended.

She didn't want to play the part of the mourning widow. She wanted everyone to go away, leave her alone. Give her a quiet moment for herself. But since the night of Adrian's passing the only privacy she got was when she went to the bathroom.

Janice and Martha stayed with her for those first two nights. Rachel took the third night's watch. The fourth night she stayed at her parents' house. By the fifth she was hungry for solitude.

Now, as she sat in the front pew of the funeral chapel, a hundred-plus chairs behind her filled with people she knew and didn't, she just wanted it over and done. Her husband lay in the bronze casket looking like someone she never loved. The rail-thin, peaceful-faced man lying inside, wearing the three-hundred-dollar suit, including new underwear, undershirt, and shoes, wasn't the man she'd loved, just an remote effigy.

The organ music drifted in mournful tones. The whisper of conversation dusted the air in shimmery reverence. Sandy looked down at the gorgeous, smiling man on the front of the program and resisted the urge to weep.

She was setting the tone.

Not Adrian's mother, not Adrian's father, not his brothers or his sister. Sandy was the conductor of this orchestra, and if she stayed strong, did not weep, moan, keen, then everyone there would follow her lead.

Just want to give you that final peace.

"Sandy?"

Her head snapped up. Her mouth fell open, and all the pain and misery she had been holding on to threatened to leave her. She had no idea her grandmother was coming, did not expect her here, but there she stood, a matriarch in black, looking down at her with sad, knowing, *loving* eyes.

Leona Olivia Hutchinson had not come to her granddaughter's engagement party, nor attended the wedding.

But she had come now when Sandy needed her most, and it was overwhelming.

Sandy's eyes welled, overflowed. She was seconds away from losing it.

"No, no, don't start," her grandmother insisted. "You was doing just fine, and I want to you to continue to do just fine. Let's go outside where we can sit and talk a spell."

The feel of those old, warm, gnarly hands over her own was the best medicine. There was a healing in the touch, and Sandy opened her soul to it.

"It's a hard road you picked for yourself, Sandy. One I'd never pick for you myself."

"I know, Grandma Tee."

"And I was mad atcha and you just as mad at me." Her grandmother wiped a tear from Sandy's face. "Just couldn't see you bringing on this pain and misery. Didn't want that for you. But you was always a hard-head little thing. Nobody could tell you nuttin'."

"Because I loved him."

Her grandmother nodded. "I know you did, baby. I know you did. And he loved you too. Still loving you. I see his love around you like the sun setting, just shining up everything." She patted Sandy's hand. "Now, I want you to go back in there and be strong, you hear? There's a lot of pain in that room, a lot of lost people sitting there trying to find some peace. Go in there and be a good example. What Adrian wants."

Sandy looked into the eyes that were the spitting image of her own, sensing so much more than her grandmother was willing to share. "I'm trying to be strong," she confessed.

Her grandmother shook her head. "No, baby, you ain't trying nothing. You *are* strong. Only true faith could have broughtcha this far, and that faith is still right there in you. So now, you go on in there and honor the man you love. Go make Adrian proud."

She went, her head filled with one thought: *A thousand dreams when I looked at him . . . how many came true?* The answer came to her swiftly, filling her with a warmth she hadn't felt in weeks.

Two. Me and Adrian, and it was enough.

It had been a long week for Janice, with Cliff and Rachel in her face every time she turned around. Cliff being a good brother, Rachel the attentive sister-in-law. Their proximity a temptuous but needed presence for Sandy, who was taking Adrian's death hard.

But Sandy wasn't the only one in the midst of changes. Janice was going through some of her own. Adrian's passing had done things to her, things she had never counted on. It changed Janice's whole way of thinking, the very way she viewed the world.

The greatest love of her friend's life was gone. This was what stuck in Janice's craw. Great love just snatched away, this was what pulled at her mind and heart.

Suddenly the adage about life being too short became a mantra, a verse constantly playing in her head. Janice felt maybe she had acted too hastily, too conceitedly, had walked away too quickly without understanding what she had.

Yes, Cliff had disappointed her, had broken the ultimate promise. But life wasn't about ease; it was about riding out the storms and appreciating the good times with someone you loved and someone who could love you back.

This was what Adrian's death had delivered, another piece to the ever expanding puzzle called life. It was a hard lesson at a high price, but Janice embraced it whole.

She had seen them go off together, Rachel taking Cliff's arm, pulling him out of the living room and up the stairs. When she found herself checking her watch, Janice knew she could not sit in the living room awaiting their return.

She had gone off to the kitchen, sampling the deviled

eggs, cutting a few slices of ham. One minute she had been by herself, and the next there stood Rachel. She had been avoiding such moments, but now Rachel had her cornered.

"Ya luv 'er?"

"Love who?"

"Sandy? You luv 'er?" Rachel asked again, in her brisk Caribbean accent.

"Of course I do."

Rachel took a step forward, a daring gleam in her eyes. "Me luv 'er too. I ain't go'wan no ware. So what'eva ya tinking 'bout me, what'eva ya feeling 'bout me, if ya luv San-dee, truly luv 'er, den ya got ta make peace wit me."

Janice looked at the woman as if she had lost her mind. *Oh, this bitch is fucking crazy. Make peace with her? She got to be out of her mind.*

"I'in't stole Cliff frum under ya. I'in't come like a teeth in da night and jusa snatch 'em. Ya let 'em go, remembah? Ya turned away from 'em. Can't be standing dere like de air be smelling bah'd every time we cross pats, cause I'in't done a ting to ya, not ta ting."

Denial was the first thing that bubbled up Janice's throat, but she knew the truth was better. "You want to know something, Rachel? You are absolutely right. No, you didn't steal him, but that don't change what we had or how I feel. If you expect me to become some kind of Stepford wife every time you around, if you expect me to be cool with you, then you better not hold your breath, because you nor anybody else have the right to dictate how I feel and when I'm feeling it."

Rachel considered her with a raised eyebrow. "Well, nuh, least you confessing to feelin'. Taw't maybe you *was* some Stepford wife or sumtim', being awl coool and ting 'round Cleef, acting like ya din't care."

Janice felt her face grow red.

"For da record, Cleef an' I? Nuttin' serious go'wen on dere. He bored, I'm bored, we just trying to do away wit each udder's boredness." Rachel chuckled. "Ya seen us go off, nuh? Betcha was wondering what we up to? We taw'ked. Taw'ked in a way we neber taw'ked before. Came to a real conclewshun.

"See, his 'eart, it belong to one person. An' mine? To one person, 'cept mine dead and Cleef's alive, and me looking 'er in da face." Rachel raised her eyebrow. "Ya look surprised."

"Just that, well, y'know."

"Know what? Me an' Cleef going 'round acting like we justa mad for each udder?" Rachel shook her head. "Just some roles we've slipped into, an' I telling ya we bot getting tiyard of de game."

"So what was all that talk about me having to get over you and Cliff being together?"

"Who say dat? Me say dat? When me say so?"

"But you just said—"

"No, what me say was dat I'in go'wn ta be around for a long time an' you need ta make your peace with me, dat what I said."

Janice grew suspicious, the whole scene playing out too nicely for her taste. "Cliff put you up to this?"

Rachel laughed. "Nobody put me up to anyting," lost her smile. "Adrian die and everyting get clear . . . I look at San-dee and my 'eart justa break, cause dat was true luv. I tink about my Colin 'oo a bullet took frum me y'ears ago, my 'eart it justa break some more." She shook her head. "Ya standin dere and don't even know 'ow lucky ya are. Cleef, him still 'ere." Rachel pointed towards the door. "Still right dere and still luving ya. Ya gotta chance me an' San-dee no longer have and ya don't even know it. Ya better reach out and snatch it before it's too late, 'cause when it gone, it gone fa good." Rachel looked at her softly. "Dat all I'm sayin'. Dat all."

Rachel's words were a bee in her ear, buzzing constantly and refusing to go away. Janice left the kitchen, found Martha and Britney, and wedged herself between them on the couch.

She saw Cliff talking to Maurice and looked away. "Seen Sandy?" she asked absently, in need of a diversion from her thoughts.

"Not in a while. Maybe she went upstairs to lay down," Martha said wearily. It had been a long week and she was grateful to see it coming to an end. All she really wanted was to go home, crawl into bed with Calvin, and make love till dawn.

Britney looked at her watch. It was getting late. No doubt her baby daughter was missing her. It was the first time she had been away from her for so long. "I'm going to have to go soon," she said carefully.

Both Janice and Martha nodded and understood. Britney had a new life now, consisting of a husband and child. The days of hanging out forever were long gone, and no one would fault her early departure.

She got up off the sofa, moved across the room to tell Maurice she was ready to go. Cliff glanced at Janice, and she looked away.

"What was that about?" Martha asked.

"Nothing," Janice said quickly.

"Has to be a whole lot of nothing because Cliff is looking at you like he ready to eat you up."

Janice felt her heart trembling, knew she could not stay in the room another minute. A strange, buzzy energy was rolling towards her, and she knew the source. She swallowed, grew hot. Felt the need to run before something happened.

"Be back," Janice said, getting up off the sofa. She would find Sandy, something, anything to get away from what she knew would occur.

Up the stairs she went and down the short hall. The bedroom door was closed, and she knocked with sharp quick raps. There was no answer and she tried the knob. It twisted easily and she pushed the door open.

The room was empty.

Turning, *got to find Sandy,* Janice was making her way to the second bedroom when Cliff appeared at the end of the hall. She stood there, barely breathing, wanted to duck and take cover.

She shook her head, whispered, "No," as Cliff headed toward her. "Please, Cliff, don't," she pleaded not wanting to take the moment any further.

He was a liar, he was a cheat, he was a scoundrel and selfish and self-serving. He had committed the ultimate crime—offering her a dream on a platter and then snatching it away as she reached for it. *He's bad news.*

The distance between them grew smaller, the fuzzy buzzy energy stronger. Her heart hammered in her chest, her breathing grew shallow. Her knees threatened to give out on her. "Please, Cliff, don't." Her last attempt to stop him, to prevent what he was determined to do.

"Don't what? Tell you that I'm sorry? Because I am. Don't say I love you? Because I do. Don't say you were right? Well, you were. You were so right, Janice. Didn't realize any of it. Just blind to everything. Would have gone on being blind if Rachel had not pulled my coattail."

He shook his head. "Did I want to marry you? Yes, I did. Just wasn't ready. Not then. But now . . ." His hand moved through the air. "Now I know what's important. Understand life's fragilities and what's worth holding on to. And you are worth holding on to. Never felt about anyone the way I feel about you."

Just death talking. He won't mean it tomorrow . . . She stopped herself. Remembered Rachel's words. Felt their truth.

She *was* staring in the face what Sandy no longer could. There before her was a love that had taken a bad turn but somehow had managed to find its way back to her.

Janice knew enough about Cliff to know that if he wasn't serious she would be standing in the upstairs hallway alone. *But you're not, he's right there before you. Reach out and snatch it while you can.*

She moved towards him, saw his arms open to her. He didn't kiss her. Didn't caress her. Just held her. Two hearts beating to a surrender that was simple and sweet. The brass ring before them, together they reached out and snatched it.

TWENTY-THREE

Martha closed the door, Phoebe Snow's voice full inside the apartment. "Harpo's Blues" had been playing the last time she had come, and even though this was a new visit, the atmosphere was the same—arrested.

She had hoped that her friend would find the lever, the button, a notion, a thought, to help move her from a state of resignation into the warm glow of hope. That something, anything, would awaken her from her deep, dark despair so that she could start living again.

But all things took time, and Martha accepted that the time wasn't now. She took a deep breath, released it. *Maybe Phoebe Snow's tired-ass song about clouds and mountains and costumes is helping her.* Martha hoped so.

It was their first soiree in months, and though there were still things to mourn, the four friends were coming together to rekindle the spirit of who they were to each other.

"Where you want me to put these hot wings?" Martha asked. Every time she shifted her eyes, there was Adrian smiling back at her.

"Kitchen."

"You want me to set the plates and cups out?" Martha asked, moving through the living room.

"No, I'll get them."

"So how are you doing?" Martha said, taking in her friend, who looked a little better than the last time she had seen her. The weight Sandy had dropped hadn't returned yet, but her eyes had lost some of their haunted look.

"Okay."

Sandy's parents had inquired, as had Adrian's parents, but none of her friends had found the courage to ask what Martha set about asking. "You're okay, then?"

It took a moment for Sandy to get Martha's drift, to shift from the feeling of loss and discern what Martha was hinting at. But it was gasoline on an open flame. "Negative. Happy? Want to see the results? They mailed the shit to me like I couldn't fucking bear a human voice telling me that I was going to live a whole lot longer than Adrian ever did."

Sandy turned away, her anger catching her by surprise. She was in the midst of the process of recovery—denial, anger, fear, and then acceptance. Only two away from the healing, it looked a long way off.

She sighed. "I'm sorry, Martha." Shook her head. "I know you're concerned . . . just that I feel like everybody breathing down my neck waiting to see if I'm gonna die."

"No, we just want to make sure you're not."

"I'm fine, okay? I have had every single AIDS test known to man, and all of them came back negative." Sandy's eyes glistened, her voice faint. "But sometimes I just wish I was . . . dying, y'know?"

But Martha didn't know. Wouldn't even think about saying she did. It was an irresponsible solution to a hard situation, lacking common sense, hope, and guts. "But you're not dying, and you are here. And it's the hardest shit you will probably ever face in your life, Sandy, but you got to face it. Face the fact. Adrian is gone and you're not."

The doorbell rang. They both turned at the sound of it.

"You want me to get it?" Martha said.

Sandy shook her head. It was her place and her duty. She moved towards the door.

They were all looking at her, and Sandy knew what their hope was. That she'd be all right, would not wallow in her sadness, would come back swinging, be the person she had been before.

But it was a tall order. Sandy had been through so much. *Need time,* she sat there thinking. *Need more than a day, a week, a month.* How much she wasn't sure, but she did know their expectancies had arrived too soon.

She needed real time to work her way through, and though she didn't know exactly how much, she hoped her friends would allow her as long as it took.

"Am I heartbroken?" she asked. "Yes, I am. Do I still cry? Almost every other minute of the day. Am I sad, lonely, depressed? The answer is yes. And though I know you all mean well, you have to let me work through this my way."

She seemed so fragile now, nothing of her determined self visible. The three friends sat, knowing the weight of the world was heavy on her shoulders and she wanted no assistance in carrying it.

"People still ask me why I married him. That I knew he was going to die." Tears like diamonds glistened in the corners of her eyes as she shook her head. "What me and Adrian had? I couldn't walk away from that."

Janice nodded. "I know," her voice very soft. "I've learned so much because of you. Some days I just sit back and think about all you taught me, and I am so grateful for you my heart just aches."

Martha waved her hand. "Please don't start crying," she begged, her own eyes wet. "We've shed enough tears to last a lifetime." But even as she spoke she could hear Britney sniffling, could see the glistening on Janice's cheek.

"There's nothing wrong with tears," Britney said wisely. "Tears make you feel better. There's no shame in tears."

Martha only half agreed. "Yeah, but I'm not one for crying."

Janice laughed. "Yes, I know, Miss Hard-as-Rock Martha."

Martha looked around the room. "You guys aren't for shit, but I sure love the hell out of all of you."

Janice jumped up. "Group hug?"

The word was hardly out of her mouth before they were all standing, scrunched up together, hands fitting over shoulders and around waists, drawing each other in, closer, tight, complete.

Compassion, comforting as a soft quilt, surrounded them. There in the midst of her friends, Sandy realized she wasn't alone. And her one true prayer had been answered. A wonderful man had come into her life, and he would love her until the end of time.

"Who been eating onions?" Martha piped up, making everyone laugh, break away, find seats, comfortable.

"Me," Janice confessed, testing her own breath with the cup of her hand.

Martha reached into her bag and pulled out a Certs. "Well, here, your breath nearly knocked me out."

Janice snatched it, cutting her eyes, smiling as the realization found her. *This is how it's supposed to be, just like this. Martha cutting up and everybody laughing. Feels good.*

"Been thinking," Sandy said, uncertainty in her eyes. Absolutes were far and few for her these days, and she didn't quite trust how she felt or why.

"About what?" Britney asked.

Sandy's eyes dusted the room, saw her pictorial memorial to what was. "About moving. Never gonna get on my with life living here like this. I need to get out of here."

Martha's hand went to her chest. "I am so glad to hear you say that. You had me worried. This place is like a shrine. Adrian everywhere I look. I went to use the toilet and damn if he wasn't on the bathroom wall."

Despite herself Sandy laughed, shook her head. "You're right, Martha, and I know Adrian don't want me living like this." She sighed. "Hard as it is to let go, I know I have to."

"Letting go doesn't mean forgetting, Sandy," Janice said quickly.

"And your love for Adrian is forever. He knows that," Britney added.

"And you know we have our creed," Martha said. "In

the famous words of Gloria Gaynor, we will survive."

Janice jumped up, an invisible mike in her hand. "First I was afraid, I was petrified . . ." Britney jumped up for the second chorus. By the third, Martha was up, and Sandy joined them as well, her voice choked with tears.

They latched arms, did kicks, sang loud, off key, full. Tearing down the sadness, banishing the pain. They sang, their friend's life depending on it, snatching up Sandy from the depths of depression and moving her one step closer to new hope.

Even when she stopped, broke away, went to retreat back into the tiny box she had shoved herself into, they reached out, corralled her back, surrounding her, holding her up when all strength had left her, using their will, their arms, their hands, their voices, their love to help her, urge her, shift her one step away from the pain and the heartbreak, kindred spirits moving her towards that better day.

Martha pulled back, looked at her friend. Smiled until tears sparkled in her eyes. "You gonna be all right, you hear me, Sandy? You gonna be just fine."

"We love you, Sandy. Gonna be there for you," Janice told her.

Britney nodded. "Life is gonna be so rich for you, Sandy. I can just feel it."

Sandy looked around the room, felt all the love her friends had for her and knew, *life already is . . .*

The food was better than any West Indian restaurant. The peas and rice were seasoned and cooked so well there was an underlying sweetness to them. The oxtail was so tender and well spiced Sandy felt there wasn't enough on the table to fill her. The simple salad of lettuce, tomatoes, and cucumbers seemed garden fresh, and even the plantains were golden sweet.

Sandy sensed Adrian's father watching her. Looked up from her plate.

"You wasting all dat meat, gal?" He asked, watching

Sandy maneuver the knife and fork over the meaty bone, a joy in his eyes, gentle teasing in his voice.

"Like this, Sandy," Winston instructed, picking up the nub of meat and forcing the whole thing into his mouth.

Mrs. Burton reached over and patted her hand. "You're a Burton now. No need for formalities."

Sandy smiled, took up the biggest piece between her fingers, opened her mouth, and sucked, seasoned meat finding her tongue like heaven.

Mr. Burton sat back and clapped. "Dere ya go, gal!" Mrs. Burton handed her a napkin. Winston patted her back, nodded, and went back to his plate. By the time the meal was through, not a single morsel of meat remained on Sandy's plate.

Now, as the meal drew to an end, she looked at the faces that had come to mean so much. Understood them all so much better, respected the lives they had lived.

"Fine meal, Alice," Mr. Burton said, tossing his napkin onto his plate.

"Absolutely delicious, Mrs. Burton," Sandy added, meaning it.

"Call me Alice."

"I, an cawl me Pop," Mr. Burton added, his eyes dancing with appreciation.

"Pop," Sandy said with enthusiasm.

"An cawl me lay-zee, 'cause dis meal done wearied me down to to bone," Rachel said, standing slowly and gathering up plates.

Sandy got up too. "I'll help." Together they headed towards the kitchen, Rachel to wash and Sandy to dry.

"How ya friend?" Rachel asked.

"Janice?"

"Dat her."

"She's fine."

"Cleef treatin' 'er good, den?"

"Better than ever."

Rachel nodded. "Good, good."

Sandy paused from her drying, considered her. "She told me what you said to her."

"I expected dat much."

"But I saw you and Cliff. Looked like more than boredom to me, Rachel."

Rachel chuckled. "More, yes. Real luv? Nah, sir."

"So you just said that to—"

"Get 'er tinking? Yes. So mucha life justa wasted. People playing stupard games all abouta ego and not da 'eart. When Adrian die, just change tings. Couldn't see me hanging on ta Cleef when dere was somebody else 'oo luved 'em more."

It was not a big house, but as she looked around the living room, things still in boxes, unopened cartons everywhere, she wondered if she would ever fill it, fill the three-bedroom, one-and-a-half-bath on 112th Avenue in Hollis.

Finding the house hadn't taken long at all. A glance through the Sunday paper, a trip to a local realtor, by the week's end Sandy had narrowed her choices to one. With the money Adrian had left her, she was able to put 20 percent down, and voilà—she had become a homeowner.

But it was a dream just half-realized. Yes, her name was on the title, but a house was not a home. It took moments, experiences, people, and things to truly belong to it, and Sandy stood there feeling the hollowness waiting to be filled.

She stood there, not moving, just breathing, trying to sense Adrian. He visited her dreams nightly, but come morning she would awaken brokenhearted. Sandy sighed. Took in the boxes by the corner. Knew their contents item by item. *Adrian's things*.

She hadn't been certain if she would line the cowrie beads along the windowsill that faced The Motherland; if the carved wooden African warrior would greet visitors in her front hall.

But now that the moment had arrived, she knew that

they would remain in the box. *Just a part of what was, not what is.* She had to live in truth, and the truth was that Adrian was not coming back and she had to make a new life. Truth was that she was scared.

She looked up again, laughed. "Hear that, Adrian? I'm terrified. A new house, a new life, no you . . . What am I gonna do, huh? What am I gonna do?"

The phone rang. "Hello?"

"Baby?"

"Grandma Tee?"

"In your new place, huh?"

Sandy nodded. "Yeah, I'm here."

"Kinda scary, ain't it. New place, nothing familiar. Goes away after a while."

"I hope so."

"Been through some hard times, sugah," her grandmother said softly. "Tough tough times, but it's gonna get better from here on in."

"I hope so, Grandma Tee."

"Don't hope. Gotta know, 'cause I sure do."

"You know?"

"Sure do. An angel told me. Came to me in my dream."

"Angel?"

"Well, that's not his real name, but he said you'd know."

He looked liked some kind of an angel. Adrian.

"Yes sur. I was just taking my afternoon nap and suddenly I'm dreaming and there's this angel, a colored one. Not dark or nothing, but not white like in the books. And he says to tell you that life is going to get better, and soon. Now I'm looking at him and he don't look familiar, but I feel like I know him. That's when he told me you'd know. Said maybe I should wake up and call you. That you was in your new place and feeling out of sorts."

"You dreamt about Adrian, Grandma Tee?"

"Can't say. He said something about blue."

"Blue?"

"Yeah. Chello? Jello?"

The word fell from the sky. "Harpo's?"

"Yeah, that was it. Mean anything?"

Sandy smiled. "Means everything."

"Well, baby, just delivering a message. You take care, hear? And don't forget you promised me a visit."

"Yes, ma'am."

Sandy hung up the phone. Found the box marked REC-ORDS, dug deep inside. She hooked up the turntable, put the vinyl on the rubber mat. Carefully she laid the stylus, the hiss of the needle filling the air.

She did not realize what was happening until she was in the midst of it. Did not experience the shift until she was halfway through. Her life was doing one of its phenomenal changes, and she did not resist the transition.

Music drifted around her "I wish I was a willow—" the words familiar as the mole on the back of her hand. She remembered the first time she had heard that song and how it pulled at some mystery deep inside of her, but the mystery had been solved.

Once Sandy had longed to be that willow but in the end had evolved into an oak. Roots deep, limbs upward, she had become a strong tree searching for new rainbows in the sky.